HUNTING THE MAIL ORDER MURDERER

Also by C. M. Wendelboe

Bitter Wind Mysteries
Hunting the Five Point Killer
Hunting the Saturday Night Strangler
Hunting the VA Slayer

Spirit Road Mysteries
Death Where the Bad Rocks Live
Death on the Greasy Grass
Death Etched in Stone
Death through Destiny's Door

Tucker Ashley Western Adventures
Backed to the Wall
Seeking Justice
When the Gold Dust Died in Deadwood

Nelson Lane Frontier Mysteries
The Marshal and the Moonshiner
The Marshal and the Sinister Still
The Marshal and the Mystical Mountain

HUNTING THE MAIL ORDER MURDERER

A BITTER WIND MYSTERY

C. M. Wendelboe

Encircle Publications
Farmington, Maine U.S.A.

Paperback ISBN 13: 978-1-64599-364-3
Hardcover ISBN 13: 978-1-64599-365-0
E-book ISBN 13: 978-1-64599-366-7

Cover design by Deirdre Wait
Cover photograph and author photograph by Heather M. Wendelboe

Published by:

Encircle Publications
PO Box 187
Farmington, ME 04938

info@encirclepub.com
http://encirclepub.com

ACKNOWLEDGMENTS

To my wife Heather for taking the photos, and telling me where to go. To Deirdre Wait for her work on the cover design, and to Cynthia Brackett-Vincent and Eddie Vincent for their advice on the telling of this tale.

*I would like to dedicate this book to the
women and men of law enforcement whose job it is
to catch predators like the ones you will meet
inside the dank, dark walls of this novel.*

1

"I got a body. A dead body. Finally—"

"Whoa," Arn Anderson said. "What do you mean *you* have a dead body?"

"Down at Frontier Park," Ana Maria blurted out over the phone. "A jogger found another runner DRT. 'Dead Right There' in police parlance, in case you forgot."

How could Arn forget? After a long career as a street cop and homicide detective in Denver before moving back to Cheyenne, he'd encountered more people *DRT* than he wanted to remember. But Ana Maria? He wasn't quite sure why the television reporter was so... giddy about a corpse. "Tell me just why you're so happy about this."

Rustling in the background. Ana Maria donning a coat? Grabbing her reporter's notebook? "Arn, for the last two months, DeAngelo has sent me to cover all sorts of exciting stories—a quilting contest at the library. A hog judging event at Archer Complex. You know, exciting, breaking stories."

"I'd have thought you'd love to set back and be out of danger for once." Two months ago, Arn had been hired to look into suspicious deaths at various VA facilities in the region, culminating in Ana Maria nearly becoming the killer's next victim. Television station owner DeAngelo Demos vowed he'd keep his ace reporter out of danger if he could. Still, a jogger dying while running at this altitude—though rare—was not unheard of. "I don't recall you getting excited covering traffic accident deaths or heart attacks."

"I got a good feeling about this one," she said. "Wanna tag along?"

Arn rubbed the sleep out of his eyes and checked the clock beside his bed. "For heaven's sake, it's seven o'clock on a Sunday morning. I have things to do."

"What, now you're going to lie and tell me you need to go to church?"

Arn wasn't going to lie—he wasn't going to church. He had promised the Man after last time Ana Maria nearly bought the farm that he'd attend worship services. That had lasted all of a month before sleeping in on Sundays became the norm. "But I had a late night last night."

"Not that Tito Hondros gig again?"

"Again," Arn answered. He didn't usually do divorce cases, but he needed the money for an addition he and Danny were putting on the house, so he'd agreed to meet Tito's wife, Lizzy. For enough to pay for materials, all Arn had to do was tail her husband and get photographic evidence he had a mistress on the side. Last night had been a bust. Tito had proven wily, moving his mistress from motel to motel, and Arn still had no idea where Tito was keeping her.

"Come on. Put your ratty jeans on and I'll pick you up."

Arn groaned. "Do I at least have time to shave?"

"Shave on the way. I'll be there in a bit."

Arn slipped on the same jeans that he wore yesterday when he was mudding dry wall. He stumbled down the stairs and stubbed his toe on the bottom tread. He yelped just as Danny came out of the TV room. Danny Spotted Hawk stood with his hands on his meatless hips, wearing what looked like an old man's nightshirt nearly to his feet. He stared up at Arn and said, "That all you got to do this morning is interrupt my entertainment?"

In the background, from the TV room, a bachelorette was just deciding on which hunk to select for the big date. "It sounds so... stimulating. *Bachelorette* reruns again, I take it."

"And you sound as if Ana Maria guilt-tripped you into going on some cockamamie reporter's call again."

"You a mind reader?"

"No," Danny answered. "What I am is the cook around here. I planned to have eggs Benedict, but that can wait for later. I'll pour you coffee in a go cup. With Ana Maria, you'll need it."

Arn had just taken his first sip when Ana Maria's shrill horn honked outside the door. Arn rushed out, sipping coffee as he went. He wedged himself into the tiny seat of the Volkswagen and buckled up. Not that the Bug could go fast enough to hurt him if she hit anything. "Don't you beat all," he said. "Waking me up to go along on some accidental death call. Still don't know why you're so happy."

She glanced at Arn and shook her head. "When you were on the job, would you have been happy working auto theft or check fraud instead of homicide?"

"I see your point."

"And like I said, I got a good feeling about this croaker."

"Good as in bad?"

"Is there any other kind?" she answered and grinned wide.

"By the way, how'd you find out about it? You musta been sleeping like me."

"Police scanner."

"I gotta call bullshit on that. The police dispatch most of their calls via car computer nowadays, so your old scanner can't pick up squat."

"All right then—Bobby."

"As in Officer Bobby?"

Ana Maria nodded. "He still thinks our occasional lunch date will blossom into something more."

"You're using him."

"Like he uses me. In case you haven't been paying attention, I got him on camera half a dozen times for different police calls this spring alone. One of these days the chief will take notice, and Bobby will soar to the top of the police department food chain."

When they pulled into Frontier Park, it was easy to find the victim. All they had to do was follow the trail of police cars, ambulances, and fire rescue units. Not that paramedics or firemen are any good at raising a dead body.

A fire truck with four firefighters in yellow bunker gear milled about. *Just in case the victim spontaneously combusts*, Arn figured as Ana Maria parked just outside the yellow police evidence tape and opened the door. "If the detective asks, you're with me. A trainee journalist."

"At my age?" Arn smirked. "Besides, all the cops on the force already know me."

"Not the investigator handling this call. It's that hot-shot detective they hired out of Houston."

"Frida Kubek," Arn said. "I read in the *Tribune Eagle* how she aced out three other out-of-area candidates and two already on the force here to become Chief Detective."

"Probably 'cause she's got more balls than any of the guys that applied," Ana Maria said. "Bobby says she's hard as hell to work with so, *please*, keep a low profile and try not to piss her off."

"*Moi?*" Arn said in his best juvenile falsetto. "I'll have her eating out of the palm of my hand—"

"Arn…"

Arn held up his hand. "Okay. I'll be on my best behavior."

2

Arn followed close behind Ana Maria as she threaded her way through pine trees and lilac bushes like a hunting dog on the scent of a quail, headed right for a cluster of emergency personnel looking down at the ground. She stopped outside the evidence tape barrier just as a short woman with her hair tucked under a ball cap embossed with *Cheyenne PD* approached them. "Move along," she said in a clipped voice hinting at a slight southern accent. She stood no taller than Ana Maria, her lithe frame suggesting she was fit. Her blue eyes complimented her naturally blonde hair, and her makeup—applied sparingly—was unnecessary. She would be a looker even without any Maybelline. "Go on. Git!"

Ana Maria grabbed her journalist ID from her purse and showed it to the woman. "For the sake of the public, we need to be here."

The detective stepped closer and took the ID, turning it to the light that filtered through the trees before handing it back. "Television reporter," she guffawed. "This old guy your cameraman? I don't see any equipment on his shoulder. You trying to worm your way in where you don't belong?"

Ana Maria pocketed her ID and leaned closer over the plastic tape. "My cameraman's on his way—lives twenty minutes north of town. This… old guy here's wishing to be a journalist. I'm showing him the ropes."

"Only rope he's likely to see is the ones separating concession counters at the movie theater."

Arn swallowed hard, doing his best to remain composed.

Ana Maria took her notebook from her purse and said, "Chief Detective Kubek is it?"

The woman stepped back a pace and asked, "Why do you need to know?"

"For my broadcast tonight, so I can tell viewers who kept the press from covering a deceased victim."

"It's only an accidental death," Kubek sputtered. "Unattended. That's the reason we have to open an investigation."

"Chief of Detectives Kubek," Ana Maria said aloud as she wrote in her notebook, "refused to allow the press access—"

"All right, all right. Duck under the tape. But you two best not get in the way of our investigation."

"And my cameraman when he gets here?"

Kubek's face turned red, in contrast to her pale skin, when she said, "I'll allow him in, too."

Ana Maria thanked her, and Chief Detective Kubek turned on her heels and returned to the victim. Ana Maria held the tape up for Arn to duck under, but he slapped her hand away. "This *old* guy's not so far gone that he can't do a limbo under the tape. Now, let's look at this AD so we can go grab a bite to eat. Danny'll fix eggs Benedict for us."

They walked to where three paramedics and a uniformed officer stood beside Detective Kubek looking down at the victim just off the running trail. Grass had stained her white shorts when she had fallen, and her well-worn Nikes were scuffed from the fall, an evergreen twig sticking out of one shoelace. On her right wrist, a watch glittered in the sun from the light reflecting off diamonds ringing the clock face, the gold band engraved with some type of ornate filigree. "Your people already take photos?" Arn asked while he squatted to look closer at the dead woman.

"Of course," Kubek answered. "One of the first things I ordered. Why?"

"Then you won't object to me taking one of that watch?"

Kubek shrugged. "Help yourself, though it's just a watch."

Arn took his phone from his pocket and moved to get a better angle of the watch. *Kubek's wrong*, he thought, as he zoomed in on the victim's wrist. It wasn't *just* a watch—it was an extremely *expensive* watch, if he knew his jewelry. He snapped a close-up, then shifted slightly to photograph the three faint scratch marks on one of the victim's legs.

When he stood and arched his back, he felt a *pop*. Perhaps Kubek was right about one thing—maybe he was getting too long in the tooth.

"Looks like you don't need us here anymore," a paramedic announced before he and his two partners climbed into the ambulance and drove out of the park just ahead of the fire truck.

"Need me here, boss?" the young policeman asked.

"Naw," Kubek answered. "The coroner's on the way. No bigger than this girl is… she'll be easy to lift onto the gurney."

Kubek watched the policeman as he walked to his cruiser before turning back and saying to Ana Maria, "Still don't know why this is much interest to you. It's pretty cut and dried, what happened."

Ana Maria took out her notebook again and said, "Can I get a quote from you about the victim?"

"Is this on the record?"

"Of course," Ana Maria replied.

A slight smile tugged at the corners of Frida Kubek's mouth, and Arn recognized that look. Kubek would make statements on the record, statements that would find their way into the public domain of Facebook memes and cable television quotes. Enough that, one day soon, she would have so many such quotes in her portfolio that she could interview at some big department for a police chief position.

"Then, for the record," Ana Maria said, "what are your initial findings concerning this young woman?"

"Your cameraman?" Kubek asked.

"He ran out of gas. We'll have to catch up with you later for an on-air interview, if that's all right."

"Of course," Kubek said, the roughness of her voice gone now that she thought the press could propel her to greatness. She cleared her throat and began a slow walk around the body. "Early to mid-twenties. Of Asian descent, it would appear. She was out for an early jog and collapsed. Not uncommon in such high altitude, if she wasn't used to it."

"You believe she was new to this country?" Ana Maria asked.

"Or new to this climate. This mountain air is thin. I'm having a hard time myself adapting to the altitude."

Arn squatted beside the body once more. "These scratch marks on her leg—what do you make of them?"

Kubek waved her hand around the grounds. "What do you see here? I'll tell you—there's branches and trees and bushes. At some point in her jog, she must have brushed past something and it gouged her skin. Simple enough."

Ana Maria turned a page and stood with pen poised. "And who reported the death?"

"Another jogger," Kubek said. "He ran by here at about 6:15 a.m. but didn't see the girl then. He ran around the park and came by this way again at… about 6:45 and saw the girl lying on the ground."

The coroner's van pulled into the park and Kubek waved her over.

The coroner—a lady in her forties—opened the back of her van and rolled out a gurney. Atop the gurney was a gray body bag, and the coroner collapsed the stretcher beside the victim. She tucked the heavy bag under the body and it stuck. Arn bent beside Kubek and helped roll the victim over. A feather lodged in the victim's hair fluttered out and Arn grabbed it. "Want to bag this?"

Kubek stopped long enough to laugh and asked, "Bag it for what? It's a damn feather. Looks a lot like a feather from one of these noisy geese infesting the park."

"Probably right," Arn said, but pocketed the feather anyway.

"When we roll her over," Kubek said, "I want to check for ID in her back pockets. There were none in the front pocket of her shorts."

Arn knelt beside the coroner and Kubek and they gently rolled the body on her side, rigor already having set in, her body stiffening. Liver Mortis had already begun with purple splotches on the victim's legs where she'd contacted the ground after falling. Kubek gently felt inside the running shorts and asked, "What's this?" She turned a business card over in her hand, and her face and neck turned crimson. "What did you say your name was?"

"Arn Anderson," he answered and caught a glimpse of his business card in Kubek's hand.

"That's what I thought. Just what the hell are you pulling here, passing yourself off as a journalist?"

"It was my idea," Ana Maria said. "I often bring Arn along. He's got different perspectives than most… investigators."

"I ought to run you in," Kubek said. She flicked the business card against her knee and asked, "Just what relation are you to this woman?"

"Not any relation at all," Arn said and forced a grin. "I'm a little big to be Asian."

"Damn it, you know what I mean. Why was she carrying your business card?"

"Can't say."

"Can't—or won't?"

"Listen, officer—"

"Chief Detective," she corrected.

Arn sighed. How many times in his career had he run into some beside-themselves staff officer with a head too big to fit through most doorways. "I don't know this woman. Never met her. Never saw her before. I pass out business cards to many people. Perhaps she intended for me to work a case for her."

"I'll buy that. For now. I'll just log this into evidence," Kubek said and pocketed the card.

"Are you finished, Detective Kubek?" the coroner asked. "'Cause if you are, I'd like to get her to the morgue and begin calling around for a pathologist to conduct the autopsy."

"An autopsy!" Kubek said. "For this… this accidental death?"

The coroner nodded. "We do autopsies on all unattended deaths, or didn't they tell you that when you were hired? Now please, help me roll her into the bag."

As Arn bent over to roll the victim's shoulders so she could be put into the body bag, he looked into her dead eyes. And those eyes told him as much as if she were talking with Arn right there in the park.

3

After the waitress left, Ana Maria said, "I hope Danny's not too miffed that we didn't go to our place for breakfast."

Arn sipped lightly of his coffee. Strong. Dark. But then coffee was always strong and dark at the Diamond Horseshoe Diner. He watched a railroader wolf down an omelet from his corner booth, the only other patron in the eatery. "Danny was banging on the computer when I called. He's probably just as happy we didn't drag him away from whatever he's doing."

"Well, tell him I'm sorry if he is angry," Ana Maria said. "I couldn't wait any longer. Dead bodies always give me an appetite for some reason." She took out her notebook and flipped pages. "How about that *Chief* Detective Kubek? Kinda an arrogant bitty. Bobby concurs. He said she figures she's God's gift to investigators down in Houston, if his contacts are right. And she swishes her ass around like she figures every guy in the department wants to lay her."

The waitress brought their plates and Ana Maria chuckled at Arn's. "The 55 and older special's not exactly for someone your size."

"That's the problem," Arn said. "Someone my size better be cutting down."

Ana Maria drizzled Tabasco over her Denver omelet. "Maybe seeing such a young person have the big MI worked on you?"

"That runner didn't have heart failure," Arn said, then added, "she was most likely murdered. Excuse me. I need to visit the little boy's powder room."

When he returned minutes later, Ana Maria hadn't touched her omelet. "Not hungry?" Arn asked as he slid back into the booth.

"You throw out 'she didn't have heart failure; was probably murdered,' and then you just leave for the crapper?"

"So? I had to see a man about a horse." Arn grabbed for a small packet of jelly in the holder on the table "Bad. My plumbing works okay, but it waits for no man. Or woman. When you gotta go, you gotta go."

"Well?"

"Well, what?"

"Are you going to fill me in on this conclusion of yours? If this was anything but an accident, I'd like to know."

Arn took the first bite of sourdough toast smeared with apple jelly and let it slide down his throat. He washed the toast down with coffee, and then said, "The first things I noticed that were more than a little askew were her shoes and watch."

"Oh, this oughta be interesting."

"It is," Arn said. "Looking at her Nikes, they were tied as if she were right-handed."

Ana Marie threw up her hands. "That's it? She was right-handed, ergo, she must've been murdered?"

"I didn't say that. I said, they were tied *as if* she were right-handed. But she was probably a lefty."

"How do you figure—"

"She wore her watch on her right hand. Opposite of me." He held up his hand. "Or you, both of us—who are righties."

Ana Maria's hand went to the wristwatch worn on her left wrist. "Maybe she just liked wearing her watch on her right wrist."

Arn waited until the waitress had refilled their cups before saying, "It's possible, but not likely. And speaking of watches, did you see that one?"

"Hard not to," Ana Maria said. "Unless it was a cheap knock off."

"It wasn't a knock off."

"Then it must've set her back a fortune… you're not taking exception with a woman wearing expensive jewelry?"

"Not if she can actually afford it, which she could not."

Ana Maria leaned over and wiped a dab of jelly off Arn's chin. "This I gotta hear."

"It's simple, really. The girl was a working girl, and I don't mean one who worked in the back seat of cars or one you could rent by the hour. Not that kind of working girl."

Ana Maria laughed. "Now you're going to tell me you developed clairvoyance, knowing just what she did in life."

"Even *I* don't know what she did for a living. All I know is that by the looks of her chipped nails and hair badly in need of a trim, she must have done some kind of manual labor for a living with no disposable income for stylists or manicures."

"That's it? She wore her watch as a lefty and her nails were chipped? Convince Kubek that the victim's death wasn't accidental based on that."

Arn sopped egg yolk up with his last piece of toast. "Then there are the scratches on her leg—"

"From a bush in the park," Ana Maria interrupted. "That one I'll have to give to the evanescent Frida Kubek. Makes sense."

"Don't give her credit too soon," Arn said. "Can you recall how evenly spaced those three scratches were?" He ran his fingernails across the table. "Even. As if someone had raked their nails across her legs."

"Now you've almost got me convinced it wasn't accidental," Ana Maria said. "*Almost.* But you have to convince me with more than just that, for me to go to DeAngelo with it."

Arn pushed his empty plate away, wishing he'd bought *two* senior specials. "She was suffocated."

"How do you know?"

"She told me."

Ana Maria sat back in the booth and looked at Arn as if he was a crazy person. "I'm thinking a mental evaluation of one retired homicide detective ought to be ordered. A corpse talking to you—"

"In her own way. When I looked into her eyes, she told me." He held up his cup for the waitress. "Refill?"

Ana Maria jumped as if seeing the waitress with a pot for the first time. She topped off their coffee cups and began making her way to the other table where the railroader was just finishing his meal. "What about her eyes?"

"Petechiae," Arn said. "Very faint in this case—hemorrhaging in the white part of the eye. Only a few tiny red dots. Caused by blood being forced out of the arteries. Only comes from sudden loss of oxygen to the brain, such as when someone suffocates. You going to finish that English muffin?"

"Help yourself."

Arn reached for another packet of jelly and asked, "Do you know just how hard it is for someone to suffocate another with something such as a pillow, despite movies and television telling us otherwise? Difficult as hell with the victim thrashing around. Fighting the attacker. Unless the size disparity is such that the victim has no chance. With someone as tiny as that girl was, most any man—and many women—could hold a pillow over her face long enough to suffocate her to death."

"Those scratches... might she have gotten them in the struggle?"

"Quite possible," Arn said, "and she might have given as good as she got in that respect. I know our coroner—I'll stop by today and tell the pathologist to pay particular attention to Paquita's fingernails. She may have gouged her attacker as well."

"Let me get this straight—the victim was suffocated with a pillow, though none was found at the scene?"

"That's about it."

"What makes you think it was a pillow?"

Arn used the whole jelly packet on the English muffin. *So much for my diet.* He reached into his shirt pocket, withdrew the small bindle he'd folded from a piece of notepaper and opened it. "This was stuck in her hair," Arn said and handed Ana Maria the feather.

She held to the light and shrugged. "I know. I heard Kubek's very plausible explanation—that with the number of damned geese overrunning the park, it was a probably a goose feather."

"Pretty small to come from one of those big Canada geese that patrol the park in packs."

"All right, all right." Ana Maria fidgeted in her seat as if she was starting to be convinced the dead girl *was* a victim of murder. "What if it came from a pillow? All we need to do is find it."

"Good luck finding that *one* pillow," Arn said.

"Hate to admit it, but you're almost making sense. You've nearly convinced me. Anything else to close the deal that I can go to DeAngelo with for tonight's broadcast?"

"It usually takes at least two hours for rigor to set into the large muscles," Arn said. "But when we rolled her over, rigor had already set in."

"That makes no sense," Ana Maria said, "if she were running just this morning."

"It can make sense," Arn said, and began explaining to Ana Maria what happens after death, like he'd educated juries countless times. "There are a couple ways to speed up rigor. One is by exertion, such as jogging. But I'm discounting that."

"Why?" Ana Maria asked. "It's pretty obvious she *was* jogging."

"You ever do any running?"

"Some," Ana Maria answered. "When I was in college, just to stay in shape. Why?"

"When you ran, did you sweat?"

"Of course. I sweat like an old hog. Everybody does."

Arn licked a spot of grape jelly off his hand and said, "What shape were her jogging clothes in? All sweated up enough to indicate she may have overexerted herself?"

Ana Maria paused and set her coffee cup on the table. "Her clothes were… like she'd just put them on. I didn't see a sweat stain anywhere. But you said there was another way in which rigor can develop sooner."

"If the girl put up a hard struggle while she was being smothered, the onset of rigor could come earlier."

"Or the other thing," Ana Maria said, "she could have been killed some hours before, like you said. Maybe dumped in the park this morning."

"We do think alike sometimes," Arn said, and polished off the last of the English muffin.

4

When Arn walked in the house, he heard the not-so-gentle clack-clacking of computer keys coming from the office room and he headed for it.

"Looks like you're on a mission." Arn bent over Danny's shoulder to look at the screen and whistled. "Some babe you got pulled up there. Anyone we know?"

"Not unless you're from the Ukraine. She's a mail order bride."

"A mail order bride?"

"Yep," Danny said as he enlarged her profile. "And don't she look... delicious."

Arn put on his reading glasses to study the profile. Twenty-six. Five foot ten inches, and one-hundred-thirty pounds with the blondest hair and bluest eyes Arn had ever seen. Almost like her photograph had been enhanced. "Tell me you just have a passing curiosity in mail order brides."

"More than a curiosity," Danny said. "I'm going to sign up on one of these sites."

Arn sat in the occasional chair beside the computer desk and took off his Stetson. "You never indicated you were even remotely interested in women. What brought all this on?"

Danny swiveled his chair around and set his readers beside the keyboard. "You might say you were my inspiration."

"I'm some inspiration because I'm widowed?"

"No," Danny said as he twirled his single, gray ponytail held with a bone hair tie. "That woman who hired you to find out where her husband is hiding his mistress. His 'mail-order mistress' is how I recall you telling it."

"So, the guy's got a mail order bride that he has no intention marrying. What's that got to do with you?"

Danny leaned forward and said, "In case you haven't noticed, I'm not getting any younger. I have one foot on a banana peel and the other one on the grave site."

"Nonsense," Arn said. "For seventy-three, you're healthy as a horse."

"An old swayback horse," Danny said. "Maybe I just want some companionship."

"And I'm not a companion?" Arn asked.

"You know what I mean," Danny said. "Get the door."

"For what?"

"Somebody's out front."

"How you know—"

"Sonny just moved in the kitchen, and you know how he don't like being disturbed from his nap."

Arn stood and left the room, passing Sonny in the hallway. The old Basset Hound tilted his head back and emitted a lame, sick howl just as the doorbell rang. Arn bent and patted the dog on the head. "You done good. Now go back to sleep."

As if Sonny needed Arn's permission, the old dog walked back to the kitchen to lay his sad head down under the table once more.

Arn had had enough death threats that he remained wary of anyone coming to the house and his hand rested on the gun butt in his trouser pocket when he answered the door. "Chief Detective Kubek," he said, tried sounding happy. "This official or casual visit?"

"Definitely official," she said.

"Then come on into the kitchen. Excuse the mess, we're in the process of remodeling."

"We?" Kubek asked. "I didn't think you were married."

"I'm not, but I have a… roommate who is a genius at everything concerning home renovation. Please follow me."

Arn led Kubek into the kitchen, the sound of Sonny already snoring echoing off the kitchen walls. "Coffee?"

"Tea if you have it," Kubek said.

Arn looked into the cabinets, finally locating some herbal concoction Danny liked. He poured himself a cup of coffee and put the tea pot on the stove for Kubek's tea before sitting down. "I am curious about this visit, detective."

"Frida," Kubek corrected, and Arn detected a faint softening of her voice. "The reason I'm here is to get a straight answer as to how your business card wound up in the jogger's pocket."

Arn sipped his coffee, dragging out his answer. "Like I told you at the crime scene, I've never seen that girl before. I have business cards all over town." He chuckled. "Even in the pockets of homeless folks."

The tea pot whistled for attention and Arn poured hot water over the tea bag and set it on the table in front of Kubek. "You used a curious choice of words just now—crime scene. I see it as an unattended death."

"Most murders are unattended," Arn said.

"Murder?" Kubek puckered up when she took the first sip of Danny's herbal tea.

Arn slid a sugar dispenser across the table. "I have to use it, too, when I drink that... tea."

Kubek spooned sugar into the hot liquid and stirred it. "Tell me why you think the girl was murdered?" she asked at last.

Arn gave Kubek the headline version—the girl was jogging but showed no sweat stains on her clothes. Hemorrhagic petechiae indicated a sudden loss of oxygen often associated with manual strangulation. Her shoes were tied as if she were a right hander, but she wore her wristwatch on her right wrist like a lefty would. "And speaking of that watch," Arn said, "I have the feeling that you and I combined couldn't afford it."

Kubek jumped and looked under the table where Sonny had moved his operations to. "Your dog..."

"He's harmless," Arn said.

"That's not what I'm worried about. He's sitting on my feet with his... *cajones* right on my shoe tips."

"I'd let that sleeping dog lie," Arn said as seriously as he could, "or else he might pee on your shoes."

Kubek looked a final time at Sonny before asking, "after examining it at the coroner's office, I realized that watch is expensive. Even distinctive. Even if we couldn't afford it that's not to say the girl couldn't. Maybe she was a professional girl on the side after all."

"Tell me… Frida, if you possessed such a fancy watch, would you dare take it jogging where it might get damaged?"

"I wouldn't own one so ostentatious. But if I did… no, I would not wear it jogging. Still doesn't really mean anything."

"It does if the victim was a working girl."

"You saying you can tell the girl was a prostitute just from seeing her this morning?" Kubek asked.

"That's not what I'm saying at all." Sonny had moved to where he now sat on Arn's feet. "She was definitely one used to hard labor."

"How did you determine that just by looking at her?"

"Her hands. The victim worked hard for a living by the looks of her chipped nails. And that her hair was badly in need of a cut and style. Her crusty elbows that hadn't been washed thoroughly in some time."

"But a beautiful girl like that… she could get most any man she wanted. She didn't need to work manual labor."

"Something to find out as soon as you learn her identity," Arn said and held up his coffee cup as if in a toast. "But that's why they pay you the big bucks."

Kubek eased out of her chair so as not to disturb Sonny. "My investigators have shown a photo around, but no one recognized her."

"Maybe Ana Maria will have some luck," Arn said. "She's going to put the victim's photo on her nightly news broadcast."

"Before we even notify next of kin…" Kubek stopped. "I guess we'll never find out *who* her next of kin is if we can't identify her."

She headed for the door and paused for a moment to ask, "I looked you up—"

"Like on a dating site?' Arn asked, playing with the detective.

"Not hardly. I just wanted to find out who was posing as a journalist to get access to a death scene. I thought it was because you knew the victim—after all, she had your business card in her pocket."

"I told you I didn't, and you still don't believe me?"

"I do now. And…"

"Yes?" Arn pressed.

"I found out you solved every homicide you investigated when you worked in Denver Metro Homicide. And several since you moved to Cheyenne as a private investigator."

"Can't argue there," Arn said. "And I hear a 'but' in there somewhere."

"Dammit, Anderson, are you going to make me ask you... a private citizen, for advice."

"Walk this way, Frida." Arn led her towards the door and waved his hand around the room. "The only reason I take cases is to be able to afford the renovations to my mother's old house. But I could be persuaded to... consult with the police."

"Consult for a fee? I'm not sure I could get the city council to approve—"

Arn held up his hand. "Call this a freebee. I'll... suggest things now and again. That's if you're interested."

Kubek nodded. "I am. So, for the first suggestion from this private citizen, how would you go about finding out who the dead girl is?"

"Sounds like you're doing all you can, and maybe Ana Maria's broadcast will jar someone's memory," Arn said. "I think the only other thing I'd do is send out a Triple I—"

"Triple I?"

"Regional bulletin with the victim's description and a photo of that watch. As distinctive as it is, someone might recognize it."

"Good idea," Kubek said as she walked out the door. "We'll stay in touch."

"I'd like that." Arn waited until she'd climbed into her car before shutting the door and walking to the computer room.

"Sounds like one Chief of Detectives has a thing for you," Danny said and swiveled his chair around to look at Arn. "At least if I read her tone right when she was talking with you."

"Your ears are too sharp for your own good." Arn sat in the chair and looked around Danny at the computer screen. "Those photos don't look much like exotic Russians or Ukrainians to me."

"I did some research while you were flirting with Kubek."

"I wasn't flirting—"

"Relax," Danny said. "If I'm not too old to be chasing skirts, you sure aren't."

"I said I am not, repeat not, chasing skirts or flirting with Kubek."

"Whatever," Danny said as he waved the air. "It'll be our little secret."

Arn felt the need to change the subject before his temper got the best of him and he asked Danny, "What kind of dating site is that now, 'cause those sure aren't Russian beauties you're scoping out."

"It's a domestic dating site you've seen advertised on television a hundred times," Danny said. "I got to checking into those Eastern European sites and I gotta tell you, it costs mega bucks just to go over on one of those dating jaunts. Then there's no guarantee that you'll meet someone who's worthwhile and honest."

Arn tapped the computer. "And you're certain those women are?"

"Sure. You don't think they'd lie just to get a date?"

"All's I'm saying," Arn said, "is don't assume those ladies post everything that's a hundred prevent truthful on those sites. Even down to their glamour photos."

"I'll ponder your advice," Danny said then added, "you sure you don't want to throw out your profile just to see who takes the bait?"

"I'm at the stage of my life where a woman would have to be special for me to have such lascivious thoughts."

"Special as in self-assuredness. A professional woman who knows just what she wants. Maybe someone who doesn't need a man, per se, but who wants one for the companionship?"

"That about sums it up."

Danny grinned. "That about sounds like Chief Detective Frida Kubek."

"Just turn off that computer and let's go watch Ana Maria's broadcast," Arn said and headed for the TV room.

5

Ana Maria yelled up the stairs.

Arn poked his head out of the room. "What'd you say?"

"I wondered if you and Danny are ready for a little mid-morning snack," she said as she held up a box of donuts. "If you guys eat one with me, I won't feel so guilty."

He batted drywall dust off his jeans and started down the stairs. "Coming!" he said over his shoulder.

Danny emerged from the room looking even grubbier than Arn. He came down the stairs and stopped in front of Ana Maria, his hands on his hips. "As the technical part of this team, it's a shame that I even get dirty. But he," he jerked his thumb at Arn, "isn't exactly proficient in this remodeling game. I usually have to follow behind him and fix his screw-ups."

"And don't think I don't appreciate it, too," Arn said. "I'll start coffee."

While Arn loaded the Mr. Coffee with grounds, Ana Maria grabbed paper plates from the cupboard and opened the box of donuts on the table. "You sound cheery this morning?" Arn said. "Did you get lucky last night or something?"

"I wish," Ana Maria said, selecting a chocolate long john and sliding the box over to Danny. "Something almost as good though—I got a tip that our Jane Doe was a Paquita Robles."

"Name doesn't ring a bell."

"Unless you're Filipino," Danny said.

"How'd you know she was Filipino?" Arn asked.

Danny's jelly-filled Bismark spewed yellow goo and he licked it off his finger. "I just know things."

Arn had no argument for that. Ever since Danny had squatted in Arn's mother's abandoned house, Arn had allowed the emaciated Lakota to remain if he pulled his weight. Not only had Danny pulled his weight around the house with the remodeling projects Arn came up with, but his knowledge of all things unusual often baffled Arn. Danny was—he was certain—the only genius that Arn knew, despite looking like any of the homeless people wandering downtown Cheyenne.

"Just to appease my curiosity," Ana Maria said, "just how *did* you know Paquita Robles was Filipino?"

"Robles," Danny said off-handily, "is a name that dates back to when the Spanish occupied what is now Manilla. Shortly after that, Miguel Lopez de Legazpi arrived from Mexico—"

"Okay, Danny," Ana Maria said. "We get it—you were right— Paquita was a Filipino and she did manual labor as a maid at the Cadillac Motel if my tipster was right."

"That dive across from what's left of the Hitching Post?" Danny asked. "The place that you can rent a room by the hour—clean sheets extra?"

"How do you know they charge by the hour."

"I just… heard it from a friend is all."

Arn broke a glazed doughnut in half and left the other half in the box. He'd come back later for it, he was sure, knowing if you ate the sinker in two sessions there weren't nearly as many calories. Like Danny, he'd heard that somewhere, too. "This makes it even more puzzling as to what she was doing with a wristwatch that cost as much as I make in a year."

"Or why a looker like her worked as a room maid in a snake pit of a motel," Ana Maria added.

"I'd be more curious," Danny said between nibbles, "as to why your business card was in her pocket."

Arn grabbed the other half of the doughnut and dunked it in his coffee. "She must have wanted to contact me about something." He dropped the doughnut onto the plate and grabbed a napkin.

"Dammit, a young, beautiful girl wouldn't want to look me up unless she were in trouble."

"As logical an answer as I can come up," Ana Maria said, spearing a filled long john with a fork. "Can you think of anyone lately who has left you messages to call them? Notes in the mailbox? Anything like that?"

"Nada," Arn said and stood abruptly. "But I'll do some more thinking about it on the way over to Burri Jewelers."

"What are you going to there for?"

"A watch that exclusive," Arn said, "could only be sold by someone like Burri."

*   *   *

Arn walked into Burri Jewelers to a faint bell tinkling above the door. A young couple stood bent over looking at weddings rings, while a man at the service counter pocketed his receipt for his Rolex to be cleaned. Arn stepped up to the counter and a man with a magnifier strapped to his head called out, "Kaddie, can you get the counter."

An impeccably dressed young lady half Arn's age stepped up to the counter. "I'm Kaddie McCurdy. What may I help you with?"

Arn handed Kaddie his business card while he took his phone from his pocket and scrolled through his pictures. When he found the photo of Paquita Roble's wrist, he blew it up and handed Kaddie the phone. "This wrist watch... it looks quite expensive. Is there anything you could tell me about it?"

Kaddie studied the phone before turning to the man with the magnifier strapped to his head. She showed him the photo and he whispered something before turning back to the ring he was working on. "What would you like to know?"

"It's a long shot," Arn said, "but did you happen to sell that watch to anyone?"

She chuckled and said, "not unless I was a hundred years older."

"How's that?"

"This watch," she answered, handing Arn his phone back, "is well over a hundred years old. When it was brought to us for repair and cleaning—"

"You know the watch?"

"We do. It was dropped off here, along with a matching set of earrings and a matching broach about…" she turned to the man and asked, "when did we clean this set?"

"Few months ago," the man said without looking up from his jewelry vice.

"By any chance, do you recall who dropped the set off to be cleaned?"

"I can do better than that," the man said. He pulled out a card file and thumbed through the cards until he handed Kaddie one. "An Alex Barberi dropped this off."

"Can I see that?"

Kaddie handed Arn the card with the date and cost of cleaning. He handed it back and said, "you sure it was Alex Barberi?"

She shrugged. "That was the name he gave. Why?"

"Describe this man," Arn asked.

Kaddie shuddered and said, "a scary-looking dude. All wild-eyed. Hair looked like it'd been through a blender. And the tats…"

"Even I was a little hinked by the ink." The man took off his magnifier and walked to the counter. "He had tattoos all up to here," he indicated past his neckline, "and his arm had various odd ones."

"The ones that scared me the most," Kaddie said and shuddered again, "was that weird tat on the inside of his forearm."

"Can you describe it?"

"How can I forget it," she said. "It was a red rose with the image of a woman. And the odd thing was that the woman had one of those old school nurses' caps on like they used to wear. Oh, and there was a red cross across the cap."

"Rose of No Man's Land," Arn breathed.

"How's that?"

"The tat. Rose of No Man's Land. Popular in the Great War. The guy's a combat vet."

"How do you know that?"

Arn smiled. "I just know things."

As Arn headed out the door, Kaddie called after him. "One more thing, Mr. Anderson—though I don't know if it's germane to your investigation but I wouldn't have paid to have that jewelry cleaned."

"How's that?"

"The jewelry," Kaddie said. "It didn't even need cleaning. Like it had been stored away in a vault somewhere."

*   *   *

Arn heard voices chatting from the kitchen area as he walked into the house. He hung his hat on the rack beside the door and walked through the house. Danny sat at the kitchen able across from a girl looking like she was still in college. She'd fit in at any amateur beauty contest, and she sat at the table, clearly agitated as she shifted from foot to foot. Even Sonny was upset by her actions and had staked out a corner of the kitchen well away from the girl.

"I think that I should leave now," she blurted. "Thanks for wasting my time."

She brushed past Arn without looking at him and rushed out the door.

Danny looked after her and finally said, "Women. Now why would she act like that?"

Arn opened the fridge and grabbed a 7 Up. "Explain."

"I met her online," Danny said flatly.

"You met her on that goofy dating site you've been farting around on?"

Danny nodded and kissed the air after her. He wandered over to Sonny and scratched behind his ear before the dog ambled to his favorite spot under the table and dropped down. "She answered my ad, and I thought it best to interview her here at the house. In the daytime before we got more… intimate."

Arn felt the fizz go up his nose as he tried to digest what Danny just told him. "Let me get this straight—that woman has what, a fetish for much-older men?"

"Not exactly," Danny said.

Arn recognized the look in the old man, the look that refused to meet Arn's stare. "Okay. Let's take this slowly… what is the complete story?"

"I sort of fudged with my profile."

"Fudged how?" Arn asked, but he was already getting a picture of what happened. "Show me your post."

"Do I have to—"

"Show me."

Danny looked at the floor like a little boy about to be scolded by his father as he led Arn into the office. He sat in front of the computer and tapped keys until a photo of a man Arn barely recognized popped up.

"Is that the photo you posted to your profile?"

Danny nodded.

"How old were you in that picture?"

"Twenty-nine. Just graduated college," Danny said at a whisper as if Arn wouldn't hear.

"I can picture that woman responding to that," Arn tapped the picture on the screen, "expecting to see a young feller."

Danny sat silent.

"No damn wonder she stormed out of here. Danny, what the hell were you even thinking posting *that*?"

"Women lie in their profiles," Danny stammered. "I thought I might as well, too."

"My guess is women don't lie that bad, posting a photo that's forty years old…" Arn bent to read the narrative. "And since when do you ski?"

"Never had."

"Scuba diving?"

"Never done that either," Danny said.

"Then my friend, I'd suggest you edit your post… take out all those activities you've never done that might attract young women. And go someplace and have a recent photo taken, one that won't give the women any illusions as to who they're corresponding with." Arn walked out of the room, shaking his head as he went. "For all your intelligence… don't you beat all."

6

Arn pulled into the Cadillac Motel parking lot, narrowly missing a pothole big enough to fish out of in wet weather. He looked over the siding in bad need of a repaint, and the roof missing shingles like some little kid missing his teeth after the bully finished with him. The upper balcony drooped and was held from falling by a thick cable anchored somewhere on the roof.

He walked to the Office, the neon sign missing letters so that it flashed 'OFF E'—and Arn wished he'd brought his hand sanitizer with him. As he walked through the doorway, he started to put his mask on when a man sitting behind the counter said, "Don't worry about the mask, pard'ner. Governor Gordon just lifted the mask mandate, and I'm by God not going to make anyone in my business wear them for one more minute." He used the counter to stand and lean over, his big belly pushing against the cash register as he reached out his hand. "Frankie May. Welcome to the Cadillac, pard'ner. What'll it be? A room for just a couple hours?" he winked.

Arn handed Frankie a business card. "I don't need a room."

Frankie grabbed reading glasses missing one of the bows from off the counter and held them to his face as he read it. "Arn Anderson. Wasn't there an Arn Anderson that wrestled up around Minneapolis way?"

"There was," Arn said. "But I'm not him."

"You could be, big as you are." Frankie handed the card back and said, "What the hell do I need a PI for?"

"I'm sure you don't," Arn answered. "But one of your employees did." He took out a photo of Paquita Robles and slid it across the counter.

Frankie slid it back and turned his head. "I don't even want to look at her in that condition. Bad enough that her death mask was pasted across the television."

"I understand you were the one who called Ana Maria Villarreal at the TV station."

Frankie took out a pack of generic cigarettes but laid them back on the counter as he dug into an ashtray for a long snipe. "Sure. Soon's I seen Paquita's photo on the television last night, I called that reporter woman. Who, in turn, must have called the cops, 'cause it weren't too long before they descended on my place." He lowered his voice. "Kind of cramps my business having cops sniffing around, if you get my drift. But having a private investigator... I can't think of anything to tell you that I ain't already told the cops."

Arn moved away from the smoke lingering over Frankie like dust over Pig Pen. "Humor me... tell me what you told the police."

"Ouch!" Frankie snuffed the butt out in the ashtray and sucked on his finger. "Teach me to smoke them down to the nub."

"The police?" Arn pressed.

"Sure. The police. Follow me—it'll be easier to remember if I show you."

Arn followed Frankie as he walked from around the counter and led Arn up a flight of steps, Frankie huffing all the way and Arn hoped he wouldn't have to do CPR on the fat man. They made their way down a walkway in front of rooms in a row and Frankie stopped at one. He dug into his pocket and came away with a Ziploc full of loose cigarettes. He caught Arn staring and said, "folks bring smokes at every AA meeting and I... scoop up what I can." He tapped a room door with a jaundiced finger. "This is where Paquita was cleaning when she left."

"Left where?"

"Can't say," Frankie said. "All's I know is she left her cleaning cart smack in the middle of the walkway in front of the door to this room."

"Did she say where she was going?"

"I never seen her that morning," Frankie said. "First I knew that she left work was looking up at the cart and seeing it there. But no Paquita."

"Did the other cleaning ladies see her?"

Frankie shook his head. "As slow as business is during this damn pandemic, she was the only cleaning lady I needed for the last month."

"She often walk off the job?"

"Not that one," Frankie said. "She's not the first Filipino woman I've had cleaning for me, and none of them have been anything but good workers."

"Did you show the police her job application?"

Frankie tilted his head back and laughed, his belly jiggling, the stained Mickey Mouse on the front of his shorts dancing to his laugh. "Anderson, we're not exactly keen on formalities here. The girl needed a job, I needed a cleaning woman." A dreamy look crossed his face. "But when she asked for the job, I was sure she wanted access to the rooms for... professional reasons. A real shame a looker like that stooping to cleaning. But then, a lot of druggies do."

"She a druggie?" Arn asked.

"I never seen her do any drugs, but a beauty like that... someone should have taken her in as hot lookin' as she was."

Arn explained that Paquita was found wearing jogging shorts and a tank top. "Did she often dress like that to work?"

"Not that one," Frankie said, "though I told her she could wear whatever she liked. And she seemed to like jeans and a T-shirt."

Arn took out his notebook expecting some rudimentary information about Paquita. "Where did she live?"

"She never said."

"And you never asked?"

"No reason to pry," Frankie answered, "as long as she showed up and done her job."

"Which she didn't do that last morning."

Arn felt the balcony walkway sway with a sudden gust of wind, and he held onto to the railing. Just in case. "You said her cart was right here in front of room 206. Did she clean that room?"

"Partially," Frankie said, "which was odd, too. She always did a nice job."

"You said partially," Arn said. "What did you mean by that?"

Frankie flicked his butt over the balcony and it sizzled in a mud puddle in a parking lot pot hole. "She cleaned the bathroom and the small television area but left the bed rumpled and the pillows on the floor when she took off."

"Can I see the room?"

Frankie grinned. "Just a room like the others. The cops already went in and looked, but you're welcome to." He pulled up his belly hanging over his belt and unsnapped a ring of keys from a chrome key fob. He opened the door for Arn and stepped aside. "This is just like she left it that morning, except I had to straighten the bed. Oh, and clean up the damnable fingerprint powder the evidence people spewed around."

Arn flicked the single, dim light on and walked in. He stood in the middle of the room and closed his eyes, imaging Paquita cleaning, being a responsible employee, making sure that everything was straightened and spotless despite this motel being a dive. Did the killer frighten her? Is that why she suddenly dropped everything, leaving her cart, running to the park? Perhaps she was not jogging for fitness. Perhaps she was jogging for her life. But that didn't square with Frankie saying Paquita always wore jeans and a T-shirt to work. Still, the puzzle was the bed.

Arn opened his eyes and asked Frankie, "you say the bed was messed up as if someone had slept in it?"

"No," Frankie said. "More like someone just passed out on it. I had to tighten the bedding is all. She'd already put fresh sheets on before she took off."

Arn turned to the bed and pulled the covers back.

"Hey, I gotta make that bed again, and for what? You ain't gonna find anythin' the cops ain't already."

Arn felt the pillows and said, "did you put new pillowcases on?"

"Of course, I did," Frankie said. "What do you take this place for?"

Arn held his answer as he pictured the pillows on the floor. "Changed pillowcases but not pillows?"

"Pillows rarely need changing. They're the same ones."

Arn started taking the pillowcase off one when Frankie said, "you better put that back on when you're done."

"I will," Arn said over his shoulder as he fluffed the pillow. He checked the edges—the pillow appeared fairly new, and he grabbed the other pillow. He peeled the pillowcase back and fluffed it. "Tell me, Frankie, did you have to replace the pillowcases after they'd been on the floor?"

"Just one," Frankie said, "and only 'cause it had a tiny spot of something on it. Paint. Maybe grease."

"Could it have been blood?" Arn asked.

Frankie snapped his fingers. "Now that you mention it, it could have been. No, by God, I know it was blood. I didn't tell the cops that."

"Can I look at the pillowcase?"

"I already washed the thing by the time the cops came snooping around. Do you think it's significant?"

"Possibly," Arn said, fluffing the pillow again, causing tiny feathers to *poof* from a broken seam. He picked two feathers up and held them to the light. He was no feather expert, but they looked a lot like the goose feather that was stuck in Paquita's hair.

* * *

Arn drove down the circular driveway lined with lilac bushes and sunflowers as if welcoming people to the Hondros house. Or more accurately, the Hondros mansion. Elizabeth Hondros had texted Arn, wanting to meet at the house and he'd texted her back, worried Elizabeth's husband would catch them together. *He's out of town on business*, she'd texted back.

Arn parked in front of a four-door garage and climbed out onto crunchy pebbles underfoot. The sweet odor of fresh flowers greeted him and he headed for the front door. Even before he reached it, Elizabeth opened it. She stood smiling in the doorway, her housecoat open to reveal more cleavage than she should have. Arn forced himself to look away, though he would have preferred to stare. Elizabeth was a stunning woman with her collar-length blond hair and green eyes that smiled at Arn as he approached the door. "Relax," she said as she stepped aside to allow him to enter. "Tito went to Salt Lake City on business and he's not due back until tomorrow. Come in, please."

She led Arn past the first room off the entryway, where a fat black cat lay on the floor. It looked up at Arn but didn't move.

"Don't pay Winston any mind. He's my husband's cat and he just lays wherever he wants to. Speaking of Winston's," she shook out a cigarette and offered one to Arn, but he waved it away.

He followed Lizzy into a study with a twelve-foot ceiling, classic books lining two walls, dust on the books showing they'd not been out any time recently. She walked to a liquor cart and motioned to the couch. "Sit. What'll it be? I'm having bourbon, but I have most anything."

"Club soda if you have it." Arn said. He plopped down onto the overstuffed leather couch. "When a client has critical information, I prefer to stay clear-headed."

She laughed and said, "first, it's Lizzy as in Lizzy Borden."

"The ax murderer?"

Ice clinked in her glass as she poured three fingers of booze from a crystal decanter. "My namesake and—sometimes when Tito's home—my inspiration. Of course, I can't act on it, that's why I hired you. But maybe you just don't want to lose your... control?" she teased, then let Arn off the hook as she handed him a glass with bubbly club soda. "Relax, I'm not going to jump your bones. Not unless you want me to."

Arn quickly took his notebook from his back pocket and said, "just what important information do you have for me?"

"A name," Lizzy said. She reached in an open drawer on the desk and grabbed an envelope. She walked to the couch with drink in one hand, envelope in the other, and sat close enough that their shoulders touched. "My husband's current mistress is named Ivana Nenasheva. Another mail order bride that he conned into coming over to the states."

"Ukrainian?

"Belarusian," Lizzy answered. "I found some letters in his safe a few days ago."

Arn jotted the name down and asked if Lizzy had ever seen Ivana.

"I can do better than that." She slipped a photo out of the envelope and handed it to Arn. "A dating service glamour photo."

Arn studied the picture. The mistress of Tito Hondros looked much like his wife with blonde hair and deep blue eyes. The information sheet said she was five feet ten inches and one-hundred twenty-five pounds. As Arn glanced at Lizzy, her husband's mistress was nearly identical to Lizzy except about ten years younger. And she didn't have the pursed lips of a chain smoker nor the sagging cheeks of a heavy drinker. He pocketed the photo and said, "she looks a lot like you, for what it's worth. I don't understand—"

"You don't understand why my husband brought some mail order bride over for a mistress when he has me here at home?" She sipped her drink and moved closer to Arn. "And this isn't the first one he's brought over—brought over and wined and dined and bought expensive clothes for and such before dumping them when he tires of them." She downed her drink and eyed the liquor cart. "I was snookered in just like they were, except I actually married him."

"You were a mail order bride?"

"I was. Met him through a dating service in San Diego. But now… I just want you to get the goods on him."

"That's not been so easy," Arn said. "Until now I've only heard about Tito's mistress from friends. *My street eyes.* Every night I make the rounds to try to find where he's hiding her but have come up totally blank. Are you certain he would keep this Ivana Nenasheva in a motel and not rent—or buy—a house?"

"For all Tito's extravagant spending on his various mistresses," Lizzy said, "he is one frugal Greek. He would rather put them in some cheap motel and have money to lavish them with… things."

Arn tried moving away, but the arm of the couch prevented it. "It sounds as if you've known he was a philanderer for some time."

"I have. For many years now."

"Then tell me," Arn said as he felt Lizzy inch even closer, "why hire an investigator now to find his mistress and develop evidence?"

"The prenup," Lizzy said as a wide smile crossed her face. "When we were married, Tito insisted we sign a prenuptial agreement. One of the stipulations was that, if either one us of was caught in an adulterous relationship, they would get the princely sum of one dollar and be out on their ear."

"Seems easy enough to hold up in court."

"That's if I had the agreement. Tito insisted he lost it, telling me it wasn't important as neither of us would violate our marriage vows." She guffawed. "Fat chance."

"Don't help you any if you don't have the signed agreement in hand."

"Mr. Anderson… Arn," she said as she laid her hand on his forearm, "I'm like my namesake, Lizzy Borden, as I told you. Kind of ruthless. I finally found the combination to his safe. Lo and behold what's right on top—the prenuptial agreement that Tito claimed he lost. I copied it and put it right back in his safe. But when the time comes, I'll have my proof for court."

"It goes both ways then," Arn said. "If he catches you, you could lose everything."

"Relax, Arn." Lizzy reached over and pushed a wispy blond lock behind Arn's ear. "He's out of town. And you know what they about when the cat's away—"

"When the cat's away I can't stay," Arn said and jumped up, keeping out of reach of Lizzy. "I'll keep you informed if I find your husband and his mail order bride."

Arn started through the door when Lizzy called after him, "Arn. Wait, please. I'm serious."

Arn waited, skeptical that Lizzy wanted to merely talk. But when she came off the couch and approached Arn, a stern look had overcome her face, her eyes angry slits. "Be careful."

"Always."

"No, I am deadly serious. You watch your back when you're getting the goods on Tito. He didn't get to own the only quarry and rock business in town without being as cunning as… me."

7

"Okay," Ana Maria said, taking her second piece of Old Chicago pizza. "Time to compare notes. What did you come away with from your little visit at the Cadillac Motel besides bed bugs?"

"That owner—Frankie May—he's something else. Have you ever been in that place?"

"Can't say as I have."

"Then if you go, make sure you pack a can of Black Flag 'cause you'll get the heebie jeebies like I did." Right on cue, Arn's arm itched and he scratched it, getting pizza sauce on his hand and he wiped it off. "Thought I was going to have to stop and buy some calamine lotion as itchy as I got."

"And that's all you managed to come away with—a case of lice or whatever?"

Arn lowered his voice even though they were one of only two couples at this early lunch hour. He reached inside his shirt pocket and slid a folded piece of paper across the table. "Don't get any sauce on it. I have to drop it off at the lab first thing in the morning.

Ana Maria unfolded the paper and stared at two tiny feathers.

"That," Arn said, "was in the room that Paquita had been cleaning."

"What do you mean it was in the room?"

"Came out of a pillow with the stitching coming apart. Can't be definitive until it's compared with the one I took out of Paquita's hair, but my guess is it'll be a match."

Ana Maria shook Parmesan cheese on another slice of pizza and said, "Paquita could have picked the feather up while cleaning the room. Or other rooms. Doesn't mean anything."

"Means a lot when you take into consideration that the motel owner had to change the pillowcase as it had a spot of blood on it."

"A spot of blood doesn't a homicide make."

Arn admired another slice of pizza but thought better and left it. He sat back and dabbed at the corner of his mouth with his napkin. "If the killer jumped Paquita and held the pillow over her mouth, it was probably with enough force to make her nose bleed. And remember I said early onset of rigor mortis could be caused by exertion? Picture Paquita on the bed with her killer atop her. Smothering her. She's fighting back but she's only a small woman. That exertion that would cause rigor to set in quickly."

The waitress came to take their plates and gave them a box for the left-over pizza. When she laid the ticket down on the counter, Ana Maria snatched it before Arn could and said, "this one's on DeAngelo. Official business."

"By all means, then," Arn said. "Now your turn—did you find out anything from that tip line your IT guy set up?"

"Actually, one tip came through. The person in the recording sounded Hispanic. Said Paquita used to work at Barberi's Restaurant up until a few months ago."

"That's kind of going downhill, working for some high-class place like Barberi's to cleaning rooms at the Cadillac Motel."

*   *   *

The afternoon crowd had come and gone when Arn entered Barberi's Restaurant. Except for an elderly couple sitting in a booth whispering among themselves, holding hands like teenagers on their first date, the restaurant was empty. Sounds of metal pots being cleaned echoed from the back kitchen, while off in another room a vacuum cleaner whined.

"We close at one o'clock," a man said as he walked around a shoji separating the employee's area from the restaurant proper. "Um… we'll be back serving at five o'clock again," his voice resonant even through the mask he wore.

Arn faced him. Taller than Arn but thinner and *in shape*, he stood in a casual gray sport coat and maroon dress shirt buttoned all the way to the neck. His slicked-back hair looked as if it had a jar of brilliantine pasted on it until Arn realized it possessed a natural sheen to it. He liked to think that he was as in shape as this man was when he was his age, then reconsidered. This man spends considerable time in the gym, he was certain. Arn handed him a business card and said, "Can I speak with the owner."

"Uh… I'm the owner. Alex Barberi," he said and offered his hand. Something gentlemen did even in this pandemic. He looked at the business card and said, "What would a private investigator wish to talk to me about?"

"Paquita Robles."

"What of the girl?"

"Mr. Barberi—"

"Alex."

"Alex, do you not watch the daily news?"

Alex waved his hand around the restaurant. "Mr. Anderson, I practically live *here*, and Gold's Gym is my second home where I work off the stress an hour a day. I don't have time to watch the news."

"Can we sit then?"

Alex led Arn to a corner booth and asked, "Would you like coffee? Soda perhaps?"

"Diet root beer would be nice."

"Melissa," Alex called over his shoulder.

A woman looking as young as Paquita Robles emerged from the kitchen. "Root beer for Mr. Anderson," Alex said and turned back to Arn. "Now tell me why you're asking about Paquita."

"She was found dead in Frontier Park two mornings ago."

"Oh my," Alex slumped in the booth. "What on earth happened?"

"Police think it was an accident when she was jogging—"

"She ran mornings when she worked for me. A woman that stunning… she was a little vain. Always kept her looks up. Uh… guess it was because the men gave her about twice the tips as the other girls usually got. But you don't think it was an accident or you wouldn't be here."

Arn explained that he felt as if Paquita had been murdered at the Cadillac Motel and carried or carted somehow to Frontier Park. "I think the scene was staged to make it look as if she died from the effects of the altitude while she was jogging."

Melissa returned with a soda. Her eyes met Arn's for a brief moment, and he recognized that look: *she wants to tell me something in private.* "Paquita worked at the motel cleaning rooms—"

"I heard that she started there after I had to let her go."

"Problems?"

"Drugs. Or at least I thought she was using. Her and that wild man I hired as a dishwasher. Shame, too, she was such a beautiful woman."

Arn kept quiet, knowing people often told their stories at their own pace. In their own good time.

"Paquita came from the Philippines, and she just didn't seem to... fit in here. Didn't talk much with the other girls. But she did bond with Darwin."

"Your dishwasher?"

Alex nodded, kneading one hand into the other. "Darwin Ness. An apropos name for him as Charles Darwin himself would have a hard time classifying the man." He stood and paced in front of the booth. "I hired Darwin off the street... guess I have a soft spot for homeless vets. And druggies in rehab. And other people with their hand out. What a mistake that was. I had to fire him after no more than a month."

Arn sipped his root beer, waiting for Alex to get it off his chest.

"Darwin started having flashbacks. At least that's what I thought they were... going off about this battle in Iraq. That gunfight in Afghanistan. He'd get all wild-eyed and I got complaints from customers when he came out to pick up their plates and such." Alex forced a laugh. "He didn't even make an effort to be presentable, hair unkempt looking like he'd combed it with a wire brush. And that scraggly beard..."

"You said you thought he was doing drugs. With Paquita?"

Alex stopped pacing as he looked down at Arn. "I'm sure of it. Especially when a policeman in uniform and his wife came into the restaurant one evening. Darwin caught sight of him and he got agitated. Said he refused to go out on the floor while the officer was there. Said he'd kill any officer who got in his face again. My guess is that Darwin had a run in with the law more than once." Alex sat back down in the booth and asked, "uh… are you going to try finding Darwin?"

"I wouldn't know where to look. Would you?"

"The street somewhere. Last I heard he slept in an abandoned train car down at the depot. But Mr. Anderson, if you come across him, I'd call the law before I approached him. The way he was talking about law enforcement I'd wager that he'd do just what he claimed—kill anyone who approached him in uniform."

"Or even a retired cop like me," Arn said. "I'll remember that," Arn said and flipped his notebook to a fresh page. "Do you know where Paquita was staying?"

"Her job application said the homeless shelter, but I don't know if she was still there when she left here." A waitress got Alex's attention and he stood from the booth. "I wish I could be more help. The girl might have had her troubles, but I don't think she was really a bad sort. Certainly didn't deserve to get strangled to death."

Arn sat for a moment finishing his root beer, imagining Paquita waiting tables, a stunning woman floating among customers, dropping jaws, wondering why such a beautiful girl needed to be waiting tables rather than be sitting on the arm of some wealthy sugar daddy.

Arn left his glass on the table and headed out the door. He stood by his car for a long moment, expecting Melissa to meet him in the parking lot. He was right. Within moments, she walked out of the back door, approaching Arn she peeling off her COVID mask. "I'm Melissa."

"I gathered as much," Arn said. "And I would wager you know something about Paquita."

Melissa leaned against Arn's Oldsmobile and dug a pack of cigarettes out of her uniform pocket. Her hand shook as she flicked a blue Bic lighter to her Virginia Slim. "I saw Paquita's picture on Ms. Villarreal's broadcast, wanting to identify her." She looked at the ground and kicked a pebble with her shoe. "I really wanted to call the TV station and tell them who she was but… I just didn't want to get involved."

When Arn said nothing, she blurted out, "I'm on probation, so don't look at me like that. I can't be involved with shit that might land me back in Lusk."

"Let me guess—you were in the women's prison for drugs?"

"How'd you know?"

"Melissa, most women incarcerated in Lusk are there for drugs. But you need to look at yourself objectively. Realize you made a mistake but now have a steady job and off the dope. Is that why you didn't tell your boss about Paquita?"

Melissa shook her head and avoided Arn's gaze. "Cops would have come around questioning us about our relationship since we worked together, and the last thing I need is for my PO to be suspicious of me."

"You are off the drugs?"

"Oh, God, yes." Melissa looked around the parking lot before she added, "but Paquita wasn't doing drugs. Believe me, one druggie can tell another, and she was clean."

"Your boss seems to think Paquita and Darwin were drugging together."

"He's wrong about Paquita, but I'm not so sure about Darwin. I think he suffered from PTSD and it wouldn't surprise me if he did a doobie or two every day just to take the edge off. As for them doing anything together, she'd borrow a car now and again to give him a ride to the VA for some doctor's appointment, but that was it."

Arn jotted the information in his notebook. He clicked and unclicked his pen, thinking. "Paquita was Filipino... what brought her to this country?"

"Marriage," Melissa said. "The girl rarely talked with any of us. Kept to herself. Most of the other girls thought it was because she was so uppity, being so much better looking than us... ranch girls. Me, I always thought she was just shy."

Melissa looked over her shoulder at the back door before saying, "one night we left work at the same time and I offered her a ride home. 'Waiting for my husband to get done,' she told me. I gotta tell you that took be back some—I never knew she was married, and I said as much. 'I was bought here from a dating agency to marry my husband' she said, and clammed up after that."

"Did you see her husband when he came to pick her up?"

"Naw." Melissa dropped her cigarette butt on the pavement and snubbed it out with her shoe. "I left for home before he came. Never talked with her about it afterwards. Never saw her husband pick her up as she always seemed to hang around the restaurant longer than she had to. Like the man was always late or else she was ashamed of him."

"You said she kept to herself... did any of the other girls hang with her?"

"Bonnie Peters," Melissa said immediately. "Paquita talked with her now and again so you'll have to ask her."

"Where can I find Bonnie?"

"County jail."

"Explain."

Melissa shook out another cigarette while she looked around the parking lot. "Where I served time in Lusk for drugs, Bonnie spent a year in the county hoosgow."

"Drugs?"

"That and turning a few tricks for her dope." Melissa lowered her voice. "This ain't going to get to Alex, 'cause he'd fire Bonnie in a heartbeat?"

"Thought he had a soft spot for druggies?"

"He does," Melissa said. "He hired Bonnie when she got out of jail on probation with the stipulation—like he tells all of us—not to reoffend."

"And she reoffended?"

"Not exactly." Melissa drew in smoke and held it there for a long moment before exhaling through her nose. "Part of her probation was community service so she works a day a week at the courthouse. Helping with license and registrations one week, other times working at the Assessor's Office. Wherever they need extra help."

"Doesn't explain how she wound up in jail again."

"Sleeping, if you can believe that. She was supposed to be helping the Records clerks when they caught her napping in the janitor's closet. Wham! Her PO sent her to the county for a weekend to teach her a lesson." She kept watching the back door for Alex. "Please don't come to the restaurant to talk with her."

"She might have information I need—"

"Then here." Melissa took her cell phone from her back pocket and scrolled through her contacts. "This is her cell number. I'm sure she'll appreciate you not coming by work. But give her a few days— the detention officers always take people's cell phones. Leave a voice message and she'll get back to you."

Arn thanked Melissa for the information and climbed into his car. She held the door for a moment and asked, "you're not going to the cops with any of this, 'cause I might not have my job if they came around asking questions."

"I'll put you down as anonymous witness."

"Thanks, Mr. Anderson," Melissa said, then added, "I just wish I would have been friendlier to Paquita."

8

Arn downshifted into third gear and tromped on the foot feed. The Olds fishtailed and threated to dive off into the ditch before he got it under control.

"Dammit, don't drive like a crazy man," Ana Maria said, cinching up her seat belt and grabbing for the lap belt in the spring clip above the door. "You're not a cop anymore."

Arn slowed down, feeling foolish. Ana Maria was right—he wasn't a cop anymore. But if there was one thing that he missed about the job it was driving fast. Legally.

"Pull a stunt like that again," Ana Maria scolded, "and there night be a cop just lurking around the corner like last time."

The last time was on Interstate 25 when he had floored the accelerator in second gear and chirped the tires speed shifting into third just as a Wyoming Highway Patrolman sat darked out in the median. "A man your age pulling a stunt like this," the trooper had admonished him when he handed Arn his citation that had cost him $200. He couldn't afford the fine then and his economic situation hadn't changed much in the last two months. Which is why he'd taken the divorce case from Lizzy Hondros.

"Still no luck finding Tito Hondros' mistress?" Ana Maria asked.

"I've been out every night. Passed the word to all my eyes but no one's seen her which is odd. Looking at her picture, anyone would remember Ivana Nenasheva." Arn's 'eyes' were his 'street eyes,' street people, men and women he did favors for now and again: a meal at a café here, a carton of cigarettes there. People—many living on the street by their own wits, others living in the homeless shelter—but all human beings with their own tragic tales that they told Arn on lonely nights when they were feeling talkative. Mostly though, they just kept to themselves in small groups or with close friends. As he had been told many times before, trusting *anyone* when you lived on the street was dangerous.

Arn came to a stop by the rest area, the bust of Abraham Lincoln rising thirty feet into the air. "What do you make of this Melissa at Barberi's?" Ana Maria asked. "She trustworthy?"

"I got a good read on her—"

"Come on, she's a druggie," Ana Maria said. "One day she can be trusted, the next they're off in their own world stabbing anyone in the back for their daily dose."

He turned onto Interstate 80 for the last few miles to Laramie. "She had no reason to lie to me that I could see. I believe that one night, Paquita decided to talk as she waited for her husband that she told Melissa the truth."

"Then why haven't you checked the courthouse for her marriage license? You find out who her husband is, and you might find her murderer."

"Don't you think I know that?" Most murders are committed by people they knew. Women—more often than not by a boyfriend or husband. "I'd be at the courthouse now doing just that if *someone*," he looked over at Ana Maria, "hadn't guilt tripped me into tagging along to Laramie."

"I told you this is big. We might have a serial killer in our area. And I just knew how you loved serial killers."

Arn had a lifetime of dealing with serial murderers these last years and he didn't want to be involved with another. But Ana Maria's call had intrigued him. "Remember that Jane Doe found in Laramie a few months ago?" she had asked as Arn was on his way to the courthouse.

"How could I forget. College student, the Laramie police thought. You had her photo on your nightly broadcast too, but she was never identified to the best of my knowledge."

"We might be a step closer to doing just that."

"What's that got to do with her being the victim of a serial killer?"

"That watch and band that Paquita wore, the one Detective Kubek intended sending an image regionally… Laramie's Jane Doe wore an earring at the time of her death with the exact same pattern. Thought you might like to tag along."

Arn pulled into the Laramie Police visitor's parking area as Ana Maria reached inside her purse. She withdrew a small spray bottle of Scope. "You sure don't have to have nice breath for me," he said.

"It's not for you, silly," she said. "The detective I spoke with sounded *sooooo* sexy. And with name like Fabian, he's bound to be hot. And possibly available."

"Is that all you think about?"

"So, I've got needs," Ana Maria said and stepped out of the car.

They walked into the police station and asked the desk sergeant for Detective Fabian Hanes. The officer picked up the phone and announced he had visitors. "He'll see you shortly," the sergeant said and went back to reading *Evidence Technology* on his computer.

Ana Maria pulled hair behind her ears and smoothed her pants when she heard Detective Hanes walking towards the waiting room. He opened the door and nearly had to step sideways to get through. Shorter than Arn, half again as big around the girth. With even less hair, Detective Hanes nonetheless had a twinkle in his eye that exuded intelligence. "Ms. Villarreal," he said and offered his hand. "Please call me Fabian," then added, "you look just as pretty as you do on the television."

Arn found amusement in the way Fabian's appearance seemed to deflate Ana Maria, and he stepped in to rescue her. "Arn Anderson. I'm a—"

"Private investigator of sorts," Fabian said, his gaze never leaving Ana Maria, "who caught that nasty bastard last year who was killing those veterans. Excuse the language," he said to Ana Maria.

Ana Maria stood speechless until Arn said, "you were going to interview Detective Hanes?"

"Sure," Ana Maria said, struggling to keep her composure. She took out her notebook and flipped to a blank sheet. After jotting down Fabian's full name and title, she said, "you told me over the phone that you thought your Jane Doe from last year had a single earring when she was found—one that matched the design of the watch on the victim found in Frontier Park a few days ago."

Fabian nodded. "I called right after I notified the Cheyenne police." "Can I see it?"

"Ms. Villarreal, as you know we like working with the press whenever we can, but in homicide investigations..." he grinned widely and said, "but I already got approval to make an exception for you."

"And for my chauffeur?" she said motioning to Arn.

"Won't hurt any. A Chief of Detectives from the Cheyenne PD... Kubek I believe her name was, already dropped by looking at the evidence. Come this way please."

Arn nudged Ana Maria. "You go on beside Fabian and talk about it while I just follow along behind like a good chauffeur."

Fabian led them into an empty room where a box sat in the middle of a table. He indicated seats and Arn took great pleasure in moving two chairs close together before sitting on the opposite side of the table from them.

Fabian reverently took a binder out of the box and sat beside Ana Maria. "This is how we found her—"

"It was your case, then?" she asked.

"Unfortunately. The girl's body was found underneath some thick bushes off Optimist Park." He forced a laugh. "What irony, huh? Dying in Optimist's Park."

"Underneath thick bushes," Ana Maria prodded.

Fabian nodded. "Some joggers found her only about thirty feet off the walking trail. Are you comfortable looking at photos of a corpse that we figured had been in the elements a couple days before she was found?"

"I took some anxiety medication on the way over here," Ana Maria said when in actuality she was giddy that she might be able to feature a serial killing on her broadcast again.

"May I?" Arn asked as he slid the binder towards him. He began flipping pages slowly, the book chronological evidence of what the investigators and evidence technicians did at the crime scene and afterward at autopsy. Even being left where she'd been found for days, it was obvious in the photos that the woman had been stunning.

"We called the state crime van in," Fabian said. "But they never came up with anything that would help us identify her either."

A beautiful college girl like that..." Ana Maria stopped as she cocked her head to look at a frontal photo. "She had to be a college kid, right?"

"If she was," Fabian said, "no one came forward and claimed to know her."

When Arn flipped to a closeup photograph of the victim's earring, he pulled out his phone. He scrolled through his pictures until he found the one he had taken of Paquita's wristwatch.

"Do you need to see the earring itself 'cause I can drive you over to the evidence vault?" Fabian asked, his chair miraculously closer to Ana Maria's than it was a moment ago.

Arn closed his phone. "That won't be necessary. I can see from this picture that her earring and our victim's watch were identical designs."

"How did she die?" Ana Maria asked, scooting her chair back.

Fabian looked at the photographs. Arn would bet the detective hadn't looked at them in some time, the showing and retelling of the girl's death would probably bring on renewed nightmares. At least they often had for Arn when he was on the job. "Strangulation. Possibility occurring during rough sex." He turned several plastic pages, and his finger tapped a photograph. "These marks the coroner determined were rope burns. We figured she was tied up at the time of death. Found one tendril of rope but nothing unusual there—just common rope you'd buy at places like Home Depot or Ace Hardware."

"It fits," Arn said. When he worked Denver Homicide, he'd had several asphyxia deaths that occurred during rough sex. Strangulation intended to heighten the sexual experience, pressure applied just until the moment of orgasm, but that had gotten out of hand. In those instances, the killer had typically come forward and admitted what had happened in the heat of passion between consenting adults.

"I take it you ran her prints?" Arn asked.

"Through the state and through the FBI data base. Nada. This girl was never in any trouble that she would have to be printed. And if your next question is DNA, the ME sent a sample to CODIS but the FBI had nothing in their database. The medical examiner contacted

UNTCHI. Nothing yet, though Jane Doe is at least in their system."
Arn had submitted several cases to the UNT Center for Human
Identification with good luck in identifying his victims at the time.
Often, unclaimed bodies like Fabian's Jane Doe took years to be
identified. Arn prayed it wouldn't be the case here.

Arn thumbed past other photographs, the rest of them like the first
except from different angles and different lighting until he came to the
one he wanted most to look at. He turned the binder so that the light
didn't reflect off the plastic sleeve and he donned his reading glasses
again. Even though the victim's skin had started to slough and the
discoloration from the purple marbling after death nearly obscured it,
a tattoo was visible on her ankle. "12-26-91. Her date of birth?"

"That's the first thing we thought," Fabian answered.

Had he moved closer to Ana Maria?

"But we had no luck with that either."

Arn turned back several pages and looked once again at the victim's
face, making a mental calculation: it would put the victim at thirty
years old. Not unheard of, but a little old to be attending traditional
college. "Can your medical examiner square with her age?"

"Funny you mention that. The ME did some measurements and
testing, and it appears as if the woman was older than her DOB tat
showed. Somewhere, there's a missing person's report on this woman,
I would wager."

Arn slid the binder over to Ana Maria and she made some quick
notes before closing it and saying, "All I need is a photograph of you
and I'll put this onto my nightly broadcast. We got a tip on your Jane
Doe from someone watching my broadcast, perhaps someone will
recognize this victim as well."

"I can come over and sit for an interview," Fabian said. "Perhaps
something more… in-depth for your broadcast might jar someone's
memory of the victim."

"That won't be necessary—"

"Then afterward I can buy you lunch. Someplace nice, say…
tomorrow?"

Ana Maria snapped her fingers. "Tomorrow's a bad day. I told…
Arn here we'd go interview people at the homeless shelter—"

"We can do it another day," Arn said with a wave of his hand, enjoying seeing Ana Maria turn red and squirm. "I can stop by the shelter alone. Go on—you and Fabian have a nice lunch."

"Then it's a date," Fabian said. "I'll stop by your TV station tomorrow."

9

"You just get your COVID shot?" Frida Kubek asked.

"Why do you ask?"

"Because you're rubbing your arm like it's sore from the injection."

Arn wanted to tell her that Ana Maria had hit his arm so many times on the ride back from Laramie he felt it even today. For some reason she'd been angry that Arn hadn't helped her out of her date offer with Fabian. "He weighs more than my Bug," she'd said and hit him hard again. But Arn didn't tell Kubek that.

He rubbed his arm again as he glanced at the clock on the detective's office. Ana Maria and Fabian would be having a nice, romantic lunch while he sat here. He only hoped she would cool off enough that she didn't smack him again when they got home. "Yes," he lied. "The shot made my arm just a little sore."

"All right. But you were saying about the autopsy report?"

"I was saying that I'm impressed—lining up an autopsy in this short of time must have taken some doing."

Kubek smiled, basking in the glow of Arn's compliment. "I drove down to Denver with the coroner myself."

"You didn't use the ME in Ft. Collins?"

"She was at a seminar in Boca Raton. And, yes, it did take some doing. But then, that's why the city hired someone from a larger agency—we were used to getting things done."

And so did the Cheyenne PD investigators, Arn wanted to tell her. "Can I see Paquita's autopsy report?"

When Kubek said nothing, Arn added, "just professional courtesy."

She laughed. "Professional courtesy? You haven't been a cop for ten years—"

"Nine."

"Nine, then." She seemed to be mulling it over when she asked, "none of this information will be leaked to the press?"

"None." Arn gestured that his lips would be sealed while at the same time regretting lying to Kubek. He would bounce information off Danny and Ana Maria tonight and just hoped nothing in her broadcast could be traced to what Kubek was about to show him.

Kubek stood and walked to a tall, gun-metal gray file cabinet in one corner of her office and unlocked it. She grabbed a manila file folder and sat back down at her desk. She handed it to Arn and sat back awaiting questions while he studied the file.

"The medical examiner said she thought the marks around her wrists were from a rope."

"Similar to Laramie's Jane Doe."

"I saw that," Kubek said. "But doesn't mean they're connected if that's where you going with this. Binding victims with rope is common in these cases. Besides, the ME found skin under two of Paquita's fingernails. She put up a fight."

He turned to the back page where the medical examiner had recorded her conclusions. There were no drugs found in the victim's system, nor evidence that she had been raped. There had been no injury such as tearing to her genitals. No semen was found in her system. That alone didn't mean Paquita hadn't been sexually assaulted—Arn knew semen broke down within hours, but parts could be found for two weeks. That's if the attacker didn't use a condom. If he did, all bets were off. "You conclude that Paquita was smothered," Arn said. "I recall I tossed that out in the park."

Kubek sipped on a bottle of Perrier. "I didn't have all the facts at the time," she said at last. "But now things have changed. That feather you took from Paquita's hair matched forensically those you found from that pillow at the Cadillac Motel. I sent our crime scene tech back into that room, but he came up with nothing the second time either."

Arn jotted that down when Kubek asked, "why such an interest in

Paquita Robles? It's not like you're going to get paid for your time."

"My business card. I believe that she was trying to get ahold of me but never got that far. If she were still alive, I'd tell her this private investigation is on the house."

"Then when you ask around, tell folks she was pregnant at the time of her murder. Three months is as close as the ME could determine."

"I will," Arn said and pocketed his notebook.

He started for the door when Kubek stopped him. "Is that it *all* for showing you an official police report?"

Arn turned back and said, "I don't understand."

"I went out of my way to give you what you asked. The least you could do is buy lunch."

Arn had to admit that this was a pleasant surprise. For all her gruffness and proving that she was the consummate professional, he could see spending time with her. It would be a challenge breaking through that strict exterior. "Sure. Where to?"

"We can walk to Two Doors Down," Kubek answered as she grabbed her purse. "They have great burgers."

"Maybe someplace else," Arn said, knowing Ana Maria and Fabian would still be there for their *date*. The last thing he wanted was for Ana Maria to start wailing on him again in the presence of Kubek.

* * *

"I can find no record of marriage license for Paquita Robles," the record clerk said. She snapped her fingers. "That's the girl found dead in Frontier Park?"

Arn nodded.

"She came in last week," another clerk called over from her desk, one corner piled high with paperwork. "She got rowdy, and we had to call the deputies to escort her out of the courthouse."

"Why was she upset?"

"Can't say," the clerk said. "We were at lunch and Helen was here alone. She'll be back tomorrow and can fill you in."

Arn thanked her and left, the scenarios of just why Paquita had to be escorted out of the building playing in his mind. He could come up with no particular reason, and he was at the whim of Helen returning to work tomorrow.

Arn climbed into his car and headed toward the F. E. Warren Air Force Base at the west edge of town consisting of missiles. That was it. Arn always thought it odd an Air Force base had no aircraft save for a few Huey helicopters they deployed during missile defense exercises.

Arn pulled to the gate at F. E. Warren and was directed to the information officer to get a pass to come onto the base. "State your business," the Air Force captain said as she studied Arn's driver's license.

"I'd like to speak with some ladies at the enlisted-officer's club."

She grinned at Arn and said, "you trying to get a date, Pop?"

He wasn't. Ana Maria said that the missile base had a large Filipino population, largely because so many airmen stationed overseas married Filipino woman and brought them to the States when they rotated from their Asian assignment. She'd talked with one of her base contacts who said many Filipino expats met at the club for an afternoon lunch.

"You're out of luck meeting anyone at the club—there wasn't enough business, so they closed last year. But you might luck out and check the mess hall. There's a group of ladies who meet there every lunch hour."

With his day pass in hand, he drove to the mess hall, heads turning to stare at his vintage gold Olds. He pulled into a parking spot and entered. Country western music played through speakers throughout the club, the aroma of burgers from a grill reaching him, making him wish he hadn't already had lunch with Kubek.

Airman lined up at a grill to order burgers or brats while another grill was maned by a cook flipping oriental noodles and vegetables. "Is there a group of women who meet here every day?" he asked an airman.

The *kid* half Arn's age hesitated as if the civilian in front of him was asking about something that would endanger national security. "That back room," he pointed at last, and bellied-up to the grill to order his lunch.

Laughter preceded Arn as he followed the sound of gaiety into another room. Eight ladies—all appearing to be Filipino, all stunningly beautiful in their tight skirts and expertly applied makeup—sat at a table laughing. Salads and burgers and soups of various kinds sat in front of them. They stopped their laughter while they watched Arn approach them. "My name is Arn Anderson," he said, handing out business cards.

They bent their heads together and spoke in a language Arn didn't understand—probably Tagalog—until one of the women turned to him and said, "I am Elana. What would an investigator want with us?"

"I'm looking into the death of a Filipino girl found dead in the park this last week." He showed a picture of Paquita after the mortician had gotten her cleaned up for burial.

Elana said something to her friends. She turned to Arn and said, "that is that Pena we saw on the news. Awful the way she died."

"Did anyone here know her?"

They all shook their heads. "That is… was… one beautiful Pena," another girl said and Arn looked her over closely. She appeared to be in her twenties even though the veins and brown spots on the backs of her hands indicated she was much older. But if she'd walked into a room of men, everyone would have eyes on her. As they would all the other ladies at the table. "We belong to the Filipino Club in town," she said, "but this girl never came. We don't know who she was."

"She was pregnant at the time of her death."

"What does her husband say about it?" An older woman asked, dressed to the nines, still lovely at her age. "He must have reported her missing."

Arn took off his Stetson and ran his fingers through his hair. "The records clerk at the courthouse could find no marriage license on file."

The woman spoke among themselves for so long Arn thought they'd decided to brush him off when Elana said, "if this Pena was pregnant, she had to have been married. She would not have had sex outside of marriage, unless she was a working girl. And we would have heard about another Pena working as a prostitute."

"Are you sure—"

"Mr. Anderson," Elana said, "it would appear as if you have much to learn about us Filipino women. As I said, she would have thought it a sin. She would have spent much time in the confessional. As do all Catholics."

"So, you think she was Catholic?"

"Devoutly," Elana answered. "Like the rest of us. But we never saw her at Mass."

*   *   *

Arn returned home, his arm still aching where Ana Marie had hit him for passing Fabian off as her date. He thought it was her voice he heard when he stepped in the house and walked to the kitchen. Danny sat at the table with a notepad and pen in front of him while across from him a very large woman filled the chair.

"Can you give us a minute, Arn," Danny said. "We're just about through with our interview."

"I need to take a shower anyway."

When Arn came out of the shower twenty minutes later, he picked his way past sheets of dry wall leaning against the wall with five-gallon buckets of mud propped up against them. He stepped into the kitchen; Danny sat alone sipping on an iced tea while he scribbled notes. "I'm almost afraid to ask who that lady was?"

"Number eleven."

"Number eleven what?"

"Number eleven on my interview list," Danny said. "I took your advice and modified my profile on the dating site."

"Is it BS now or did you present yourself honestly?"

Danny jabbed the air with his pen. "You bet I'm honest now—or reasonably honest. At least honest enough that I've interviewed eleven women as a potential partner so far."

"Interview?"

"Yeah. Interview." Danny handed Arn the notepad. He had created columns with rankings for looks and personality and profession.

"That's amazing that you've had that much interest in your ad."

"See," Danny said, "You should have joined."

"No offense," Arn said, "but how on earth did you get these many younger women to respond?"

"They weren't intrigued by my looks or anything. They were drawn to the fact that I'm a structural engineer."

"But Danny, you haven't worked as an engineer for forty years."

"*Au contraire.*" He waved his hand around the room. "I've engineered all this remodeling, haven't I?"

10

Arn poked his head in the computer room and said over the sound of the radio station playing oldies, "Is it safe to come in?"

"Only if you promise not to try setting me up with any more detectives."

"Promise." Arn sat in the chair beside the computer. "Whatcha working on?"

"I'm trying to hook men into looking at my dating profile."

Arn put his hand on Ana Maria's shoulder. "Wasn't your experience with Doc Henry when you were in Denver enough to break you of dating on-line?" Doc Henry—who was not a Doc, though he posed as one for one of his victims—had answered Ana Maria's on-line dating ad when she and Arn both lived in Denver. Doc wasn't the hunk his profile photo showed. He wasn't educated, like his profile ad claimed. And he wasn't into straight relationships. What the profile failed to reveal is that he was happiest when he abducted and eventually killed women, his most recent obsession at the time being Ana Maria Villarreal.

She began trembling before she took deep, calming breaths and said, "I'm over him. I haven't heard a thing about him since he fled Cheyenne last year. The Mars-halls contacted me a few months ago and said they have credible information that Doc was living in Toronto and they'd notify me if they caught him but they haven't so far." She covered his hand with hers. "I understand your concern, but this time I'm a whole lot more careful, especially since this is for my special on dating and mail order brides I'm working on."

"All right, but if you run into trouble…"

"If I do, you'll be the second to know about it."

Arn squinted at the screen before putting on his readers. "Who's Emily Prose?"

"Me," Ana Maria said. "I asked our IT guy at the television station to set me up a fake account."

"You're as bad as Danny," Arn said. "Telling lies on a dating site. Passing yourself off as someone else—"

"Relax," Ana Maria said. "I have no intention of making a date with any of them."

"Then why are you doing it?"

"Ivana Nenasheva," Ana Maria said. "It got me thinking about how Lizzy Hondros told you Tito brought women into the country on the ruse of marrying them, only to use them until he tired of them and tossed them away." She stood and walked to the small fridge in the corner. "Want a soda?"

"Sure," Arn said and accepted the root beer Ana Maria handed him. "But where did we get an apartment fridge? Never saw that before."

And Maria nodded in the direction of the kitchen as if she could see through walls. "Danny said the Fridge Fairy dropped it off."

Arn groaned. "I just hope it's legal."

"Of course it is. Ever know Danny to steal anything?"

"Can't say as I have," Arn answered. "It's just that his acquisitions are a little... suspect."

Ana Maria waved the air. "I got to thinking about Paquita Robles... if there was no marriage license on file with the records clerk, I would bet a month's meager salary she was lured over just like Ivana had been with the promise of marriage."

She turned the radio down and sat once more in front of the computer. "I ran the project by—"

"What project?"

"Dating With the Internet is what I'll probably call it. I told DeAngelo that the viewers would be interested in the many dating sites and portals there are and the perils of joining and putting your profile on them."

"So, this is purely research? "He asked with skepticism.

She winked. "Unless I find a real hunk. Look here." She pulled up a spread sheet with six dating sites that she'd ranked, much like Danny had ranked the women he interviewed. "You can see how each site has their pros and cons."

"How did you come up with these out of all the ones advertised?"

"The State Department of Criminal Investigation," Ana Marie said. She finished her water and dropped the bottle into the trash can. "I contacted the Acting Director—Frosty Williams—and he steered me to his supervisor of internet crime, Agent Chris McDonald. He has a list of complaints against dozens of dating sites. Some with misinformation, others that out and out operate fraudulently. These six have received fewest complaints from consumers."

Arn moved his chair closer to look at the spread sheet. "How come there's no dating site dealing with Eastern European woman?"

"I wanted to stick with domestic sites," Ana Maria said. "Especially after I did some research." Her voice rose, excited as she explained. "Eastern European women—Russians and Ukrainians and Lithuanians—outnumber the men in those countries as much as five to one. A bachelors' dream you'd think."

"Even *I* could score over there," Arn said.

"Score? You'd be a king. Listen, men with the most success in finding mail order brides from that region have steady jobs. Are reasonably good looking—which," she messed his hair, "you could be if you tried hard enough."

"Thanks for the compliment. I think. But looks aren't important to these women?"

"Not particularly," Ana Maria said and pulled up an article written by a former dating site manager in Odessa. "That is the dating capitol for mail order brides in the world. And women want men who actually work. Preferably with money to lavish upon them."

"That'd leave me out."

"You could fool them. A lot of men do. The whole business is a series of give and take, of the potential groom artificially posing as someone a lying bride would want."

"So, in most… transactions, both parties are lying?"

Ana Maria nodded her head. "It's almost a contest of who can out-lie who."

"But when the guy promises marriage—that brings it to a whole other level. Like Ivana Nenasheva and the situation she's in," Arn said. "'Cause you can well bet Tito has no intention of marrying her. Just like the other women he brought over with the promise they'd be married to a wealthy man."

"And there are many." Ana Maria pulled up another article by an Interpol agent advising caution to avoid fraud when dating women from Eastern Europe. Ana Maria rubbed her eyes and sat back from the computer screen. "Ever since the fall of the Soviet Union on December twenty-six of '91 the mail order bride business has exploded."

Arn swiveled his chair around to look at Ana Maria. "What did you just say?"

"About the explosion of mail order brides—"

"About when this article claims it all began."

She looked back at the screen to be sure. "December twenty-six of 1991. Why?"

"12-26-91," Arn breathed, feeling his pulse quicken, the veins in his forehead throbbing with the realization that the fall of the Soviet Union was the same date as the tattoo on the Jane Doe's ankle in Laramie. "She must have been Russian."

*   *   *

Arn caught Frida Kubek just as she was leaving the police station for home. "Miss me that bad already?" she teased.

He hated to admit it, but he did miss visiting with her. Lunch had been nice, talking with a woman once again. He felt his face and neck warm, and he quickly said, "the Jane Doe in Laramie was Eastern European."

"Like you said, that's Laramie's case," Kubek said.

Arn explained that Paquita Robles might have been lured into this country by the promise of marriage, only to have that promise turn into nothing more than being a sex object for the man.

"That's a lot of assumptions, but I'll check with customs," Kubek said. "I know they fingerprint everyone coming into the country even though they don't contribute to the data base."

Arn walked Kubek out to her car. When she hit the door lock, Arn reached over to open the door when she said, "Arn Anderson don't you dare."

"I thought it was customary to open doors for a lady."

"I'm no lady… you know what I mean. If the other officers saw their Chief of Detectives had to have a man open her car door, what confidence would that inspire among the troops?"

"Maybe it'd show you're human," Arn said.

"Tell you what," Kubek said. "Give me a call later in the week and I'll give you a chance to open your car door for me when we go to dinner."

As Kubek drove away, Arn watched after her, a forceful woman. One who knew what she wanted and said so bluntly. Arn admired frankness but wondered just how energetic she might become if their relationship developed. His mind wandered into an area he had not gone to since Cailee died, just a year after he was promoted to detective at Denver Metro. Sure, he'd had some casual dates since, but none more intimate than talking with the lady clerk at the shoe store or checkout at the supermarket. But that was all right—he was always content to keep the ladies at a safe distance. But with Kubek, he might not be able to stave her off and Frida Kubek in stockings and garter belt, whip in one hand, chair in the other, herding Arn just where she wanted him popped into his mind. "You've been reading too many crime reports," he said to himself and climbed into his Olds.

He headed down Lincolnway looking for Nappy the Pimp, who was actually no pimp and had no girls to run. He'd been given that name by other homeless people who caught him wearing a lady's evening dress, ruffles, feathers, and all, that he'd dug out of a dumpster. "Let me put you up for a couple nights," Arn said to Nappy one day last winter when the temperature hovered around minus ten. "We're supposed to get snow dumped on us and I don't want to see you freezing to death. All you got to warm you are those nylon stockings and a holy hat."

Nappy had brushed the offer off. "If it gets too cold, there's a whole bunch of car lots around here that keep their cars unlocked."

Arn turned the note over in his hand. Nappy had called for Arn at the house earlier and talked with Danny. Nappy always claimed never to have a cell phone, yet each time he called, it was from a different number, and Arn was certain he was calling from burner phones he'd lifted from Walmart or Target. All Nappy told Danny was for Arn to meet him somewhere downtown.

Arn began driving down alleys, paying particular attention to dumpsters, knowing that was the best place Nappy might be shopping. As Arn drove the entire west-east alley route between sixteenth and seventeenth and started to head up a block, a shrill whistle cut the air. Arn stopped and put the Olds in neutral.

"Yo, Arnold, my man!" Nappy emerged from under a pickup in back of the pool hall, brushing dust off his ripped trousers. In his hand he held… "It's a catalytic converter, in case you're wondering," Nappy said. He looked both ways in the alley before walking to meet Arn. He set the exhaust piece down and slapped dust off his pants,

"Did you just swipe that from under that truck?" Arn asked.

"'Course," Nappy answered. "They give fifty-bucks… well, it's best you don't know who buys these."

"That's stealing?"

"That old jalopy's been sitting there for the last month. I figure someone just abandoned it."

"It's got current tags on it," Arn said. "You can't be stealing car parts."

"I gots to eat somehow."

"How about work?" Arn said. "That would be a start toward modifying your economic situation."

Nappy stepped back and formed a cross with his fingers as if to ward off such a terrifying notion. "Bite your tongue, Arnold Anderson. My economic situation is just fine. Now did you come looking me up to lecture me or hear what I have to tell you about your man Tito."

"Let's hear it."

"Okay, here's the skinny," Nappy said. "He got him a woman, alright… *Loooordy*, she's a looker. Tall and ever so lovely like she be walking down some fashion runway. Or posing for a Playboy spread."

"You've seen her then?"

"Obviously," Nappy answered. "And now you wants to see her, too?"

"Obviously," Arn answered.

"That rat trap down the road towards the interstate, the Diamond Lil Inn. That's where I seen her. You know, if I had a babe like Tito's got, I damn sure wouldn't be putting her up in no flea bag of a motel that I wouldn't even want to stay in."

"Thanks, Nappy."

"By-the-by big man, if you park in that stand of trees about thirty yards from the motel, you'll be able to get a nice photo. That's assuming you want a photograph."

Arn nodded. "Thanks," Arn said, then added, "you say someone's going to pay you fifty bucks for that catalytic converter?"

"They is, but I'm not going to tell you who—"

"I'm not asking," Arn said as he dug in his pocket for his wallet. "Would you sell it to me for a nice, crisp Grant?"

Nappy looked suspiciously at Arn. "Whatchu need this for?"

"So you don't get nailed for theft. I'll pay you the fifty bucks if you put it back on the truck."

"Why would I do that—it'd just be extra work for me. This way, I take it… down the road and get the fifty smackers and don't have to do no more work for it."

Arn peeled a fifty-dollar bill from his wallet along with a twenty. "This will make up for cutting into your valuable time."

When Nappy hesitated, Arn said, "it's the right thing to do. I'd hate to see some poor slob finally return to his truck and find his converter gone."

"All right," Nappy said at last. "You guilt tripped me." He took the money Arn offered and said, "but don't expect me to be so generous next time."

Arn pulled out of the alley, now only a few blocks from his home when Danny called. "I need a lift home."

"Thought you had a dinner date?"

"Had," Danny said. "She took off and left me afoot."

Arn wondered—as he often did—if he'd adopted Danny somewhere along the way. Danny had been conversing with a woman on the dating site and they had made arrangements to meet at Lucky's Mexicali Grill. "Stand by the curb. I'm only about ten minutes away."

Arn drove to the restaurant and pulled to the curb. Danny climbed in and sat looking straight ahead. "In case you're wondering, I didn't have enough money for a cab."

"I gave you a fifty before leaving the house."

"Just drive, I'm so mad."

Arn pulled away and kept quiet, knowing Danny couldn't keep it inside for long. "That woman ate. And ate. And she ate some more. She just kept ordering food and shoving it down." He held up his hand. "I know you told me the first date should have been Dutch, but I thought I'd impress her and be the gentlemen." He turned in the seat and said, "I had only a two-taco plate while she gobbled and gobbled like she was a contestant in one of those eating contests. She broke me. That's why I had to call for a ride."

Arn pulled to the curb beside their house. Danny started to get out when he paused and said, "you got another thirty bucks I can borrow?"

"If I have to. Don't tell me you're taking her out for another endless feast?"

"No," Danny said. "I need the money to cover the bad check I wrote to the restaurant for her third helping."

* * *

Arn settled back among the pine trees across the road west of the Diamond Lil Inn. He opened his Thermos of coffee and warmed his cup up before taking his binoculars out of the case and setting them on the seat beside him. The trees sat between houses to the west and the motel as if shielding normal people from the happenings here. He'd heard stories about the Diamond Lil Inn from local police officers complaining about the motel being a hangout of druggies and working girls. The police raided the motel last year and—allegedly— cleaned out the riff-raff, but Arn was doubtful. Even at this distance he felt itchy just being near the place, and he prayed he wouldn't have to wait too long.

Arn took the lens cap off his Nikon telephoto, setting it on the seat and taking up his binos. If Tito appeared at the motel, he'd be easy to spot even if he came darked-out. With the full moon high overhead and Arn shielded from it by the trees, he knew it was a matter of time before the Greek showed. Unless he moved his mail order bride to another location like he'd done twice this past week already.

Sometime into his third cup of coffee and second protein bar, a wine-colored Mercedes pulled to the motel parking lot. Arn put the binos to his eyes and watched as Tito Hondros stepped from his car. After he closed the door, he stood for a moment, looking around the motel, across the street. Arn thought for a moment that he looked straight at him when he turned and walked up the stairs to the second-floor rooms. "So, you stashed your babe upstairs," Arn said to his coffee cup as he put his binos down and grabbed his camera.

Tito paused when he reached the second-floor walkway and looked out over the parking lot, across the street to the trees, at Lincolnway a block away with light traffic tonight. He rapped on a door, waited, and rapped again. The door opened slowly and a woman, taller than Tito, stood framed in the doorway—Ivana Nenasheva wearing little more than a flimsy nightie. She wrapped her arms around his neck, but Tito pushed her away. Arn started snapping photos as Tito jerked her hands away and shoved her into the room. The door slammed loudly—even for as far away as Arn was parked, he heard it shut—and he settled back once again with his coffee cup.

He finished his coffee and looked at the photos in the viewer. He had caught the two at the exact moment when Ivana nearly kissed Tito on the lips. Would that be enough proof of adultery to present to a divorce judge when the time came for Lizzy to press it? He thought not, and set his camera on the dash, ready for when Tito came out of the room. If Arn got a photo of Tito coming out, the time stamp would show how long Tito remained in Ivana's motel room, surely proof that the man wasn't there selling baked baklava.

Arn continued watching the motel, the hours dragging by, his head doing the pecking bird on his chest as he shook his head to keep awake. Keep awake, he told himself. Keep...

Arn caught the faint movement outside his window a heartbeat before something crashed through his side window. Something long and round and hard enough to make his head swirl and he felt himself lose consciousness.

11

"**Y**ou're lucky the guy living behind the trees heard your window getting smashed." Ana Maria sat in a chair alongside the hospital bed. "I can't even let you out for one night doing your window peeping thing—"

"Surveillance," Arn said and winced. His hand went to his head, but Ana Maria slapped it away.

"How long was I out?"

"Better part of an hour," Ana Maria said.

"This?" He pointed to his head. "How bad?"

"Eight staples and about a hundred tiny cuts from the glass."

"How... where's my car?"

"I towed it to our evidence lot." Kubek leaned against the door jamb. "I'll have our evidence tech go over it tomorrow to see if we can identify what exactly smashed through your side window and into that thick head of yours."

Arn reached for a glass of ice water when Ana Maria handed it to him. She bent the straw so he could reach it and he said, "Give me the quick and dirty version."

"Don't you remember?" Kubek asked.

Arn shook his head and winced again. "Last thing I remember was watching the second floor of the Diamond Lil Inn expecting Tito Hondros to come out smooching on his mail order bride. That's when I saw *something*... a blur by my window... how's my Olds?"

"Except for the window and a gazillion shards of glass inside, it's all right," Kubek said.

"Could you let Ana Maria into the evidence yard to get my camera," he asked her.

"There wasn't any camera listed on the in-sheet."

"My camera... Nikon with a 70-200 zoom. Cost me a mint."

"And you can bet someone else will be selling it for a mint," Kubek said. "I was wondering why someone would hit you out of the clear blue so now we have a motive. Do you have the serial number for your camera?"

"At the house."

"Get it to me in the morning. I'll put it on NCIC and have our guys start checking the pawn shops."

"So, I am going home in the morning?" Arn asked.

"The doctor wants to keep you overnight in case of a concussion," Ana Maria said, "but I'll be by bright and early to pick you up. Right after you have a nutritious pureed hospital breakfast."

*   *   *

Arn carried his Stetson rather than try to sit it on his aching head as Ana Maria walked beside him toward the house. "I'm fine now," he said. "A little bit wobbly at first—"

"You darned near fell just now," Ana Maria said. "You have to take it easy for a few days with that concussion."

When they came into the house, Danny emerged from the sitting room slapping sawdust off his shirt. He stood in the middle of the room and looked at Arn with a stern expression on his dour face. "I'm hoping that wasn't a stunt to get out of helping me raising that wall for the new addition."

Arn hung up his hat and carefully made his way toward the kitchen. "Let me change first and I'll help you—"

"You will not!" Danny stepped closer to Arn and craned his neck up to look at the bandages on his head. "I was just spoofing you. I don't need your help right now. You need to take it easy and go on the mend. Besides, every time you help I gotta go back and fix your work."

"But I have things to do—"

"Enough!" Danny threaded his arm through Arn's and led him to the kitchen and eased him into a chair. "Soon's I get cleaned up a bit I'll fix you an omelet like you've never had before."

"I already had breakfast," Arn said. "Came out of a baby food jar."

"Hospital breakfast," Danny said. "If it was like any hospital food I ever had it was bland. And not very much of it."

"Good point," Arn said. "I'll be waiting at the table hungry."

*   *   *

After he had eaten Danny's superb omelet along with flapjacks he's whipped up, Arn sat in the kitchen sipping on strong coffee and listening to Danny's circular saw cut through two-by-fours in preparation of raising a wall for the new addition. After he couldn't take the boredom anymore, Arn took the phone receiver off the wall and called Kubek. "Have you found out anything yet?"

"It's only been a day since you were attacked," she answered. "The evidence tech finished processing your car and we drove samples over to the lab, but I can tell you there won't be anything to identify what smashed your window. As for your camera, it's still MIA."

"I'm going to call a tow truck and have it taken over to Safelite to replace that side glass and ask them to vacuum the glass shards up."

"It'll be here at the impound yard when the tow truck's ready," Kubek said. "I'll keep you posted if I hear anything."

Arn hung up the phone, wishing the conversation would have taken longer, wishing he had something to help fight the boredom. This wasn't the first time he'd been laid up with one injury or another. And each time, it nearly killed him to have to sit around until he was mended up enough to get back to work.

Danny's saw stopped buzzing and sounds of a keyboard clacking from the office reached the kitchen. Arn stood, feeling himself become dizzy before catching himself on a chair and slowly walking to the computer room.

"Working on your broadcast? Arn asked Ana Maria from the doorway, then answered his own question when he saw photos on the screen. He hobbled over to a chair and moved it close to the screen before plopping down. "Mind?"

"No problem," Ana Maria answered. "Just gathering research for my Internet Dating special in another week."

"Who are all these guys?"

"Research material." Ana Maria scooted her chair back so Arn could get a closer look. "I selected one of those fellers to have a date with."

"Thought you weren't actually going on a date?"

"Just for research, I assure you," she answered.

"That's a lotta men to pick from."

Ana Maria laughed. "This is just the list I paired down. I had dozens more contact me through my profile."

"They all look fairly similar. How did you decide?"

"This one." Ana Maria tapped the screen. "Robert. He's a few years older than me and claims to own a successful business here in town. He's never been married, has no kids, and wants to settle down and make a family."

"He sounds like you." Arn carefully rubbed his head where the bandage covered the staples, the itching coming over him. "Perhaps this is more than just research?"

Ana Maria looked sideways at him. "Of course not. But then again... I'm not getting any younger."

"You have struck out with most of your dates since this COVID epidemic hit—"

"Thanks for reminding me—"

"...and probably will never find your Prince Charming in this lifetime."

"That's enough, Mister Optimist. Don't you have anything else to do?"

"At the moment, no." He nudged Ana Maria and asked, "what do you think this guy's going to say when he learns you're not who you claim to be on your profile. Are you going to tell him it was all part of your grand experiment?"

"Of course, I'm going to tell him. He'll probably recognize me from the nightly news anyhow."

"When's the date?"

"Tonight," she answered. "I thought it best we meet someplace neutral, and he suggested Barberi's Restaurant." She pursed her lips and kissed the air. "I can't afford to eat there, but DeAngelo Demos can. I already told the tightwad he'd be paying for my meal. A business expense."

"The food there is supposed to be out of this world. Want a chaperone?"

"And be a part of you leaving the house? Not on your life. You need to stay and mend up, and I am confident that's just what you'll do. You know why? Because I told the glass company to take just as many days as they need to replace your window."

12

D anny stood on the brakes, tires squealing in protest as they bit the pavement. The rental car came within inches of the truck ahead of him before traffic once again moved at a crawl. "See. That's why I don't drive."

Even before Danny moved into Arn's old house, he had been content to let other people drive him where he needed to go. As a homeless Army vet living on the street for so many years, he didn't need to drive anywhere. His whole world was within walking distance. But that didn't mean Danny didn't know how to drive. He was just a little rusty in Denver traffic is all. "You're going to get me tossed into the pokey for driving without a license. And having an accident to boot."

"Keep your eyes on the road."

"If I get pulled over—"

"Relax," Arn said. "I was a cop here in Denver remember. I think I'll be able to talk our way out of a ticket."

Danny braked hard again as the heavy noon traffic stopped entirely for road construction. "Sure, you were a cop here—about a century ago. Any cop stopping us won't recognize the famous homicide detective. And what about insurance? I know you lied to that Enterprise kid who dropped the car off at the house."

Arn massaged the bandages on his head and said, "I'll just tell them I hit my head so hard I can't think logically. Perfect defense. Watch the road—our exit is coming up."

"How would you know?" Danny said. "You can't hardly even see straight."

Arn once again fought the urge to itch the staples in his head. "I saw good enough to read those signs, didn't I?" For the last ten miles of Interstate 25 into Denver, signs for International Dating, Inc., had been pasted alongside the freeway. Like miles of Burma Shave signs along the roadside during the Great Depression, International Dating, Inc., had posted tantalizing photos of mail order brides in scantily clad attire just waiting for that lucky American to sweep them off their feet. The dating company bragged that it handled any nationality of foreign bride one would wish for, and Lizzy Hondros was sure Tito had contacted his last two Russian women through the dating company. Perhaps Arn would be just as fortunate. "There," he pointed to a parking lot and Danny cut across three lanes to horns blaring and middle fingers jutting up in the air as he drove past them.

"I'd better sit out in the car," Danny said. "If they take a look as us together, they'd figure the good looking one—that be me—was their potential client."

"With the crappy luck you've been having on that dating site back home, perhaps you should give this place a try."

"What I've read about these international sites? No thanks. Besides, sitting here will give me a chance to brush up on my traffic laws. Just so I don't get stopped driving back to Cheyenne in rush hour traffic."

Arn climbed out of the Nissan and gingerly set his Stetson on his head so as to hide his bandage. He smoothed his sport coat and tightened the knot on his tie. He wanted to appear the affluent gentleman looking for a permanent relationship. Even if wearing a COVID mask spoiled the look.

When he entered International Dating, Inc., soft sounds-of-nature music filtered through the reception area to go with the subdued lighting overhead. A mister sat on a stand in one corner, droplets of fragrant lavender scent filling the office empty except for the receptionist.

The receptionist behind the counter, a Black lady, her exotic earrings dangling from her ears, her head in a turban stood and smiled. "Welcome to Denver's premier dating site for glamorous ladies," she said as smoothly as if she'd greeted clients the same way a thousand times. Tall and lithe with a hint of Jamaican accent remaining, though it was hard to tell underneath her mask. She came around the counter with a clipboard in her hand and said, "You have come here to find love, no?"

"Yes, I have," Arn said, looking around the empty waiting room. "But I have not done this before and frankly," he lowered his voice, "I am kind of nervous."

She laid her hand on Arn's shoulder and handed him the clipboard. "Most men your age who come to us for help are a little apprehensive." She motioned to a row of chairs along one wall under a mural of the Orient Express chugging across Siberia in the wintertime. "Please fill this out. A dating advisor will be happy to help you find what you truly wish for."

Arn sat with pen in hand and did his best to answer the questions as fraudulently as possible. When he completed it, he stood and handed the receptionist the clipboard.

"Your advisor will be with you shortly," she said and disappeared into a side room. Within moments, she emerged and said with a broad smile, "you are truly in luck, Mr. Tartan. The owner himself will advise you. Please step this way."

Arn once again smoothed his sport coat while fighting off the urge to scratch his head wound. He followed the receptionist into a spacious office, thick carpeting underfoot cushioning his steps. A thin man sat behind a desk wearing a smile as wide as the receptionist's. When the woman left, the man stood and smoothed his three-piece herringbone suit before offering his hand. "Grigori Musin-Pushkin," he said with a thick Eastern European accent. "But please to call me *yust* Grigori."

Arn shook his hand, noting the softness, the perfectly manicured nails, the fake Rolex on his wrist.

He pulled his mask down. "If you are comfortable…"

"Of course," Arn said and took his own mask off.

"Sit, please, *while* I examine your application." He motioned to a cart beside his desk. "Tea. Or *haf* some of my Turkish coffee."

"Water is fine." Arn sat in an overstuffed chair and poured himself a glass of water from a crystal decanter with floating slices of lime while he looked about the office. Pictures adorned the walls, ranging from a photo of Moscow Square to Hong Kong's business district to Manilla's Ft. Santiago to Bogota's Salt Cathedral, enticing places all.

"Amos Tartan," the man said after a moment and laid Arn's application onto his desk. "Such a strong name. I like that about you Americans."

Arn remained quiet.

Grigori leaned back in his chair and tapped the application. "You *vish* to find a good *vife*, no? I see," he said, as he put on glasses dangling by a chain around his neck, "you are twice divorced."

Arn shrugged. "The job... it takes me all over the world."

"Yes. Yes. It says that you *vere* an oil engineer before you retired." Grigori let his glasses drop onto his chest again. "But you *vere* not specific as to *vhat* nationality you desire."

"That's why I am here," Arn said. "To seek your wisdom. Tell me, what country do you feel offers the most for a man in search of a wife? I have heard much about Filipino ladies."

Grigori sat back and rested his clasped hands on his stomach. "You *haf* good tastes. Filipino ladies are... not discriminating. They often cling to men much older than they. I can arrange for you to visit Manila on one of our Love Tours. You *vill* be an instant success, even *vith* ladies half your age, distinguished looking as you are." He handed Arn a brochure. Different Asian countries were included in the dating site's Love Tours: Vietnam and the Philippines and China and Laos, each with a price for the jaunt listed. Each more than Arn was going to make on this assignment from Lizzy Hondros.

"So, you recommend Filipino women?"

"I did not say that." Grigori leaned his elbows on the desk and tented his fingers. "The problem *vith* many Filipino woman is that— once the man brings them here to the States—they get with other expats from the Philippines. They talk among themselves. They gain independence they did not *haf* over there. And before you know it, that beauty who got ladied-up *yust* for you is now attracting other men—*younger* men—here and, *poof!* They are gone from your life. But if that is your desire—"

"I see the dilemma," Arn said. "Then tell me about the Eastern European ladies."

"Ahhhh," Grigori said, kissing his fingers and throwing a kiss to the poster of Russia hanging beside his desk. "I *haf* a soft spot for those from the Fatherland. My Russia. Those ladies from Minsk and Lithuania and Belarus are equally as good for potential mates." He nodded to the brochure. "*Vhatever* you seek, Grigori will make happen."

Arn studied the brochure that outlined a dating jaunt with a group of other men seeking young brides. He laid the pamphlet on the desk and said, "I have a confession to make—I lied."

Grigori slid his chair back and he sat up straight, looking to the door. Looking for an exit in case I am a fraud investigator. "How Mr. Tartan… if that is your name?"

"It is. But what I lied about is that I am not divorced. I am happily married and would like to remain that way."

"Then *vhy* are you here if your marriage is fine?"

Arn leaned forward and his eyes met Grigori's. "I didn't say it was fine. There is just… something missing with my wife. A spark that used to be there that is lacking now, I'm afraid."

"Ah, I see now," Grigori said and Arn saw a relieved look on his face. "You *vish* to… meet a young lady *vith* the utmost… discretion?"

"The utmost," Arn said. "I don't need my wife finding out. I don't need my bank account lost in divorce court. And I sure don't have the luxury of going on one of your Love Tours to another country. In short, Grigori, I need to find a woman who will come over here on the promise of marriage."

Grigori nodded and a slight grin tugged on the corners of his mouth. "So, you *vish* to bring a young woman here on the promise of marriage *vithout* the possibility of such? You *vish* to bring her over under false promises?"

Arn sat back in his chair and fidgeted with his tie. "You have a perfect grasp of my situation."

Grigori sat silent for a moment, thinking, but Arn got the impression this wasn't the first time he'd had this proposed. He could envision Tito Hondros having the same conversation with Grigori. "I think," he said slowly, "that this could be arranged. But it *vill* be… slightly higher than our regular fee."

"That's fine," Arn said. "But I must emphasize the utmost discretion. There can be no record of the lady entering this country."

"I cannot arrange that—"

"For the right price, you can."

Once again, Grigori seemed to be weighing the solution in his mind. "There is one way, but it *vill* cost you even more."

"Fine. How?"

"I cannot tell you—"

"You can if I'm the one paying the bill. And I imagine it will be a very pricey bill, at that."

"Very well," Grigori said at last. "I can arrange for the lady—I'll have to put together a photo album *vith* the ones willing to come here this *vay*."

"What way?"

"Through the southern border. You see, Mr. Tartan, that is *vhy* it *vill* be so expensive—the cartels charge so much to take people across the border." He stood and offered his hand again. "It *vill* take some time to gather the potential ladies. Give me your cell number and I *vill* call you back in about a *veek* or so. And Mr. Tartan, I don't need to tell you that discretion goes both ways. I for one do not *vish* to sit in a federal lockup."

13

When Arn returned to the rental car after meeting with International Dating, Inc., he expected Danny to be cutting Zs. The man could literally sleep any place. Or so Arn thought. "Why the hell did you leave me here alone? If I'd known it was this bad," Danny said as he unlocked the door.

"Whoa," Arn said. "Slow down and tell me what you're upset about."

"This." Danny motioned to the cars speeding by on E. Colfax. To the drunks staggering to the liquor store for another forty of beer. To the ladies that—even though it was daylight—still walked up and down the street hoping for a john to pay their way for another fix that would last them until tonight. "Do you know how many bums came up to the car for a handout?"

Arn buckled his seatbelt and locked his door. He'd worked Denver long enough as a policeman to know all sorts of things happened on E. Colfax. But rarely during the daylight. "Maybe these bums you worry about actually needed some lucky bucks for a meal."

"Arn," Danny said, "I lived on the street long enough to be able to spot a scam with these guys. But ol' soft-hearted-Danny finally gave one of them a dollar. And you know what happened? I'll tell you what happened—the word got around pretty quick there was a sucker in a Nissan and before long others came out of the woodwork. It was like the Night of the Living Dead, all coming to the car and pawing it like I have a bottomless pocket. They saw you come out of the building, and they scattered like I'd hit them with some Black Flag."

Arn grinned. "I'm glad you made it through your ordeal."

Danny started the car and half-turned in the seat. "I see you made it through yours. How'd it go?"

Arn explained about the lavish waiting room, the large, opulent office for the Russian owner of International Dating, Inc. Of the brochures that explained what to expect with the ladies and the dating service.

"Then it's all on the up-and-up?" Danny said.

"Not hardly. The office is a set-up. The carpeting had been put down somewhere once before if I spotted the carpet staples right. Probably got the carpeting for free to haul away. The furniture was Walmart modern with faux leather. Then there was the owner. My dating advisor touted himself as Russian. He was about as Russian as you are."

"How you figure that out?"

"His accent," Arn said as he took off his tie. "I put it North Dakota. Maybe Minnesota. And crooked as a corkscrew, I'd wager." Arn explained the proposition he had arranged with Grigori to smuggle a mail order bride into the country by the porous southern border, thereby avoiding her being fingerprinted. "As far as the government knew, she would never be in the U.S."

"I'm betting that's how Tito got his current mail order bride into the country with no record and maybe that Jane Doe in Laramie—"

"Katya Petrov," Arn said. After Fabian had run the victim's tattoo by the Marshals with an emphasis on looking at missing women from Russia, Katya Petrov's name surfaced.

"She didn't have any prints on file either you said. Tito *had* to have a hand in it."

"Somebody had to," Arn said. "I just don't know enough about Tito's current MOB—Ivana Nenasheva—to know if he brought her in that way or not. I'll have to get her prints and run them."

"How you ever going to do that?" Danny said, eying a bum walking towards the car.

"Pick up something she's discarded—a cigarette pack. Maybe a soda can."

"First you have to find her," Danny said, "without getting your noggin busted again." He started out of the parking lot onto Colfax for the drive back to Cheyenne. "Still have no idea who attacked you and stole your camera?"

"Detective Kubek left a voice message for me to call her after we eat. I know I promised you a steak dinner if you drove—"

"You can buy me a steak once we get out of downtown Denver. Let's just get back heading north before we stop somewhere."

For having not driven in years, Danny picked up on it remarkably quick, weaving in and out of traffic, bypassing a construction area to go a quicker route, shaking his fist at a motorcyclist who cut them off. Within an hour, they were well out of Denver and Arn said, "let's pull into Wellington. I know a place where we can get a steak dinner."

"Where?"

"There." Arn pointed to Culver's Cafe.

"They don't have steaks."

"Tube steak," Arn said. "A hot dog. It's all I can afford today. I had to put down a hundred dollars earnest money for Grigori—or whatever his name is—to come up with potential ladies to smuggle through the southern border."

"Why'd you do that? You're not actually going to have a woman smuggled in."

"I just want to make sure that fool can actually arrange it. If he can, I'll get hold of an FBI agent I know at the Denver Field Office to raid International Dating, Inc. It'll cost me a hundred bucks, but it'll be worth it if I can put that place out of business."

They pulled off the Wellington, Colorado exit and drove to Culver's. After ordering tube steak and a soda, Danny led the way to a back booth where Arn could talk without anyone hearing. He took out his phone. Besides the call he'd gotten from Kubek, there was another from a number he didn't recognize, someone who had left a voice mail. "Probably some insurance scam again."

"What's that?" Danny asked with a French fry at his mouth.

"Another number, but I'll listen to it later." He dialed Kubek's phone and she picked up on the first ring. "Thought I'd give you the good news," she said. "A street man pawned your camera at Lincolnway."

Arn felt his fortunes rise. He'd get his Nikon back, download the photos of Tito and his mail order bride, and be off the case by the end of the week with a check in his account. He didn't want to spend any more time dealing with Lizzy Hondros than he had to. Like going in Grigori's office, he felt the need to slather on hand sanitizer when talking with her. "You got a name?"

"Mikey the Sneak," Kubek answered. "He didn't give his real name when he pawned it."

Arn covered the phone and asked, "Ever hear of Mikey the Sneak?"

Danny dabbed mustard off his lip. "Sure. Mikey's been around Cheyenne since before I stumbled into town. Has some crib in the UP railyard."

"Could you find him if we drove there?"

"We can unless he's dumpster diving. This being Tuesday, it's the best shopping day of the week."

"Let me know if you find Mikey," Arn told Kubek. "If you haven't had any luck by the time we pull back into town, we'll walk around and see if we spot him."

"We?"

"Danny. My roomer."

"That old man?" Kubek said. "If you do much walking, you better stay close to him. You do know CPR I hope?"

"I only hope *he* does," Arn said. "That *old man* can walk circles— and work circles—around me. I'll call when we're back in town," and he disconnected.

"She doesn't like me much," Danny said matter-of-factly, but Arn knew Danny didn't really care. All he wanted was for folks to leave him alone and let him work his magic with the house remodeling. "I heard what she said about your camera. Sounds just like Mikey. But," he finished his hot dog and took the wrapper off his milkshake straw, "it doesn't sound like him busting your window and stealing the camera. Mikey might be a sneak as his name suggests, but he's about as violent as Nappy the Pimp."

Arn checked his watch. "Lot of daylight left when we get back to Cheyenne to hunt up Mikey." He pulled up the voice mail from the other call he'd missed. *"Paquita Robles' husband abused her. Find her husband and you find her killer."*

Arn replayed the message twice more before pocketing his phone.

"Didn't quite catch that," Danny said.

"Someone left me a message to look for Paquita's killer. Says it was her husband."

"She didn't have a husband," Danny said, "at least not legally if you believe the records lady at the courthouse."

"I do believe her," Arn said. "Now all I have to do is locate my tipster and find out what he knows."

* * *

When they got back into town, Arn had Danny drive towards the Union Pacific railyard. He parked by the depot clock tower lording over the railyard and the square below. "I think we'd have better luck finding Mikey the Sneak if I walked the railyard alone."

"I don't believe this," Arn said. "You don't trust me."

"Nothing personal." Danny hitched up his jeans and said, "you are still, after all those years, still a cop at heart. And you move like a cop, something Mikey would pick up right off. In the back of your mind Mikey's… home… should be taken down. Mikey should be put into the homeless shelter."

Arn started to argue when Danny held up his hand. "Now you trust *me*. Hang around the depot and I'll bring Mikey to you."

Arn sat on the fender of the rental car, itching his head, the staples holding his scalp together urging him on to more vigorous scratching. He knew he better not do it. He knew he would heal quicker if he didn't. But it felt oh *soooo* good.

"You're going to wind up back in the ER." Danny had come up on Arn without him being aware of him. Or aware of the unusually tall man beside him. "Meet Mikey the Sneak."

"Oh, Danny," Mikey said. He slapped Danny on the shoulder and nearly knocked him down.

"Now you can see why he can get into the dumpsters easy," Danny said. "When the rest of the street people have to go diving, all Mikey needs to do is reach in if he wants to shop."

Arn came off the fender and approached Mikey. "Do you know me?"

"Cain't say I do, pard'ner," Mikey said.

"You've never met me?" Arn asked, watching closely the man's eyes for any telltale hint of a lie.

There wasn't any when he said, "I ain't never seen you before. Why?"

"You pawned a camera yesterday to Lincolnway Pawn."

Mikey nodded. "Got thirty dollars for it too."

"That was my camera."

Mikey backed away and held his hands in front of him as if to ward off the accusation that… "I never stole it. I found it in the dumpster back of the parking garage."

"How'd it get there?"

Mikey shook his head, great strands of braided black hair bouncing on his chest.

"I believe you," Arn said.

Mikey slumped and used the car for support. "I was afeard you'd think I stole it—"

"I said I don't think that you did," Arn said. "But you'll still have to talk with the police about it."

Mikey backed away, his eyes darting somewhere in back of him. Looking for an escape route. "Me and the law… we've never seen eye-to-eye. I cain't go to the police—"

"Do you want me to tell them I do think you stole my camera?"

"No, Mr. Anderson."

Arn reached into his wallet and handed Mikey Detective Kubek's business card. "All you need to do is call her or stop at the PD. Tell her where you found the camera. I have to go up there now and get it back. I'll tell her I don't believe you were the one who knocked me senseless and stole it."

"Okay," Mikey said. "Just as long as they don't toss me into the hoosgow. The mattresses on their bunks are *terrible*."

14

Kubek wasn't in her office, but the evidence officer released Arn's camera to him. He waited until he got back to the car and sitting beside Danny to power it up. "Crap!"

"What crap?" Danny asked.

"The memory card is missing."

"You should still have photos in the hard drive, right?"

Arn scrolled through his photos. Those he had taken earlier in the day of his attack—the ones showing progress of the house project— were there. But the pictures he had taken of the Diamond Lil motel and of Tito and Ivana Nenasheva had been erased.

"Now what's your plan?" Danny asked.

"We're going to the Diamond Lil and see what she knows about Ivana about Tito. In case she's still there, I might find out something. If that memory card's gone, my bet is that it wasn't someone committing a crime of opportunity when that attacked me and stole my camera. It had to be Tito."

"How could he manage to come out of the room without you seeing him?" Danny asked.

"I can't answer that unless I take a look at the motel. And talk with Tito if he happens to be there."

"What if the manager doesn't want to talk with you about her renters. And what if Tito doesn't want to tell about his mail order bride? Tito's a big ol' boy from what I see of him now and again in the grocery store."

"That's why I'll bring you along."

Danny chuckled. "In case you didn't notice, I'm just a little old—
and a little small— to be wrestling with some big bruiser like him."

"But you're not too old to dial 911 if he's there and starts something."

"Understood," Danny said, then added, "you'd better steel yourself
if we're going to the Diamond Lil."

"What are you talking about?"

"Lil," Danny said. "You've never seen her dressed up for Halloween?"

"Can't say I've ever trick-or-treated at that motel."

"Well, a lot of kids have, and a lot of kids have been scarred out of
their wits. Lil dresses up in her *very large* witch's costume, broomstick
in her hand, her cat as her *familiar* at her feet. Scares the hell out of
kids."

"Luckily," Arn said, "this isn't Halloween. Ready to talk with the
witch?"

"As soon as we stop at Walgreens?"

"For?"

"Disinfectant wipes. I'll need them if you expect me to set foot in
the Diamond Lil."

*   *   *

After stopping at Walgreens to pick up disinfectant wipes, they drove
to the Diamond Lil. A two-story affair like many in town, the Lil—
as it was unaffectionately called by locals—was almost as run down
as the Cadillac Motel. Trash blew in the parking lot and a door on
the lower floor creaked off its rusty hinges, swaying at an acute angle
waiting for a handyman who may never come to fix it.

As Arn and Danny were walking towards the office, Danny said,
"You better hide your left hand."

"How's that?"

"Your left hand. Where you wore a wedding ring once."

"I still don't understand—"

"Lil," Danny said, "has been married four times, two of which
ended in divorce, two in death and she's always on the lookout for
number five. I'd hate for you to gamble wrong and be one of the ones
who croaked."

"Doesn't have anything to do with me?"

"As soon as she sees you're not spoken for, she'll be all over you like a cheap used car salesman. Hide your ring finger is all I'm saying."

Arn paused before entering the office and said, "this would seem a good opportunity for you. After all, *you're* the one who's been on the dating site non-stop looking for a babe."

Arn," Danny said, "with my current rating system, Lil wouldn't break any higher than that one-armed woman from Greely who answered my ad."

Arn led the way into the office, the odor of *something* nauseating coming from the back room. Arn stepped around an overflowing kitty litter box and a garbage can stuffed with empty beer cans before making it to the counter. They stood there and Danny's hand hovered above the bell. "Aren't you going to slap the bell?"

"I'm trying to gather enough courage—"

"Just ring it, already," Arn said.

Danny slapped the bell softly, then again more forcefully.

"Keep your damn pants on," a woman yelled from the manager's apartment a moment before she emerged from the room. Bright red lipstick and thick rouge adorned her seventy-something face to set off the four ear studs in one ear and a lovely silver nose ring. Her pursed lips and nauseous odor told Arn the woman was a heavy smoker. She wiped her hands on a stained apron and smiled when she saw them. "Danny," she said cheerily, "who is your handsome friend?"

Danny introduced Arn and Diamond Lil focused her attention on him like a pit viper looking at a crippled mouse. "Do you fellas want supper? Got a fresh pot of tripe boiling."

"We just ate," Arn said while he patted his stomach for effect. He moved away from the thick odor of lilac perfume and asked, "we'd like to ask you about one of your renters—Ivana Nenasheva."

"Never heard of her."

"She rented room 212—"

"That *wench!*" Lil stripped off her apron and came around the corner. "Gave her name as Lima Dorn. Listed an address in Mexicali, but I suspicioned she wasn't any more Mexican than me. Had an odd accent." She tapped the side of her head. "Can't fool me none."

"Is she still here?" Danny asked, careful to keep Arn between Diamond Lil and himself.

"Naw, she moved out two... why do you ask?"

Arn handed Lil a business card and said, "just following up on a recent case. When did she leave?"

"Two days ago."

"The morning after my attack."

"What's that, sugar?"

"Just thinking aloud," Arn answered. "Is the room rented now?"

Lil winked and said, "do you want to rent it by the hour for you and Danny? I'll have to charge you extra for clean sheets if you want them."

Arn felt his neck warm and knew someone as pale as he was blushing. "No. We'd just like to look at the room."

"Suit yourself, sugar. Just let me turn off the stove."

After more than ten minutes waiting, Danny said, "do you think she forgot?"

"I don't know," Arn answered. "Might be a blessing if she did."

Lil finally emerged from her office apartment like she was walking down a fashion runway. She'd changed her grubby day clothes for a tight dress that was cut *waaay* too low for a woman her advanced age.

Danny bent his head and shielded his mouth. "I told you she would be hot after you."

"If you follow me," Lil said, "I'll show you the room. But Danny, stay here and mind the office will you."

Lil threaded her arm through Arn's and they walked beside each other like teenagers on the prom date until they reached the room where Arn earlier saw Tito and Ivana Nenasheva meeting. Lil produced a ring of keys from her pocket that would choke a horse and unlocked the room. "Not sure what you expect to find in here, sugar. Lima—Ivana according to you— took all her things when she checked out. Doubt you'll find anything."

Arn didn't think so either, but he thought he might pick up on *something* if he looked about.

He did.

He walked past the bed sporting a faded and raveled bedspread, past the nightstand with one broken leg propped up by a Gideon's

Bible, to the only window in the room on the wall away from where Arn had parked two nights ago as he watched Tito.

He pulled back the stained curtain and studied the windowsill. He was secretly pleased that Lil hadn't cleaned the room as the dust on the windowsill showed where someone had stepped onto it. The screen was missing, and Arn opened the window, poking his head out. A safety ladder leading to the ground floor swayed, barely secured to the side of the motel by one rusty bolt. And on the ground outside the window were footprints of a large, pointed shoe beside the screen that had been laid off to one side. *Tito's.*

Arn pulled the curtain back and said to Lil, "did she say where she was going when she checked out?"

"The same big, stocky guy that rented the room checked her out." Lil stepped closer. "He had a wedding ring on, though. Attached. But," she motioned to Arn's left hand, "I see you're not hitched."

"I'm spoken for. I'm gay," Arn lied.

Lil shrugged. "I could convert you."

* * *

"That's not really prima facia evidence that Tito sneaked out of the room and attacked you," Ana Maria said, picking at her plate of spaghetti Danny had cooked tonight.

"Close," Arn said. "If it'd been some random attack to steal my camera, they sure wouldn't toss it in the dumpster after deleting pics and taking my memory card."

"What're you going to do about it, bust Tito's head?"

"I feel like it," Arn said, massaging his bandage. He was scheduled to get his staples out tomorrow and was grateful for it. "What I am going to do is follow that bastard until I find out just where he's stashing his mail order bride and fill up my new memory card with his... indiscretions."

"You oughta bust him." Danny grabbed another piece of garlic bread, and Arn marveled how he could eat for two people and still look like he'd been on a starvation diet for a month. "Just for making me go into the Diamond Lil Inn again you oughta bust him."

Ana Maria twirled her noodles in her spoon. "I've never been into the Diamond Lil, but Danny said it was about as bad as the Cadillac Motel."

"It'd be a tossup." Arn tore a piece of garlic bread in half. He didn't have the luxury of eating like a horse like Danny did. "What I don't understand is how someone as outwardly stunning as Ivana Nenasheva would stand for being put up in such a rat trap like the Diamond Lil's, let alone being lured to this country under a false promise of marriage."

"'Member that special I did in Denver about the abused women?"

Arn 'membered. Shortly after he'd met Ana Maria while she was at the CBS network affiliate in Denver, she aired a four-part special on abused women, including many interviews on her broadcast. She had gotten threats then after her segment featuring battered women staying with their guys, and the segment on the recourses for women wishing to escape an abusive relationship.

"Didn't sound as if Tito's mistress was abused," Danny said. "Arn says the woman looked like she could be on the cover of a fashion magazine." He asked Arn, "mind if I have your second half of bread?"

Arn pushed the plate towards Danny.

"I aired a whole segment once on women abused *psychologically*," Ana Maria said. "From just what you told me, I'd bet Ivana is so dependent on Tito Hondros that she'd follow him like a puppy. She'd accept what scraps he threw her way and wouldn't say a thing if the law ever interviewed her. She'd stick by him to the death, even though she's been treated like dirt. And the sex would be just as impersonal."

Ana Maria washed her spaghetti down with a sip of wine. "The sex would probably be rough. Romantic sexual partners don't treat their mates, married or otherwise, like Tito's been treating his mail order bride. I'm reluctant to even call her that the way she was smuggled into the country."

"I'm not a hundred-percent certain that she was," Arn said, "but that fool Grigori down at International Dating, Inc., convinced me it could be done for a price. Tito certainly has enough money to do just that."

Arn finished his supper and scooted his chair back as he studied Ana Maria. "You look kind of down in the dumps. I figured a date with that guy you met online—Robert—was the guy for you. Thought meeting him would have perked you up."

"Oh, he wined and dined me at Barberi's all right. He was actually charming at first, even though he wasn't a prince as the evening wore on."

"Let's hear it," Danny said. "Might be a lesson for me."

"A big lesson, but one that I couldn't foresee. Robert began with some interest in me, especially when he learned I was not the Emily Prose I had set my profile up with. I told him I was going to do a special on internet dating and that was the last time he showed any interest in me. He spent the next two hours bragging about himself. How successful his business was. How many classic cars he had stashed in his garage. I'm telling you, the man was a bore to the *nth* degree. I couldn't get away from him." She suddenly smiled. "Until I was rescued."

Arn refilled his glass of wine and Ana Maria's, bypassing Danny's. The man had been an alcoholic in another life and hadn't touched the stuff in a decade. "I'm betting there's a fairytale story in there somewhere."

"The *prince* that came to my aid," Ana Maria said, "is the owner of Barberi's—Alexius. Though he insisted I call him Alex."

"What did he do—horn in on Robert?' Danny asked.

"In a way. He had been watching us off and on the whole night. He stopped at our table and announced that he was closing early and asked that we please leave. That was a relief, though I wanted to talk with Alex. Actually, I wanted to get as close to him as I could. What a hunk."

"There's gotta be more to the story than that." Danny licked butter off his fingers while he grabbed the last piece of garlic bread. "Or you wouldn't be grinning like a Cheshire cat."

"There is. When I said goodbye to Robert in the parking lot, I was about to leave when one of the waitresses—Melissa—knocked on my window and said that there's been a problem with my card as payment. Said the owner needed to see me back inside the restaurant."

"You just got a new card," Arn said.

"Wasn't my credit card," Ana Maria said. "It was the TV station's card and I've used it a gazillion times. Alex just wanted me back inside where he could talk with me. He saw how the evening was going with the egotistic Robert and wanted to change my opinion of men."

Danny took their plates and set them in the sink. He grabbed a peach cobbler he'd made earlier from the fridge and said, "I'm guessing he managed to change that opinion."

"He did," Ana Maria said. "We talked for the next three hours, well after Melissa had left for the night. The man never even had a girlfriend the whole time he was going to college at Colorado State."

"Thought you said he was a hunk?" Danny said. "He ought to have no trouble finding a lady."

"That might be his problem—he's *too* good looking. Like women who are so beautiful they intimidate men and wind up with no man at all. Did I mention we're going out on a date?"

"See, you didn't even need the internet to find a man after all," Arn said. "Unlike Danny here with his list of potential women who never quite seem to measure up."

"Measure up!" Danny said. "I'd just be happy that the ones who got back to me were just ambulatory and able to get around on their own. Or ones who didn't care for a company of soldiers."

Danny warmed the cobblers in the microwave before topping it with a dollop of ice cream and setting the plates on the table. "You said you were going to tail Tito," Danny said. "I take it you expect to get pictures of him and this babe he keeps stashed?"

Arn let the warm, gooey cobbler slide down his throat before saying, "I'm going to stop off at the Geek Garage and buy another memory card, then I'm going to stick with that SOB until I get the pictures I need to give to Lizzy."

"And hope he doesn't put the sneak on you again," Ana Maria said. "Just keep your cell phone handy in case he does."

"That reminds me..." Arn handed Ana Maria his cell phone. "Ask your IT genius at the TV station if he can figure out where a call came from." He explained that he had received a call from someone who did not leave their name telling Arn to look at Paquita's husband— whoever he may be— as responsible for her murder.

"But you said she wasn't married," Ana Maria said. "At least not officially."

"The caller must think she was."

Ana Maria pocketed Arn's phone and stood. She took her plate of cobbler and ice cream when she left and Danny called after her, "where you going in such a rush?"

"To delete my dating profile," she answered. "I don't need to look for another man. Even for my research."

Danny watched her disappear around the corner and said, "I've seen that look on her before… she's going to get all goo-goo eyed over this Alex guy." A dreamy look came over his face. "Now all we have to do is find me a babe and we'll all be happy."

"All?" Arn asked. "What about me?"

"You already found your romantic contact—Diamond Lil."

Before Arn could slap Danny on the back of the head, the old man scurried out of the kitchen.

15

Nappy the Pimp was comfortably resting in the back seat of a jacked-up '86 LeSabre missing the wheels and tires. "How'd you find me?" he asked Arn.

"Simple," Arn answered. "I asked if anybody'd seen the street guy dressed like he was going to a concert or something."

Nappy rubbed the sleepers out of his eyes and opened the back door. He smoothed the long tail of his black coat and turned the collar of his white shirt down. Or what used to be white.

"Goodwill modern?" Arn asked, running his hand over the coat.

"You making fun of me 'cause I go shopping at Goodwill? It's all this poor soul can afford—"

"Danny told me how you were once the top architect in Longmont."

"Used to be," Nappy said. "But I got tired of the rat race. I tuned out, or so my therapist said." He laughed. "I stiffed her for her fees, no more good than she did me. She tried serving me papers. The cops couldn't find me to serve..." He eyed Arn suspiciously. "You're not going to tell the law where I am?"

Arn shrugged. "Your business with your creditors is none of mine."

Nappy sat on the seat with his legs dangling over the edge and said, "then why did you interrupt my sleep? What the hell do you want?"

"I'm looking for that woman of Tito Hondros."

"I tolds you she was crashing at the Diamond Lil."

"She since moved out," Arn said.

Nappy dug into his pocket and came away with a half-smoked cigarillo. All Arn could think of was that he found it lying on the street somewhere. "I'll put the word out and see what we can see." He motioned to Arn's head. "I heard you got your head busted and lost your camera." He fished a kitchen match out of his pocket. "Mikey the Sneak said he found it in a dumpster and you made him go to the law."

"I needed a paper trail so I can prosecute the bastard who stole it," Arn said, "but it wasn't Mikey."

"I knew that," Nappy said. "Mikey's no thief. I'll call you if I find anything out."

Arn thanked him and started walking away when he dug into his pocket and handed Nappy a ten spot. "Go to the Smoker Friendly Store across the street and get yourself a couple packs of smokes."

* * *

The nice thing about driving a rental Nissan, Arn thought, was that it didn't stick out like a sore toe like his Oldsmobile. Which was a good thing because there was no subtle way to drive past Tito's rock and stone quarry without being seen. If he'd had driven his 442 past here, Tito and everyone else working at the quarry would point and his cover, such as it was, would be blown.

Arn drove past the entrance, past a mound of river rock and gravel and quarried stone in various piles. Trucks sat in a single file waiting their turn to be loaded by an enormous Michigan front end loader, while Tito's Mercedes sat in front of the trailer that was his office. Arn paid them little attention, instead focusing on driving to the abandoned trailers east of the quarry. He had gotten on Google Earth and scouted out a suitable place from which to surveil Tito's office and hoped that the ratty trailers were still there.

They were, and Arn parked between two of them with three windows still intact between them. The one wall had caved in where the weather had taken its toll, and a tree had grown through the other trailer.

Arn set his camera with the new memory card on the seat beside him and his binoculars on the dash. He reached into his boot and retrieved his snubbie .38 and tucked it under his leg. "Try attacking me again," he said out loud before placing his sack lunch Danny had thrown together onto the floorboard.

He settled back in the seat while he opened the lid on his Thermos. Unlike last time when he'd fallen asleep watching the motel, this time he'd brought a Red Bull to go with coffee. Just in case he felt himself dozing off.

When Arn worked at Denver Metro, junior officers often drew the thankless task of sitting for hours—long hours—waiting for a suspect to leave or waiting for a crime to happen. He never liked the duty then, and he especially didn't like it now that he was retired and didn't *have* to be here.

But he *did* have to be here. When Tito busted the side window of Arn's *baby*, that made it personal. That made it so Arn *had* to be here.

Towards quitting time, trucks pulled into the yard. Drivers climbed out and went into the office for a brief moment before coming out and driving away in their personal cars or pickups. Arn expected Tito to stay and work on the books before leaving to be with his mistress, and he was prepared for a long night.

Arn looked through the binos at the quarry and the line of trucks parked waiting to be loaded for the first delivery run in the morning. Tito might have been a philanderer and criminal for smuggling Ivana Nenasheva into the country, but he was not lazy. He hadn't built up a business like he had by ignoring it to spend time with his mail order bride. He'd have enough time for that after work. After all, he had her stashed *somewhere* waiting just for the time when Tito could join her.

The sun was well set and the only vehicle left in the yard was Tito's Mercedes. Arn had just drank the Red Bull when movement under the yard light at the quarry caught his attention. He put the binos to his eyes and focused on the yard. Tito locked the office up and climbed into his car, spinning gravel on the way out.

Arn waited until he had driven past the first bend of the county road before turning his headlights on. He'd stay a comfortable distance behind. If there was one thing he'd learned working Metro, it was how to tail a suspect without being seen. Arn hoped Tito would pay the bland Nissan no mind.

* * *

Tito drove through downtown traffic, turning north on Warren, oblivious that the nondescript white Nissan behind him contained a man bent on seeing Tito get his comeuppance for breaking the window of his car. He pulled into the drive-through of a liquor store on Yellowstone and Arn drove past, parking in the Pizza Hut lot across the street to wait for Tito to pull out. When he once again merged into traffic, Arn gave him a moment before falling in behind.

He kept several cars between him and the Mercedes, the big sedan easy to spot in the traffic of small cars and pickup trucks. Tito turned onto the road leading to a row of high-end homes built a few years ago for discriminating home buyers, with only one car between them now.

Tito headed toward the enormous house at the end of the cul de sac and pulled into the circular driveway—his own house. Arn cursed under his breath. The last thing he wanted was for Tito to pick this one night to go home to his wife.

Arn doused his lights and backed into the driveway of an empty home with a realtor's 'FOR SALE: CONTACT GEORGE COSTOPOULOS' sign on the well-manicured lawn. Once again, he set his binoculars on the seat and settled back for a long vigil when Tito unexpectedly backed away from his house, leaving his headlights off. He only turned them on after he had started down the street, well away from his house. Arn readied to follow him when he paused. Tito had backed away and sped down the street to get away from his house, but why?

As Tito motored past, Arn made the decision to remain darked out where he was, not to follow Tito, and see just why the man was so afraid to go home.

Arn poured a cup of coffee from his Thermos and waited. An hour later, Lizzy walked out of the house holding hands with a man as they walked to a rusty Dodge station wagon. Arn put the binos to his head: the man was younger than Lizzy, smaller and much more attractive than her husband. Before the man climbed into his car, the two kissed, long and passionately before he patted her rear end and drove away from the house past Arn in the driveway of the sale home. "Now just why the hell would you be so afraid of that guy?" Arn asked himself as if Tito were there in the seat beside him. He'd have to ask Lizzy herself just what kind of game she was playing. But for now, Arn hoped Nappy could find where Tito was keeping Ivana Nenasheva.

16

When Arn entered Starbucks, Lizzy was already sitting at a table in front of a window. She waved to get his attention and he grabbed a black coffee before sitting across from her. "You sure your husband's not going to come along and catch us talking?" Arn said. "Especially sitting in front of the window."

She laughed and waved the air with her straw. "Tito wouldn't set foot in here. The arrogant bastard only likes his strong Greek coffee. He'll only buy Venizelos from a shop in New York. Has it shipped in once a month." She stuck her straw in her latte. "Now why did you need to see me so urgently? Have you managed to get the photos I need?"

"I did," Arn said. "I got a nice picture of you and some young feller kissing at your house last night."

Lizzy leaned forward and jabbed the air with her finger. "I didn't pay you to snoop on me—"

"Couldn't be helped. I followed Tito to your house, and he promptly got the hell away like he was afraid of something. Maybe having a run-in with your boy toy?"

Lizzy shouldered her purse and scooted her chair back to leave when Arn said, "What kind of game are you playing? You want me to get the goods on your husband and his mistress while you play the field yourself?"

"I ought to fire you—"

"You wouldn't get anyone else to tail Tito. Now sit down and climb off your high horse. That's if you still want proof he's got a mail order bride stashed away."

Lizzy hesitated a moment before sitting back down.

"Now tell me just what is going on with you and Tito? You have some kind of open marriage or something?"

"Not hardly." Lizzy sipped her latte and swirled liquid around in her cup. "I told you before we had a prenuptial agreement that reads if either one of us catches the other in an adulterous affair, they get the whole farm—business and house and toys and all."

"Then wasn't that a little risky on your part having your boyfriend come to the house for your little... interlude?"

Lizzy waved the air. "I'm not worried."

"That makes no sense," Arn said. "If Tito caught you two last night doing the wild thing, he'd have the goods on you. *You'd* be out on your ear and his mistress would be sashaying around in your house coat."

"Mr. Anderson, it's like this—Tito doesn't *want* a divorce. He doesn't want to be free to allow another woman in his house. He loves things just the way they are... he has his mail order brides and, when he tires of them, discards them for a new one, all the while I'm taking care of the home and the business expenses and handle the taxes. I do everything domestic except clean the house and... low things like that."

"But why did he take off like he'd seen a ghost last night?"

Lizzy sucked up the last of her latte and set the cup on the table. "If Tito would have admitted to catching me and... Ryan last night, he would have *had* to confront us both. His Greek machismo wouldn't allow him to let it slide. He would have likely beaten Ryan to a pulp— or worse—and then Tito would be camped down at his attorney's office the next morning to file divorce papers after he bonded out of jail. He might have seen us, but he was smart enough not to act on it. He knows he has an uncontrollable temper. So, in a way, we do have an open marriage. Except the other one just isn't supposed to know about the other's indiscretions."

"Except now you've grown tired of your little arrangement," Arn said, "and you want out for whatever reason."

"The reason, Mr. Anderson, is this—unlike Tito, my indiscretion— particularly Ryan at the present—is someone who is fun to be with. He treats me with respect."

"And if you take Tito to the cleaners, you'd have his money and still have your kind of fun?"

"You got it," Lizzy said "and the bonus is he's brought so many women over with the promise of marriage, he needs his pee-pee whacked." She smiled. "Maybe I'll let him keep his car—that's his pride and joy."

"How many women has he had?"

Lizzy shrugged. "Four that I know of."

"All Eastern European then?"

"Hardly," Lizzy answered. "He's an equal philandering bastard who has no particular nationality preferences."

"He must know that you've hired me to get damaging photos of him and his mistress."

"He all but admitted it to me the morning he came home after your beating." Lizzy held up her hand. "But I won't go on the record or testify in court. You'll have to get your proof somewhere else. The proof I need is his mistress and him swapping spit. The juicier the better. Anything to sway a divorce court judge when the time comes."

Lizzy stood and Arn walked with her out of the building to her car. He thought for only a moment before deciding not to tell her about his suspicions about Tito's involvement with Paquita and Laramie's Jane Doe. He wanted to ask her if she'd ever found paperwork that showed Tito paid to have a mail order bride smuggled in through the southern border, where there'd no paper trail and nothing to show that the woman ever set foot in America. Until she came up dead.

He wanted to. But he didn't. Lizzy was as ruthless and calculating as any man Arn had dealt with, and he was afraid she would confront him and Tito's Greek ego would lead to serious violence. Something Arn wasn't sure he could handle right now, his concussion still causing him to stumble now and again, and cause weakness in his legs at odd times. When Arn mended up… then he and Tito would dance. After Arn healed.

*　*　*

Arn waited at the curb outside the county jail, checking his watch, knowing Bonnie Peters should have been released by now. Corrections Officer McPhearson had called him as Bonnie was being processed to be released and said, "don't expect to get anything out of her. She's got one nasty attitude. One of those who think the world owes them a living."

After a few moments, Bonnie walked out of the jail and sat on the steps. She lit a cigarette under a No Smoking sign and blew smoke at the building as if that would erase the time she'd spent for her latest probation revocation. Arn pulled the car ahead and rolled down the window. "Bonnie Peters?" he asked while he leaned over in the seat.

She ignored Arn and went about looking at the traffic passing by. "Bonnie Peters—I'd like to talk with you."

She stood and ambled over to the door, flicking her cigarette at a sheriff's transport van parked in front of the jail. She bent over and leaned in the window. "Before you ask how much for a short time, I gotta tell you I can spot a cop a mile off. And you be one. Now go hump somebody else's leg—"

"I'm not a cop. Anymore. I do private work now and again and I think you have information I need."

"Information costs just as much as… the other thing."

Arn took out his wallet when Bonnie said, "Put your wallet away, dummy! If you even look like you're offering me money, the deputies will spot that and assume you're giving me lucky bucks for a happy ending. And I'd be right back in the pokey."

Arn pocketed his wallet and said, "I still need to talk with you, and your information could be worth money."

She looked around before she climbed into the car and said, "Drive someplace very public so no one can accuse me of turning tricks again. Last thing I need to do is get busted again between the lap of some old dude."

The old dude drove away from the county jail and turned onto Lincolnway, passing used car lots and pawn shops and antique stores before he pulled into the depot parking lot where he'd talked with Mikey the Sneak. People came and went from the bistro and brewery in the depot building and Arn parked so the car was visible.

"That's better," Bonnie said. "Now you can pass me some bills."

"How much?"

"Depends on what kind of information you're looking for."

"I'm needing information on Paquita Robles."

Bonnie's face blanched and she looked around the lot. "What about her—she was found murdered if you believe that Villarreal woman on the TV."

Arn studied Bonnie. The way her hand shook holding a cigarette and the way the color had drained all of a sudden from her face, she believed Paquita was murdered. "I hear you and Paquita were close."

"No one was close to Paquita," Bonnie snapped. "She kept to herself. We talked once and a while at work is all."

"Someone told me that Paquita claimed she was married, but the Records Office has no marriage license on file. The records clerk says she raised a ruckus when she learned there was none."

"Ruckus? I should shout," Bonnie said. "She raised hell loud enough that it woke me and—just my luck—there was that ole schoolmarm overseeing my work standing just outside the janitor's closet I was napping in. When I stumbled out of the room, she spotted me and reported me to my PO. Bitch."

"Wasn't you supposed to be working instead of sleeping?"

"Doesn't mean she needed to call my Probation Officer. And it damn well ought to have helped my cause when I ushered Paquita out of the building before she could cause real trouble. But my PO didn't see it that way and sent me to the County lockup."

"Did Paquita talk about her husband—or the man she thought she'd married?"

Bonnie looked around the depot plaza before she flicked her cigarette butt out the window. "That afternoon at the courthouse when she raised hell at the Records Office, we sat on the bench outside. In her broken English, she said she'd trusted him. That he betrayed her when he staged a marriage. I couldn't talk her down very much. I'd never seen her like that. She was upset and going to file a formal complaint on Monday for marriage fraud."

"Did she name her... husband?"

Bonnie shook her head. "She didn't. Said I'd read it in the papers once the bastard was arrested—my words for the man. I never heard Paquita cuss. Anyway, when she didn't come to work that night, I told Alex that Paquita was probably still spun up about her faux marriage. He wasn't happy she didn't show as he had to bring another girl in to wait tables."

Thanks, Bonnie," Arn said and once more took his wallet out when she laid her hand over his. "That pearl of information was on the house if it helps to catch Paquita's killer. Except for being a little aloof, she wasn't a bad sort. For a foreigner."

17

By the time Arn walked into the house, the odor of supper had filled the kitchen and seeped out into the rest of the home. He hung his hat beside the door and started running the gauntlet of buckets of nails with a hammer sticking out of it and collapsed sawhorses leaning against the wall and over electrical conduit just to get to the kitchen.

"Don't know what you're cooking," he told Danny, "but it smells world-class."

The old man turned around and wiped his hands on the flowered apron tied around his thin waist. "It will be cordon bleu, but I'm making it with veal rather than chicken. And," he tapped a pot of water simmering on the stove, "we'll add to our dining pleasure with wild rice and asparagus stalks."

"Wow, you're outdoing yourself," Arn said. "What's the special occasion, and don't tell me you've invited Kubek over or—God forbid—one of those creatures you met on that dating site."

"The special occasion," Danny said filling Arn's coffee cup, "is Ana Maria's… date she had last night with Alex Barberi."

"I don't get it—"

"Arn," Danny said, "Ana Marie came home last night late long after you'd gone to bed. I was on the 'puter checking my profile when she came in. All she could rave about was Alex's charm and how wonderful the food was at Barberi's. How she'd never ate anything like it in Cheyenne before. But this," he waved his hand over his cooking with a flourish and a slight bow, "will change her opinion. At least I hope it will."

"Where is the star-struck lady of the house by the way? Her Bug is parked at the curb?"

"She came home from the TV station and typed up a few notes before hopping in the shower."

"Speaking of showers," Arn said, "when are you going to fix the hot water in mine?"

"Nothing wrong with it."

"The hot water's good for just a few minutes before turning tepid at best."

"That's to be expected," Danny said, "if you take a shower right after me. I run the hot water out."

"Then take shorter showers."

"Pony up for a bigger water heater and that won't happen," Danny said as he kept an eye on his "masterpiece."

"You could always drive out and use the shower in the truck stop." Ana Maria came into the kitchen patting her hair dry with a towel.

"I'm not going to go out for a shower when I have one in my own house," Arn said.

"Then do what Danny says, cheapskate—buy a bigger water heater." She walked to the pot simmering on the stove and sniffed the air. "Now *that* smells delicious."

"Smell better than your meal at Barberi's last night?" Arn asked. "Danny told me how you went on about the food. And the company."

She sat and draped the towel over a chair back while she ruffled her hair. "It was something to be sure."

Arn stood and grabbed the pitcher of iced tea from the fridge. He poured Ana Maria a glass and set it in front of her. "A lot of the success of a fine meal is dining with those whose company you enjoy. With that being said, I take it your... dining partner was pleasant to be with?"

And Maria sipped her tea and looked at the corner of the room with a faraway look in her brown eyes. "He was the perfect gentlemen. Unlike Robert, Alex actually *listened* to me. Wanted to know about me. How refreshing."

"Sounds as if you fell under Alex's charm," Arn said.

Ana Maria shook her head and went back to sipping her tea. "I'm no star-struck schoolgirl—"

"Aren't you?" Danny asked over his shoulder as he grabbed plates from the cupboard. "Tell Arn how you... mothered Alex with his sad background."

"I did not—"

"With you," Arn grinned, "there's always more to the dating story. Let's hear it."

Ana Maria glared at Danny who ignored her and went about setting the table. "Alright, so he had a hard time in Denver."

Danny guffawed. "Hard like he was born with a silver spoon in his mouth."

"So, his parents ran a successful business," Ana Maria said, and explained how Alex's parents owned eleven high-end beauty salons in and around Denver.

Arn snapped his fingers. "Crap. I didn't even connect Alex with those salons. Or with those murders."

"What murders?" Danny asked.

"Some years ago—"

"While Alex was at Colorado State in Ft. Collins," Ana Maria interrupted, "there was a home invasion at the Barberi estate. Two men broke in, held Alex's parents at gunpoint until Alex's father finally gave them the combination to the safe. Then, just killed them."

"I recall how the Barberi boy—I didn't realize it was Alex—was brought in as a person of interest, being the sole heir to the estate," Arn said, leaning over the stove and sniffing.

Danny took off his apron before washing his hands. He dried them on a kitchen towel and said, "that's normal for the next of kin to be singled out. Most murderers know their victims. Statistically it's in the upper eighty-percent range."

"You studying criminology now?" Ana Maria asked.

"*Forensic Files* on the tube," Danny asked. "You'd learn a lot about people watching that show."

Ana Maria shook her head and continued. "Alex was cleared when the two killers were identified. The police caught their scent and closed in on the flop house in Denver where they were hiding out. One committed suicide while the other fled. There's been more sightings of the other brother than there have been sightings of Elvis, but the law hasn't caught him yet... that *really* smells good, Danny."

He lifted a veal cordon bleu with a turner and lovingly set a veal cutlet on each plate.

"I would have thought Alex would have continued with the family business," Arn said. "When I lived down there, all the young detectives raved about how Barberi's was the place to go."

Ana Maria unfolded a napkin and draped it over her lap while she eyed Danny setting a bowl of rice in the middle of the table. "At the time of the murder Alex was a senior in college. Business major. He finished his senior year and tried running the business, but said it was too painful. Brought too many bad memories so he sold out and looked around for a place to buy. Poor Richards was up for sale and, *shazam*, there his restaurant is."

Danny finished the presentation with asparagus spears before sitting at the table across from Arn. "Well," he said to Ana Maria, "how does this compare with Barberi's?"

She held up her hand as she placed a tiny corner of the cordon bleu on her tongue. She closed her eyes and chewed for a moment until Arn thought he heard her *coo*. "My God, that's good."

"Of course it is," Danny said, "but how does it compare with your new boyfriend's restaurant?"

"I'll let you know after tonight," she answered. "He's treating me to a very late meal at his restaurant. Just the two of us and his chef."

Arn nudged Ana Maria and said, "This is getting serious after only one real date?"

"Yeah," Danny added. "A date where he doesn't have to spend a dime on, you... just feeding you at his business."

"Look, you two, this isn't getting serious. I'm more cautious—you know me."

"That's the point," Arn said. "We *know* you."

"Can't we just talk about something else besides Alex Barberi," Ana Maria said, "like Danny's new squeeze."

"How do you know I have a new squeeze?" Danny asked. "I never told anyone—"

"You left the computer on last night and her profile was plastered across the screen. So, what's she like?"

"Can't say," Danny said. He sliced off a piece of asparagus and dipped it into melted butter. "This will be our first date tomorrow but… she might be 'The One'." He turned to Arn. "She has a sister. Maybe we could go on a double date."

Danny," Arn said, "at my age I have a hard enough time going on a *single* date. Besides, I don't have time for that. I have to get the goods on Tito Hondros."

"Thought Lizzy Hondros fired you?" Danny said.

"Reminds me," Ana Maria said, "Eugene—our IT guy—managed to come up with the owner of that anonymous call you got. After supper, I'll dig the guy's name out of my notes."

Small talk, thankfully, took up the rest of the dinner conversation: how Frontier Days would be on this year after being canceled last year due to the pandemic. How the new mayor was making changes in the city government. How Spradley Ford was hoping to fill orders on the new Bronco that was back-ordered for more than a year. And most important—what the city was going to do to fix the potholes big enough to fish out of.

"That was an amazing meal," Ana Maria said after finishing her crème brulée.

"As good as Barberi's?"

Ana Maria paused. "I'll let you know after our dinner date." She stood and motioned to Arn. "Come into the computer room and I'll dig up that name for you."

Arn followed her into the room and she sat by the computer desk. She began digging through her notebook until she found the page and tore it off.

Arn squinted while he read the note. "Mihael Mendoza. I've seen that name somewhere."

"Every time you drive out towards the air base I'd bet."

"How's that?"

Ana Maria flicked the note with her finger. "Mihael Mendoza is *Father* Mihael Mendoza. St. Luke's Catholic Church."

Arn stood and rushed out the door when Ana Maria called after him, "And where you going in such a hurry?"

"I'm going to get religion," Arn said and grabbed his hat on the way out the door.

18

Arn stood outside the door of St. Luke's Catholic Church listening to the congregation finish their evening service. When Mass was over, he stepped out of the way as the doors opened and people filed out, some holding prayer beads, others small crucifixes, none paying Arn any mind as they made their way to cars parked along the curb. The last to file out was a small man younger than Ana Maria, clerical collar too loose around his thin neck. He smiled as he walked towards Arn and looked up at him. "You were free to come inside. As you can see," he motioned to the parishioners leaving, "we are a small parish and we welcome all people, not just Catholics," he said with a thick accent Arn recognized as the voice on his anonymous call.

"Honduras, Father?"

"Guatemala," he said. "You know your region well."

"I had to for thirty years working as a lawman." He offered his hand. "Arn Anderson."

Father Mendoza's smile faded, and he stepped back. "Mr. Anderson," he stammered, "what... what do you want from me?"

"First, I want to know why you left me an anonymous voice message and how you got my number in the first place."

"I don't understand—"

He held up his hand for the father to stop while Arn dug his cell phone out of his pocket. He selected the voice mail that the father had left and replayed it.

Father Mendoza's frail shoulders slumped, and he rubbed his forehead. "I sent that, Mr. Anderson."

"Why? What is Paquita Roble's death to you?"

"Please," Father Mendoza said, "come with me into the rectory. Please."

He led Arn around the side of the church to a small addition attached to the building. The decayed and chipped stucco hung off the side of the rectory like hair hanging off a shedding dog. The door splintered where the paint had been attacked by the bitter Wyoming wind, while a mailbox barely hung onto the side of the building by a single bolt. Father Mendoza saw Arn eying the rectory and said, "like I said, ours is a small parish Someday we will… repair my house, but it is still far better than my one back in my Guatemala. Please come inside."

The father appeared small in his quarters even though he was a rail thin man. He motioned for Arn to sit in an occasional chair with its tweed fabric unraveling, while he turned a burner on the two-burner stove. He set a teapot on to heat before taking a deep breath and saying, "Where to begin, Mr. Anderson."

"You can begin by telling me how you got my phone number."

A smile replaced Father Mendoza's dour expression as if remembering something pleasant. "We get many people in here for lunch… we offer noon day meals for anyone in need. Not a large meal, but enough to sustain. I have many homeless people who come in. Hungry. Tired. Many quite… unkempt. But we at St. Luke's welcome them all."

"Still doesn't explain how you got my cell number."

"One of the men who came in… we have become friends, though he refuses to come out of the elements into the church to sleep. I unburdened him one day after lunch, telling how I had a parishioner in need of help of the police, but she was leery of the law. This man gave me your card and I gave it to Paquita after she came to me again. But I had jotted your cell phone number down before giving the card away.

"Why did she need to hire a private investigator?"

"I cannot tell you. Privileged communication between parishioner—"

"Father," Arn pressed, "Paquita Robles is dead. There *are* no confidentiality issues. I believe you have information that might help me find her murderer."

"Why is it that you look for the person who killed her—that is a job for the police."

"Because she believed that I could help her. She must have been desperate if she intended to hire me," Arn answered. "Call it tying up loose ends. Obviously she needed my help but never got the chance to come to me."

Father Mendoza jumped when the teapot whistled, and he turned to the stove. "Tea, Mr. Anderson?"

"I'm more a coffee man, Father."

"Ah," the priest said. "And you know the best coffee comes from my Guatemala."

He poured hot water over a tea bag in his cup and sat back down across from Arn. "Paquita was a member of our congregation since she came to this country, though she always sat in the back. Never talked with anyone. I did not hear her confession until a week before she was killed."

"Something must have weighed on her to finally confess to you."

Father Mendoza nodded. "Her burden was that she was naïve enough to come to this country under the promise of marriage. She was ashamed that she consented to be married in a civil ceremony rather than the church."

"So, she was married?"

"No," the priest said, sipping his tea. "She only *thought* she was. See, her... husband arranged for a man to perform the ceremony out in the state park west of town. Her husband claimed the man was a lay preacher authorized to perform marriages. But—"

"But when she checked at the courthouse, she learned there was no marriage license on file?"

Father Mendoza nodded. "She felt such shame that she had lived in sin with that man—"

"Any information about him would help."

The father shrugged. "She did not tell me his name. But she did say that after the... marriage... her husband grew abusive. Demanded things from her. Awful things in the bedroom."

Arn leaned closer to the priest and asked, "Do you know the term S&M?"

Father Mendoza shook his head.

"It is a way to… enhance the sexual experience. At least that's what it's supposed to do." Arn told the priest about S&M deaths he'd known of while working in Denver. They'd been caused by sexual activity gone too far. Of women being trussed up and beaten in the name of sexual gratification. "Did she mention anything like that?"

Father Mendoza stood and paced the small room. He rubbed his temples while he gathered his thoughts. "She did," he said at last. "When I asked her about the rope burns on her wrists, she broke down. She felt such disgrace that she had allowed herself to submit to her husband. To being tied up while he… had his way with her. She felt she had no choice, being such a small woman and her husband so strong."

Arn took out his notebook and flipped to the page where he'd interviewed Frankie May at the Cadillac Inn. "Paquita worked at the motel and lived in one of the rooms. Did she say why she did not live with her… husband?"

"He tired of her," the priest said immediately. "Tired of her company and he kicked her out of the house. Told her he wanted nothing more to do with her. She wanted to return to the Philippines and was saving money for the trip. Even more, though, she wanted to be reunited with her husband."

"I don't understand why?" Arn said. "It sounded as if he abused her repeatedly."

"The baby," Father Mendoza said under his breath. "Paquita was pregnant by her husband and desperately wanted to be reunited with him. She couldn't imagine bearing a child out of wedlock."

"In all those times she talked with you she never identified her husband?"

"I wish she had," Father Mendoza said. "She might have been sitting in that back pew for this morning's Mass."

19

Arn and Danny both stayed up that night waiting for Ana Maria to come home from her late diner date with Alex Barberi. "Hope her date turns out better than mine," Danny said.

Arn exaggerated a groan. "Not another one who ate continuously the entire night?"

"No. This... lady... ate like a sparrow. Which is why I couldn't see how one so small could," he scrunched up his nose, "pass so much gas. Even at the table."

Arn laughed, imagining Danny sitting across from a flatulence-laden babe he was trying to impress. "What did you do?"

"What could I do?" Danny answered. "Sonny wasn't there to blame." He refilled their coffee cups from a Thermos and set it aside. "If I had a bottle of Febreze, I'd have doused her, but all I could do was sit there and watch everyone stare at us. Or I should say, stare at me—I was the one the other diners blamed."

"You being the gentlemen, I would wager you didn't indicate she was the one doing the dirty deed?"

"I did not."

"Did you at least get some smooching at the end of the night?"

"Are you kidding me?" Danny said. "I was afraid if I squeezed her even a little, she'd let loose again."

The nightly Greg Gutfeld Show came on and they settled back in their recliners with a bowl of popcorn between them. Just as the show ended, Ana Maria came back from her dinner date. She strolled into the TV room and sat in her own recliner, tossing her sweater aside.

"You're grinning like you had a good time," Danny said, then added, "hold that thought—I'll be right back."

"Danny's right," Arn said, "you're... glowing. Haven't seen you like this since the last Prince Charming made you promises."

"That Prince Charming was a total dud, you know that. This one—Alex—is the real McCoy."

Danny entered the room carrying three plates of hot peach pie topped with ice cream. After he set the plates on the tray between recliners he said, "Now I'm ready. Let's hear the lowdown."

Ana Maria kept silent as if purposely creating tension while she set her pie in front of her. Even Arn fidgeted, anxious to hear how her night went. "Well?"

"The evening was as sweet as... Danny's pie."

"The dinner must have been memorable as it was the other night," Danny said, "but did it taste as good as my cooking?"

Ana Maria paused, the pie inches from her lips when she winked and said, "I'm sure it's going to take another meal to figure that out. But more memorable than the dinner was... afterward. At Alex's house."

"He took you to his house?" Arn asked.

"He did."

"Don't tell me you jumped his bones after only a few dates?" Danny asked.

Ana Maria put her plate back on the TV tray and dabbed at her mouth with a napkin. "Give me a little more credit than that. No, I asked where he lived. He said hop in his car and he'd show me, so I did. He was the perfect gentleman, never forcing himself on me as he showed me around the house. And you ought to see it."

"Is it as memorable as the meal?" Danny asked.

"Just the opposite," Ana Maria said. "It's a pretty plain two level with a basement and three bedrooms—which I *just* poked my head into and nothing else in case you're wondering."

Arn held up his hands as if in surrender. "Okay. I get it. Tell me there's more to the place than that. I can't say for sure, but I'd wager Alex inherited mega bucks from the sale of those Denver salons."

"He did but it doesn't show by his house," Ana Maria said, taking up her pie plate and fork once more. "He has an unfinished basement that floods a lot when it rains, so I didn't feel like going into someplace musty like that. But for as much money as he has, he lives a pretty simple life—working out and running his restaurant."

"I definitely here a 'but' in there," Arn said.

Ana Maria nodded. "*But, if* our relationship… expands, I am sure I can cut through his shyness and start having some fun. Traveling and such."

"Take me along as a chef," Danny said, "I always wanted to see Antarctica."

Ana Maria chuckled. "I can think of a whole lot more romantic places than that I'd like to see with Alex."

Arn raised an eyebrow. "Then, this *is* serious?"

"It could be." She set her empty plate beside her and took a notebook from her purse. "But now to business—I'm ready to air the first segment of my Mail Order Bride special and thought I'd run things by you guys… get a different perspective."

"I'm all for puzzles," Danny said and lowered his recliner. "Perspect away."

"Okay, here's what I'm going to point out about Paquita Robles and Laramie's victim, Katya Petrov—they were both mail order brides, but there is no record of either entering the country. And they had things in common, like both had short, dark hair. Dark eyes."

"Like you," Arn pointed out.

"But unlike me," Ana Maria continued, "they had rope burns on their wrists."

Arn told her what Father Mendoza said when Paquita admitted her husband and she engaged in what can only be described as S&M. "Using that angle, you may receive tips from some other women who have had men engage in those practices."

"Good point," Ana Maria said as she jotted in her notebook.

"Maybe not," Danny said. "S&M can be attributed to the Marquis de Sade who not only practiced deviant sex but wrote about it. Often both parties are consenting. Often as not, the dominant male will assume the role of the one being abused. Maybe it would be just as productive to ask the public if anyone's heard screams coming from their neighbor's homes."

"He's got a point there," Arn said. "I'd bet there aren't too many S&M practitioners here in Cheyenne."

"Even though there's an Adam and Eve store just opened up here in town," Danny blurted out.

"How do you know that?" Arn asked.

Danny's face turned crimson. "A… friend said he went there for toys a time or two."

Ana Maria winked at Danny. "Sure. A friend. But back to my special—if our killer lives a ways away from other people, he wouldn't be heard. I'd be more likely to get a response with the mail order bride angle… find someone who knew a bride who'd been brought into the country, legally or otherwise." She turned and faced Arn. "Any more luck with that fake Russian at International Dating, Inc.?"

"He left a message for me to meet him at his office. Said he had some excellent prospects. As soon as I see the list and know if he can bring women over the southern border without paperwork, I'll know it was possible that Paquita and Katya Petrov sneaked into the country illegally."

"When will you know?"

"I going to drive down to Denver tomorrow and meet with Grigori, or whatever the hell his real name is. But first I have to find that Darwin Ness character who dropped the watch and earrings and broach off at Burri Jewelers to be cleaned. I think he might be the key to finding who killed them."

"He could be the killer himself," Ana Maria said. "How else would he have possession of the jewelry?"

"He could have stolen them," Danny said.

"Just my thought," Arn said.

"By the way," Ana Maria said, "aren't you going to go out and try to find Tito and his mistress?"

Arn scrunched down into the recliner and kicked off his slippers. "Lizzy says Tito is out of town on business tonight, so it won't pay for me to go out. Tomorrow night maybe. But for now… Danny hand me the remote. There's a noir Bogart movie on Turner Classics."

20

Arn parked around back of the Cheyenne VA facility and donned his mask before entering. He started down the hallway when a burly male orderly stopped him. "I can't let you in with *that* mask."

Arn tapped his cloth mask and asked, "What's wrong with it? It's a mask, isn't it?"

The orderly frowned and handed Arn a mask from a box beside his desk. "Yours isn't an approved cloth mask, even though it's more appropriate."

"Suit yourself," Arn said and took off his mask he'd bought in the shape of a *colon nose*. He put the VA-approved one on and continued down the hallway until he reached the end to cut over to the offices. When he got to the Administration area of the facility, he rang the bell on the wall and waited until a receptionist opened the door. "I have an appointment with Dr. Land."

She stepped aside for Arn to enter and led him down a hallway to a closed door. She rapped and a shrill voice called out, "Damn thing's open. It's always open."

"Good luck," the receptionist whispered and closed the door.

Dr. Land—head of clinical psychology at the VA facility—stood but didn't offer his hand as if in so doing it would conjure up bad mojo from last year. One of the traveling psychologists, Ethan Ames, had managed to kill vets in three regional hospitals—including Cheyenne— before Arn stopped him not far down the hall from Land's office. "You were pretty cryptic when you told my secretary why you needed to talk."

"I need to know about a patient."

"One of ours?"

Arn nodded. "Darwin Ness."

"I can't tell you if he even is a patient."

"Doctor," Arn said, "you couldn't tell me anything last year about Ethan Ames, either, and look what he did—murdered vets right here in your facility."

"I can't—"

"If you had told me about Ethan earlier and about the patients he was seeing, I might have been able to stop the killings sooner. Besides, you owe me for saving the hospital here a massive investigation when I talked with the federal investigators."

Dr. Land plopped down in his chair and rubbed his temples before looking up at Arn. "Set then, damn it. I will talk to you about Darwin but—know this—if a word of his condition leaves this room, I will personally hire the biggest psychotic veteran I can find to break your legs. Now what do you want to know?"

"Darwin might be a suspect in at least two killings." Arn explained how Darwin had dropped a watch with a distinctive gold and diamond face off at Burri Jewelers to be cleaned along with matching earrings and broach, and that the watch that would later find its way onto the wrist of Paquita Robles. The same distinctive pattern as the earring Laramie's Katya Petrov had on when her body was found at Optimist's Park. "Of all the people here, I expect you'd know if Darwin was capable of murder."

Dr. Land tented his fingers together and nodded. "Everyone is capable of murder under the right circumstances. But Darwin... more so. He suffers damaging PTSD, brought on when he was in the Battle of Fallujah in 2004. He and other Marines with the 3/1 were riding in a personnel carrier when it took a direct hit from an RPG. The hot rocket sliced right through the thin armor of the carrier and killed everyone except Darwin. Somehow, he managed to extricate himself from the PC and carry another Marine that he thought was alive to an aid station two klicks away."

"He should have celebrated carrying his fellow Marine, even if he wasn't alive."

"He didn't," Dr. Land said. "The other Marine he slung over his back had died instantly when the rocket exploded and blew off both legs. Darwin thought the man was alive when he made his way to the aid station. Medics figured the Marine had bled out even before Darwin carried him."

"That's horrible," Arn said, "but doesn't alter the fact that he might be involved with the two victims. Can you tell me where he lives?"

"211 West Lincolnway according to his file."

Arn started to jot it down when Dr. Land stopped him. "Don't waste your ink. I actually went by that address to check on him after a particularly bad session with me—it's the Atlas Theater."

"Where those Cheyenne Little Theater players put on plays and melodramas?" Arn asked, though he knew well that the historic theater was still in operation, one of the few in the country still offering live performances.

"Darwin said he used to be homeless and had moved there recently. But I knew that couldn't be his address unless he was like the Hunchback of Notre Dame, living in the theater itself." Dr. Land took his glasses off and rubbed his eyes. "I never did find out where Darwin lived even though I told him I'd caught him in a lie during the next session."

"Perhaps when he comes in for another therapy session—"

"Darwin hasn't been to therapy for more 'n a year."

"Is there anything you can tell me to help me find him?" Arn asked.

"Besides his plethora of tattoos? Let me see, he's several inches taller than you, and at one time was quite muscular. But for many of his forty-five years he's been homeless and so everything that he wears looks like it could fall off him at any moment." Dr. Land rubbed his wrist. "Despite looking almost anemic, he is still strong as a bull. I laid my hand on his shoulder once and he reacted instantly by grabbing me. I thought he was breaking my wrist until he realized what he was doing. And Arn, if you do manage to find him, keep in mind that he can become quite violent, particularly if he thinks you're a law officer."

"That's what Alex Barberi at the restaurant said. Darwin must have had a bad encounter with the law once."

Dr. Land laughed nervously. "Once? Try dozens of times. When he got discharged after his last tour in Iraq he refused any counseling, thinking he could handle his PTSD alone. He knocked around Southern California and—every time he went off on somebody and hurt them—he was tossed into the lockup."

"Alex said Darwin worked at the restaurant for a month, so he must be able to keep it under control for a little while."

"For a week here. A month there he can," Land said. "Eventually, he'll go off and then there's trouble, especially now that he's off his meds. The pharmacy said he hasn't called for refills for six months."

"Did Darwin ever mention any type of skills he has—or used to have before he went to war that might tell me where to look for him?"

"Just that he did landscaping before he enlisted."

Arn thought about what kind of man Darwin Ness might be and where he might be in hiding, if he were even still here in town. Being a combat Marine, Darwin would most likely be able to live most anyplace beside motels and railroad cars. "I'll pass the word around and see if anyone hired a wild-looking landscaper recently."

"You watch him if you catch up with him," Dr. Land said. "If he's in his manic mood you'd better go armed."

* * *

Arn lucked out and caught Detective Kubek just as she was leaving her office "As much as I'd love to stay and visit," she said, "I have to meet with the Chief and Mayor about Paquita's death. They seem to think it should have been solved by now, so make it quick."

"Does Darwin Ness ring a bell?"

"Like Quasimodo rings a bell," she answered. "Since I've been in this position, Darwin Ness's name has come across on reports half-a-dozen times for petty thefts from parked cars. Beating up a bouncer at one of the fine drinking establishments here in town catering to bikers. Breaking into motels—twice—and staying for the night. Why, do you know where he's staying?"

"I hoped you'd know." Arn said, then added, "did you ever run a Triple-I on him?"

She nodded. "We did run a five-state records check and it showed only petty crimes."

"Did he ever graduate into anything more serious, like felony-grade thefts?"

"If you know something—"

"I do, and honestly, I intended sharing it with you at... lunch this week. But while you're here..." Arn explained how a man meeting Darwin Ness' description dropped the watch and broach and earrings by Burri to be cleaned and later picked them up.

Kubek grabbed her cell phone and dialed. "Sorry, Chief. I can't make the meeting. Something important's come up related to Paquita Robles' murder," and she hung up. "They can wait. I'm headed to the squad room to talk with the shift sergeant. Get everybody doubling down on finding Darwin Ness. If he was in possession of the Paquita's watch at one time, he's just been elevated to a person of interest. We'll catch lunch another time... if you wish," she said, and disappeared down the hallway leaving Arn to wonder how a man like Darwin— living on the street, barely surviving if he was even in town—could afford the cleaning of the jewelry. "Of course, he stole the money just like he stole the jewelry," Arn said to himself. "I wonder..."

21

"Are you sure you're up to driving in Denver traffic?" Ana Maria asked, cinching her seat belt tighter. "You just got those staples out of your noggin this morning."

"I was all right when Danny drove me down there."

"But you weren't driving then. And whatever possessed you to make Danny drive? He hasn't touched a steering wheel in decades."

"I *had* to get down to Denver somehow. I'll drive cautious like. All the more reason for me to drive careful is that DeAngelo will have my hide if I get into a wreck with his ace reporter."

"Relax," Ana Maria said. "He's just as happy as a pig in slop over this special I'm doing."

"Could it be," Arn said, slowing to allow a tractor-trailer to enter the on-ramp ahead of him, "that the old man is letting you have your way in your investigation so you can learn what the legitimate dating sites are."

"Why would he do that?"

"DeAngelo's pushing eighty. Might he have a soft spot for you like a father would have for his daughter? Perhaps—just perhaps—he wants to see you find a nice guy."

"I don't know about that. It'd be more likely that the old coot just wants me to research the best legitimate sights so *he* could post a profile."

"DeAngelo? Didn't know he was on the prowl," Arn said, thinking that if DeAngelo Damos was on the hunt for a babe at his age, perhaps Arn wasn't too old to look at some dating sites himself.

"DeAngelo has been widowed longer than I have been alive, and I hear from the secretaries at the TV station that he fancies himself quite the lady's man." Ana Maria laughed. "If he had an erection, I think that it'd scare him to death. Construction up ahead."

Arn tapped an alternate route into his Garmin and got off the interstate well before the bottleneck in the construction zone. "Where do you suppose Darwin got the money for cleaning the jewelry, 'cause Kaddie at Burri Jewelers said it wasn't cheap?"

"Same way he got the jewelry in the first place," Ana Maria said. "He stole it."

"I'm not convinced he stole the items," Arn said. "His rap sheet indicates that he has no arrests for committing serious crimes. Stealing jewelry as pricey as Kaddie says it is would be a felony serious."

"Didn't you say he was a suspect in several thefts of cars in Cheyenne?"

"That's the odd part—two of the cars he's a suspect in had quite expensive things lying about... a camcorder in one. Pistol right on the seat in another, and yet the thief bypassed those things to steal groceries the owner had just bought from Safeway. Another vehicle owner lost a carton of cigarettes. If it was Darwin, he left the expensive items."

"Maybe our Darwin is a lot more clever than we give him credit for," Ana Maria said. "Maybe he knows stealing expensive items will land him a felony if caught, and he sticks to penny-ante things."

Arn followed the instructions the Garmin gave out in the mellow English assent he'd selected. "This would be easier to use if it was a man's voice telling me where to turn," he told Ana Maria. "The directions would be more logical."

"At least with a woman ordering you where to go you're bound to actually arrive where you need to be."

They turned off the Colfax exit and pulled into an empty lot. They didn't have long to wait before a Suburban with darked-out windows pulled beside them and rolled down the window. "Is this how far down you've slid since you retired?" Agent Barns said. "A far cry from that old cool Oldsmobile you used to drive. What'd you do—have to sell it when you got hard up?"

"Barney," Arn said, recalling how the agent hated to be called Barney. Something about being associated with Barney Fife. "I am amazed you are still working at your age."

"Got two kids in college," Agent Barnes said, "and an ex that sucks me dry with alimony so I'll be working until your advanced age." He stuck his head out the window and asked, "who's your good-lookin' sidekick?"

Arn introduced Ana Maria and added, "She's spoken for at the moment. Until she gets tired of Mr. Barberi."

"There was a couple named Barberi... eight years ago, if I my mental synapses are triggering right. Killed in a home invasion. Left everything to their kid in college I think."

"That's him. Alex Barberi is Ana Maria's current squeeze." Arn nudged Ana Maria. "Until she finds a new Prince Charming."

Barney took a pipe out of his pocket and began stuffing it from a pouch of Borkum Riff. "We assisted Metro Denver in that investigation. Two brothers did the dirty deed, with one committing suicide shortly before SWAT made entry into an old run-down house the brothers were squatting in. We never did find that other brother, though the Marshals say they've had a ton of tips on his whereabouts." He touched a kitchen match to his pipe and asked, "you ready for this?"

"As ready as I can be." Arn stepped out of the car. "Wire me."

Arn unbuttoned his shirt, and Agent Barnes taped the transmitter to Arn's chest. Barnes slipped the earpiece in his ear and tested the receiver. With the units working properly, Arn tucked his shirt in and climbed back into the car.

"Tell me again why the hell you're wearing a wire for the feds?" Ana Maria asked when they'd pulled back into traffic.

"Let's say I'm killing two pigeons with one big-ass rock. I'm going to meet with that fool Grigori to see if he can actually smuggle mail order brides into the country with no paper trail. If he can and if it's recorded, that piece of human garbage will be out of business. The other reason is that Barney does me favors now and again, and this would be a feather in his cap. Might land the old dude a desk job." Arn dipped his head to his chest. "You hope so don't you, Barney Fife?"

Two cars in back of Arn the dark Suburban flashed the lights in response.

They pulled out of traffic and into the parking lot of International Dating, Inc. Arn tightened his tie before climbing out and throwing on his sport coat. "Go on back and have a seat in Barney's outfit," he told Ana Maria. When Arn called Agent Barnes yesterday, he was overjoyed to hear someone might finally get Grigori Musin-Pushkin on tape with something that he could go to the U.S. Attorney with. The Bureau had sent undercover officers into the dating office on several occasions, but Grigori had spotted a ringer each time.

"It just might work," Barnes said yesterday when Arn called him offering to wear a wire. "Our younger officers didn't look like they needed a dating set up and Grigori made them right off. But you... you're over the hill enough that you look like you need help finding a woman."

But when Arn suggested Ana Maria tag along to gather material for her TV special, Barney had balked. "I don't know, Arn. Having the press along... well, you know how they distort things."

"I can just as well go into International Dating, Inc.'s office and talk with that fool without wearing a wire," Arn told Barney. "I'll still get the information *I* need for *my* investigation." After minutes of side stepping the issue, Agent Barnes agreed to allow Ana Maria to tag along while Arn and Grigori's conversation was taped.

Arn smoothed his sport coat and winced as he carefully put his hat on. "How do I look?"

"Like some fifties horny old guy looking for a young babe."

"Just the look I was going for," Arn said, and headed across the parking lot.

When he walked into the dating office, the receptionist greeted him as if he were an old friend. Or like an old guy who was about to drop a bundle smuggling his new bride into the country. "Grigori is waiting for you." She opened the office and winked at Arn. "Good luck. I think you'll like who Grigori found for you."

Grigori sat behind his desk smoking a cigar, his feet propped up on an open desk drawer, a glass of wine in his hand. He dropped his feet onto the floor and slid a ring binder towards Arn. "There are ten lovely ladies who have agreed to… enter the country by a southern route. But," he snubbed his cigar out in an ashtray, "it *vill* not be cheap."

Arn opened the binder and looked at each photograph and read their brief descriptions. Each of the ten women were, indeed, beautiful. Each of the ten women were no older than twenty-six. Each of the ten women had signed an agreement at the bottom of the page to slip into America without going the legal route. "How much is 'not cheap'?" Arn asked.

Grigori shrugged. "The boat over to… a South American country is not cheap. Then there are the cartels who *vill* be escorting your lady north." He held up his hand. "I know, the cartels are unscrupulous, but they are—how you Americans say it?—the only game in town."

"How much?"

Grigori shrugged. "Fifty-thousand. For a start. Then if *ve* have trouble along the way… bribes and such, *vell*, you understand *ve* have to add that to the cost."

"You mean *we* have to add it to the cost, as *we* Americans say it."

"*Vhat's* that you say?" Grigori asked.

"What I'm saying is you're as American as I am."

Grigori's smile faded and he blurted out, "I am not from your country. I am from Mother Russia—"

"More like Mother North Dakota or Mother Minnesota, if I nail your accent right."

"I don't understand—"

"Look Grigori—or whatever your name is—what you're running here is nothing less than human trafficking. You've been lying about these ladies, and you've been lying about your so-called Russian heritage. Now, if I don't get a straight answer, without that phony accent, I'm going to leave and place a call to the FBI Field Office here in Denver."

Grigori slid his chair back and it hit the wall. He stood on shaky legs for a moment before he sat back down. He grabbed his glass of wine and downed it. "What do you want from me?" he asked, his phony Eastern European accent gone, sounding right now as if he'd had a starring role in *Fargo*.

"First, a name."

"Greg," he said at last. "Greg Willis. And you nailed my accent—I'm from Mandan, North Dakota." He leaned his elbows on his desk and rubbed his hands together nervously. "Now that I've given you my name and admitted I... can arrange for women to come into the country unnoticed, what else do you want from me? Free service?"

"Not hardly. One of the men I suspect has used your service numerous times... I want confirmation that you brought his mail order bride in by the southern border."

Greg put his hands in front of him as if to ward off the mere suggestion of giving up a client. "I draw the line at that. My client list is sacrosanct."

Arn stood and loosened his tie. "Suit yourself. You'll be telling that to the FBI."

He started for the door when Greg stopped him. "Hold on. Is that the only client you wish to know about?"

"It is."

Greg sighed heavily. "What is his name?"

"Tito Hondros is the name I'm interested in."

Greg hesitated and Arn started for the door. "Hold on. Let me get into my... special client list."

He stood and walked to a picture on the wall depicting a Jackson Pollock abstract—always the proverbial picture hiding the safe, Arn thought. Greg swung the picture aside and dialed the combination. He reached in and withdrew a ledger book, shielding it from Arn as he flipped pages. After scrolling down the list, Greg nodded. "Tito Hondros has used our service—"

"Your special service through the southern route?"

Greg nodded again. "Yes. He's used it four times. Now is that all?"

"While you have your records in front of you, tell me if Tito had a preference for any particularly nationality of women."

Greg shielded the book with his arm once more and finally said, "he brought in two ladies from Eastern Europe—I can't tell if they were Russian or Ukrainian or Lithuanian."

"And the other nationality?"

"Filipinos."

"How was the money transferred to you?"

"Secure account, of course," Greg said. "I'm no amateur."

"Names," Arn pressed. "What were the names of the women Tito paid for?"

Greg smiled. "Numbers eleven, nineteen, eighty-six, and three. I don't keep records of their names. I just assign them a number. What do you take me for, a monster ready to give out the ladies' names?"

He turned his back on Arn and replaced the ledger in his safe before sitting back in his chair. "Now, if there's nothing else—"

"Ledger book with names of the clients are stashed," Arn said to the microphone taped under his shirt, "in a safe behind a faux Jackson Pollock print—"

"What's that you're saying…" the color left Greg's face and his hands trembled. "Tell me you're not wired."

"I'd be lying if I did. The FBI will come through that door in just a moment."

"You can't do that—it's entrapment! I know the law."

"Then you know it's not entrapment when a civilian volunteers to assist law enforcement."

"But we had an agreement. You lied!"

"I did," Arn said, "just like you lied to all the women you've brought over illegally as mail order brides."

22

"**D**amn!" Ana Maria said as she reached over and turned the radio up. "KGAB's scooped me again."

"What are you talking about?" Arn asked as he braked for a motorcyclist who had cut in front of him.

"Didn't you hear anything that guy on the radio said?"

"I'm hard of hearing—"

"Shush," she said and cranked the rental car's radio up even more.

"A positive identification has been made," the radio announcer said, and went on to explain how a woman's body had been found dead at the Diamond Lil Inn. A Russian woman, though they couldn't release her name until the next of kin had been notified. "The murder suspect has been arrested, but we cannot yet release his name, as per Detective Lieutenant Kubek." The announcer next skipped to a summary of the windy weather for today and Ana Maria turned off the radio.

"Kick it in the butt," she said. "I need to get back to town and cover the murder. Maybe I can get an interview with the killer."

"You don't even know who the suspect is."

"No?" Ana Maria said. "A Russian woman victim... I'd say that sounds like Ivana Nenasheva. And I'd wager Tito is the murder suspect."

Arn thankfully left the heavy Denver traffic headed north. "Were I you," he said, "I wouldn't put too much money on that bet."

Ana Maria guffawed. "No one else it could be besides Tito."

"Sure there is. Think back to how I characterized Lizzy—ruthless. Capable of killing her rival."

"And you base that on what?"

Arn shrugged. "Call it the feeling of an old, retired cop."

"I call it watching too many *Forensic Files* with Danny," Ana Maria said. "All's I know is that I better get back and get on it or DeAngelo will be having me cover funerals and those cheesy weddings people have out at Curt Gowdy Park."

* * *

Arn parked at the curb outside the Police Department intending to go in. He wanted to go in, but a dozen people blocked his path, the cacophony nearly hurting his ears. Reporters shoved microphones into Frida Kubek's face, shouting questions, crowding her until she held up her hands for them to be quiet. "I can't release any more information than I've already given you until we complete our initial investigation."

"Just tell us who the victim is," one woman said, "and we'll get out of your hair."

"So you can find the next of kin before we go and ruin their day? No thanks." Kubek stepped closer to the woman reporter from the ABC affiliate in Denver, now close enough they were nearly rubbing noses. "As for getting out of my hair—go. Now. All of you."

"This is a public place," a man from CNN said. "We can hang out here if we wish."

"Suit yourself," Kubek said, then spotted Arn in the back of the crowd. "I won't be available for the rest of the day as I have an interview with a man regarding another incident. Arn," she said, and got onto her tip toes to motion to him. "Come with me, Mr. Anderson."

Arn didn't know what special place he had in the crowd, but he dutifully elbowed his way through the reporters. They glared at him as if he had taken their own special place in the police department lobby as he followed Kubek down the hallway. She looked over her shoulder every few feet to ensure the reporters hadn't followed her until she ducked into her office and hurriedly closed the door. "Thanks for saving me from those vultures."

"I didn't do a thing except... play along. You really don't have anything to discuss with me about this recent homicide, now do you?"

Kubek dropped into a chair behind a gun-metal gray desk and rubbed her forehead. "I have been trying to get rid of them for the past hour. You were just a... convenient out for me."

"Then if that's the case, you owe me."

Kubek smiled. "Dinner?"

"Information."

Kubek hung her head and said, "Let's hear it. I bet you'll be as snoopy as the reporters."

"More," Arn said. "Except I won't go out and tell the whole world whatever you tell me."

"But you will tell your roommate—that Villarreal woman. And she does work for the television station."

Arn took off his hat and set it on the desk as he plopped in a chair across the desk from Kubek. "We have an agreement, Ana Maria and me—if I tell her anything that is off the record, it stays off the record and she'll have to find her information on her own."

Kubek opened a small fridge beside her desk and took out a bottle of Perrier. She handed it to Arn, but he declined. "Bad for the regularity."

"Well, isn't that romantic."

Arn shook his head. "The romance we can talk about later. Right now, I need information, like if your victim is Ivana Nenasheva?"

Kubek nodded. "That's if she received letters from Russia addressed to that name it is. We found an envelope addressed to her in her back jean pocket. But as for a driver's license or some other kind of ID, she had nothing. We sent her prints to the DCI and FBI but nothing back yet."

Arn explained what Grigori—Greg Willis—had told him in Denver when he looked at his special client list. "International Dating, Inc., has a record of Tito Hondros bringing two Eastern European women into the country illegally. I doubt you'll find your victim's prints on file where she applied for a temporary visa."

Kubek jotted the information down before asking, "what else are you going to pry out of me?"

"The suspect you have in custody—is it Tito or Lizzy Hondros?"

Kubek sat back and chewed on the end of her pen. "Why do you think either one might have murdered Nenasheva?"

Arn explained how Lizzy had hired him to surveil her husband and snap incriminating photos she could use in a divorce. "She was calculating those times I talked with her. But during those brief conversations, I got the... feeling that she was as tough and ruthless as Tito."

Kubek laughed. "A feeling? You're going on a damned impression based on talking with Elizabeth Hondros?"

Arn leaned forward and looked Kubek in the eye. "Being in law enforcement as long as you have, surely *you've* had nothing more than a gut feeling to go on now and again?"

Kubek broke the stare and looked at her college diploma from ASU hanging on the wall. "All right, maybe you have something there, but we had enough evidence to arrest Tito Hondros this afternoon."

"Can you tell me the particulars?" He held up his hand. "And Ana Maria will not get it."

Kubek paused, seeming to weigh the request when Arn said, "I can walk out now and steer those reporters here to your office."

"Okay," Kubek snapped. She reached into a briefcase and took a stenographer's notebook out, long and slim with every page filled with notes she had taken. "Diamond Lil called it in when she found the body."

"To appease my curiosity—what's Diamond Lil's Christian name?"

"For one thing—that woman's not a Christian. For another, she had her name legally changed to Diamond Lil after her arrest on sex charges. Either way, she found Ivana's body."

"Surely not when she was cleaning rooms, as dirty as that place is."

"Hardly by the looks of that dump." Kubek capped her bottle of Perrier and set it aside. She flipped pages until she found the one she wanted. "Lil saw Tito Hondros go into the room last night but didn't think anything of it as Tito was a frequent visitor to Ivana's motel room. In fact, he was the only visitor that Lil knew of."

"Tito's clever, moving his mistress around to motels and now back to Diamond Lil's."

"How's that?"

"I'll explain later," Arn said and added, "tell me, was Ivana strangled like the others, Paquita Robles and Katya over in Laramie?"

"As a matter of fact," Kubek said, "she was. But," she flipped to another page, "she had no rope marks on her wrists like she'd been bound up, practicing S&M like the others."

Arn resisted the urge to write down what Kubek said, fearing it would break the magic and she would clam up. "Did you work out a scenario as to what happened?" he asked. When he worked Metro Homicide, Arn always put the pieces he had at the time of the murder scene together to envision how the crime happened, how the victim lost their life. The killer's actions afterward. And he was usually pretty close to how the victims met their end.

"Tito came to visit Ivana," Kubek began, choosing her words carefully, "but he stayed for only a few moments according to Lil."

Arn thought back to the crude and nasty owner of the Diamond Lil and to how he had to drag information out of her.

"Lil thought nothing of it as Tito often visited Ivana, and now—by what you said about his wife hiring you to get the goods on Tito—I can clearly see why."

"You said before that Lil didn't report the body right then... did she not hear a struggle?"

"For once, she was busy with an... unsuspecting customer off the interstate needing a room for the night."

"Pity that poor slob."

"Tell me about it," Kubek said. "It gave me the heebie jeebies just being in the motel office talking with her. I felt better viewing the victim."

"When did she report the murder?"

Kubek double-checked her notes before saying, "About twenty minutes later. She saw Tito running out of the room and grew suspicious. By the time she'd checked the room and called 911, rigor had set in, and we had a pretty good idea of what happened."

Arn remained quiet, seeing the memory of the murder victim effecting Kubek, even though her persona was tough as fence staples. Her lower lip quivered and she said, "I figure Tito stopped by for some quick sex. Quick and dirty is my thinking. Ivana didn't want sex for whatever reason and was strangled for it. Way I see it, Tito paid her objections no mind and strangled her while they were having sex like they'd done dozens of times before. Things just went too far and she was dead before he knew it. Ever investigate an autoerotic death, Arn?"

He nodded, thinking back to numerous deaths involving strangulation. Some sickos feel they give greater pleasure by cutting off the O2, causing a more intense organism for their partner. Most devotees of the technique let up before their partner is strangled to death. Some do not. Others slip a ligature around their own neck, cutting off air supply during masturbation, heightening their orgasm. Sometimes, their safety knot fails and they're found swinging from some rafter. Sickos.

"Can I see the crime scene photos?"

Kubek forced a laugh. "You ought to know they're in possession of our evidence techs."

Arn grinned and said, "you did snap just a few photos with your phone?"

Kubek sat back away from Arn and chewed on the end of her pen again. "Why would I do that?"

"To show it to friends. Maybe to family at Christmastime."

"Now that's sick—"

Arn held up his hand. "Frida, I was a cop more 'n thirty years. I know what cops do at crime scenes. They want... souvenirs. Like serial killers want souvenirs, except cops want to pass the phone pics around the squad room to show their fellow officers. Or they like to gross people out at supper or prove what a thankless, nasty-ass job they have to do. I did and... can I please see the photos on your phone?"

"Damn you, Arn Anderson, why the hell am I even doing this?"

Arn batted his eyelids. "Because I'm just irresistible?"

Kubek dug in her purse and pulled up photos on her phone. "You horse's petute," she said and handed him her Android.

Arn donned his reading glasses and studied the pictures Kubek had snapped of the victim and the crime scene. "Looks like he didn't quite get her clothes off before he started the dirty deed." Arn expanded the photo to where he could see Ivana Nenasheva lying atop the bed that was still made, though rumpled by the struggle. Her skirt still covered her knees but her thin top had torn and barely covered her chest.

He squinted and expanded the photo to study the mark on her upper arm. "That's '12-26-91' tattooed on her arm."

Kubek nodded. "The same as the tat on Katya Petrov's body over in Laramie."

"That was the day the Soviet Union fell," Arn said. "Ana Maria's been researching it and it appears as if thousands of students in Russia and the Ukraine took to the streets in celebration. And many got such a tat to show their support." Arn handed Kubek her phone back. "It's a possibility Ivana and Katya Petrov knew each other. Many expats cling together when they get to a foreign country."

"I thought of that, too," Kubek said, "and our guys are trying to run that down. If they did know one another, we might have a serial killer on our hands."

"Still on the serial killer angle?"

"I am. And it's Tito, I'd stake my job on it."

I wouldn't, Arn thought and left the police station.

23

Ana Maria had just finished her nightly broadcast and Danny and Arn had just polished off a bowl of popcorn when his phone rang. He spoke briefly to the man on the other end of the line before hanging up and grabbing for his boots.

Danny wiped a dab of butter from his lower lip and asked, "looks like you're going someplace."

"No," Arn said, "*we're* going someplace."

Danny groaned. "But I'm just settled in for the night. You'd think the pajamas and the fuzzy slippers would be a clue to you. What you need me along for anyways?"

"Mikey the Sneak. One of my street contacts just called and said your ol' friend Mikey knows where Darwin is. And like you pointed out the other day, Mikey won't talk to just anyone."

* * *

Arn waited at the train depot parking lot as he had the other day when Danny went to bring Mikey the Sneak to him. Perhaps it was because he was getting used to Arn talking to him or perhaps it was because Mikey felt safe in the darkness that he walked willingly beside Danny.

"This ain't about finding your camera in a dumpster again?"

"No," Arn said. "We're good on that. The reason Danny hunted you up again is I need to know where one of the street people is staying."

"Whoa," Mikey said and backed away. "I don't know if Danny's told you but we street folks don't give up our own."

137

Arn stepped closer to Mikey and looked up at him. "I did you a favor by not pressing charges for you selling my stolen camera."

"You going to want charges filed now that I refuse to give up one of my own?"

Arn took out a pack of Juicy Fruit from his shirt pocket and peeled back a stick before offering one to Mikey. "I'm not going to go back on my word and see you charged. I just thought you street folks were honorable, even if you are homeless."

Mikey chewed on the gum like he was chewing on his options when he said, "This gonna get this street person you're looking for in hot water with the cops?"

"Can't promise anything."

"Who is it you need to find?"

"Darwin Ness."

Mikey rubbed his forehead and said, "You ain't gonna turn him in to 5-O?"

"Like I said, I can't promise anything."

"Then I might not tell you where to find him."

"I don't understand—"

"Mr. Anderson, the dude's bad news."

"Explain 'bad news'?"

Mikey spat his gum out and sat on the trunk lid of Arn's Oldsmobile. No one sat on his trunk, especially since it was polished so nicely after the glass company finished with it. Arn gritted his teeth. He needed to find Darwin and now wasn't the time to give Mikey the Sneak hell. "The man's okay most of the time," Mikey said. "Comes and goes and don't say squat to no one. Almost normal. But now and again, he just goes nuts. I'm talking bat-shit nuts, ranting and screaming, and threatening to kick everyone's ass within earshot. I'm telling you, the guy needs help."

"There are facilities that would take Darwin in," Danny said. "Man's got PTSD bad. Had it for a time myself when I came back from the 'Nam but they called it jungle fatigue back then."

"But getting him there to some mental facility would be the challenge," Mikey said.

"How come?"

"The dude's *gnarly*. No one messes with Darwin."

"I'll do what I can," Arn said, "if you tell me where to find him."

"You're not gonna tell him I ratted on him?"

"Only ones to know but you and me and Danny."

Mikey came off the trunk and said, "This Darwin dude is living in one of those abandoned cabooses the Union Pacific parked at the end of their railyard when they did away with them. It has some FTRA graffiti bullshit painted in red and blue on the side like all them cabooses and boxcars have."

Arn knew the kind—letters big enough to be seen from across the street, drawn by hobos riding the rails. "Look for one with bright yellow graffiti," Mikey said, "even yellower than the UP color. But be careful. This might be his night to go ape shit."

Arn fished a twenty out of his pocket and handed it to Danny. "Go take Mikey to the Village Inn and you both have supper on me."

"And you go alone?" Danny asked. "I don't think that's a good idea. From what Mikey here says of Darwin—"

"I'm afraid if too many people show up at his crib that he *will* go ape," Arn said, "and then I'd never get any information out of him."

Arn waited until Danny and Mikey disappeared across the street walking toward the restaurant before he opened his trunk and grabbed his flashlight and gun. He stuffed the snubbie .38 into his trouser pocket and started around the depot, headed for the railyard.

He arrived at the enormous yard with four freight trains in various stages of locomotion, passing each other within feet. He paused to allow his eyes to adjust to the darkness as he looked about for a bright yellow caboose with FTRA graffiti painted on the side.

He had to walk another hundred yards until he saw the only caboose like Mikey had described. Arn walked to within ten yards of the train car before stopping and squatting on his heels to stud it. A faint light flickered inside casting an eerie shadow over the windows while a thin tendril of smoke escaped the smokestack. After long moments, Arn gripped his flashlight tightly and walked the remaining distance to the caboose. He grabbed the rusty handrail and ascended the steps as quietly as he could, peering inside over the window door. His hand found the knob when someone inside called out, "You can come in but leave your baggage outside."

Arn entered and shined his flashlight around. A man squatted in front of the small stove in the corner said, "Don't know who you are, but I didn't serve three combat tours not to recognize someone putting the sneak on me. Who the hell are you? And douse that damn light —it kills my night vision."

Arn did as he was asked when the man said, "And who the hell are you to come sneaking around like a damned thief?" He waved his hand around the caboose, light from the stove flickering, accentuating the man's wild look with his unkempt hair and eyes as wide as saucers as he stared at Arn. And the Rose of No Man's Land tat on his right inner arm. "As you can see, I got nothing for you to steal. But if you're hungry, you can have half this can of Spaghetti-Os."

"I just ate," Arn said. "And I'm not here to steal your shit. I'm here looking for Darwin Ness."

The man stiffened but said nothing.

"That's Marine Corps Staff Sergeant Ness."

"You've found him. Now what do you want?"

"I want to ask you about some jewelry you took into Burri Jewelers for cleaning a couple months ago."

Darwin finished his can of pasta and licked the plastic spork before standing to his full height causing Arn to look up at him. Though he had lost weight over the years since his Marine Corps photo—Darwin still exuded power as he glared down at Arn. "What difference is it to you? You didn't own the jewelry."

"And neither did you. Where did you get it?"

"If I told you I took it at a friend's request, would you believe me? At least, someone I thought was a friend. Once. Besides, you wouldn't know my friend."

"I might if you told me the name."

Darwin's eyes darted from Arn to the open door behind him and he began shaking ever so slightly. "It's a secret, believe me. If I told you and it came out... I'm here to tell you, I'd be a dead man."

"Your friend must be some kind of nasty bastard for a three-tour combat Marine to be scared."

"I don't have much, but I have my life and I aim to keep it."

"Then give me a name, if you didn't steal the jewelry."

"Just why the hell's it so important for you to know?"

"Because some of that jewelry was found on two women recently who had been murdered."

"Now wait a damn minute… the cops ain't pinning any murder on me. I didn't kill anyone. At least not in this country."

"Then who is your friend?"

Darwin began to shake violently then. Even in the dim light of the lantern he had hung from a hook overhead, Arn could see the man's growing anger. "Was it Tito Hondros?"

Darwin crouched, his legs ready to spring, run through Arn if he had to. "Why don't you come with me," Arn said in a soft voice. "Tell the police who your friend is and they can protect you. Then we can go talk with Doctor Land and get you help. Maybe get you back on your meds—"

Darwin screamed. He sprang from his crouch. Ran headlong. Arms flailing.

Arn cocked the flashlight back just as Darwin crashed into him. The flashlight flew through the air and careened off of the far wall just ahead of Arn tripping and falling onto the stove. He broke his fall against it and burnt his hand. He groped for his gun, expecting Darwin to be upon him, when he looked at the open door.

Darwin's running steps had already faded into the night air.

24

Danny finished smearing Neosporin onto Arn's blistered hand before lightly wrapping it with a burn bandage. "Good thing you didn't catch your fall with that noggin of yours," he said, "or it mighta messed up your boyish looks."

"Are you going to keep giving me crap all night?"

"You're the one who let Darwin escape, not me," Danny said.

"I'd like to see you try stopping a two-hundred-pound wild man as he's running over you."

"Arn's right." Ana Maria came into the TV room carrying a tray with bowls of ice cream on it. "I'm glad he didn't try to stop Darwin—he might have really been hurt." She patted Arn's head. "And at his age, people bruise easily."

Arn slapped her hand away and said, "I'm not ready to be planted just yet."

Ana Maria set the ice cream on TV trays before sitting in her recliner. "Exactly what information did you get, 'cause it better be a good trade for burning your hand on that old caboose stove."

Arn turned in his chair and gingerly ran his hand over the burn bandage. "Darwin said he dropped the jewelry off for a friend. One he is no longer is friendly with."

"What friend?"

Arn shrugged. "Darwin refused to tell me. Said he was scared to death the person would kill him."

"We don't even know if his 'friend' was a man or woman?" Danny said.

"I'm thinking a man," Ana Maria said.

Arn wiped ice cream that had dripped onto his good hand. "Don't be so stereotypical. There's a lot of women I'd be afraid of in the right circumstances. Like one TV reporter when she gets angry."

Ana Maria waved the air with her spoon. "You know what I mean. I can't imagine someone like Darwin being afraid of a lot of people."

Danny put the Neosporin and tape into a Ziploc bag and sat in his recliner between Arn and Ana Maria. "Do you believe Darwin?"

Arn had thought of that very question, concluding that he really got no read on Darwin in the brief moments he was in the caboose with him. Arn didn't know if the man was lying or telling the truth. "Let's say Darwin was honest about just being a courier for an estranged friend. That he dropped the jewelry off at Burri to be cleaned then picked it up for this friend. And if he is telling the truth, the friend would at some point put the fear of God into a three-time combat Marine, which would be no easy feat. Especially after I saw how crazed Darwin could become in a moment's notice."

"Then we must be looking at some street person who put the fear of the Lord into him," Ana Maria said, "as it doesn't sound like Darwin knows anyone *but* street people."

"That's a good point." Arn finished his ice cream and asked Danny, "Who do you know on the street who's dangerous enough to scare Darwin?"

Danny set his bowl on the TV tray and grabbed his bottle of soda. "There's quite a few folks living off the grid in Cheyenne who'd almost fit the bill. Couple that have assault convictions that I know of. One with an attempted murder arrest but never proved. But if Darwin's as goofy as you say... I just don't know for sure."

"What is for sure is that—if it's someone living on the street who conned Darwin into dropping the jewelry off—they must have also stolen it."

"Now that's a whole lot easier to come up with than names of thieves," Danny said. "When I was living on the street, I had to watch my stuff close. Bunch a street people—women as well as men—had sticky fingers. Some bragged how they'd regularly break into cars and steal things they'd pawn later."

"You're both going out of your way to make Darwin a victim here," Ana Maria said. She stood and gathered the empty bowls and set them aside. "Maybe you secretly feel sorry for him?"

"Can't argue there," Arn answered. "I feel sorry for him and for every vet who suffers PTSD."

"It's all right to empathize with him," Ana Maria said, "just don't lose sight that he could actually be the killer."

"Believe me, I've thought about that, too." Darwin had gone from suspicious of Arn being in his crib to a crazy man who could have broken Arn if he wished. But he hadn't, even though Arn was down and vulnerable. Was it that the veteran with PTSD was more fearful of the police and institutions, more intent on fleeing the authorities than of hurting Arn? "If Darwin's the killer, he'd have to borrow a car to get to Laramie."

"Or steal one," Danny said. "Back in my street days when I was drinking I'd… find keys dangling in ignitions. More likely under car mats or ashtrays. People would be foolish to think no one would look there. Keys just begging for someone to joy ride." He laughed. "I was more concerned then about getting arrested for drunk driving and no license than stealing some beater for an evening's pleasure."

"You're saying Darwin could have found a set of keys in a car and driven to Laramie?" Ana Maria asked.

"Sure could have," Danny said. "We have more used corner car lots here in town than we have convenience stores. And more often than not, the keys are left somewhere in the car."

"But why drive to Laramie," Ana Maria said, "just to dump a body."

"Unless Katya Petrov had fled to Laramie and Darwin eventually found her," Danny said. "Could be she had some kind of relationship with Darwin, got hinked around him, and decided it would be easier to move out of Cheyenne. Maybe he partied with her and things got out of hand."

"I don't know," Arn said, realizing he was defending Darwin Ness. "The brief time I was with Darwin and from what Mikey the Sneak says, the man doesn't seem like the partying kind. Most loners aren't."

"Then the only other scenario is that he killed Katya here in Cheyenne, stole a car, and drove her body to Laramie where he dumped her in Optimist's Park of all places," Ana Maria said.

A spot of ice cream fell onto Danny's nightshirt and he wiped it away. "If that's the case, someone must have seen them together."

"Not necessarily," Arn answered, "any more than anyone saw Darwin with Paquita before she was killed. *If* he's involved in that murder also. I'll hit the car lots tomorrow and check if any of them had a car stolen and recovered in Laramie shortly before Katya's body was found."

"Why not just ask your new squeeze Kubek to check for stolens?"

"Because many of the small used car dealers rarely report their cars taken they're so used to it. Police never find the thieves anyway." Arn shrugged. "Just a fact of life."

"We're forgetting another way that Darwin—or anyone—could have gotten to Laramie and it doesn't involve stealing a car," Danny said.

Ana Maria looked at Danny. "You going to leave us in suspense all night?" she said.

"The train," Danny said at last. "The UP. He could have hopped a freight car to Laramie, found her, and killed her. Be back home at his crib in Cheyenne with no one the wiser."

"Possibility," Arn said. "That's why I keep you around—for all the odd ball theories."

"No," Danny said, "you keep me around 'cause you can't even drive a nail straight."

"Either way," Ana Maria said, "I think the jewelry is the key. It's just too coincidental that Paquita and Katya both had the identical patterns of jewelry on when their bodies were found."

"Let's hope someone recognized the design from your broadcast and calls your tip line," Arn said.

After Danny came back from the kitchen, he turned the volume down on the Gutfeld show and sat in his recliner. He grabbed knitting needles and yarn from a canvas bag beside his recliner and the needles click-clicked away, sounding like an old-time telegraph operator.

Arn groaned and said, "I hate to ask what you're knitting now."

"Another pair of mittens for you, of course. Since you lost your other ones, you'll need another pair come winter."

Since taking the homeless man in and seeing how handy he was in remodeling—as well as in the kitchen—Arn had grown close to the anemic-looking old Indian and he hated to lie to him. But he had this last winter not two weeks after Danny gave Arn a lovely pair of knitted chartreuse-colored mittens. Arn might have been able to live with the color *if* no one saw him wearing them. What he couldn't live with was that Danny knitted so loosely that the gloves provided no protection from the cold whatsoever and so Arn had dropped them into the box at Goodwill. Now as Arn watched Danny knit another pair in periwinkle, thoughts raced in Arn's mind as to how he could lose this pair once Danny gave them to him.

"What do you have there?" Ana Maria said to Arn as she laid out papers on her TV tray. "Looks like one of those brochures from those mail order bride scams. You aren't thinking about taking a love jaunt to, say the Ukraine or the Philippines?"

"No," he said. "I'm just trying to get a handle on how men would think they could find their Princess Charming through one of those trips." He winked at her. "We don't all have the luxury of stumbling across Mr. Right like some lucky TV reporter did."

"I didn't say Alex Barberi was Mr. Right—"

"No?" Danny said as he dropped another stitch. "He's all you've been talking about for the last week."

"Danny's right." Arn set the Eastern European Bride pamphlet aside and grabbed one specializing in Vietnamese women. "Seems like you fell head-over-heels for that funeral director last year and it didn't pan out."

Ana Marie sorted through papers and said, "He ended up being a little creepy, taking about his clients slabbed-out all the time."

"How about that doctor last fall?" Danny said. "Nothing wrong with a proctologist—"

"Gastroenterologist," Ana Marie blurted out. "Every time we held hands it just didn't seem… quite right."

"But here comes Alex, your stainless-steel savior—riding into town in his Mercedes to save you from being an unmarried spinster," Arn said with a wide grin.

Ana Maria picked a sheet of paper from the pile in front of her and set back to read it.

"Alex is different than all the others," she said. "I don't know if he's 'The One,' but it sure feels like it." She blushed and Arn knew there was something more.

"Tell me you didn't do the wild thing so soon?" he asked.

"If I did, it'd be none of your business," she snapped, then laid her hand on Arn's forearm. "Sorry. I know you're just looking out for my wellbeing but, no, we got a little… smoochy is all."

Danny set his knitting aside and leaned closer to her. "Come on. Let's hear the juicy details."

"Nothing juicy to tell," she said. "We went to his place after supper… did I tell you about that long, elegant driveway of fine river stone that leads to his house. All lined with willows and flowers and manicured shrubbery?"

"You said he lived in a pretty normal house off Story Road a few miles out in that subdivision. But you didn't mention he was handy enough to lay stone."

"He did, and he hung the drywall and did all the lighting himself."

"Pretty handy guy," Danny said. "Feel free to ask him to come by and help me with this."

"I might do that once he gets his basement done. Some water leaked into his foundation after this last heavy rain. He's got a call in to a contractor to see what can be done. For now, he says the sump pump will have to do."

"You were telling us about getting kissy-face," Danny pressed her. He sat on the edge of his seat expecting something seedy.

"That's it."

"That's all?"

"That's all," she said. "Just a little goodnight kiss. It didn't last very long, either. Alex had to get up early to open the restaurant to do inventory. I just think he's just shy. He didn't want me looking at this," she tapped the pile of papers.

"Just what are you reading?" Arn asked.

"Alex had all this… paperwork on his folks being murdered. *Denver Post* articles of when one of the two home invasion scroats committed suicide with his brother on the lam."

Arn nodded to the pile of papers. "Mind?"

Ana Maria shrugged. "You'll see it all eventually in my special."

"What special?"

"I convinced DeAngelo it'd be a nice gesture to feature a businessman every week."

"Don't tell me... Alex will be the first in your... series?" Danny asked as he picked up his knitting needles again. "Might this be a series of *one*?"

"Don't be silly," she answered. "A little exposure will be good for his business and patrons wanting a fine dining experience. The one I'm doing on him I'm calling a 'Riches to Even More Riches' story. I'll cover him from his college days to when he inherited his parents' business after they were brutally murdered."

Arn picked up the top paper in her stack, a follow-up police report on the initial crime. It listed things that had been recovered from a fence who bought stolen items known to the Denver police—paintings that had been valued at thousands, along with two sixteenth-century clocks that were valued at more than the paintings. Guns and cash from a safe. "No wonder those two brothers risked the home invasion."

"Did they just come knocking," Danny said, "and the parents opened the door for them? What's the cop report say?"

"Both killers were computer science majors at CSU," Ana Maria said. "Brilliant by what the police report said. They disabled the alarm system before opening the garage door and entering that way."

Danny's interest was now piqued, and he followed Arn by picking up another report form. He whistled and said, "This is from the lead detective. Says that the larger paintings were left on the hallway and speculated they were too big to carry away. But Alex's father had a collection of Rolex watches that were taken and his mother's four jewelry boxes missing. And," Danny turned a page, "it would seem his mother was somewhat of a history buff. She had signed documents by George Washington and JFK and FDR. All framed. All missing. Sounds like they weren't common thieves."

"Sounds like they were educated ones," Arn said.

"Alex said they found one of the jewelry boxes in a pawn shop in Orlando and figured the surviving brother fled there," Ana Maria said, "but they didn't get much for it, filled with just costume jewelry."

"Let's see the report," Arn said. He read where the detective brought in an appraiser to assess the value of those items taken.

Ana Maria picked up a copy of the police teletype. "No luck finding the surviving brother, Jesse Brown, but the FBI put out a wanted poster."

"He'll be found," Arn said. "Eventually, all criminals float to the top." Arn thought of his current situation and how Lizzy Hondros' check would not cover the cost of the home addition. He started formulating a pitch to Alex Barberi: for a percentage of the stolen goods that Arn recovered. If Arn could find even some of the stolen items it would be worth it. Would Alex agree to that? Arn hoped so because the addition wasn't getting built until he had more income than his police pension.

He laid the report back on the stack. "Looks like a lot of material to go through for just a ten-minute special."

Ana Maria grinned. "At least my research with Alex will be interesting."

25

Kubek motioned to Arn's bandage on his hand and said, "Don't you feel a little humbled that some down-and-out vet would get the best of you?"

"Down-and-out! You should have seen him," Arn said. "He was like a crazed dog. Took me by surprise, though. I ought to feel lucky he didn't take advantage of me lying on the floor to put the boots to me."

"It's a shame you couldn't have talked him into the PD—we've been looking hard for him. I stationed an officer on the depot roof glassing that caboose for when he returns."

"I think Darwin needs a mental health facility more than he needs jail."

Kubek grabbed a bottle of Perrier but didn't ask Arn if he wanted one this time. "I have been thinking hard on what you said and have concluded that this Darwin Ness character lied to you about dropping the jewelry off for a friend." She held up her hand when he started to speak. "I know your cop instinct is that Darwin was telling you the truth, but I don't buy it. The possibility that he is the killer is even more telling now. Thing I'm wondering is why he gave the name of Alex Barberi when he dropped it off for cleaning."

"Perhaps Darwin was so pissed that Alex fired him, he wanted to make sure there was a paper trail linking Alex to the stolen jewelry."

Arn had discussed with Kubek this morning the theories he and Danny and Ana Maria had talked about last night, leaving out that he'd shared any information with them. That Darwin could easily have stolen a car and either drove Katya Petrov's body to Laramie or met her over there and killed her was discussed amongst them.

"Don't forget that Darwin and Paquita Robles worked at Barberi's Restaurant at the same time," Kubek said.

"Then by your thoughts, we're looking at two killers—Tito for offing Ivana Nenasheva and Darwin for killing Paquita and Katya Petrov?" Arn said, though he could think of no connection between Darwin Ness and Petrov.

"That's just what I've been thinking," Kubek said. "The case we have against Tito Hondros is solid, especially with the information you have about tailing him to meet up with Ivana."

"Speaking of Tito, did he make bail?"

"Last night. Paid cash. I just wish we could have held him longer— maybe he'd have cracked."

He wouldn't, Arn thought. From what he knew of Tito Hondros, the man was as tough as boiled whale hide. Just like his wife, whom Arn intended on visiting just as soon as he left Kubek's office.

* * *

Arn parked in front of the circular driveway and looked warily around. Although Tito had gotten the best of him last time, the big Greek had sucker punched him through the window of his car. The next time Arn would be prepared and see just how tough Tito was when a man faced him. He rang the doorbell and, when he got no answer, rang it again.

When Lizzy Hondros came to the door, she was dressed as if she'd just crawled out of bed. She made no effort to hide anything, the sheer nightie too short and the neckline too revealing. He had to force himself to look away until he realized one side of Lizzy's neck showed deep scratches. Old if he read the scabs that had formed right that he'd missed it the other day and asked, "Did Tito do that?"

Lizzy covered the scratches with her hand. "Winston that... worthless cat of Tito's hates me. Jumped up when I was just walking into the family room and did this," she brought her hand away. "On a lighter note, I was wondering when you were going to come around," she said and winked. "Step in."

She held the door for Arn, the loud music playing shielded from the outside world by the construction of the house. She had told Arn during his last visit here that Tito had insisted on extreme soundproofing when he contracted to have the house built, and Arn would give the architect kudos for doing just that.

She led Arn through a family room with two fireplaces, deer and elk and bear mounts hanging on the wall. Lizzy saw him eying them and said, "don't give Tito any credit for those—he bought the mounts from an outfitting guide he knows."

She motioned for Arn to follow past the family room and into the study. A ceiling fan sucked cigarette smoke upward into the twelve-foot-high ceiling, the odor of Lizzy's cigarettes lingering. A set of dumbbells lay on the floor in front of a sixty-inch television monitor. She saw Arn looking at it and said, "I need to keep up my strength and my looks. "Sit anywhere," she said as she stopped at a wet bar in one corner of the room. "A breakfast bourbon?" she said over her shoulder as ice tinkled in a tumbler.

"Trying to quit," Arn answered.

"Probably just as well," Lizzy said. "Unless this is a romantic call, you won't be staying for long."

She turned around and finally drew her nightgown together. "By now you've heard of Tito's little flip being murdered?"

Arn nodded.

"Then I won't need your services any longer."

She walked to the desk and opened the middle drawer, taking out a large check book and writing. When she finished, she handed Arn the check and said, "this ought to cover your fee, even if you didn't get the goods on Tito like I wanted."

Arn laid the check on the desk. "Like you said, I wasn't successful. But what are you going to do, now that your husband is facing a murder charge?"

"I'm going to hire the best lawyer I can get to get him off."

"Get him off? I thought you'd be happy he was arrested. If he were convicted, you'd get the house. The business. Even his Mercedes—"

"I have to stand by my man," Lizzy said.

"I don't know what game you're playing—first hiring me to get the goods on your husband so you could take over the business and house. Then paying me off—"

"Like I said, Anderson—Tito's still my man and we'll fight this murder charge together."

"There's more to it than that the Tammy Wynette crap. Yesterday you would have as soon seen Tito keel over with the big MI as look at him. You don't come across as the compassionate loyalist—"

"All right then," Lizzy said. She poured two fingers of bourbon and paused before pouring two more and dropping ice into her tumbler. "Want to know the truth—if Tito is convicted, sure I'll get the house and the business and that smelly old Mercedes. But I wouldn't be able to keep it. With a murder conviction, the relatives of that Nenasheva woman will be wide open to filing a civil suit for wrongful death. And whatever I had the court would take away." She downed her drink and looked at the liquor cart. "Tito's going to get off."

"You're sure he didn't kill Ivana?"

"Hundred percent positive. I'll testify he was home with me."

"That would give both of you an alibi," Arn said.

"Why would I need an alibi?"

Arn moved away from her and his foot bumped into the cat. Winston cracked one eye before going back to napping, "What's to say you didn't find Ivana before I did? If you found her, you might have been so angry as to attack her—"

"You accusing me of the girl's death?"

"All I'm suggesting is that you are so positive that Tito didn't kill her because maybe—just maybe—you did."

"Get out!" Lizzy shouted and once again Arn's foot nudged the sleeping cat who did not move an inch. The last thing he needed was scratches Ike Lizzy's. But—as he looked at the cat snoring peacefully— he doubted that would happen.

"Good day, Ms. Hondros."

"Wait, Anderson. You forgot your check."

Arn stopped and faced her.

She thrust the check at him. "Here."

"I didn't earn it yet," Arn said. "I didn't find Tito's mistress for you like you hired me to do. But I'm quite sure I can trace your husband's activities leading up to Ivana's murder and we'll see if he was involved with her death."

"I told you, you're off the case."

"Consider this *pro bono* work. I'll get your proof that he had an affair. And more perhaps. That's a promise."

As Arn resumed walking to the door, Lizzy screamed at him while she stumbled down the hallway, check in hand.

As he shut the door, he thought how remarkable the architect was who designed such a sound-proof house. As if Tito didn't want the neighbors to hear the screams of his drunken wife.

In that respect, Tito and Arn were in agreement.

26

The atmosphere in the Red Lobster was appealing, with the lights turned low just illuminating the nautical decorations adorning the wall. A tugboat in Boston Harbor. A lobster fisherman in Maine hauling up his traps. If pressed, Arn would say it was romantic. "You were telling me about your time at the Houston PD."

"I started in vice," Kubek said. "The Assistant Chief suggested I go into vice and so I did. I worked as a decoy for two *looooong* years before I earned my way up to general investigations—you know, bad checks. Carnival scams. Really important things."

"I came across an article in the *Houston Chronicle* on-line about you—"

"You've been looking into me?" Kubek asked, her face lighting up, the redness of her neck creeping slowly into her face.

"How else can I get to know you better?" Arn asked. "You're always busy when I stop by or call your office."

"That's Lucille," Kubek said and sipped her wine delicately, "mother-henning me. She feels she has to screen all my calls and shoo people off stopping by so I can devote more time to these homicides." She set her glass down and Arn poured more wine for her. "Lucille doesn't realize what a strain it is working these cases and how an investigator has to take a break now and then."

Arn empathized with Kubek. When he'd transferred into investigations at Denver Metro, crime was skyrocketing. He had been assigned property crime his first three years, and he rarely quit at the end of the day without having something work related to take home. And it just worsened when he transferred to Homicide. As if the City and County of Denver were wringing every minute of time from him. He loved those days when his vacation would kick in so he could spend time with Cailee on the best vacation ever—just staying at home and doing absolutely nothing work related.

The server arrived and set a steak on Arn's plate while Kubek had salmon. "That's a mighty big steak," she said as he shook the salt shaker for all it was worth. "And you doused it with enough sodium to last a week."

"So, I'm a carnivore," Arn said as he began buttering his baked potato.

Kubek picked at her salmon and had eaten only a bite when she laid her fork down and said, "do you think I'm a little... brusque with my investigators?"

"Why do you say that?"

"I've heard snippets of rumor when the guys don't think I'm listening. They get the impression I'm a..."

"Ball buster."

"You've heard it, too?"

Arn nodded and wiped steak sauce off his chin. "I think that you are a little short. Expect maybe just a bit too much from your investigators. They're like you—they're working long hours on these murders, and it wouldn't hurt none to cut them some slack. But I thought we weren't going to talk shop tonight."

Kubek grinned and ran her finger over her lips. "You are so right."

They continued eating slowly as if to keep one another's company as long as possible and they didn't talk of the murders. Instead, the mask situation and the low vaccination rates in the state occupied their conversation until it was time to order desert. "Split a fried ice cream?" she asked.

"You read my mind."

They sat looking at one another until Kubek said, "you know what is stressful—this COVID-19 crap."

"Tell me about it," Arn said. "Everywhere you go people are talking about it. Give me an old-fashioned homicide anytime—" his hand shot to cover his mouth. "I know, we had an agreement."

"To hell with the agreement," Kubek said and leaned closer. "I'd much rather talk about the murder cases than the damn virus. I got a belly full of COVID crap."

"Amen to that," Arn said.

"So whatcha think about the connection between Ivana Nenasheva and Paquita Robles and Katya Petrov? I'm leaning towards it being one killer. A serial killer." She got a dreamy look about her face. "The person who solved crimes committed by a serial killer would be flying high."

"As in moving up the police food chain to something more... rewarding?"

"What's wrong with that?" Kubek asked. "Everyone wants to be successful."

As long as you didn't climb over the backs of others to get there. "I don't think you'll solve that serial murder case thinking like you have been."

"I don't understand—"

"These murders might not be the work of one man, just like you figured before. Remember telling me in your office that Tito was good for Ivana's murder, but another person likely killed Paquita and Petrov?"

Kubek grinned sheepishly. "Can't a girl change her mind?"

"She can, but—when it comes to homicide investigations—there'd better be a good reason for it. Look here," Arn took the salt and pepper shakers and said, "let's assume salt is Paquita, the first victim in town, while the pepper is Ivana Nenasheva. This A.1. bottle will serve as Katya Petrov who was found in Laramie. Now Petrov and Nenasheva probably had some connection, given they both had a 12-26-91 tattoo, and because they might have gravitated to one another, both being from the same area in Eastern Europe. Speaking the same language. But," he moved the bottle of steak sauce next to the saltshaker, "Paquita and Katya Petrov both had rope burns, possibly linking them to the same sicko who is into bondage, while Ivana Nenasheva had none." Kubek had grudgingly allowed Arn to read the coroner's report on Paquita Robles yesterday. When she had taken the victim's watch off at autopsy, the coroner noted old scaring on Paquita's wrist, which she determined was as a result of a rope.

He sat back and sipped his iced tea. "There is nothing linking Ivana and Paquita that I see. There is not one thing linking *all* of the victims except illegal entry into the country. I'm with your initial belief—that we're dealing with two killers."

"You made my point." Kubek knocked over the salt shaker and laid the A.1. bottle on its side. "I believe... no, I *know* that Tito Hondros killed his mistress, Ivana," she said, tapping the pepper shaker. "And although there were no rope burns on Nenasheva's wrists, I *think* there might be a strong enough connection to Laramie's victim—they were both Russian, or Eastern European. Both with the tattoos. Just like you pointed out."

"So, what you're saying is that Petrov was Tito's mistress, too, and he killed her last year in Laramie?"

Kubek grinned and sat back in the booth. "That's just what I'm saying. I can see either Ivana or Petrov being Tito's love interest and bringing the other in, perhaps for a *ménage à trois*."

"That's a load off my mind."

"How's that?"

"I'm relieved that you have evidence that Tito killed both."

The smile left Kubek's face.

"You *do* have evidence?" Arn asked, enjoying the way Kubek squirmed in her seat. Other than needing Tito to be a serial killer, he knew she had no evidence.

"I... we don't actually have enough to go to the County Attorney in Laramie and ask for additional charges."

Arn shrugged. "What evidence do you have?"

"What is this, an inquisition?"

"Think I'm asking tough questions? Think what Tito's attorney will be asking you on the witness stand."

Kubek trembled slightly and looked away.

"Have you ever been grilled on the witness stand by a good defense attorney?"

She shook her head. "All right, so all I've testified is against one street walker and a man who broke in and repossessed his television from his ex-wife. Tell you the truth, I break out in hives just thinking about speaking in public." She leaned forward and laid her hand on Arn's forearm. "Are there any tricks to testifying in front of a jury?"

"There are," Arn said.

"I'm all ears."

"Testify as to the *truth* and be confidant in your investigation and everything else will fall in place."

"Then I had better forget about asking Laramie to charge Tito for the Petrov murder." She rubbed her forehead. "At least I can testify about Ivana Nenasheva's murder. I got Tito nailed to the wall on that one."

When the waitress came, Arn ordered another iced tea and a gin and tonic for Kubek who seemed rattled enough to need another stiff drink. "Tell me just what you found at the Diamond Lil."

"For one thing," Kubek said, her speech slightly slurred, "we tore the room apart that Ivana rented. Or some big, burly guy rented it according to Diamond Lil. Ain't she something?"

"She something but I can't think what."

"I'll tell you what she is—she's a sex offender."

"You said that once before. This I gotta hear."

Kubek looked at a photo on the wall showing a fishing trawler unloading its daily cache. "She was convicted of second-degree abuse of a child."

"She on the sex offender registry?"

"No," Kubek answered. "If I would have known that I would have proceeded differently with her."

"Why isn't she a registered offender?"

"She was convicted about twenty years before that law went into effect. In short, she was grandfathered in and does not have to register."

"What alerted you?"

"The peephole."

"What peephole?"

Kubek drew out her explanation between sips of her drink. "We tore the room apart where Nenasheva was staying, the same room Diamond Lil put her in before. We found a peep hole behind a picture on the wall. And on the other side was another room that the motel records showed was never rented. Diamond Lil was watching people through that peephole. Must be doing it regularly for all the cigarillo butts we found on the floor. Sicko."

"So, there's no possibility that Lil was looking though the peep hole during those few minutes that Tito was there?"

"If she was, she's not coughing it up."

"What'd the maid say?"

"What maid?" Kubek asked. "From the looks of the place, a maid last worked there about the last time Haley's Comet passed."

"There's gotta be somebody cleaning rooms besides Lil—she'd deposit more dirt than she'd take out of the rooms."

Kubek said, "I don't know her last name, but Lil said she has a woman who comes in now and again." She laughed. "Her now and again is probably every other month. One of my guys stopped there to interview her but just hasn't caught up with her yet. Want a drink?"

"Trying to quit," Arn said.

"Suit yourself," Kubek said and held her empty glass up for a refill. "As aggravating as Diamond Lil is, I'm more angry with Frankie Mae."

"Why's he on your shit list?"

"Darwin Ness. Frankie let Darwin crash in one of the motel rooms with no running water and someone called in that there was a squatter at the Cadillac. Seems he let Darwin crash there more than a few times. One of the patrol officers responded and confronted the whacko bastard and Darwin laid the officer out cold before running away in the night. Damn it, Frankie knew we were looking for Darwin."

"How's the officer?"

"More embarrassed than hurt. Seems like our man Darwin hit the officer once before running over him and into the night."

"Sounds like when I confronted him in that caboose."

"Either way, there's enough officers pissed that one of their own got waylaid they're hitting the street hard looking for Darwin. But on a positive note, I drove down to Denver with Agent McDonald and we met up went the Metro detectives to serve our search warrant on International Dating, Inc."

"What did you find that Barney Fife didn't?"

"Who?"

"FBI Agent Barnes when he poured through Grigori's... Greg Willis' files."

"Our search warrant had a limited scope. I just wanted to find out who and how many mail order brides Tito Hondros had sent for."

"And?"

"Confidentially?"

"Always," Arn said, holding up one hand as if to swear to it, his other hand crossing his fingers.

"Greg Willis had a second book that the FBI didn't find. But Agent McDonald did. It listed all the men—and a few women—who had paid for brides to be smuggled through the southern border."

"So that proves Tito brought in Ivana Nenasheva?"

"In a manner of speaking. Sure you don't want a drink? Man your size ought to keep hydrated."

Arn waved the suggestion away. He needed to remain clear-headed if he were to get information from Kubek. "I'm just trying to find out who Tito brought into the country."

"The ledger was in a code we haven't broken yet and Greg Willis isn't cooperating."

"So, you don't know for certain that Tito paid Nenasheva to be smuggled into the country besides?"

Kubek shook her head. "Oh, ye of little faith. Or rather, little faith in McDonald. He managed to decipher who the man listed as Greek—Tito."

"I know that—Greg Willis confirmed that for me."

"But he didn't tell you the name of the lady Tito paid for."

"Gotta be Ivana Nenasheva."

"Wrong," Kubek said. "The ledger shows Tito paid for Greg Willis to smuggle in Katya Petrov."

Arn sat back, mulling this development over in his mind. "That certainly changes things."

"It does." Kubek finished her gin and tonic and said, "I'm back to thinking Tito's good for both the Nenasheva *and* Petrov murders."

"You know what that means?" Arn said and smiled wide. "It means my roommate will have another research date with detective Fabian of the Laramie Police Department."

Arn sipped his tea and his mind wandered to the last possibility when he asked Kubek, "There's one other person of interest—Jesse Brown."

"The other brother nobody's found yet. What made you think of him?"

"The watch and the earrings and broach were all stolen the night of the home invasion and here it shows up in Cheyenne. Doesn't that give you pause?"

"It did," Kubek said, "for all of about ten seconds. I could see no reason why Jesse Brown would be here in town when he was safely hiding somewhere in Florida."

Arn shrugged. "Something to run by Alex when you reinterview him."

"Who said I was going to reinterview him?"

Arn smiled. "Call it old cop's intuition."

27

Arn hung his Stetson on the hat rack by the door and followed the conversation going on in the TV room. Danny sat knitting, now almost finished with the pair of mittens for Arn, while Ana Maria sat hunched over a card table arranging newspaper clippings. "That looks serious," Arn said.

"It's just a pair of mittens," Danny said.

"I was talking about Ana Maria's project."

She looked up at Arn and he wiped a print smudge off her cheek. "You still studying the Barberi murders?" Arn asked.

"I have to know about them if I'm going to have viewers emphasize with Alex's sad story."

Arn left the clippings in the order that Ana Maria arranged them and read how the two killers apparently overrode the sophisticated security system at the Barberi's mansion. The article quoted the manager of the security firm that had installed the system four years prior as "incredulous that someone could defeat our system."

"Who were these guys, NSA or something like that to be able to get in?"

"Close," Ana Maria said without looking up. "They were computer science majors. Gamers to the extreme, one of their classmates told Denver detectives."

"Let me know the lowdown after you've finished organizing the clippings and police reports."

"Why?"

"Because in the last eight years, no one's found the rest of the stolen

163

items. I'm thinking Alex Barberi might shell out twenty-percent to get his parent's art and expensive items back."

"Don't you dare approach him with that."

"Why not? It'd be a legitimate business arrangement—his money to hire my investigative skills. Call it a finder's fee."

"I think what the feminine member of our household is saying," Danny began, "is that she doesn't want to spend any more money from the family coffers, her 'family' being Alex Barberi in the near future." Danny exaggerated a bow. "Do I have that about right?"

Ana Maria swatted at Danny's head but the old man dodged it. "At least wait—"

"Until you've made it official, you and your new Prince Charming?" Arn asked.

Ana Maria stood with her hands on her hips. "I didn't say he was definitely 'The One.' All I'm saying is hold off for a while until… damn, you guys you know me too well," she blurted out.

Arn sat in his recliner and kicked his boots off. "Knowing you like we do, I don't expect you'll be changing the name on your driver's license anytime soon. Alex isn't the first man you figured to snuggle up with forever."

"How about we just change the subject," Ana Maria said. "For starters, tell me what you can about what Kubek found when she and McDonald went to Dating International, Inc."

"Agent McDonald found the hidden ledger Greg Willis secreted in a false-bottomed desk drawer. And I'm hurt that Greg—Grigori—would hold out on me. The agent deciphered enough to show that Tito Hondros brought Katya Petrov into the country illegally."

"I wasn't expecting that," Ana Maria said. "I figured Tito paying for Ivana Nenasheva to come into the U.S.," she stopped and a wide grin lit up her face. "That *almost* makes Tito a serial killer—"

"Whoa," Arn said. "Just because he brought Petrov over doesn't mean he killed her."

"No," Ana Maria said, "it doesn't. But it establishes that the only one who knew them both—that we could prove—is Tito."

"What kind of game do you think Tito was playing?" Danny asked as he finished the last stitch in the mittens. "For it would be a game if both ladies were alive and talking with each other. A deadly game apparently. Like you said, expats tend to gravitate toward one another."

"I intend on finding out tomorrow." Arn grabbed the remote and turned on the channel guide. "You guys up for a classic noir tonight?"

Danny stood and started for the kitchen. "I'll pop popcorn," he said over his shoulder.

"How about you?" Arn asked Ana Maria.

"Whatever you boys like watching tonight, I won't be here to enjoy it."

"Going out on an assignment?"

Ana Maria winked. "Sure. Assignment Alex Barberi."

*   *   *

Arn dropped Danny off downtown to make the rounds with the street people. With any luck, one of them would have seen the wild man, Darwin Ness. And although it wasn't something that Arn wanted to think about doing, he needed to talk with him, a bit more gently than the last time Darwin "talked" with Arn.

He headed towards the Diamond Lil Inn—another thing that he didn't want to do. Arn prayed Lil would be out of the office. She wasn't.

She stood menacingly close to a broomstick propped against the counter when Arn walked into the office. Gone was the thickly-applied makeup she used to charm Arn last time, replaced by a skin the color and texture of a dirty chalkboard. She'd ditched her tight-fitting skirt Arn saw last visit with a pair of bib overalls that allowed her ample bulk to spill over the frayed straps. And her voice that seemed to *coo* when she talked to Arn last time as if he were her next hubby had been replaced by a guttural, accusing voice reminiscent of *The Exorcist.* "You damned near got me arrested," she said, inching closer to the broom.

Arn calculated his chances of coming out on top if she started anything. With her size and anger on, he didn't like his chances as he said, "I'm not the one who drilled a hole in the wall so you could watch people do the wild thing. You're lucky you didn't get arrested." Kubek had told Arn that the only reason Lil couldn't be arrested was that there was no victim *alive* who had standing. "If ever someone comes forth complaining they've been watched in that room, I'm going to nail that big, old biddy," Kubek had said.

"What do you want now—see if you can stir up something new on me?" Lil said.

"Josephine," Arn said. "I'd like to talk with your maid Josephine."

"What makes you think she's working today?"

"There were three cars in the lot not an hour ago that are gone now. Customers. Their rooms need cleaning, and I can tell you're not going to do it."

"What's that mean?"

"Means you're too... sophisticated to clean rooms, being the entrepreneurial genius at this establishment."

Lil started speaking but hesitated and Arn could see her tossing around the backhanded compliments he just threw her way. Her voice softened and she said, "Josephine is all the way down to room 115 at the end of the first floor."

Arn thanked her and started to leave when Lil called after him, "you coming back, sugar?"

"Eventually," Arn answered and left hurriedly, knowing if he could get enough of a head start, he could outrun Lil.

He found Josephine just as she was coming out of the room with a trash bag in hand. The small woman—Thai, perhaps Vietnamese—started to empty the bag into another hanging off her cart when she jumped, noticing Arn for the first time. "May I help—"

He handed her his business card. She looked at it only a brief moment, her eyes darting to the office and back to the room when she said, come in here. Please."

He followed her inside the room. When she began to shut the door when he said, "your trash bag... aren't you going to toss it?"

"Lil... she is... frugal. Wants me to reuse the bags."

"In this country," Arn said, "we call that cheap." He motioned to the bed and said, "Please sit and I'll take the chair. That way you won't be getting a stiff neck looking up at me."

He took off his hat and sat in the chair, now eye level with the lady. She sat with her back arrow straight, her delicate hands folded in her lap.

"By the way you ushered me into the room I'm betting you know what this is about."

She looked down at the floor and said, "It is about Miss Lil and that... hole in the wall of that one room, isn't it?"

"What can you tell me about it?"

Josephine continued looking at the floor. "I need this job. My husband... he was hurt in a mining accident in Gillette before we moved here. I am the only one working—"

"Josephine," Arn said, "I'm not going to go to Lil or anyone else with what you tell me. I just want to know what you know about that room."

"And about that Russian woman who was murdered the other night?"

Arn nodded. "Was that the room Lil always put her up in?"

Josephine nodded. "She always puts people in there who... rents by the hour. And the Russian lady."

"So, you were aware that Lil peeked through the hole watching... what was she watching?"

The woman paused before choosing her words carefully. "Sex, Mr. Anderson."

"I take it there were others that she spied on?"

Josephine knotted her hands together in her lap as she kept an eye on the door. "There were."

"Was it always Tito Hondros who visited the Russian woman?"

"There was another woman, too. Russian, I think by her talk."

Arn took out his phone and pulled photos up until he found the least gruesome one of Katya Petrov that showed her face. He passed the phone to Josephine and she gasped. "Is that the woman who visited the Russian lady, Ivana?"

"It is." Josephine looked away. "They were friends, I think. But Miss Lil never watched them." She lowered her voice as if Lil could hear through all these walls. "She prefers watching men and women—not two women. Understand?"

Arn nodded and next pulled one of Tito that he'd snapped that night he followed him from the quarry. "Did he visit Ivana?"

Josephine blew up the grainy photo. "He did when Ivana stayed here. It was odd… she would only stay a day or two at a time, then check out. Come back a few days later. I do not know where she went those other days."

"Other motels."

"What?"

"Thinking out loud." Arn said, then asked, "That photo I showed you of the dead woman—Katya Petrov—was she ever there with Ivana and Tito?"

"No," Josephine said. "Never. The two Russian women were always alone. That man was alone with Ivana—never Petrov."

"Did you ever overhear what they talked about?"

"Mr. Anderson. I do not eaves drop."

"But you must have some idea what they talked about."

Josephine sat up straighter and said, "I think they were planning on going away together."

"Is that what they talked about?" Arn asked.

"No, it was more an… impression I got. I caught Ivana taking extra bars of soap from my cart, and the other woman—Petrov—brought things to eat like they were going to travel—protein bars. Bags of chips."

"What makes you think they were buying food for traveling and not just snacking while they watched the TV?"

"There were no empty wrappers, even though they brought enough into the room to feed them for a week." Josephine finally looked Arn in the eye and said, "That other woman… the woman you know as Petrov, did leave for good. But Ivana stayed."

"How do you know Petrov left for good?"

"Because, Mr. Anderson, this Petrov just never came back to be with her friend."

Because she was lying dead in Laramie's Optimist's Park, Arn thought.

28

A rn walked the long way back to his Olds, fearing Diamond Lil would accost him and hang onto him despite her being initially angry at him. The thought of Lil becoming aroused watching people having sex left a bad image in Arn's mind that he wanted no part of. He had safely motored out of the motel parking lot when his cell phone rang. "I found Darwin," Danny said, "staying in an abandoned trailer by that frame shop on 1st St."

"Just keep an eye on him and don't approach him. He's too dangerous—"

"Darwin and I have already had a nice little talk—veteran to veteran, Soon's I hang up the phone I'm going to go grab us a soda while we wait for you."

"Be there in fifteen," Arn said and squealed his tires as he sped off towards 1st St.

On the way over to meet with Danny, all Arn could think of was how easily Darwin could crumple Danny in a wad. It would be like Sarge stomping on Beetle Bailey. Except Danny wouldn't be picking himself up like Beetle would do in the next frame of the cartoon.

But had Arn heard right—Danny and the wild man have been talking? Danny going for sodas like old friends? By the time Arn slid around the corner onto 1st Street he didn't know what to think.

He spotted the blue and rust mobile home that hadn't seen paint since it was manufactured in the sixties. Arn slid his car to a stop beside a junk pile behind the trailer and slipped his snubbie into his trouser pocket before warily approaching.

Voices came from inside the trailer—Danny's and a calm Darwin Ness. Arn took a deep breath before stepping onto a rock at the bottom of the trailer door, then he was inside staring at Danny sitting on an overturned milk crate. Darwin on a bean bag chair. He stood abruptly, the tiny plastic beads *poof*ing into the air. He clutched his can of soda like he intended throwing it at Arn while his eyes darted wildly to the back door.

Danny stood. He put his hand on Darwin's shoulder as he eased him back onto the bean bag chair. "Take it easy, sergeant. Arn is one of the good guys we talked about."

"He's the one who tried taking me to the police."

"It was for your own good," Danny said. "He won't try taking you in today. Right, Arn?"

"Jail's not the place for Darwin," Arn said as he brushed dust off a five-gallon paint bucket before sitting.

He took his hat off and ran his fingers through what was left of his blond hair that was slowly turning gray. Darwin—"

"Sergeant Ness," Danny corrected.

"Sergeant Ness it is, then." If all Arn had to do to keep Darwin calm was call him by his Marine rank he'd do it. "Sergeant, you cold cocked that policeman and every available man on the force is searching for you."

Darwin smiled. "I saw that cop when I Injuned-up on my crib in the railyard. He was watching the place. I sneaked close enough I could have grabbed one—"

"I explained to Sergeant Ness that he's no longer in combat and that the police are not his enemy."

"I'm not going to the police!" Darwin started to stand when Danny eased him back down again. "No one's going to turn you in, but you can't be going around assaulting cops."

Darwin bent over and put his head between his knees. "Gunny," Darwin said, "I know it's not right to be wailing on a cop but sometimes I get so confused."

Danny patted Darwin on the back. "It's okay, big'un. Do you feel up to visiting with Arn?"

Darwin sat up and brushed long black hair that was falling over his eyes. "As long as he ain't gonna take me to the law."

"I won't," Arn said. "But I still need to know about those earrings and watch you took to Burri Jewelers for cleaning."

The color left Darwin's face and his shoulders began to tremble. "I already told you I… can't tell you. I don't want to be killed, too."

"Who are you afraid of, Sergeant Ness?"

"I can't say."

"Can't or won't?"

Darwin stood and headed for the door when Danny rose from the crate he was sitting on. "No need to leave. Arn here just wants to talk to you."

"I'll be back," Darwin said, unzipping his dungarees. "Soon's I get rid of some of that soda pop."

When Darwin disappeared through the doorway Danny lowered his voice and said, "That man needs a mental health expert."

"That's my thinking. I'm surprised he sat as long as he did. What did you say to him to calm him?"

Danny took a pack of Juicy Fruit from his pocket and popped a piece of gum. "I figured he was in the military long enough that he grew accustomed to talking with other military people. I just happen to talk the lingo—"

"You never told me you made Gunnery Sergeant."

"Well, I did," Danny said. "And that outranks Darwin, who made Staff Sergeant. We got to talking shop—he what he did in Afghanistan and Iraq, what I did in Vietnam and Laos. As good as he's done with anybody lately, we bonded to a degree." Danny stuffed the gum wrapper in his shirt pocket. "What do we do now? The cops want him bad, but I promised you wouldn't take him to the hoosgow. You not going to, are you?"

"I said I wasn't. He needs to get back into treatment at the VA, but the police will lock him up on sight and he'll never get any help. But in that stubborn skull is the answer to who owns the watch and earrings that just happened to be found on two dead women."

"You're still not thinking Darwin is the murderer?"

Arn reached into Danny's pocket and grabbed his pack of gum. "It would tie things up nicely—a beastly, a wild-assed homeless combat vet with PTSD killing women out of fear or rejection. But no, I figure Darwin's just lucid enough that—if he killed those women—he'd be long gone from town by now."

"But you do you think that Darwin knows the killer?"

"He has to—why else would he be so afraid to tell me who gave him the jewelry to be cleaned. And I want to know why he gave Burri Jewelers Alex Barberi's name."

"What are we going to do?"

"Let me think a moment," Arn said and sat back down on the bucket.

Arn wasn't sure if Darwin would come back inside the trailer or not when he appeared as silently as a whisper in the doorway. Danny went to him and said, "You all right, Sergeant?"

Darwin nodded. "Now I am." He sat back onto the bean bag chair and kicked an empty beer cap with his ragged tennis shoe.

"Darwin... Sergeant Ness," Arn said, "you crashed at the Cadillac Motel a few times... did you ever see your friend Paquita when you were there?"

"She cleaned rooms."

"I know. But did she ever talk with you besides those times she gave you a ride to the VA to visit with Dr. Land?"

"Sure," Darwin said. "She talked a lot about how she was saving her money to get back to her home in Manilla."

"Did she talk about her husband?"

Darwin stood and paced the room. He rubbed his forehead and said, "she found out her husband had scammed her. That she was not actually married."

"Who was her husband?"

Darwin became more agitated, pacing quicker now, his eyes once more darting to the back door and freedom from this questioning. "I won't say... he will kill me. He done some wicked things."

"I thought the only person you were afraid of was the person who gave you the jewelry to be cleaned. Was that person Paquita's husband?"

"Gunny," Darwin pleaded with Danny. "What do I do?"

Danny stood beside Darwin and draped his thin arm around the big man's shoulder. "Just tell Arn what you're comfortable with. We talked about remaining mellow before, remember?"

"I 'member. Sure. Stay mellow. But I ain't gonna say who gave me that jewelry or who Paquita's scamming husband was—he'll find me and kill me."

"Tell me this, then, do you recall two Eastern European women at the motel?"

"At the Cadillac?"

Arn nodded. "I know they stayed at Diamond Lil's a few nights, but were they ever at Frankie May's place?"

"I think they moved around motels a lot. Russians. "They were standoffish. Talked amongst themselves in one of the rooms."

"Was Paquita part of that... discussion?"

Darwin shook his head. "Paquita cleaned the rooms, but the Russians never talked with her. As if talking to a cleaning woman was beneath them."

Darwin slumped in the chair, his head resting on his chest as if the recent conversation had taken something out of him, and Arn knew he would get no more from Darwin today. Arn leaned closer to him and said, "Sergeant Ness, how about I take you to see Dr. Land?"

"Dr. Land?" Darwin said, looking at Arn.

"Yes. Dr. Land. You used to talk with him regularly."

Darwin nodded. "He was almost like a friend."

"How about you visit with him again. Me and... the Gunny can take you to the VA."

Darwin looked at Danny, who nodded and said, "it's time that you got back on your feet, big'un."

* * *

Arn left Danny at the VA to sit with Darwin. Calm him. Assure him that the best thing for him to do was talk with his friend, Dr. Land. Arn had talked with the head of the VA psychiatry department an hour ago over the phone, explaining that Darwin appeared to be at his lowest and needed help desperately. The doctor was appreciative that someone managed to talk Darwin into coming back to treatment and asked, "Has he hurt anyone?"

"Just a patrol officer who got sucker punched," Arn answered, "but nothing serious. Doctor, Darwin has information locked in his head that he isn't willing to release just yet." Arn explained that Darwin could possibly be *the* link to finding out who killed the three mail order brides. "Can you talk with him and see what he'll tell you."

"I can't. Patient confidentiality—"

"Remember the last time the 'patient confidentiality' crap was thrown into my face—people died. I need to know what Darwin knows."

"I'll do my best," Dr. Land said at last. "I'll meet with him in the lobby in thirty minutes."

"I'll catch a cab home when the doctor is finished admitting Darwin," Danny said when Arn stopped at the entrance to the VA. "Just go to the Police Department and tell Kubek she can't get her hands on him just yet."

On the way down to the Police Department, he rolled it over in his mind how to break it to Kubek that she couldn't arrest Darwin right now. She wouldn't be at all pleased. Assaulting a police officer was a serious offense and she'd be livid. He had only few miles' drive to formulate his defense.

* * *

"Lucille said you needed to see me immediately," Kubek said.

Arn checked his watch. "I guess immediately means in an hour."

"You know how she thinks everyone's monopolizing my time. Sorry for the wait."

"If I could have gotten in to see you *immediately*, I'd have told you that I found Darwin Ness."

Kubek jumped from her seat. "Let's go. You can fill me in on the way—"

"We're not going anywhere," Arn said. "I dropped Darwin off at the VA. The head shrink there's finished admitting him for treatment right about now."

Kubek came around and sat on the edge of her desk as she tapped a pen in her hand. "You had Darwin Ness and you let him go?"

"I did."

"Knowing an assault warrant was outstanding on him."

Arn nodded and offered Kubek the last stick of Danny's Juicy Fruit. "Want gum?"

"No, I don't want gum!" She came off the desk and walked to the window. "Damn you Arn Anderson," she said over her shoulder while she looked out the window, "you knew we wanted him. I ought to arrest you for harboring a fugitive."

"I'm a civilian. I can't make an arrest on your warrant."

She spun around. "Start talking or I just might go to the DA and see what we can charge you with."

"Darwin's the key to solving the mail order bride murders—"

"I solved mine—Tito Hondros killed Ivana Nenasheva and probably Paquita Robles."

"But what if Darwin could tie all three murders together—including Katya Petrov's."

"That's Laramie's case."

"But if—just if—you could tie them all in, that would be that serial murder case you wanted so badly."

Kubek seemed to be mulling that over when she said, "Still doesn't absolve you of what you did. When the Chief finds out I had a star witness that I let slip out of my grasp—"

"He'll commend you for your comprehensive thinking."

"How's that?"

Arn smiled and said, "let's say I would have turned Darwin over to you. You would have arrested and booked him, which would have lasted about an hour before the jail nurse realized Darwin has serious mental health issues. He'd be transported to the hospital. Stuck in their psych ward for treatment. Can you imagine how much money that would have cost the taxpayers? This way, Darwin gets help on the federal government dime and when he is able to talk, you'll have your tie-in with all three murders. And it won't cost the department a penny. You might get a commendation for that."

"I'd rather get—"

"A job offer at a bigger department?" Arn said.

29

Ana Maria took off her sweater and slung it over her arm. "Danny said you'd be in here." She stepped around sheets of dry wall leaning against a sawhorse and stopped close to the bare, unpainted wall where Arn had begun sketching the murders. "You think you have enough information to speculate about the killings?"

"I'm stuck without Darwin's help and thought I'd run some things by you and Danny. That's if you're not going out again."

Ana Maria kept away from dusty walls and pulled up a chair in front of where Arn jotted with his magic marker. "Alex said he had a headache—"

"That's supposed to be the woman's line."

She forced a smile and said, "Just when I think I'm getting close to him, he pushed me away. Politely, like saying he has a headache. Or has to get up early to go to the restaurant. Or he needs to hit the gym."

"Maybe it's as simple as him having a headache and as simple as he has to get to his restaurant early. Perhaps you're rushing things a bit."

"Ana Maria rushing things?" Danny came into the room and stayed out of her reach. "Since when has our darling girl ever rushed a relationship?" He sidestepped her swing and said, "maybe since last time."

"You don't think I rush men too soon, do you?" she asked Arn as she batted her eyelashes.

He set his marker on a card table alongside drywall knives and faced her. "I do." He held up his hand when she started to object. "Here's what I think—in your television career, you have covered

176

some of the very worst human beings doing terrible things. And when you find a man who is antithetical to those nasty bastards you spotlight in your nightly broadcasts, you want to latch onto him because he is just the opposite of the men you have been covering. That make sense?"

Her frown softened and she said, "Maybe you're right. Maybe when I find a decent one, I want our relationship to progress too fast. Maybe I do that because I'm afraid the guy will get away from me."

"Trust me," Arn said, "if Alex or anyone else gets away from you it'd be their loss. Take your time with him."

"That would be my advice," Danny said.

Ana Maria laughed. "That's from a guy with some convoluted rating system practically living on a dating site hoping to land his own Princess Charming?"

"Truce?" Danny said, "and I'll grab some chairs and some snacks."

Twenty minutes later as they all sat around the white wall with Arn's notations written in black magic marker, their fingers sticky from a tort Danny had baked, their bellies happy, Danny said, "good a time as any."

"Sure is," Ana Maria said. She wiped her mouth with her napkin and set her empty plate on the floor.

"I suppose you guys are right… might as well see what we got."

Arn feigned reluctance to start with their brainstorming, but in actuality, he enjoyed it. Discussing a case—or cases as in the mail order murders—helped him think through things. Getting Ana Maria and Danny's perspective had helped solve recent killings in Cheyenne, and Arn thought it was much like the Metro Denver homicide team sitting around a table discussing active cases. Talking about evidence or lack of it. About witnesses whose stories might be reliable. Or fabricated.

"What're those columns you made?" Danny asked as he scooted his chair closer to the wall.

"Crap," Arn said and grabbed his marker. "Forgot to label them." He marked one column for each of the murdered mail order brides.

"What's those last two?" Ana Maria asked.

"Wild cards. Tito Hondros and Darwin 'cause I don't know where they set just yet."

"What's not to know? Tito's good for Ivana's murder," Danny said.

"That's according to Kubek," Arn said, "which doesn't necessarily mean she—with all her vast investigative skills honed by years in vice and property crimes—is right."

Danny walked to the wall and studied it. "So, you don't think Tito's good for Ivana's murder and possibly Katya's?"

"All I'm saying is that we should keep an open mind. Here's what we know for certain." Arn picked up a yardstick and began pointing to items while he spoke as if he were in a kindergarten classroom. "Paquita Robles was brought in illegally through the southern border with the promise of marriage, which was unfulfilled."

"Lizzy mentioned Tito had brought in at least one Filipino girl," Danny said. "Might be Paquita."

"That's why I noted it like that. We do know that Paquita's husband snookered her, and possibly murdered her."

"But he's more 'n likely Ivana's, killer," Ana Maria said. "Listening to what Kubek told me on the record… that Tito knew Ivana intimately. That's according to surveillance by the great Arn Anderson, Tito may have been the last one to see her alive."

"And it's indisputable that Tito knew Petrov," Danny said, "when International Dating, Inc., has him listed as the man paying for her to come in illegally."

Arn made a line connecting Petrov and Ivana. "Any thoughts?"

"One, they may be totally unrelated," Ana Maria said, "with the exception that Ivana and Petrov were friends. Perhaps drawn together by their nationality."

"Or their circumstances," Danny said.

"So, all we have to do is find out who brought Ivana and Petrov into the country," Ana Maria said. "I think it's time to ramp up my coverage on my nightly broadcast. Say that I have information that's come across the TV station's tip line that a witness will come forward who can identify the killer."

Arn laid his hand on Ana Maria's arm. "Remember what happened the last couple times you did that on air—"

"You came to rescue me before the boogeymen killed me."

"It's not funny," Arn said.

"Darn straight it's not," Danny piled on. "You came close to being the breaking news yourself."

"But I managed to flush the killers out into the open, didn't I?"

"Ana Maria," Arn said, "I've never been able to tell you what to do. But if you're going to up the ante and put out some bait for the killer—assuming Tito didn't kill them all—do this for me—don't tell a soul except me and Danny. The last two times you had loose lips the killer hunted you up."

Ana Maria nodded. "That's why you two are my protectors."

"Thank God we got that out of the way," Danny said. "Now can we retire to the TV room and watch *The Bachelor*?"

* * *

By the time Ana Maria had changed clothes and joined them in the TV room, The Bachelor was just ending. Ana Maria had a towel wrapped around her wet hair and she sat in her recliner drying it. "He pick a babe yet?"

"Two more episodes in the season to go." Danny grabbed a skein of yarn from a wicker basket beside his recliner. "I'm hoping he'll pick Antoinette."

Ana Maria pulled two TV trays closer. Newspaper clippings occupied one tray, police reports and listings of the items stole from the Barberis at the time of their murder another tray. "You watching this... dribble?" she asked Arn. "Seriously?"

Danny shrugged and poured Epson salts into a foot bath before submerging his tired dogs into the hot water. "It was either this or watch reruns of WWF. Frankly, I've had about as much of scripted wrestling as I can handle for a lifetime. If some special reporter would ever go on with her special, I'd tune into that."

"Tomorrow night," she said, as she examined a sheet listing stolen goods from the Barberis. "Tomorrow's broadcast will flush the killer out in the open."

"I hate to ask what you'll be telling viewers," Arn said.

"I'll say that we got several substantive tips that came in on the tip line, one who believes they know where the killer is staying. The other tipster claiming they know what the killer looks like."

"Your tip line got neither?" Arn asked.

Ana Maria guffawed. "Of course not. I'll lay it on thick how the TV station's lined up a sketch artist that I'll meet with along with the person who can ID the murderer. That ought to get some movement in the cases."

"Does DeAngelo know what you're going to broadcast?"

"He does not," Ana Maria said. "Just like you advised, only the three of us know it'll be bogus information."

Danny set his knitting aside and took up a Thermos of coffee. "I'm more than a little worried about you. Flushing the killer out could backfire, don't ya think, Arn?"

Arn brought one foot out of the water and wrapped a towel around it. As he patted it dry, he said to Ana Maria, "you have two killers to worry about... the one who killed the three MOBs—as I am still not convinced Tito is good for them—and Jesse Brown. The more you hang around with Alex, the more likely you'll get caught up with that vengeance thing."

"Still thinking of Brown?" she said.

"I am," Arn answered.

"Forget that," Ana Maria said. "Brown's down—way down—on my suspect list. He's not been seen in town even, but relax—I can handle myself," she said. "But while we're talking about Brown, what did Kubek say?"

"Only that there was belief in the Marshal Service that Jesse Brown was still in hiding around the Miami area."

"Based on that jewelry box with the costume jewelry he pawned?" Ana Maria asked.

Arn nodded. "That's the last lead they got, and that was a few years ago."

Ana Maria laid her hand on his forearm. "I still have the snubbie .38 you gave me and that can of pepper spray. Besides, if I'm with Alex, he's more than a little strong in case you haven't noticed."

"Being a stud in the gym doesn't equate to being somebody able to defend himself. Or you," Arn said.

"I trust him." He recognized that dreamy-eyed look that came over Ana Maria as one of total infatuation. He just hoped Alex did nothing to deflate that feeling.

30

Arn pulled the car around the Hondros' circular drive and stopped in front of the four-car garage. Tito's Mercedes was parked in front of one door, but that didn't mean he was home. That might just mean he had started being cautious, switching cars as often as he had switched Ivana between motels. Arn smiled and waved at the two security cameras hidden among foliage growing up the side of the house before ringing the doorbell.

Arn didn't hear any footsteps coming from inside the soundproof house, but he did when Lizzy threw open the door. It banged against the side of the house and she said, "What the hell do you want now?"

"Just some honest talk."

"I told you before to keep the hell away from my home. I have half a notion to call the cops and have you arrested for trespassing."

"And miss finding out what I know about Ivana Nenasheva?"

Lizzy swirled the bourbon around in her glass, a piece of ice falling to the floor. She itched the scabs that had formed from her cat scratches on her neck as she stepped aside. "Only because you think you know something that might help my husband, I'll let you in the house."

She stepped aside to let Arn pass and slammed the door. "The study," she said simply and led Arn into the room. She walked directly to the wet bar and took the cap off a whisky decanter. "Now what is it that you think you know about that wench my husband was supposed to have killed?"

Arn sat on the arm of the couch and took off his Stetson. "I know that your husband brought Katya Petrov into the country illegally."

"And who is that?" Lizzy demanded.

"That is a Russian woman found dead over in Laramie," Tito Hondros said. He'd climbed the last few steps leading from his basement and closed the door. He began taking off his jacket, his thick shoulders and corded forearms told Arn the man would be handful. *If* Arn fought him fairly. Standing just shorter than Arn, Tito nevertheless had Arn by twenty pounds and ten years.

"What does this woman have to do with you?" Lizzy asked.

Arn started speaking when Tito interrupted him. "I'll speak for myself, not that it will make any difference. After our little chat, I intend making you a long-term resident of the hospital." He faced Lizzy as he began rolling up his sleeves. "I brought Katya Petrov into the country—"

"Using International Dating, Inc." Arn said.

"You know about that?"

Arn nodded, nonchalantly sliding his belt through the loops of his Levis. "And so do the Feds. If you don't get convicted of killing Ivana Nenasheva, they'll still nail you for bringing Katya into the country. And maybe for her death, too, which I'd put you as the prime suspect in her murder as well. So, big man, did you kill her?"

"You don't have to answer that," Lizzy said. She moved around to stand facing Tito looking up at him. "Just keep your mouth shut—"

Tito shoved Lizzy out of the way and stepped closer to Arn who stood slowly from the couch. "I got no problem answering that—I did not kill her." He looked down at Lizzy. "How could I, I loved her."

"You knew about Katya," Arn said.

"I did not—"

"Thought you know about all Tito's... playthings."

"Okay, so I did," Lizzy answered. "I'm not stupid. Tito didn't realize that I knew about her until I told him to break it off or I'd divorce him and take him to the cleaners."

"And I did break it off," Tito said. "No woman's worth having everything you've earned taken away in a messy divorce."

"How long did that last," Arn asked, "before you figured Ivana was Tito's next bedroom playmate?"

"Not long. I caught him going into Diamond Lil's flop house with her in tow. Then he moved her and I didn't know where he'd stashed her. That's when I called you to get the goods on him, but I was wrong." Lizzy moved towards the wet bar. "I don't think Tito was involved romantically with Ivana Nenasheva even though Lieutenant Kubek thinks she has an airtight case against him."

Tito turned to the bar and dropped four ice cubes into a tumbler as he picked a bottle from the many on the counter.

Lizzy poured bourbon into her glass and said to Tito, "You weren't involved with her, were you? If you were, I need to know if something happened between you two."

"That's just it," Tito said, "there was *nothing* between us." He poured two fingers into his own tumbler and leaned against the bar. When he looked to put the stopper back into the bottle, Arn reached the last loop and concealed the belt curled up in his hand beside his leg. He felt the leather wrap reassuringly around his hand, feeling the heft of the large "All Around Cowboy" buckle he'd won in a Scottsbluff rodeo as a kid.

"Katya met Ivana in Walmart one day and— both being Russian," Tito said," they—hit it off. Became friends. One day Ivana came to the quarry. Terrified of her husband. She thought the man would kill her. She said her husband had kept her tied up, but that she managed to saw through the rope with a nail file."

"You believed her?" Arn asked.

"The rope burns around her wrist proved it."

"Who was her husband—or is that just another of your fabrications?" Arn asked.

"I am so going to enjoy kicking the dog crap out of you. But first to answer your question, Ivana refused to tell me. She was that terrified. For her and for me, though I worried more for Katya if her husband found us all together. Ivana needed a place to hide out from her old man until she could get money to return home."

"Why didn't she go to the law?"

"Law!" Tito tilted his back and laughed. "If they falsely charged me with Ivana's murder, what the hell could they have done to protect Ivana?"

"And you didn't give her any money for… services?" Arn asked.

"Not for services." Tito sipped lightly of his drink and began taking his watch off while he eyed Arn. "I gave her money for food—she took all her meals in the motels rooms I rented for her. Too frightened to go out to eat. She insisted that she stay no more than a day or two at any motel before moving on. 'My husband will find me' she kept pleading."

"That's why you kept moving her from one motel to the next?"

Tito nodded. "And the only one who knew where she was at any given time was me and Katya. Then Katya was gone. I didn't know what happened to her… we had something special between us. Then, all of a sudden, she just leaves. I was heartbroken. I looked all over town for her. Put out feelers. Nothing. Not until she was found dead in that park in Laramie."

"Did Ivana say why she was so terrified of her husband?" Arn asked, tightening his grip on the belt and buckle held behind his back.

"She never told me, but I know she confided in Katya. Ivana learned her husband was not her husband and had lied to her. That the wedding ceremony was a sham. And that he'd done it to a woman before."

"Paquita Robles," Arn breathed.

"That was my thought when I heard that a Filipino woman was found dead in the park."

"There has got to be more to it than that to scare her so badly," Arn said, slowly moving so that the coffee table was between him and Tito. When he rushed Arn, moving around the table would give Arn a bit of an edge.

"There was something more that frightened her, sure, but I never knew what. Katya knew but I never pressed her for it."

"And all the time you met Ivana in the motels," Arn said, "you never had sex with her?"

"Yeah," Lizzy said, downing her drink, spilling it down the front of her nightie. "You telling us you never made out with that Ivana?"

"Never."

"I saw you that night," Arn said, "at the Diamond Lil. Walking into Ivana's room. Her wearing a sheer teddy."

"I went in and right out again by the back window," Tito said. "You know, you really ought to use something for surveillance besides that gold hot rod of yours." Tito downed his drink and set the empty glass aside. "When I saw you out there, I thought for sure you were some PI Ivana's husband had hired to find her."

"That's when you put the sneak on me and smashed my window. And me," Arn said, willing his breathing to slow, knowing Tito would soon attack him.

"Since this little conversation is between us and I will deny it, yes—I smashed your window. And took your camera and got rid of the evidence meant for Ivana's husband."

"Tito," Lizzy said, "he'll tell that Detective Kubek what you said—"

"Let him sing. The cops think they have a pat case against me, but they'll look like fools in court and I'll sue the hell out of them when the case is over." He laid his glass on the wet bar. "Now it is time to pay the piper." A smile spread across Tito's face. He walked quickly towards Arn, pausing to step around the coffee table. Now within arm's reach.

Arn bladed himself as he'd done a hundred times as a lawman.

Tito looked down at the coffee table for a heartbeat, and Arn threw his whole weight behind an overhand right. With heavy belt buckle behind it. The blow caught Tito on the side of jaw and he staggered but didn't go down.

Lizzy screamed.

Tito bellowed like an injured bull.

Lizzy picked up a lamp from an end table and rushed Arn just as he hit Tito flush on the tip of his chin.

This time, he staggered forward a foot before collapsing onto the coffee table just as Lizzy swung the lamp. Arn stepped into it and jerked it away from her. He tossed it aside while she clawed at Arn. He grabbed her arms and threw her onto the couch. "When he comes to, you tell that maniac bastard if he comes after me again I won't play mister nice cowboy. You tell him that."

Arn threaded his belt back through his loops as he walked out of the room. Lizzy stood from the couch, merely looking down at Tito, before walking to the bar.

As Arn headed for the door, he nearly stumbled over Winston, the morbidly obese cat lying in the middle of the hallway. He cracked an eye when Arn passed and went back to sleeping just as Lizzy yelled obscenities from the study. When Arn closed the door, he marveled how easily it was to tune the crazy woman out and gave silent kudos to the architect who designed the house.

As he passed Tito's Mercedes, polished and glistening in the afternoon sun, Arn spotted a garden spade leaning against the garage. For the briefest moment, he fought the urge not to bust Tito's window out. But just for a brief moment, and then he picked up the spade, turning his head, drawing the shovel back.

Smashing the side window of the car.

Much like Tito had done to Arn's Oldsmobile.

31

As Arn and Danny sat in the waiting room outside Dr. Land's office, Danny looked at the television in the corner playing a home-remodeling reality TV show. "I wonder if they could get the Dating Game on that?"

"You intend applying?"

"Why not?"

"Because," Arn said, "there is no *Senior* Dating Game show."

"Hey, I'm in reasonably good health. Considering—"

"Considering you were a drug addict and alcoholic in your younger days?"

"Something like that," Danny answered. "Still, it would be something to get my mind off

Darwin. Why do you suppose Dr. Land wanted us to talk to us for?"

"Darwin, of course," Arn said.

Danny stood and shut the television off. "Damn fools couldn't remodel an outhouse."

Arn smiled. Cailee was a nurse and they'd set around watching medical shows. She'd cursed the television when the actors portrayed something completely wrong medically, just as Arn cursed the television when watching police shows that were hokey. Danny, he cursed shows depicting men remodeling or giving some face-lift to an old, dilapidated house with little effort on the actor's part.

The door opened and Dr. Land's secretary entered the waiting room. "Please come in," she said and led them into the doctor's office.

Land sat chewing on the bow of his glasses as he watched Arn and

Danny enter the office. "Sit, 'cause you're going to want to when I get done talking."

"Sounds serious," Arn said. "He hung his hat on a bent wooden coat rack and dropped onto a hard government office chair in front of Land's desk.

"It is serious." Land stood and paced back and forth behind his desk until he finally stopped and faced them. "Darwin can make progress—"

"Can?" Arn asked.

Land nodded. "That is… *if* he had somewhere to go where he'd be safe off the street."

"Thought that's why we brought him here," Danny said.

"Gentlemen," Land began, choosing his words carefully, "we have only short-term facilities here. We can treat a veteran in crisis… get him back on his proper meds. Stabilize him emotionally and psychologically. But we're not set up for long term care—"

"But the VA does have long term mental health facilities." Arn ran his fingers through his hair. "I know there's a mental health ward at the Denver VA."

"Sure, that's where we refer the veteran who needs intensive in-facility care. If this COVID thing hadn't hit us. The Denver VA is restricting the patients they take in until this virus is contained."

"But you can't just turn Darwin loose on the street again knowing he needs help," Danny said.

"I can't argue there," Dr. Land said. "I have talked with Darwin extensively since you brought him to us. He desperately wants to be… *normal*, is how he put it. He is willing to do anything to achieve that goal—except go to a treatment center, which we don't have anyway. And he means it. Nothing frightens Darwin more than to be cooped up. Without his freedom. So, between the Denver VA refusing new mental health patients and my inability to keep him any longer, Darwin's got a bleak future. Even if we found Darwin civilian in-patient care, it's doubtful he would stay any longer than it took to waylay an orderly and escape."

"Then how is he ever going to get well," Danny asked, "if he can't go to Denver and you can't treat him here?"

A sheepish grin came over Dr. Land's face and he said, "That's where you two fellers come in."

Arn groaned. "I got a bad feeling where this is headed."

* * *

"How will you know Darwin's not going to ape and come busting out of that room?" Ana Maria whispered, barely audible.

"I don't think you have to whisper," Arn said. "Land gave him enough sedatives that he'll be sleeping like a baby until sometime tomorrow."

"Then it's safe for him to be here?" she asked.

Danny set his knitting aside. "Look, it's like this... Darwin wants to be right in the head. He agreed to meet with Dr. Land for one-on-one therapy twice a week and group therapy one night a week. Plus, Darwin swears he'll stay on his daily meds."

"And Danny here," Arn said, "will make sure Darwin makes those meetings and that he takes his medication when he's supposed to. If he stays on course with his treatment, he might just have a chance."

"It's the least we can do for a wounded vet," Danny said.

Ana Maria resumed sifting through Alex's clippings and police reports and list of things stolen when his parents were murdered. "I still don't see why in the world you ever agreed to have that... wild man under our roof."

"Let us just say it was logical," Arn said. "At least it was after Danny and me talked it over in Land's office."

"That," Ana Maria pointed to Danny with her pencil, "is your source of logic? Someone who illogically posts bogus profiles on dating sites?"

Danny set his knitting aside and grabbed the Thermos of coffee. "Hear me out. Like I told Arn, Darwin could stay in that room we keep the tools in until I get the new addition finished."

"But that's little more than an oversized coat closet. Hardly enough for someone to sleep in."

"Danny cleaned out the tools when we got home and put them in that back room," Arn said. He threw up a cot and blankets for Darwin to sleep on and resurrected that old dresser we were going to throw out. He'll be fine."

"Besides," Danny passed the coffee to Arn, "anything we provide for him is far better than what he had on the street."

"Are you going to go through formal adoption proceedings, too?" she asked.

"Darwin's going to pull his weight," Arn said. "He claims he loves yard and garden work so I'm going to unleash him on that weed-overrun thing we call a lawn."

"And all because you need to unlock Darwin's mind. To find out who the man was who gave him that jewelry to clean and told him to claim it was Alex Barberi's?"

Arn took his boots off and dug around the foot of the recliner for his slippers. "That... might just have to wait. Dr. Land was quite specific in his instructions. He tried to get Darwin to open up about the jewelry and who he is so God-awful afraid of, and he went off on Land. 'Give me a few more therapy sessions with him and I think I can get him to open up' Land said. For now, we'll monitor Darwin as we help him get back on his feet."

"Well, I for one am not sitting by waiting for Dr. Land to unlock the wild-man's head," Ana Maria said. I go on air tonight with the announcement that a sketch artist has been hired and it is a matter of time before a likeness of the killer is shown to the public. At least one of us is doing *something* to find the murderer."

"As am I," Arn said.

"You look like you're fixin' to take a nap." And, Maria said. "How's that helping any?"

"Young people nowadays," Arn said to Danny as he grabbed his sleep mask. "If I go out there and beat the bushes for the killer, all I'll get is tuckered out. This way, if some new and wondrous information comes to me, I'll be rested up and ready to pursue it with vigor."

*   *   *

Ana Maria picked at her omelet as she sat across from Darwin, looking at him warily as if she were ready to bolt once he went ape.

Darwin, for his part, seemed fascinated with Ana Maria. He had poured her coffee and stared as she tucked a napkin under her chin before Danny set the food on the table. Darwin sat across from her watching her eat, looking like any other man infected with Ana Maria's beauty. After Danny had "found" some clothes Darwin's size, complete with a set of toiletries that looked suspiciously like those given out by motels, the big man had showered and promised to shave. Once Danny "found" a shaving kit.

"Sure, rye toast was all right?" Danny asked.

Darwin nodded. He waited for Ana Maria to finish her breakfast and left the kitchen before taking three bites, and the omelet and toast were history. He sat back sipping coffee and looking at Arn as if he should know him. When he and Danny picked up Darwin from the VA yesterday, he had been so sedated and mellow that he could barely walk. "Give him these twice a day with meals," Dr. Land said as he handed Danny a medicine bottle. "He's got a double dose now, but after he sleeps these off, his daily dose will keep him on an even keel."

"Do you feel up to tackling that front lawn?" Arn asked Darwin.

"What?"

"You did landscaping before you were a Marine, I understand?"

It took Darwin a moment to answer. When he did, a wide smile spread over his face. When he answered Arn, his speech was controlled, not like the last time he and Danny had talked with him in the abandoned trailer. "I would like that. I ain't gonna be a burden to you—"

"Nonsense," Arn said. "If you overhaul that mess we call a yard, we'll be square."

"I will do it," Darwin said, "as long as the Gunny is here to tell me what to do."

"Then Ana Maria and I will leave you two to make this place look pretty."

32

A rn met Ana Maria at Old Chicago for an early lunch. They sat in back away from a large group of Japanese tourists who had stopped to see the famous western town where so much death and danger had proceeded the settling of Cheyenne. "He was doing okay when you stopped by the house?" Ana Maria asked.

"More than okay," Arn said. "Darwin had somehow managed to get that ratty old lawn mower running and had cut half the grass. He was bagging it when I drove by. If Danny can keep him occupied, the man might just pull out of his mental stupor."

"And Kubek?" Ana Maria bit into a slice of pizza, gooey, stringy cheese sticking to her chin before she wiped it off. "How'd she take it when you told her the case against Tito might just fall apart?"

"All but called me delusional when I suggested Tito hadn't killed Ivana. That he'd been her protector."

"Even I thought you were delusional when you suggested it," Ana Maria said. "Pass the Parmesan shaker."

After she'd doused Parmesan cheese all over another piece of pizza, she took a long drink of her soda to prepare to attack the last piece. "I talked with Kubek. She insists she has a clear case against Tito for Ivana's murder and she thinks he might be good for Petrov's as well. I think she has stars in her eyes thinking she might have a *serial killer* operating in the area."

"Kind of like when you thought there might be one to report on." Arn eyed another piece of pizza, then thought better. He'd always been *big* growing up and it had led him to a slot on the East High football team as a defensive guard. And extra weight came in handy when he entered bulldogging in high school rodeo. Extra bulk had also served him well many times in law enforcement. But he wasn't footballing or bulldogging or policing anymore. His one-sided fight with Tito Hondros yesterday had shown that. Arn had had to pause afterward just to catch his breath, thinking if he had a little less heft to pack around, he'd have fared better.

"Is there anything else you can tell me about when you went to visit Kubek that I can use? Arn, I need... ammunition for my broadcast tonight."

"She brought in Tito to serve a search warrant if that counts."

"This I gotta hear," she said, and took her reporter's notebook out of her purse.

"Not much to tell. Kubek said she had her evidence technician swab his mouth for a DNA sample. She still thinks Tito might be good for Petrov's *and* Paquita's murders—"

"Both victims having scratched the heck out of their attackers."

Arn nodded. "She thinks the blood spot on the pillow where Paquita was strangled at the Cadillac might be Tito's."

"This *is* a new development."

"Don't get too excited about it," Arn said. "I am convinced Tito did not kill Paquita nor Petrov. I'm a pretty good judge of people and when Tito said he loved Katya Petrov I believed him. As far as the blood spot, even after I told her it looked like Paquita had a blood smear on her upper lip she blew me off. That is one hardheaded woman."

"Like you."

"How's that?"

"You're as hardheaded as she is. What if you're entirely wrong? What if Tito did, in fact, killed them both. Cemeteries are littered with people killed by someone who loved them... a drunk husband slapping his wife around that got out of hand. A husband caught cheating and the little lady just wanted to teach him a lesson when she finds his gun. How many homicides have you investigated where the killer didn't mean to off the victim?"

"More than I'd like to think," Arn answered.

"So, Tito *could* be the killer in the Petrov and the Paquita homicides.

Guess we'll know once the lab compares skin under both victims to Tito's DNA."

"Not necessarily," Arn said. "You might have to wait a little longer to make Tito or anyone else your serial killer."

"But you said Tito provided a DNA sample for comparison—"

"Paquita's body was found rather quickly, and tissue samples taken from her nails were relatively fresh. Certainly fresh enough for a DNA workup. But Petrov... she's different. She was out in the elements far too long to assume there was any testable DNA under her nails."

He chuckled and Ana Maria said, "you gonna let me in on the joke?"

"Not much of a joke." Arn told Ana Maria how Tito had looked like he'd been beaten when Kubek served him the search warrant. "She told me she figured someone knocked Tito for a loop, as the imprint of my rodeo buckle still showed on his face. Kubek accused me of being said knocker."

"Did Tito tell her it was you?"

"He kept quiet. 'I will find the man who did this and even the score' he told Kubek."

"Great," Ana Maria said. "One more person you have to watch out for."

Ana Maria grabbed the last piece of pizza and said, "I'm keeping my fingers crossed that Tito is good for all three homicides. Be a hell of a special if that happens. All's I know is after my broadcast tonight, the killer might feel forced to make a move."

"You be careful," Arn said. "I have three roomers now and I'm not in the mood to downsize."

Ana Maria waved the concern away with a flourish of pizza at the end of her fork. "Don't worry about me. But what's your plans today?"

"I'm going to pay your boyfriend a visit—"

"Whatever for?"

"Alex's name was connected to the jewelry Darwin dropped off at Burri's. I'm going to pick his brain as to who he thinks might have paid Darwin to take it to be cleaned."

"I'm not sure how much information you'll get out of Alex. The times we were out, he knew so little about the murders it was as if he is living on another planet. He never asked me about my broadcasts on TV because he doesn't have time to watch the tube."

"Then I'll have a fresh brain to pick."

* * *

The afternoon crowd at Barberi's had come and gone, the waitresses cleaning up preparing for the evening crowd. When Arn entered the restaurant, a woman yelled from the back, "We're closed until tonight."

"I need to talk with Alex."

"I said—" Melissa stuck her head around the corner of the kitchen. "Oh, it's you, Mr. Anderson. I'll get Alex."

While he waited for Alex, Arn took off his windbreaker and wiped his brow with his bandana. This summer had been brutally hot, and he prayed daily for snow. Not much. Just a foot or so to cool things off.

"Mr. Anderson," Alex said as he stepped from his office, looking perfectly stylish and comfortable in his turtleneck sweater and tweed sport coat with the Barberi logo on the pocket. "Ana Maria tells me you are making progress into Paquita's death."

"Minimal," Arn said. "Can we talk?"

Alex motioned to a table, and they sat across from one another. "Coffee? Maybe a soda?"

"I'm fine." Arn draped his windbreaker on a chair back and wiped his forehead with his bandana. "This will take only a moment." He waited until Melissa disappeared into the kitchen to say, "Darwin Ness is staying in my house."

"Ana Maria mentioned it. Something about you feeling benevolent?"

"More like trying to get Darwin to tell me about the jewelry he took to Burri Jewelers."

"The one my namesake wanted him to drop off."

"That's why I'm here," Arn said. "Why do you think Darwin gave him your name when he took the jewelry to be cleaned?"

"I told that police lieutenant all I know is I didn't give it to Darwin. The last I saw that jewelry set it was on my mother's chest of drawers. But the day he dropped off the items—if Lieutenant Kubek's date is correct—I'd long fired him and told him never to come back into restaurant or I'd call the cops. Scared him to death."

"He just doesn't like… authorities if his military record is accurate. Seems like he didn't work and play well with officers. Knocked one on his keister," Arn said.

"Wouldn't surprise me. If you'd seen him the day he went… nuts here—"

"Oh, I've seen how he is when he gets mad," Arn said massaging his healing hand. "Tell me, do you think Darwin could kill those women?"

"If you'd have been here… sure. He is capable of that and a lot more. But why the big push to find out about the jewelry?"

"Didn't Kubek say?"

Alex shook his head.

"And you don't watch television."

"What?"

"Talking to myself," Arn said. He explained to Alex how Paquita wore an expensive heirloom watch when her body was found in the park and that Katya Petrov wore an earring of the same design when she was found. "Why would Darwin tell the jewelers the cleaning was for you?"

"I just don't know," Alex said. "The only thing I can figure out was that Darwin stole the jewelry, took it to Burri's so they'd have a record of it, and put one piece of jewelry on each victim so it would be traced back to me."

"I've thought about that but dismissed it," Arn said. "I think I will take a glass of ice water."

"Of course," Alex said and walked to the water dispenser.

"Can you think of anybody Darwin might be so afraid of that he would keep it inside rather than risk getting hurt?"

Alex set the glass of ice water in front of Arn. "There might… tell you the truth, I feel silly even bringing it up."

"Bringing what up?"

Alex pulled his turtleneck farther up on his neck and said, "I've gotten a few death threats myself lately."

"You? From who?"

Alex shrugged. "I thought at first it was somebody who was miffed that I bought Poor Richard's out from under them. But then…"

"If there's something else—"

"Jesse Brown," Alex said. "He is the only one in this world who would have a grudge against me because—besides Darwin for firing him. I paid a PI firm to track Jesse and his brother Aaron down right before Aaron committed suicide."

"Did you report these threats?"

"I stopped at the PD to talk with Lieutenant Kubek but she was gone for the day and I just left them for her to look at. She didn't get back to me so I just figured if she didn't think it important, I wouldn't."

"You do think it's Jesse Brown?"

Alex forced a laugh. "No, I think it's somebody who's mad because I outbid them on this place. Why would Jesse Brown come out of hiding now just to harass me? Why would he travel to Cheyenne?"

"Why do you think he'd be here?"

"That's just it," Alex said, "I don't. The letters had a Cheyenne stamp on it—that's why I figure it's not Jesse."

"Can you make a list of the other guys who were bidding on this place?"

"I could, but I still wouldn't dismiss Darwin being the killer just yet, Mr. Anderson. Darwin was so mad at me for letting him go… you should have seen his rage. If there were only one earring found on the victim in Laramie, that means that there is one earring left to put on another victim. Is Ana Maria at home with Darwin?"

* * *

Arn grabbed second gear, fishtailing around the corner, nearly clipping a fire hydrant, now only a block from home. He had tried Ana Maria's number repeatedly on his way over, but it went to voicemail and Danny hadn't picked up the house phone. As Arn skidded to a stop in front of his house, he saw the lawnmower in the middle of the lawn. Bags of grass laid out in a neat row by the street. With no sign of Darwin.

He burst through the door and stopped, his breaths coming in great heaves. Stopping. Listening. His hand inside his trouser pocket.

Found the butt of the snubbie .38 when… voices. Groans. Coming from the kitchen.

He ran through the house.

Bursting into the kitchen.

His hand on his gun when…

Ana Maria stood and started towards him. "What's the commotion?"

Arn quickly took in the scene—Danny sitting quietly watching Ana Maria and Darwin play a game of chess. Danny looked up and said, "You need to take a break. Don't know what's wrong with you… your blood pressure again?"

No, Arn thought, *I expected to see the worst—Ana Maria wearing the last earring, and Darwin standing over her with a ligature of some type in his hand.* "You never picked up your phone."

"I turned the ringer off," Ana Maria said. "After Darwin beat me two terribly quick games in a row, I needed to concentrate so I turned it off."

"There's no problem here?"

"Only problem here is Darwin beating the pants off me."

Darwin glanced up and smiled. "Six games and counting."

Arn hung his head and let his pistol slide back down into his pocket. Until the next time he overreacted.

33

Arn closed the door of the TV room, something he rarely did. But Ana Maria's nightly broadcast would soon air and Arn thought it best that Darwin didn't listen to it. "He took his meds," Danny said. "By now, he's sleeping like a baby."

"You know how babies sleep?" Arn asked. "Terribly. They wake up every couple hours demanding food or something else they are inclined to scream about."

"I doubt Darwin will wake up hungry. You saw how much he ate at supper." Danny grabbed the remote and turned the television on. "I still can't believe that you still suspect Darwin in these killings."

"Let's just say I took to heart what Alex said. Damn it, if Darwin, would just tell me who the hell he was afraid of..."

"Shush," Danny said and turned the volume up. "There's Ana Maria."

"...and today I met with a sketch artist whose identity will remain secret for now," she said, "for security reasons. The witness whom I interviewed yesterday, the one who came forward with information on where the Mail Order Murderer is staying and what he looks like, gave us a very detailed description of the killer. As soon as the sketch artist completes her rendition, I will post that to the station's website as well as show the sketch on-air." She cut to a commercial and Danny changed channels to the Food Network.

Arn kept his voice low and said, "did Darwin mention anything to you that might help?"

"He did not and I didn't ask him." Danny took up his knitting and the needles started their clicking. "Darwin is just now getting back on his feet. Going out and working his tail off on that field we call a lawn did wonders for him. After I told him to call it a day, he showered and afterwards I gave him his evening meds. And playing chess with Ana Maria perked him up, especially as easily as he beat her. My guess is—though all I am is a veteran trying to help another—is that things are going to start coming back to him once his body adjusts fully to the medication Dr. Land prescribed. Until then, you'll have to find out some other way."

Arn kicked his boots off and grabbed his slippers from beside his recliner. "I was hoping Alex would have been able to remember something. Someone who wanted to set him up by telling Darwin to drop that vintage jewelry off at Burris under Alex's name. Someone besides Darwin."

"What about the obvious?" Danny asked. "What about that whacko who's been sending Alex death threats?"

"That popped into my mind," Arn said. "I'd feel more inclined to think that it was Jesse Brown if there'd been any sightings of him here in Cheyenne."

"You don't think the man's actually here?"

"I just don't know. Both those death threats that Alex received were postmarked from Cheyenne so he'd have to be here if it was Brown."

"Maybe a visit to your new girlfriend—"

"And just who is that?"

"Lieutenant Kubek, of course," Danny said. "Maybe she's got an update on this Jesse Brown character." Danny winked. "Yeah, I think a visit is in order."

"Maybe I'll just do that," Arn said. "And speaking of girlfriends, how did that last one work out that answered your ad, the one who was supposed to pick you up in her car? She ever come for lunch?"

"Oh, she came by all right." Danny set his knitting aside and sipped on iced tea. "Picked me up in her year-old Kenworth conventional semi-tractor. She didn't give me a chance to tell her where I wanted to go, and so we drove right to the truck stop east of town. She ordered for us both and paid the tab herself."

"Sounds like the perfect date," Arn said, changing the channel to *Forensic Files*.

"You wouldn't think so if all you heard the entire lunch date was how her balls were as big as any man's. How she could haul freight all day and still have enough energy to give her man a roll in the hay."

"Did she," Arn asked, "give you a roll in the hay?"

"The only rolling I did was when she pulled up to the house here and puckered up for a goodbye kiss. That's when I *rolled* out of her cab and hightailed it inside."

"Guess you'll have to narrow your parameters on your profile again." Arn said, looking around the TV room. "Where's Sonny? Haven't seen him since I came home."

"Darwin," Danny answered. "Seems like Sonny's taken a shine to our new roomer. As soon as Darwin goes into his room, Sonny follows. When I woke him to work the lawn this morning, there was Sonny—sleeping right next to Darwin. Drooling on the man's shoulder. Not sure who was snoring the loudest of the two."

"Sonny doesn't take a shine to just *anybody*. He's like that very fat cat of Tito's—lying around. Not hardly moving except to jump up and claw the hell out of Lizzy's neck."

"Then by what you've told me of Lizzy Hondros, the cat should do more jumping on the witch."

* * *

When the front door opened it startled Arn awake. He scrambled to get out of the recliner when Ana Maria walked into the room. "Don't get up on my account." She dropped into her own recliner and set her purse beside it. "You're staying up pretty late watching…" she squinted against the fuzzy picture, "Home Improvement Network?"

Arn rubbed the sleepers out of his eyes and sat up. "Danny must have changed channels before he turned in. I told him I'd take the first watch."

"First watch for what?"

"For you."

"You and Danny aren't going to do the mother hen thing again?"

Arn shrugged. "Can't be helped. We saw that broadcast of yours tonight. You made it sound like tomorrow you would have the killer's sketch in your hot little hands."

"I told you I was going to air that."

"But you didn't have to make it sound so convincing that you'll have a sketch of him and where he might be staying." Arn scooted to the edge of his chair and took her hand in his. "Listen to someone who's been in the business of danger for a long, long time—you'll have a target on your back from tonight on. If the killer is in Cheyenne—"

"I'm banking on it—"

"...he'll want to pay you a visit. Soon."

"Don't you think I know that? That's why I had police protection driving home tonight."

"Officer Bobby?"

Ana Maria nodded. "Sweet kid, but he must know—"

"You use him now and again?"

"Such harsh words. Kind of like you're using Kubek for information."

"Which is what I'll be doing first thing tomorrow morning—pumping her to learn what the DNA test with Tito's sample showed."

* * *

From the lobby of the public safety building Arn picked up the phone and paged Lucille, then tucked the box under his arm and waited around the corner of the hallway for her to pass. The last time Arn had tried running the one-woman gauntlet, Kubek's secretary had kept him waiting for more than an hour. This time, he'd get in to see Kubek and be out before Lucille was even aware it was Arn paging her.

Arn paused for a moment at Kubek's closed door. When he heard no talking on the other side, he waltzed in. Kubek sat at her computer typing away and did a double take when she saw it was Arn. "How'd you get past... get in here? I told Lucille I didn't want to be disturbed."

"Bribe?" he said as he set the cardboard with 'Daylight Donuts' embossed on the outside atop her desk. "Filled long johns—your favs."

"I ought to call one of the patrol officers in and escort you out."

She looked down at the box and Arn nudged it closer to her.

"Damn you, Arn Anderson." She opened the box and grabbed two paper plates from a cart beside her desk. She picked one long john and handed Arn a plate. He thought for a moment that he didn't need it, then convinced himself that he did. *Just to be sociable is all.*

Arn thought Kubek had cooed when the creamy filling reached her mouth. She savored the pastry before setting the rest down and saying, "what is this… bribe for?"

"Just a little information for a civic-minded voter."

"God," Kubek said, looking up at the ceiling, "what did I do to deserve Arn Anderson."

Arn flashed an exaggerated smile. "Maybe you're just fortunate."

Kubek poured Arn a cup of coffee and sat back at her desk cradling her own bottle of spring water. "You came in at just the right time. Is Ana Maria spelled with one N or two?"

"Well, one N. Why?"

"I want to make sure I get her name spelled right on my affidavit."

"Affidavit for what?"

"Concealing a material witness to a homicide."

"Whoa," Arn said. "Put the brakes on and tell me what Ana Maria did."

Kubek licked frosting off her hand and asked, "Did you catch her broadcast last night?"

"I did."

"Then you know that she is concealing a witness who saw the Mail Order Murderer, and plans to air a sketch tonight."

"I don't think she—"

"Don't try to talk me out of this. The Police Chief was all over me when I came to work this morning. 'How the hell did you let a reporter find your witness?' and 'Arrange for a sketch artist!' he yelled. 'I want charges filed against that Villarreal woman,' and he nearly broke my door slamming it so hard when he left this office."

"Trust me?"

"About as far as I can throw your big ass," Kubek answered.

Arn smiled. "That's almost a compliment."

"Why do I need to trust you?"

"That witness that Ana Maria has stashed… if I tell you who it is and give you the lowdown, will you reconsider handing that affidavit over to the DA?"

"Only if it will identify the witness who saw the killer."

Arn held out his hand. "Then shake on it."

When Kubek shook Arn's hand he said, "There is no witness."

"That's it! Out of my office—"

"I am telling you the truth. Now will you give me a minute to explain?"

"You got as long as it will take me to finish this long john."

"Deal," Arn said. He explained Ana Maria's plan to try to dupe the killer into thinking she has an eyewitness that gave a description to a sketch artist. "You may not agree with her methods, but it might be a shot at flushing the murderer out."

Kubek slumped back in her chair and set her bottle of water on her desk. "So, there is no witness?"

"There is not."

Kubek groaned. "How will I explain this to the Chief?"

"Use your natural charm," Arn said. "Just make sure that information goes no further than the Chief's office or her ruse will be blown for sure."

"I'll do what I can, but I can't promise anything. The Chief was pretty pissed because the mayor called him into his office as he was pissed. But you didn't come in here delivering doughnuts out of the kindness of your black heart."

"I did not," Arn said. "I came here to find out how the DNA test came back? Is your man Tito Petrov's and Paquita's killer?"

Kubek groaned. "You must have already heard somehow and just come to rub it in."

"Rub what in?"

"After brow beating the state crime lab into running DNA test comparisons between Tito and Paquita's tissue samples, they came up not a match. As for Petrov's, their records show the tissue under her nails were too deteriorated when they processed her for any comparisons."

"There goes that serial killer angle," Arn said. He almost felt sorry for Kubek. She had placed all her hopes of hiring on with a bigger, more glamorous agency on the fact that she nailed a serial killer, and her fame would reach national levels and the attention of larger agency administrators. Now her hopes were dashed. "What's your next move?"

"Guess I'm back to the drawing board with Petrov. Just because there were no usable tissue samples to get a DNA readout doesn't mean Tito didn't kill her, too. I have a conference call with Laramie PD investigator who sounds... *dreamy.*"

"Fabian?"

"You know him?" Kubek asked. "What's he like?"

"You already said it," Arn answered. "*Dreamy.* As for Tito Hondros, he's gotten into your skull. An obsession?"

"He's an animal from my dealings with him."

"But you are finally convinced that Tito didn't kill Paquita?" Arn asked.

"Not unless he had a partner and from what I've learned about him, the man's a loner."

"Looks like you're fresh out of suspects."

"I've still got one," Kubek said. "That maniac you're harboring at your house. He knew Paquita—worked with her at Barberi's for a while before he was fired. She even took him to his VA appointments a few times. At least I can prove he assaulted my officer."

"You know he's got mental issues."

"He still needs to stand on that assault charge. Which won't happen until he gets right in the head according to the District Attorney." Kubek finished her long john and wadded up the napkin. "You must think a lot of that veteran to have gone to the DA and ask to wait on filing charges."

"That veteran thought a lot of *us* when he signed up to go to war."

"I suppose you're right but—"

"But you so wanted to solve Paquita Robles murder. That's understandable."

Kubek nodded. "Tell me, if you were consulting the department on homicide investigation, where would you look? What would do next?"

"For one, I'd get a tissue sample from Darwin Ness so you can either eliminate him or put him to the top of the suspect list."

"How am I going to do that," Kubek said, "the DA was adamant that I stay away from him."

"Unless the *butt fairy* helps you out."

"The what?"

Arn reached into his shirt pocket and came away with a folded-up napkin. He laid it on Kubek's desk and spread it out. "A gift from the *butt fairy* to you."

"A filtered stub of a cigarette," she said. "What can I do with that?"

"If you were in the mood to brow beat the state crime lab once again into processing it straight away, I'd say this will either convict or clear Darwin Ness in Paquita's murder."

"This was Darwin's Ness' cigarette?"

"It was."

"You waited until he tossed his cigarette away and you picked it up?"

"I did."

"I'd say that's a little more than sneaky," Kubek said.

"I'd say it'd be saving a combat vet a lot of misery if he was the focus of Paquita's murder and this cleared him."

Kubek eyed the butt before opening her desk drawer and taking out a Ziploc. "Why do I get the impression that you are convinced Darwin had nothing to do with it?"

"Because of Sonny's intuition."

"That mangy old dog who lives under your kitchen table?"

"He's not mangy," Arn said, "he's just an old-man doggie. Sonny's taken a shine to Darwin Ness—the dog adores him. And Sonny doesn't take to anybody, so Darwin must be of good character."

"Let me get this straight, I'm to take this to the crime lab and once more brow beat the tech into comparing Darwin's DNA with Paquita's tissue samples because your nasty old Basset Hound likes the man?"

"You have a wonderful grasp of the situation."

"I will not—"

"You afraid I'm right and that Darwin didn't kill Paquita?"

"How do I know that you just didn't pick up some random butt and bring it here?"

"Because," Arn said as he batted his eye lashes, "I'm fussy as to whose butt I let I lay their hands on."

Kubek snickered and wrote on an evidence label. She stuck it to the outside of the Ziploc and placed it atop her paperwork. "I'll do an evidence in sheet and take a drive to the state lab in a bit. While we're on the subject of Darwin Ness, did you ever ask him who gave him the jewelry—provided he didn't steal it—and why he used Alex Barberi's name?"

"The man is doing all he can to maintain. Dr. Land at the VA says it'll be weeks before Darwin will be able to talk about his last few months of his life. Believe me, I'd like to pick his brain as much as you would."

Arn stood and walked to the coffee cart. He poured from a carafe and offered Kubek a cup but she waved it off.

He stood looking out the window. Two young boys stripped down to their shorts walked by the public safety building, fishing poles slung over their shoulders. Arn wished he could wear something cooler in this blistering heat and he unbuttoned his top button. "Tell me what you can about this Jesse Brown character."

Kubek broke another long john and saw Arn eying her. "I might go back for the second half, but it'll be fewer calories than if I ate the whole—"

"I do the same," Arn said, patting his stomach, "now and again. You were going to tell me about Jesse Brown."

"Jesse Brown. The only reason I even bothered to research him was two threatening letters Alex Barberi received that *might* have been Brown." She wiped her fingers on a napkin and opened her desk drawer. She laid a manila folder in front of her and opened it. "You already have the FBI's wanted poster."

"I do," Arn said, omitting that he had copied the poster for Danny to pass out to street people he knows.

Kubek slid a paper to Arn and he donned his reading glasses. He read where Jesse and his brother Aaron were apparently gifted students with a Computer Science Major. Jesse had excelled at football while Aaron had done some modeling work with local haberdasheries. After the Barberi murders, the FBI had worked with the local police to interview hundreds of students who might have had contact with them, to find out if any knew where they might have fled. "These interviews were conducted before Aaron's death," Kubek said.

"I understand he committed suicide."

She nodded and flipped to another page. "Messy, too. Denver police got a tip that Jesse and Aaron were hiding in an abandoned house and SWAT made entry. Jesse had since fled but they found Aaron dead on the toilet. Right where he'd killed himself."

"May I?"

Kubek hesitated a moment before handing Arn black and white copies of the scene. A revolver laid on the floor beside the toilet where Aaron had sat. But Arn had never had a suicide whereby somebody had offed themselves on the crapper and he said so to Kubek.

"I'm with you," she said, back to attacking the long john. "That would be the last place I'd do myself, particular like him with his pants down around his ankles. Guess he'll never model again."

She turned to another FBI 302. That agent thought as Arn and Kubek did—that committing suicide on the toilet was more than unusual. It was unlikely. "His opinion was that Jesse offed his brother and took all the stolen items for himself. But that was never followed up on and that agent's opinion was buried along with the Barberis."

"Did the FBI analyze the death threats Alex has been getting?"

"I called the Denver field office. They couldn't verify or refute that the handwriting was Jesse's."

"Time changes a person's handwriting," Arn said. "Have any of the stolen items surfaced?"

"Just that costume jewelry down in Florida is all. The FBI agent I talked with couldn't figure it, either. Jesse should have fenced that long ago."

"*If* he needed the money. The items taken on the report that Ana Maria looked at showed more than $80,000 in cash missing. I guess my bigger question is why now? Why after four years threaten Alex?"

"I thought about that, too, and asked Alex the same question. The only thing he could figure out was that Jesse waited until Alex had something to lose—his restaurant business. I can see someone seething for years. Biding their time. Waiting to strike the man who caused his brother to kill himself. What's the old adage? 'Revenge is a dish best served cold.' Perhaps Jesse took that to heart."

34

A rn started out of the parking lot when his cell phone rang. "Mr. Anderson," a frantic voice whispered over the phone, "this is Melissa."

It took Arn a moment to connect the name with the voice of one of Alex's waitresses. "What is it, Melissa?"

"It's about Bonnie. Bonnie Peters. She... got into something she wasn't ready for."

"I don't understand—"

"She was damned near killed is what I mean," she said, then "wait a minute. Alex is giving me a smoke break."

Sounds over the phone indicated Melissa was on the move and soon the sound of a door closing was loud in the phone.

"Melissa," Arn said, "slowly tell me. Slowly."

"Okay. Okay, here's the skinny... Bonnie came to work this morning. We were getting ready for the noon crowd. I could tell there was something wrong 'cause she wouldn't look at any of us. She's taken drugs before, but she wasn't high today, though it was like she was tripping. Agitated. Wired like she was going to climb the walls. When I took hold of her arm to slow her down a bit she howled in pain. I pulled up her shirt, and her wrists were raw. Bleeding. Someone tied her up."

"Did she say what caused it?"

"She wouldn't admit it, but she's gone back to turning tricks. When I confronted her, she got mad as hell and—when Alex approached her—she told him to go to hell, too. Quit right there and then. I know she needs the job, but she just stormed out."

"Do you know where she lives?"

"In one of those old railroad houses along 3rd Street. Hold on while I check my contacts." A moment later Melissa came back on and told Arn Bonnie's address and phone number. "Please Mr. Anderson, find out what the hell she got into."

"Why not report it to the police?"

"Why?" Melissa said. "Because… because Bonnie's on probation, that's why. If I reported it to Five-O, they'd contact her PO and Bonnie would be back in the county jail. Again. Help her. Please."

* * *

Arn pulled to the curb in front of the address Melissa gave, at least he thought it was the house by Melissa's description. The last number was missing from the side of the stucco house, probably buried somewhere in the trash scattered around the front door.

He walked through the rusty gate held up by one broken hinge when a cur—Blue Healer mix if he got his dogs right—emerged from under the house. It snarled and barred its teeth until Arn yelled back and the cur retreated back under the siding.

"You want to leave my dog alone or do you want a boot in yer ass?" a man said from behind a torn screen door. He stepped outside, his greasy leather jacket matching his torn and stained jeans. "Well, do you?"

"Is those my only choices?"

"You a smart ass?" the man asked, walking toward Arn. He had to look up at the man fully six inches taller but fifty pounds lighter. His scraggly beard showed what his last meal was—chunks of some food stuck to it, and his breath smelled of beer as he neared. "Bess start explaining what the hell you want."

"I'm looking for Bonnie Peters."

A smile crept over his face. "You a… customer?"

"Might be," Arn lied.

The man looked Arn over before the smile left him and he said, "You smell like a cop."

"And you just smell."

The man took another step towards Arn when he said, "Guess you'll be the first one I kick the shit out of today. And you don't have many more teeth to lose."

The wanna-be biker stopped, blading his body as if he was a boxer at one time. Before he'd gotten hooked on meth and beer, both which did little to ensure a man could take an ass whipping very well. "What do you need Bonnie for if you're no customer, old man."

"Just conversation," Arn answered.

"You a cop?"

"Not anymore, but I can have one here with just a phone call."

The man hesitated before saying, "Stay here and I'll get her."

Meth Head retreated back into the house and Arn wasn't sure if the next person emerging would be Bonnie or the addict with a gun in his hand. Arn fingered the revolver in his trouser pocket when she staggered out of the house holding a dirty plaid housecoat pulled tight around her. "Anderson...what you want?"

"To talk is all."

"About?"

"Hop in my car and we'll visit."

"Why should I?" she asked.

"Because turning tricks would violate your probation. *If* your PO was aware of it."

"You gonna rat me out if I don't talk to you?" Bonnie asked.

Arn shrugged.

Bonnie turned to Meth Head who was glaring at Arn from the safety of the porch and told him, "I'll be all right, Mitch."

She slipped on tennis shoes and stepped over fresh dog shit before climbing into his Olds. "How did you know I... turn tricks?" she asked after she'd closed the car door.

"I just know things," Arn said. He half-turned in his seat, while Bonnie sat looking straight ahead. "Just like I know that one of your... customers roughed you up."

"How'd you find out—"

"Pull up your sleeves."

"Why—"

"Pull them up or I will."

Bonnie glared at Arn before slowly, carefully, pulling her sleeves up.

He took her hand and drew her arm close as he bent to look closely at her wrists. "Those are rope burns, aren't they?"

She kept quiet.

"Did you get into a bad situation that you couldn't handle?"

Bonnie looked out the window for many moments before saying, "I knew—just knew—that man was gonna be kinky."

"I'm listening."

"He started by leaving a note in my jacket at work. Snuck in sometime when we were busy last night during the supper crowd. Promised me a thousand dollars. Can you believe it, someone was going to give *me* a thousand bucks to me for a little... love."

"I'm betting there was no love involved."

"Can I?" Bonnie asked when she produced a pack of Marlboros.

"Just crank the window down."

She rolled the window down and lit her cigarette. She inhaled deeply as if the smoke calmed her before exhaling slowly. "I thought I was tough as nails. That I could handle any customer who got aggressive. I was wrong."

Arn remained quiet. Bonnie would tell him her story if he just remained silent. "I was to meet him in the alley behind the Albany Restaurant. 'Wear a ski mask turned backwards' the note said. I gotta tell you I was a little intrigued by the note—I always liked a little danger. Excitement."

"Did he leave a ski mask for you?"

She shook her head. "I borrowed Mitch's. He was going to use for... a stop and rob that he chickened out on. Anyway, I waited behind the Albany at midnight like the note said when he pulled up in a fancy car—"

"How'd you know it was a fancy car," Arn asked, "if you couldn't see through your ski mask?"

"I sneaked a look just before climbing into the outfit. Can't say much about the car except it was long and big. And it just *smelled* nice when I got in. The seats were like sofas. A person can just tell quality sometimes. Then we drove off presumably to his house."

"What did the guy say while he was driving?"

"Nothing," Bonnie answered. "Absolutely nothing. Even when I asked him where we were going he didn't say a word. The only thing he did was to press ten $100 bills into my hand. Told me what it was but that I better not sneak a look until after our little party."

"You thought things were going to be alright?"

Bonnie looked at Arn. Tears began cutting through the dirt on her cheek as she broke down in sobs, pouring out what happened. "I thought I'd hit the mother lode. A thousand bucks! We drove on about fifteen minutes before he stopped and climbed out. He led me by the hand across dirt or small rocks or shale or something besides pavement. I couldn't tell, I still had the ski mask on. He led me up a few steps and into the house. Started leading me down some stairs. When I reached up to take the mask off, he slapped me hard on the back of the head. His way of telling me to leave the ski mask on, though he still said nothing to me."

Arn laid his hand on Bonnie's hand and said, "It'll be okay. Take your time."

She jerked her hand away. "It won't be okay as long as that bastard is free to do to other girls what he did to me."

"What did he do to you, Bonnie?"

"First, the rope," she said at last. "He tied my wrists tight with rope. I yelled that it hurt like hell, but he paid me no mind. Tied me to something... a wall. Or a rafter. Something that I couldn't get away from, and then it started."

She took a last long drag of her cigarette before tossing it out the window. She turned so that her back was to Arn and pulled her housecoat down to her waist. Red marks, deep where something had lashed her back had started to scab up. She pulled her coat back up and said, "It don't look so bad now that Mitch put some Neosporin on them. But at the time I thought the beating would last forever."

"How long did it last?"

Bonnie shrugged. "An hour, maybe longer until... the guy stopped and I could hear he was... masturbating. The bastard got his rocks off beating me. I honestly thought he would keep on with the whip or whatever the hell he was using and I'd be a goner."

"How'd you get loose?"

"He let me loose," Bonnie answered. "All of sudden, he just untied me and led me back upstairs and into his car. Before he dropped me off in the alley in back of the Albany, he slipped another thousand dollars into the pocket of my jeans. I don't know if it was to keep my mouth shut or if he felt guilty about what he done."

"Is there anything you remember smelling or hearing or touching that was out of the ordinary?"

"His cologne," Bonnie said. "I didn't smell it in the car—guess the air conditioner dissipated it or something, but when he let me out of the car, I smelled his lavender, and I thought how manly is it that he wears lavender cologne."

"Recognize it?"

Bonnie forced a laugh. "I'm hardly an authority on men's fragrances. But it had kind of a sweet smell to it. When we got in the house, and he started with the whip, I had other things to worry about."

Arn thought about what Bonnie had told him, questions floating around in his mind. "At Barberi's, no one saw anyone strange wandering around who would slip that note into your coat pocket?"

"We were so busy with the evening crowd anyone could have sneaked back where we hang our coats." She slipped her hand into her jeans and handed Arn the note. "I don't know if that will help catch him, but it might. I don't want him doing this to any other girls. It's just so demeaning. I don't know what I'm going to do."

"I am going to do what I can to find this man," Arn said while he opened the note. It read precisely how Bonnie described it. The writing distinctive. Precise cursive.

Just like the death threats that Alex has been getting.

35

Danny had made his world-class lasagna—a dish to rival even Barberi's—with a crème brulée dessert and yet Arn barely touched them. And neither did Danny. Darwin, on the other hand, finished his in just a few bites and offered to take Arn and Danny's off their plates, after which he took his meds and went to sleep early. That had been four hours ago. Four long hours of watching the remodeling network with little spoken between them until Danny said, "She should have been home by now."

Arn checked his watch. "I'm sure she's all right—she's just with Alex."

"I know," Danny said. His project had sat in his lap this whole time, but he hadn't laid as much as one stitch. "It's when he drops her off at her car that worries me. Why doesn't she answer her cell?"

Arn didn't have an answer for that. He had dialed her cell phone six times tonight, and each time it went to voice mail. He had even called her direct line at the TV station thinking Ana Maria had gone there to work on her project after her date but it, too, went to an answering system. "I'd go out to Alex's house and see if he knows where Ana Maria is—"

"*If* we knew exactly where he lived," Danny said. "Somewhere in that subdivision north of town she said. House at the end of a long drive with a lot of trees and flowers and foliage."

"That could mean a dozen places around there."

They resumed watching the television. Arn paid just enough attention to marvel at the ease with which a ratty run-down house—

like his mother's had been before Danny tore into it—was completely remade effortlessly. Seemingly within days.

"Here's a remote possibility why she's not home," Danny said. "Maybe she and Alex were having a romantic evening when that Jesse Brown decided to extract his ultimate revenge on Alex."

"We don't know for sure if Brown's even in Cheyenne. All we're going on is jewelry Brown stole floating around town and on victims, and death threats postmarked from Cheyenne."

"By what Bonnie Peters told you happened to her, that sounds an awfully lot like what happened to Paquita and Katya Petrov. If it is Jesse Brown—"

"Don't you think I haven't been kicking that around in my feeble mind," Arn said. "I finally had to admit to myself that we have no evidence that Jesse Brown is involved with those two girls—or Ivana either. Hell, no one's spotted him in town even after you handed out copies of FBI wanted posters to street people like you were handing out voting forms. If anyone saw Brown here it would be one of your street people."

They resumed watching the television when Danny said, "There's that last possibility of why Ana Maria's not home."

"What possibility?"

"Rod Stewart."

"Rod Stewart? You think Rod Stewart breezed into town and whisked her away?"

Danny chuckled. "No, but he sang 'Tonight's the Night.'"

"Where is this going?" Arn asked.

"Where? Why, this might be *the* night when Ana Maria and Alex become... close. Intimate."

"You think she's not answering her phone 'cause she's doing the wild thing with Alex?"

"Can you think of a better reason why she'd turn off her phone?"

Arn snapped his fingers. "Officer Bobby... he might know how to find Alex's house." Arn grabbed his cell phone when he paused. "What's Officer Bobby's last name?"

"Ryerback." Ana Maria stepped into the room. "And I told you two how many times not to mother hen me?"

"How'd you get in without Sonny coming to life?" Danny asked.

"For one thing, I walked in here while you two peckerwoods were talking about me. For another, are you sure Sonny's even breathing 'cause he don't seem to be."

Arn looked at Sonny lying in the corner, one of his favorite places in the house. He had gone back to lying there after Darwin—tired of Sonny's snoring—had shut the dog out of his room. Arn had to stare long and hard before he finally saw Sonny take a gasp of air. *Some watchdog.*

"We were just worried about you." Arn stood and stretched his legs. "Your cell phone was turned off—"

"Just for that reason," she answered. "So you two wouldn't call and nag me about being out so late."

"You were with Alex all this time?" Danny asked, his knitting needles now clacking at full speed.

"I was."

"Did you do the wild thing? We want all the juicy details."

Ana Maria draped her purse over her recliner and sat to take her shoes off. "I don't know if we were going to do it or not," she said. "We were at the restaurant for a nice meal and talked afterwards until closing time. 'Want to take a drive out to my place again,' Alex offered me. You know that I was thinking—"

"Like Rod Stewart?" Danny asked.

Ana Maria nodded. "But I'm afraid tonight wasn't the night. Just as we were about to hop in his car, Melissa came driving up needing to speak with Alex. He tried to put her off until tomorrow. Said he was busy. That he had something important he needed to talk to me about."

"He's going to ask for your hand in marriage even before you two do the wild thing," Danny said. "That shows the man has character—"

"Slow down, pardners. I have no idea what he wanted to talk with me about so don't jump to any conclusions."

"What did Melissa want?" Arn asked.

"She was beside herself. She skidded to a stop in the parking lot of the restaurant and bailed out. Had to talk with Alex alone. They stepped aside and Melissa whispered to him before he came back to his car. He apologized and said we'd talk tomorrow. He said Melissa caught Bonnie Peters trying to hang herself in her back yard, but Melissa wrestled her down. When Bonnie came around again, she took off. Melissa was afraid Bonnie would find some other way to kill herself and didn't know anyone else who might help so she came to Alex."

"I pushed her too hard," Arn said, tugging on his boots.

"What are you talking about?" Ana Maria asked.

"Bonnie Peters." He explained how he had leaned on Bonnie at her house to tell him about the beating she'd received from some man yet unknown to her. "I'm calling Kubek to see if her officers can look for her. If Bonnie attempted suicide once with purpose, she'll try to kill herself again."

"You going to look for her?" Ana Maria asked.

"I have no choice. I'm responsible for pushing her over her limit—"

"That's nonsense and you know it, Arn Anderson. If she tried it tonight it was because she felt she *needed* to do it." Ana Maria put her sweater back on. "I'm going with you."

Danny stood abruptly and took his slippers off, grabbing his tennis shoes from beside his recliner. "I'll be damned if I'll be left alone in this spooky old house—"

Arn laid his hand on the old man's shoulder. "I appreciate it, but you better stay here. If Darwin wakes up and there's no one home, he might freak out. And he'll need a Gunny to calm him down."

36

They sat around the kitchen table. Silent. Morose. They had been out all night looking for Bonnie Peters as had half the police force. Arn and Ana Maria's first stop last night had been at Bonnie's house to talk with her boyfriend, but a patrol officer had already found Mitch nine sheets to the wind slumped over a pitcher of beer at the Eagle's Nest. Kubek called Arn to tell him that Mitch only knew that Bonnie didn't want to go out with him last night, and he'd left the house to get drunk alone. "Go home and leave this to the police officers," Kubek had told Arn. "I'll get hold of you if we find her."

Arn and Ana Maria had ignored Kubek, instead continuing to drive places where they thought Bonnie would go, most often passing a police cruiser doing the same. They'd stayed out until the sun came up and called it a night.

Danny heard them come in the house and stumbled out of his room rubbing his eyes, his fuzzy slippers slapping on the bare floor, tripping over a roll of carpeting waiting to be laid. "You two never came home last night. I stayed up as long as I could before I dozed off. Come on in the kitchen and I'll get start some flapjacks."

Arn felt the weight of failure, knowing that Bonnie had tried suicide before because of him pressuring her to recount the horrors she experienced with the man who had paid her for her company. He slumped down in the chair and rested his elbows on the table, cradling his head in his hands.

Ana Maria sat across from him and laid her hand on his shoulder.

"I know how badly you wanted to find her. Maybe the police will have some luck."

Arn looked up at her, holding back tears when he said, "I pushed her too hard. The beating that she took... it must have been awful. She was so demoralized, yet I kept prodding her for more details—"

"You wanted to find the bastard who did that to her," Ana Maria said, "and maybe to three mail order brides as well, if the guy was one and the same."

Danny cracked eggs into a stainless-steel bowl before grabbing a whisk. "I'll go out and talk to the street folks after we have breakfast. Surely someone had to have come across her last night"

"Can I come along with the Gunny?" Darwin entered the kitchen and stood nearly at attention beside a chair.

Arn motion to the chair and said, "You don't have to wait for an invite for breakfast. Sit and... the Gunny will have something whipped up in a bit."

Darwin sat on the chair and folded his hands, a far different man now that he was back on his medications. "I heard the Gunny is going downtown. Can I go along?"

"That'll be up to Danny... Gunny," Arn said.

Danny poured batter onto a griddle before turning and facing Darwin. "I'm not so sure that would be a good idea. After all, street people would remember the *old* Darwin, not the new and improved version. Perhaps I could give you a rain check. We'll see what next week looks like. Besides, today was the day you were going to till up the dirt and reseed the lawn remember?"

There was no emotion in Darwin's voice as he answered, "Okay, Gunny. Maybe next week."

Arn and Ana Maria sat in silence watching Danny cook the flapjacks, expertly tossing each onto a platter beside the griddle. When he had a sizable plate full, he set them on the table along with butter and syrup and a carafe of coffee. "That's the best that I can come up with on a moment's notice."

"More than I expected," Arn said. "Thanks."

Arn and Ana Maria took two flapjacks, Darwin half a dozen. They passed the syrup around when Ana Maria asked, "Wonder where

Bonnie could have gone to?"

Arn shrugged. "Wish I could have talked with Melissa last night. She might have given us a better idea where to look."

"I'm sure she and Alex checked all Bonnie's usual haunts—" Ana Maria snapped her fingers. "The Cadillac and Diamond Lil's. Bonnie was a... working girl. Both places rented rooms by the hour. She'd be familiar with both Freddie and Diamond Lil—"

Sonny howled. As best as a twenty-year-old Basset Hound can howl, indicating someone had just stepped up to the front door. "I'll get it," Ana Maria said a moment before the doorbell rang and Sonny tried howling again.

"Who is it?" Arn yelled.

"Lieutenant Kubek," Ana Maria answered.

Darwin leapt to his feet and ran for the back door. "She's not going to arrest you..." Arn got out just before Darwin disappeared out back.

"I'll go make sure nothing happens to him," Danny said and disappeared out the back door after Darwin.

"Understood."

Danny shut the back door right as Ana Maria led Kubek into the kitchen. She stood for a moment and seemed to count plates. "Looks like Darwin Ness didn't quite finish his."

"He will," Arn said. "Later."

"I'd like him to eat his meals at the county jail for attacking my officer."

"You won't catch him today so... flapjacks?"

"No," Kubek said, "but I would take a cup of that coffee," Kubek said. "Having been up all night, I'll need to stay up even longer to do paperwork on Bonnie Peters."

"Since when does an investigative lieutenant do paperwork on a suicide alert?" Ana Maria asked, pouring Kubek a cup of coffee.

"Since this Lieutenant investigated said suicide victim."

Arn leaned closer. "You found Bonnie, then?"

She took the first sip of the coffee and closed her eyes. "Now *this* is a good cup of joe. I'd marry the man who made it," she said as she winked at Arn.

"Don't look at me—Danny's the chef in this house. You can marry him if you want."

"The old man?"

Arn nodded. "But you'll have to fill out a dating profile first."

"How's that?"

Arn waved the air. "Just rambling. Tell us where you found Bonnie?"

"I didn't find her," Kubek said. "One of Tito's quarry men did. He found her body and that of Melissa Roush at the bottom of the quarry."

And Maria's hand went to her mouth as Arn said, "Do you have an idea what happened?"

"I do now that I talked with their boss, Alex Barberi." She set the cup down and said, "I think I will have a pancake or two."

Arn stood and grabbed another plate from the cupboard. He set it in front of her along with utensils and waited for an explanation.

"In reconstructing the scene, here's what me and two of my investigators think happened, looking at the position of the bodies and where they fell to their deaths." She buttered her flapjacks and wiped a glob dripping down her hand. "Alex Barberi said Melissa came to him last night in the restaurant parking lot. She'd gone to Bonnie's place and found her swinging from a tree in the back yard. She hauled her down. As soon as Bonnie came around, she took off and Melissa was sure she'd try to kill herself again."

"That's just what she told me," Arn said.

Kubek nodded and speared another piece of flapjack. "Melissa and Alex divided up among themselves places Bonnie was known to frequent. They kept in touch with each other by their cell phones. Alex said he dialed Melissa's number at…" she looked at the ceiling, "two twenty-four by his cell phone. It went to voice mail. He had no idea where Melissa was, so he started backtracking the places she was supposed to have gone to look for Bonnie. The last he tried calling her was a little after four this morning, but it went to voice mail again. He drove home after running out of places to check, hoping that Melissa would find her."

"You said their bodies were found at the bottom of the quarry… do you think they both committed suicide by jumping?"

"If they did, it would be a sure thing. That quarry's fifty feet deep with all sorts of jagged rocks down below to mangle a body. And, lordy, they were mangled." She held up her cup. "Can I have a refill?"

Ana Maria topped Kubek and Arn's cups off and sat back at the table. "But you're not sure it was a double suicide?"

"I am not. When I talked with Alex," Kubek said, "he told me Bonnie was terribly upset and ran out of the restaurant earlier that day, but he didn't know why."

"We know why," Arn said. He explained that Melissa said Bonnie had met up with a mean john and that he'd beaten her, humiliated her. "She didn't want to report it to you guys. Afraid her PO would revoke on her and land her back in the county jail. She wanted me to find the guy, but I came up short. I could see her being suicidal. That's why we went looking for her."

Kubek sipped coffee and wiped her mouth with a napkin. "Alex didn't think it was a double suicide, either. He was adamant that Melissa had no reason to kill herself. He'd just promoted her to be in charge of his waitresses, doing the scheduling and making sure they got to work on time. There doesn't appear to be any reason for Melissa to want to kill herself."

"What do you and your investigators think happened then?" Arn asked.

Kubek poured syrup on her flapjacks and tasted another bite. "Now that's a flapjack. I might fill out that dating profile for the old man after all." She set her fork down. "There was definitely a scuffle top side by the disturbance on the rocks at the edge of the quarry. We think that Melissa found Bonnie just as she was going to take the plunge and tried talking her out of it. Bonnie was determined to go through with it. Melissa determined to save her. We think that right before Bonnie jumped, Melissa rushed in to save her. They wrestled, Melissa trying her best to drag Bonnie away from the edge when the two of them did a Double Gainer off the high wall."

"Without seeing the photos, I'm guessing there's not going to be an autopsy?" Arn said.

"I'll leave that expense up to the Chief, but I'm going to recommend against it. Not enough of their bodies left to do an autopsy."

"The obvious question," Ana Maria said, "is what did Tito Hondros say about two dead girls in his quarry?"

"He was conveniently out of town on business. At least that's what his wife claimed. This afternoon I'm applying for a search warrant for his bank cards. If he was out of town, he'd have to stay at a motel somewhere and there'd be a record of it."

"Unless he has another mail order bride on the side that Lizzy doesn't know about. One that he meets at her place or her motel room, at which time he'd stay with her and there'd be no record on his bank cards."

"Let's hope that's not the case," Kubek said.

Arn watched the back door in case Danny or Darwin came back and asked Kubek, "Did the DNA workup with Darwin's cigarette butt come back yet?"

"What's with Darwin's cigarettes?" Ana Maria asked.

"The good lieutenant here was going to guilt-trip the state lab into testing Darwin's cigarette butt against tissue under Paquita's fingernails. She still considered Darwin as a possible suspect in Paquita's murder—"

"Because he knew Paquita," Kubek said. "He bummed rides from her. He lied when he gave his name as Alex Barberi when he dropped the jewelry off at Burri to be cleaned. I only wish that the courts would let me bring Darwin in for questioning. Believe me, I'd find out just what he knows about the deaths. As for the DNA, I'm still waiting."

"Darwin's been doing good now that he's back on his meds," Ana Maria said.

"Maybe you trust him," Kubek said. "But I'd damn well not have a suspect living under my roof."

37

Arn dozed through Danny's sawing and banging with his framing hammer as he worked on the addition to the house, while Darwin outside made his own noise as he operated a tiller on the front lawn. By the time Arn awoke, it was early evening and he stumbled downstairs. "Don't you ever take a break?" Arn asked the old man as he stopped in the hallway watching Danny adjust his Skill saw.

"Look who just got up."

"Give me break—I was out all night looking for Bonnie."

"I remember those nights when I was younger," Danny said, "but it wasn't looking for any babe. It was more like looking for my next baggie of dope or next jug of Thunderbird. You hungry?"

"Starved."

"Then I'll rustle something up. Ana Maria called and said she'd be home early tonight so she can prep for the next installment in her special on dating tomorrow."

"Speaking of dating," Arn said, "have you had any luck with that dating site?"

Danny slapped his jeans and sawdust *poof*ed into the air. "I have one sweet lady interested. Only problem is she lives in New York and wants me to help her with air fare out here."

"Tell me you didn't send her any money, did you?"

Danny guffawed. "What do you take me for—a fool? No, all I sent her is an iTunes card loaded with a hundred bucks."

"Danny, you didn't," Arn groaned.

"What? She needed an iTunes card so she can listen to some

mellow music. Not like I sent her money for air fare. I'm no sucker." He started towards his room and said over his shoulder, "Call Darwin in. I'll clean up quick and he can shower before supper while I make us something."

When Arn walked outside, Darwin stood hunched over a rototiller. He didn't see Arn standing on the overhanging porch looking at him. "Who the hell scared you so bad?" Arn whispered to himself. He wished this were a month or two from now, wished Darwin was completely right in the head and willing to talk about who gave him the jewelry, pieces which were found on dead mail order brides. Kubek told Arn the last time they went to lunch she still couldn't give up Darwin being a suspect in Paquita's murder. Sonny felt otherwise.

Yet, Kubek's warning sent shivers up Arn's spine. What if he were wrong all along about Darwin? What if he did what he and Ana Maria and Danny had speculated previously? What if this PTSD was all a ruse to deflect the authorities—and Arn—from suspecting him in the Mail Order Murders?

"Sgt. Ness," Arn called and finally looked up. "The Gunny said to clean up as he's fixing an early supper."

Darwin set the wrench and spark plug atop the rototiller motor and walked towards the house. When he got abreast of Arn he stopped and turned to face him. "I hurt you. There in my crib along the tracks."

"Burnt my hand on your stove's all."

"Sorry I caused that, Mr. Anderson," Darwin said and walked into the house with Arn looking after him. *If you're faking your mental health condition and how you calmed-up with medication, you ought to get an Emmy for this.*

* * *

Ana Maria sat on the edge of her recliner and leaned over the two card tables. On one table were arrayed the police reports and interviews that she had arranged for her coverage of the Mail Order Murders. On the other table, she had spread out the police reports, interviews, and evidence lists from the Barberi murders. "How can you keep all that straight?" Danny asked.

Ana Maria tapped her head. "You have to be a genius. Genius," she answered and seemed to look around the TV room, for the first time. "Where's Darwin? Thought he was going to watch TV with us."

"Darwin turned in," Danny said. "Once he has his night meds, he's ready to crash. Ready to be mellow."

"Like your new internet date feeling *mellow* with a new iTunes card?" Arn said. *Ka-ching*. He glanced down at the mess of papers that only Ana Maria knew how they were being segregated. "You got the autopsy and the lab reports on Paquita and Ivana?"

"Of course they're here."

"Hell," Arn said, "Kubek didn't even give me the reports when I asked for them."

Ana Maria batted her eyes. "You just have to sweet talk the coroner. Or in my case, promise the coroner that she'll be on nationwide television once these serial murders are solved."

"Again, we still can't connect all three," Arn said, "And secondly, how can you guarantee this will get national coverage even if it does wind up a serial killer case?"

"Let's call it a little literary license."

"I call it lying," Danny said.

Ana Maria shrugged. "Anything to nail this guy."

"If it even is a guy," Danny said.

Arn picked up the lab report on Ivana Nenasheva and glanced at it before replacing it on the table. Ana Maria moved it to another pile of papers and said, "Don't get my system out of whack."

Arn held up his hands as if in surrender. "Just looking at it. Anything significant in those lab reports?"

"Nothing that you haven't told me already," Ana Maria asked. "I'll look again later, and you're welcome to as well. *If* you make sure the reports are put in the same place as I have them."

"Then I'll look forward to reading some dynamic lab results." Arn recalled the hundreds of lab results from victims of various crimes he'd poured over through the years as a lawman, including homicides. Poring over them hoping for that *Forensic Files* moment that some piece jumped out at him, which rarely came. Sure, he'd look at them later. When he needed help falling asleep.

He poured a cup of coffee from the Thermos and said to Ana Maria, "you seem to be in a good mood tonight. But then you have been since you met 'The One'."

"Nonsense," Ana Maria said.

"Arn's right," Danny said. "Since you started dating Alex, you have been your alter ego—pleasant most days."

"Is there a compliment in there somewhere?"

Danny started to speak, then stopped when Arn bailed him out. "What I think Danny is trying to tell you is that you have that... warm glow you get when you're in love."

"In love!" Ana Maria said. "I'm no schoolgirl on my first date."

"No, you're not," Danny said. "But you are in what then... infatuation?"

"So, Alex makes me feel special. So, I like spending time with him. What's wrong with that?"

Arn saw Ana Maria's sunny disposition leaving her the angrier she got and he said, "Let's talk about something besides Ana Maria's love life. For example," Arn motioned to the papers spilled over the two card tables, "What do you hope to accomplish by looking at all those grisly reports and photos from Alex's parents' home invasion?"

"What I hope to get," Ana Maria answered, "is a better understanding as to why Alex is so... defensive. It's been hard breaking through his outer shell. But I am. Slowly."

The telephone rang in the kitchen and Danny said, "I'll get it."

After Danny left the room, Arn asked, "What's your take on Darwin?"

"Being the killer?"

Arn nodded.

"He certainly knew Paquita from working at Barberi's. As for Petrov, he could have taken a car like we speculated before and driven her body over to Laramie where she was dumped."

"What I mean is that—judging with your women's intuition— do you think he's still on the suspect list?"

Ana Maria set a newspaper clipping on the card table and thought for a long moment before she said, "No. To be perfectly honest, I was leery of being under the same roof as Darwin when I heard you were... adopting him. But now... I'm comfortable being around him, and I have to admit, he dotes on me for some reason."

Danny ran into the TV room out of breath and ran up to Arn. "We gotta go."

"Go where?"

"Downtown. Meet Bald-headed Billy."

"All right," Arn said, "I'll bite... what do we have to meet with him about?"

"Bonnie and Melissa's deaths... he was at the quarry that night. He saw everything."

"Then why doesn't he go to the police and tell them—"

"Arn," Danny blurted out, "the man sounded terrified. We need to talk with him. Now."

"I'll get my sweater and head out. Where's he want to meet?"

"He won't come out of his hidey-hole until he sees me. Arn, these street people don't trust a lot of... normal folks. You got to take me along."

"We can't leave Ana Maria here with Darwin—"

"Go! I'll be all right with him," Ana Maria said. "He'll probably sleep all night anyway."

38

"You sure Billy's going to show?"

"He will." Danny held the Thermos of coffee in his lap. "He's just shaken up. I told him I'd be in your gold Olds so he surely can't miss *this*."

Arn squinted at a figure moving in the distance. As it walked under a street light Arn saw that it was just a kid walking along the street. "Who the heck lets their kids stay out at night?"

"Arn," Danny said, "it's only ten o'clock. Didn't you ever stay out at night getting into mischief?"

"Not me. I was pure as the driven snow—" Arn stopped and grabbed his binoculars. Someone rode a bike towards them on the street, and he set the glass on the console. "I'm thinking Billy's a no-show."

"Don't leap to judgments so soon," Danny said, pointing. "Look at the biker again."

Arn once more put the binos to his eyes.

"That's Billy," Danny said.

Arn looked the rider over. A trash bag was tied on each side of the back fenders and sounds of cans rattling reached them in the still night air. Even in the darkness, Arn could see how the man's hair flowed over his shoulders. *So much for being bald-headed.*

Danny grinned. "Told you we could count on street people."

Billy stopped his bike well away from the streetlight, and far enough from the car that he could take off in any number of directions if needed. He sat. Waiting.

Arn started to get out when Danny said, "Best hold up a minute.

I'll go up there and talk to him first so he knows you're not a cop."

"He can see it's me."

"Billy's a bit... paranoid. No, he's way paranoid. I'll be back."

Arn watched as Danny approached Billy still seated on his bike for a quick getaway if needed. When Danny reached the bike, they spoke for a few moments before Billy climbed off and walked beside Danny towards the car. Arn remained seated until they got to the car and Danny said, "Hand me the coffee."

Arn did so and handed Danny the Thermos. He uncapped it and poured Billy a cup. "Go ahead," Danny said. "Tell Arn what you saw."

Billy looked around the darkened parking lot as if there were others within earshot. He downed the coffee and held the cup out for a refill. "I seen just how those two girls died. I was at the quarry when it happened."

Arn got out of his car and leaned against it as he asked, "Did one of the girls try jumping and the other one gabbed her... tried to drag her back? Did they both go over then?"

"That's what the newspaper said, but that ain't what happened at all—" A car squealed its tires a street over and Billy jumped.

Danny laid his hand on Billy's shoulder. "It's all right, kid. No one's coming out of the dark to hurt you. Just tell us what you saw."

"I was dumpster diving at the quarry," Billy began. "Those truck drivers and machine operators go through a lot of soda pop. By the end of the day when they empty the trash in that big dumpster, I get thirty, sometimes forty aluminum cans. The hotter it gets, the more they drink soda and the more I make bagging them up."

Arn waited for Billy to continue at his own pace when he was ready to talk. It was times like this that Arn kept quiet, not saying anything that would spook the person into clamming up. "A man drove up to the quarry, but don't ask me what kind of car. I don't pay no attention to cars in the quarry at night—it's usually just a couple of kids parking there making out." He wiped coffee off his chin whiskers and handed Danny the cup back.

"I was inside the dumpster when I looked up and seen some guy with his arm around some gal. 'So she's drunk and passed out,' I says to myself. Not so unusual. But then..."

Billy's shoulders began trembling and Danny draped his arm on Billy's back. "It's all right. Just tell what happened in your own time."

Billy took several deep breaths before continuing. "He laid the woman on the ground at the edge of the quarry and left. *Then* I started to pay attention. I couldn't see his car but heard a door—maybe a trunk—slam shut and this time he carried a woman over his shoulder like she was passed out. Or dead. Then he…"

Billy reached inside his tattered coat and came out with a plastic box. He opened it and looked at the cigarette butts in the box before selecting a snipe. He lit it and inhaled deeply before continuing. "Then he just tossed that woman over the edge of the quarry. And rolled the one on the ground off the edge right afterwards."

"Did you recognize the man?"

Billy shook his head. "It was too dark, and he was too far away for me to tell anything." He forced a laugh. "Hell, I couldn't even tell if it was a man or not. But the women he tossed… they were small so I knew they were girls."

Billy dropped the butt onto the ground and snubbed it out with his boot. He sat on the front bumper taking in gulps of air, his shoulder trembling anew. Arn sat beside him and said, "This changes everything about those two girl's deaths. Can you go with me to the police department—"

"I said no police!"

"Whoa," Danny said. "Calm down. Arn just asked—"

"I know what he asked." Billy stood abruptly and picked his bike up off the ground. "I want nothing to do with the law. I've told you everything I seen. Now you can make sure that the right story gets out."

Arn watched Billy blend in with the darkness as he rode off. "I'm not sure what I can do with it except talk with Kubek."

"Just like Ana Maria with Alex," Danny said, capping the Thermos.

"How's that?"

"You seem to make excuses to spend time with Lieutenant Kubek. Just like Ana Maria does with Alex Barberi." He nudged Arn. "Pretty soon, I'll need to add another addition to the house."

* * *

Lucille sat at her desk guarding Kubek's door like one of the Three Hundred Spartans waiting for the Persians at Thermopylae. She hadn't seen Arn peeking around the corner of the wall, and he retreated down the hallway to the front desk. Greg Smith sat slightly elevated, waiting to take complaints from anyone walking into the police department needing help. And right now, Arn needed help. "Officer Smith," he said, "could you please tell Officer Bobby Ryerback that I wish to speak with him."

Smith stroked his beard as he picked up the phone and spoke briefly. "Bobby just finished with a family fight. Headed this way."

"Thanks." Arn said, and tapped the wanted poster taped to the window. "No luck finding Jesse Brown?"

"Calls come in every day and we check them out but no luck."

Arn sat in the lobby until Bobby walked through the front doors. Smith pointed to Arn and Officer Ryerback approached him. Arn stood and met Bobby, motioning him away from the desk officer. "Ana Maria needs a favor from you," Arn lied.

Bobby hitched up his belt and smiled wide. "Of course. What does she need?"

"I need to speak with Lieutenant Kubek on Ana Maria's behalf. Problem is, that drill-sergeant-of-a-secretary of hers is guarding the hen house. If I try to talk with Kubek, Lucille'd have me standing at the back of the line. For *hours*. She hates me, I think."

"Ana Maria wants you to talk to the lieutenant?"

"She does."

Bobby paused for a long moment before whispering to Arn, "This will cost Ana Maria."

"Anything to get me an audience with the lieutenant."

After Bobby laid out his price for luring Lucille away from her desk, Arn stood at the corner of the hallway. When Lucille passed without seeing Arn, he stepped into the hall and walked hurriedly towards Kubek's office. "Don't know what you said to her," Arn asked.

"I told her I'd spot her if she wanted to walk down to Starbucks and grab a latte."

"Thanks," Arn said and walked into Kubek's office.

She looked up from her paperwork and stood abruptly. "How the hell did you get past Lucille?"

"Lucille?" Arn answered. "I can't say where she is. I just asked that nice policeman at her desk if you were in. I never saw Lucille."

Kubek sighed deeply. "What do you need now?"

"Not 'what happened to our date two nights ago' or some friendly greeting?"

"I figured you called our dinner date off 'cause you got tied up with that hottie... that Villarreal woman."

"Do I hear a hint of jealousy?"

"Don't flatter yourself," Kubek said. She sat back behind her desk. "What do you need now?"

"I am the bearer of new information about Melissa Roush and Bonnie Peter's deaths."

"What's new... that they were lovers and they decided to go together? Kind of like a poor woman's Thelma and Louise?"

Arn took off his hat and sat in the chair in front of Kubek's desk. "They didn't commit suicide."

Kubek laughed. "Did you call one of those clairvoyant hotlines to get that pearl of information?"

"No," Arn answered. "One of the street people saw them get thrown into the quarry pit."

"I'm listening."

Arn explained how a street person saw someone—he couldn't even tell if it was a man or woman— toss one girl into the quarry before rolling another in right afterwards.

Kubek flipped to a clean page in a notebook on, her desk. "Who's the witness?"

"Anne."

"Anne who?"

"Anne Nonymous," Arn answered. "Anonymous. The man doesn't want to be identified."

"Well, he damn well better come forward—"

"Frida," Arn said, softening his voice, "this is one of the street people we're talking about—"

"Yeah, people with outstanding warrants. That's probably why this man didn't want to talk with me directly."

"I can't say if he's wanted or not. I'm long out of the business of serving arrest warrants. But I do know many of those people choose to live by their wits on the street. With no attachments. Doesn't make what that man saw any less credible."

Kubek dropped her pen on the desk and glared at Arn. "Were there any other witnesses?"

"No."

"Then what the hell am I supposed to do with that?"

"You could use it a basis for ordering an autopsy?"

"An autopsy on two girls who took the plunge? I feel sorry for their families, but to dredge it up that somebody murdered them when there's not an ounce of proof."

"Tell me," Arn said, "is the pathologist in town?"

"So, you do read the papers."

Arn nodded. This morning's *Tribune Eagle* reported that a young man from Montana had been found dead in his car parked along Happy Jack Road. The Sheriff had told the reporter it appeared as if he had died of carbon monoxide poisoning from sleeping in his old beater. Still, he explained to the reporter, an autopsy had to be performed. "We do autopsies on all unattended deaths," the Sheriff said.

"If the ME is in town to look at that Montana feller, you could order an autopsy for Melissa and Bonnie as well."

"For what?" She stood from her chair and turned her back on Arn as she faced the window. "They were so mangled from the fall, a pathologist won't be able to tell anything."

"The hyoid."

Kubek turned around and glared at Arn once more. "What's that?"

"The hyoid bone. A small bone in the neck that is often broken in manual strangulation."

Kubek threw up her hands. "Now you know the girls were strangled. Amazing!"

Arn leaned forward and rested his elbows on the desk. "By the... street person's description, I think that both girls were dead when they were tossed into the rock quarry."

"There's no way in hell an ME could determine that they were tossed... damn it, you're getting me to talk that way. They fell into the quarry from forty feet up. Their hyoid bone and nearly every other bone were broken I am certain. You weren't there when we had to retrieve the bodies. It was like mush picking them up."

"Think of it this way," Arn said. "If Bonnie and Melissa were murdered prior to taking a dive off the quarry edge, it may be the work of your *serial killer*. And it may link to the deaths of the mail order brides."

Kubek tented her fingers on the desk and closed her eyes. "I might be able to sell this to the Chief. Autopsies are expensive but... could see where we need one on those two victims."

Arn stood. "Then it's a done deal. Let me know when you have the reports back. And Frida," Arn said as he cracked the door and looked out. "Call Lucille away. She's back at her desk and I wouldn't want to have her chase me down the hallway with that thick ruler in her hand."

Kubek escorted Arn past Lucille, who sat mouth agape, staring at him, no doubt wondering how he ever managed to sneak past her. When they'd reached the lobby, Kubek said, "You're on your own from here. All I can say is that, if Lucille comes running after you with that ruler, you better hightail it before she gets within striking range."

Arn walked outside, the air feeling as if he'd stepped into a draft furnace. The heat wave engulfing the Rocky Mountain region as well as all of the west hadn't let up these past two months. He took his COVID mask off and climbed into his car when his cell phone buzzed.

"Go by the Animal Shelter," Danny said on the other end of the line. "Sonny ran away."

"What do you mean he ran away," Arn said, "the poor dog can barely waddle."

"That may be, but he's gone now."

"Who let him out without a leash?" Arn asked, knowing the answer before he asked it.

Danny lowered his voice and said, "It had to be Darwin, but I'm sure he didn't mean anything. He's still a bit loopy from his meds."

"Did you look around the neighborhood?"

"We both did. Nada."

"All right," Arn said, "I'll stop at the shelter on my way home and ask if anyone's turned Sonny in."

39

"There's just something I'm missing," Ana Maria said.

"What's missing is Sonny," Arn said. "Never thought I'd miss his pathetic excuse for a howl but I do."

Ana Maria said, "He's wearing his collar and dog tag with your cell number. If someone doesn't find him and turn him in, maybe he'll come howling at the door to be let in. But that's not what I meant by I'm missing something." She had been bent over the Barberi reports on one table, the police information on the Mail Order Murders the other card table for the last hour. "I'm missing something that will make my special on Alex Barberi as a businessman pop. I want it to be memorable."

"Maybe you're just trying too hard," Danny said as he entered the room. He held three bowls of ice cream and set them on the buffet shoved in one corner of the TV room, one of the few things of Arn's mother's that hadn't been chopped up for firewood over the years of being idle.

"Danny's right." Arn stood from his recliner and walked to the buffet. "Darwin not coming in to have some and watch a little TV?"

"I think he's still sleeping," Danny answered. "He a bad day today."

"How so?" Ana Maria asked.

"First off, Sonny running... walking away. I tried to ask him as gently as I could if he might have let the critter out and he was adamant he didn't. Then he made the mistake of picking up the *Tribune Eagle* this morning. When he read where Kubek felt Bonnie Peters and Melissa Roush dead—murdered—before being tossed into the quarry, he went… well, ape shit. He stormed out of the house, and it was all I could do to keep up. About the time that we made it to the old steam plant I managed to stop and talk him down."

"I almost forgot he worked for a month at Barberi's with them."

"I felt like he wanted to tell me what he knew," Danny said. "*Needed* to tell me who he was so scared of. I think he was on the verge of telling me, but he didn't and I didn't press it. I finally talked him back to the house and gave him his meds early."

Ana Maria ignored the ice cream—her favorite food—and kept studying the documents in front of her.

"You need to take a break," Arn said.

"I think you're right," Ana Maria said. "My mind's going buggy trying to come with an angle that will last six episodes of broadcast." She took a bowl of ice cream and sat in her recliner.

When Danny grabbed the remote and turned on the TV, Arn groaned. "Not *The Bachelor* again!"

"I gotta get some tips for landing that one babe on my dating site somewhere."

Ana Maria's cell phone buzzed and she grabbed it from her purse. She glanced at the phone and the color left her face. "I don't recognize the number," she said and set it on her chair.

"Could have been that Mr. Right you claim you haven't found yet," Danny said.

"He's got a point there." Arn swirled ice cream around in his bowl, a wry smile on his face. "That's unless you already found Mr. Right at a restaurant."

Ana Maria blushed.

"When are you two going out again?"

"Can't say," Ana Maria answered. "I ran by Barberi's, but it was closed until after the funeral of his two waitresses. I ran by Alex's house, too, and got no answer. He doesn't return my calls—"

"Maybe he just needs to be alone," Danny said. "People grieve in different ways."

"I understand that," she said, "but he never indicated he was that close to his help."

Her cell phone buzzed again. She picked it up and her face

blanched. She started to delete it when Arn reached over and turned the phone so he could read it. "Who is threatening to kill you if you air the special on the Mail Order Murders?"

"It's nothing—"

"Nothing! You get a message like this and it's nothing? How many of these calls have you received?"

Ana Maria turned off her phone and slid it back into her purse. "This makes the ninth one today."

"And it's all texts. Nobody calls you?"

She nodded. "Just texts."

"We need to get Kubek on this. If she can trace a number… the caller's got to have service locally."

"It comes from a burner phone," Ana Maria said. "Or rather it came from two burner phones. Different numbers. No way to find out who sent them."

"How do you know that?" Arn asked.

"Officer Bobby," Ana Maria said. "I called him this morning after I received the third call when I was at the TV station. Which reminds me, Bobby said I was *obligated* to go out on a dinner date with him. When I asked where he got that notion he just winked and said 'ask Mr. Anderson.'"

"Let's say you had to take one for the team," Arn said, and explained how he needed Bobby to lure Lucille away from her desk.

"So, you just assumed I'd go out with him in exchange for that little stunt?"

Arn shrugged. "I knew—just knew—if you were right there with me… at that time, needing to lure Lucille away from Kubek's door, you'd agree to such a small request."

"Arn, I have socks older than Bobby. He's a nice kid and all, but he's just a bit young for me."

"I'd have thought you'd be flattered."

Ana Maria shook her head. "Don't you just beat all."

"Let's get back to these texts you've been getting—did you report it to the police or just—"

"Have Officer Bobby see if he could figure out who sent them?" Ana Maria said. "No, I just was hoping Bobby could help unofficially.

I don't want to report this to the law if I can help it. My IT guy at the TV station said just what Bobby did—from an untraceable phone."

Danny finished his ice cream and picked up his knitting. "You're just afraid that DeAngelo will shut down your special on these mail order murderers."

"Damn it, Danny, you know that he will. And if he shuts the special down on these killings, he'll do the same for my businessman special. Alex will never talk to me again, so don't you dare go to Kubek with this."

"Okay," Arn said. "Okay. First we have figure out if these threats are credible."

Ana Maria looked away.

"They are, aren't they?"

She dipped her spoon into her bowl of ice cream when she abruptly set it aside. "Whoever is sending these texts wants me to know he—or she—knows exactly where I am. The first two that came in today asking how I was enjoying a quiet day at the office. The next one midmorning asked how I was enjoying my brunch at Village Inn. And they knew what I ordered." She turned her head away and swiped a shirtsleeve across her eyes. "Each message ends with a death threat if I turn over the sketch to the police."

"Then this is far more serious than what you've let on," Arn said.

"I vote we override her and report it to Five-O."

"Danny," she said, turning to him, her eyes wet. "Don't even think about placing an anonymous call to the cops. You hear me? Either of you do that and I'll pack my shit and be out the door sooner than this ice cream takes to melt."

Arn held up his hands in surrender. "Understood. Danny?"

Danny set his knitting down for a moment and raised his hand like he was testifying in court. "As much as I hate to, I agree."

"All right," Arn said. "With that out of the way, we're still not helpless here. "Have you studied the texts to see if there's some unusual wording being used? Some syntax the caller is using that's distinctive?"

"I didn't even think of that," Ana Maria said.

"Is there a way to retrieve your deleted texts from a recycle bin?"

"Sure" she answered. "I could do that."

"Then let's move into the new addition. I'm sure Danny won't mind writing on his bare dry wall."

"You can do whatever you want to it," Danny said, "until I paint it."

* * *

An hour later, Arn's eyes grew tired and red staring at the white wall. "Danny, could you fix us some coffee? Strong. I have a feeling we'll be here longer than I thought."

Danny left for the kitchen and Arn asked Ana Maria, "Is that the last of the messages?"

She checked her phone once more. "It is."

Arn sat on a bucket of dry wall mud and looked at the messages that Ana Maria had transcribed from her phone onto a clean white wall with a magic marker. He looked for any distinctive pattern. Anything that would show him who might have sent the texts. It was here. He just couldn't see it and neither could Ana Maria.

"If the caller would only have spoken, I might have been able to identify the voice. But from this," she motioned to the white wall.

Danny came back into the room with two cups of coffee. "You're not staying to see if you can find a pattern?" Arn asked.

"Feel free to stay up all night, though I think if you gave it a rest you might actually see something tomorrow." Danny said. "But bright and early at 0730 Darwin has to be at Dr. Land's office for his next therapy session. And unless you want me to drive your classic old car, without a license, you have to be up bright and early, too."

"Maybe Danny's right," Ana Maria said. "Maybe it is getting too late, and we've been trying too hard. Perhaps in the morning after we've slept on it…" she trailed off.

"You go on ahead," Arn told her. "I want to give this one last try tonight."

* * *

Danny shook Arn awake at six o'clock. "Thought I'd wake you up a little early. Give you a chance to work the stiffness out."

"What stiff—"

Arn groaned as he held his hand out. Danny used all his strength to help Arn stand from the floor. He rubbed his stiff neck, his back aching from sleeping on the floor all night in front of the white wall. "Guess I fell asleep looking for patterns."

"I'll fix breakfast for you and me after you shower and get ready to take Darwin to the VA."

"How is he doing? Hope he's having a better day than he did yesterday."

"He is," Danny answered. "But he insisted on getting up with the chickens and going out to look for Sonny. I think—this is a layman speaking—that Darwin identifies with the sad, old dog."

"You think he feels like he's an old Basset Hound?"

"Not that," Danny answered. "But the way Darwin's been acting lately, he's been sleeping more than he's used to. Like Sonny."

Arn traipsed up the stairs and noticed Ana Maria's bedroom door was open. He peeked in as he made his way to the shower, but the bed had already been made. Her shoes arranged in a neat row. Organized. Just like she was organized in her job. Last night, Arn heard the frustration in her voice. Even after arranging all the newspaper clippings on Alex, she still didn't have a defining theme for her broadcast of area businessmen.

Arn followed the smell of bacon into the kitchen and sat at the table.

"'Bout done," Danny said over his shoulder. He cracked an egg in each hand, deftly and lovingly laying them onto the griddle.

"Were you up when Ana Maria left for work?"

"No," Danny said, "when she slammed the door shut is when I woke up. She musta been in some hurry 'cause she didn't even set the security alarm."

Danny slid the eggs and bacon onto a plate and set it in front of Arn. "You're not eating?" he asked.

Danny patted his stomach. "I need to be in shape my next date."

Arn took the lid off a jar of jam and said, "I almost hate to ask, but who's the lucky little lady this time?"

Danny sat across from Arn and cupped his coffee mug in his hand.

"This babe is… well, a babe. After I modified my profile—I wasn't getting quality hits on it the way it was—this woman from Longmont sent me a message and a link to her profile. Arn, she is perfect."

"This I gotta hear."

"Don't be so cynical," Danny said, "and listen up. She's only about ten years younger than me—"

"Danny, that sounds like a scam already."

"You don't think ol' Danny hasn't learned things since being on this dating site, like spotting a scam?"

"Like the last one who needed an iTunes card?"

"I learned my lesson," Danny answered. "More coffee?"

"Please."

After Danny had refilled their cups, he sat back down and a dreamy look came over him. "She's a physician, you know."

"That's nice." Arn had heard all the scams before and this one sounded like it was setting Danny up for a big fall. "When are you going to meet her?"

"I said we need to talk first on the phone."

"So, you talked with her?"

"No," Danny answered. "Her phone's broke. But just as soon as she gets it fixed, we'll have a nice visit. Which reminds me, can we slip by some place after Darwin's appointment so I can get a pre-paid Visa card loaded?"

Arn shrugged. "Don't see why not. What do you need that for?"

"Emily—the gal in Longmont—needs a few dollars to get her phone fixed so we can talk."

"Danny," Arn said, feeling odd giving a man thirty years his junior dating advice, "don't you think Emily can afford to get her phone fixed on her own? Or a new one? After all, she… claims to be a doctor."

Danny's expression turned to genuine sadness. "With this COVID going around, her practice has been significantly reduced. She just needs a helping hand up is all."

More like a helping hand straight into the hoosegow for fraud, Arn thought.

40

Arn and Danny sat in the commons area until Darwin was done with his therapy session with Dr. Land. "You going to ask the shrink when it's all right to talk to Darwin about the jewelry?"

"I have to," Arn answered. "If I knew who he was so frightened of, I'd know the killer's identity, I am certain."

Danny looked around the mostly empty waiting room. A young man with a prosthetic leg sat with his back straight, his head focused ahead as if he were still in Iraq or Afghanistan sitting at attention in front of his CO's office. "I'm going to visit with that feller for a moment."

Arn could only watch as Danny sat next to the wounded man who had faced the horrors of war head on, something Arn had never had to do. He felt the urge to join Danny and thank the man for his service, his sacrifice, but he held back. Theirs was a conversation between men who had experienced combat, and Arn's intruding—even to show appreciation for his service—would seem trivial.

After a few moments, Danny returned and said, "that corporal was a bomb tech in Afghanistan. An IED took his leg and two fingers."

"What a shame," Arn said. "Nice looking young feller like that."

"Do not," Danny said, "even feel sorry for him. He got right back up his feet after he lost his leg and doesn't want an ounce of pity. Or handout. He's a computer science major at LCCC and has his head on straight. He'll be all right. Here's Darwin."

Doctor Land walked beside Darwin Ness as they neared the waiting room. "He's all yours." He patted Darwin on the back. "Keep up the good work and I will see you next week at this time."

Dr. Land turned and started down the hallway to his office when Arn stopped him. "Mind if I walk with you?"

Land shrugged. "Suit yourself, but I can't tell you how Darwin's progress is coming along."

"Can you at least tell me if it's safe to ask him about the man who gave him the jewelry?"

Land stopped and faced Arn. "No. Do not ask him yet. He's had some terrible experiences in three combat tours that are affecting his behavior. With these twice-weekly sessions and staying on his meds, I think... soon."

Land started walking off when Arn stopped him. "Can we talk about something else?"

Land checked his watch. "I have to record Darwin's session from my notes and have another patient in a half-hour... if you make it quick."

Arn followed Dr. Land into his office and shut the door. As Land was sitting behind the desk, Arn pulled up a photo of the white wall where Ana Maria had jotted all the threatening calls she'd received. He explained that the calls had begun yesterday and he was worried about Ana Maria.

"Let me see your phone." Land donned reading glasses and scrolled through the photos before setting Arn's phone down. "Who wrote this?"

"I was hoping you could tell me."

Dr. Land took off his glasses and chewed on the end of one bow. "I would have to examine the person who wrote this, but from what I see, there is a possibility—a strong possibility—the author is a psychopath."

"How did you come to that conclusion from just what he wrote in Ana Maria's texts?"

Land put his glasses on once more and exploded the screen so they could read Arn's photo of the white wall better. "He uses a lot of *ums* and *uhs*. They are what we call fillers. Disfluencies. Words that a person uses when they can't think of a proper word. Even highly intelligent psychopaths are known to use them. Oftentimes, they stuttered when younger."

"Then I am a psychopath, as I use them more than I want to admit."

"But are you a psychopath?" Dr Land asked.

"Never thought of myself as one."

"And neither have I." Land leaned back in his chair and tented his fingers on his belly. "There are more psychopaths than you can ever imagine among the general population. But criminal psychopaths... now they're different. Where non-violent psychopaths curtail their urges because of social norms, for example, criminal psychopaths care nothing about the outcome. They have absolutely no remorse. No guilt for anything they do."

"How is this going to help me find who's been sending Ana Maria these messages?"

"They have a constant desire for sex—"

"I know several people that would fit."

"Look for someone who constantly lies. Constantly. They cannot speak even a little truth. For them, it's all about manipulating people. And they will be glib. Monopolizing conversations. It's all about them."

"From these writings, is there anything else that would help me?"

Dr. Land stood and paced beside his desk. Arn remained quiet knowing the psychiatrist was delving deep into his recollections. Land stopped and picked up Arn's phone again. He scrolled through the pictures until he found one he could blow up and show. He handed it to Arn and said, "The pioneer in linguistic analysis of psychopathic people—what we now call APSD—Anti-Social Personality Disorder— was a British Columbia psychiatrist named Robert Hare. Some of the things he noticed with true psychopaths was they also said things were 'fascinating' rather than, say, 'interesting'."

Arn laughed. "I do that now and again. Does that make me a psycho?"

"Not by itself. Dr. Hare came up with a scoring system and you— my friend—would have to score higher than just a few points. But look here." Land blew the image up even more. "This writer refers to things in the past rather than use the present tense. Shows no emotional involvement. Think Ted Bundy. Richard Kuklinski, the Ice Man. They showed no emotion whatsoever in retelling their murders. This one," Land tapped the phone, "just wants Ana Maria to stop her broadcasts. But know this," Land said as he handed the phone back to

Arn, "if this person is in Cheyenne and stalking her, I'd go out of my way to protect Ana Maria because it's just a matter of time before this person acts out their threats."

"I might do something more proactive than be Ana Maria's bodyguard," Arn said, and walked back to the commons area.

* * *

Arn pulled away from Enterprise Rental in a shiny new Toyota tin can half as comfortable as his Olds. But at least it was like every other tiny death trap on the road, and he'd fit right in. Inconspicuous.

He drove towards the TV station and parked a block away. Glassing the parking lot, he saw that Ana Maria's Volkswagen Bug was parked in a neat row with a half-dozen other cars, and Arn looked around the station with his binoculars. He didn't know what he even was looking for. Dr. Land had been of some help—he'd given Arn an idea as to who might have sent the threatening texts. But just a rough idea. Arn hated to admit it, but Ana Maria was the best bait. If the caller who was stalking her lurked in the area, they would surely follow her when she left work.

Arn checked his watch: another hour and Ana Maria would leave for home and he settled in as best he could in the tiny car and he watched.

An hour later, right on cue, people began filling out of the TV station, but no Ana Maria. He checked his phone against his watch—both were right, and he was about to dial her number and check on her when she walked out of the station.

He slowly glassed the streets adjacent to the station on Lincolnway. The housing behind. Nothing moved except for Ana Maria climbing into her car when she... stopped. She threw her purse into the back seat and bent down. Arn could not see what she was doing, fearing the caller may have left something on the seat to further frighten her when she backed out the car out of the parking space, holding Sonny. The Basset Hound did his best to lash out with a wet tongue, and Arn put his binos beside him on the passenger seat. *Thank God you found Sonny*, Arn said to himself before picking up his phone.

Danny picked up on the first ring, "Headed home now?"

"She is," Arn said. He had worked out an arrangement with Danny on the way back from the VA. Arn would leave his Olds on a side street covered up and take a cab to Enterprise to rent this little car. He would tail Ana Maria from the time she left work to the time she pulled to the curb in front of their house. They wouldn't tell Ana Maria, for she'd blow a cork over the idea of someone following her. "Like a stalker," Arn had told Danny. "Except a friendly one."

"I got that shotgun from under your bed," Danny said. "But all I could find is bird shot."

"There's not going to be any bird hunting today," Arn said. "I'll stop and grab some Double-Ought Buck from Frontier Arms after I see that Ana Maria gets home."

"You going to be back for supper?"

"Don't hold it for me," Arn said. "After I pass Ana Maria off you, I'm also going to pay an old friend a visit."

* * *

Arn sat watching the quarry at closing time. What he wanted to say to Tito he didn't want any witnesses to overhear. And he damn sure didn't want a drunk Lizzy Hondros jumping in. He wanted Tito all alone, with no one to interfere. He needed to ask Tito some questions face-to-face where he could gauge the man's reaction.

When the last truck had parked for the day and the last employee had left, Arn left the car behind one of the abandoned trailers and walked the last hundred yards toward the office.

When he reached it, he paused for a moment. Listening. He put his hand on the door. Vibrations.

Tito was heading out of his office for the day. He wore a stylish turtleneck sweater and Arn wished he were able to take the heat good enough to wear one.

Arn stepped aside. He waited until Tito opened the door and turned to lock it when Arn grabbed the back of the man's collar and jerked him away from the door. Tito looked over his shoulder with a wild-eyed look that broncs get right before you ride them into the ground and Tito yelled, "Don't hurt Winston!"

For the first time, Arn saw that Tito cradled the cat in one arm.

"Let me put him inside for God's sake."

Leary of the man's treachery, nonetheless Arn said, "Go on, put him in your office. But if do something foolish like lock yourself in, I'll take one of your trucks and run over your damn office until it's flattened."

Tito slowly opened the door and set Winston inside. When he turned around, he said, "Lizzy... um, started to get mean with him. So, I started bringing him to work."

"If your cat wouldn't claw the hell out of her maybe she'd be nicer to it."

"What're you talking about?"

"Winston clawed her neck. Pretty bad. I saw how deep—"

"That... ugh, wasn't Winston," Tito said. "I took him with me out of town when that happened. But you didn't come here wanting a rematch because you're concerned with my wife *or* my cat."

"You are the genius."

Tito took a step closer when Arn shoved his finger in his trouser pocket. "This bulge doesn't mean I'm glad to see you. It means you are facing an armed man."

Tito stepped back and said, "You know I'm going to call the cops on you for threatening me."

"For one," Arn said, "you'll know *just* when I threaten you. And second, if I do so here, now, there's no witnesses around to corroborate your story. So, you might as well sit on your steps while we have a friendly visit, you and me."

"What the hell do you want then?"

"I already told you—some talk and some straight answers."

"About what?"

"Ivana Nenasheva for one. You told me when I stopped at your house that she ran to you for help. To hide her from her husband who was after her."

"If you expect me to change my story, forget it."

"Not change. Clarify. You've been charged with Ivan's murder... tell me, are you the one who tied her up and do kinky things to her that hurt her badly?"

Tito came off the steps and Arn shoved him back. "We were

bonding so well. How's about you just stay there or I'll finish what you started the other night." Now tell me—"

"I'm not into that bondage shit," Tito said. "I could never hurt a creature as hot as Ivana was."

"And Bonnie Peters... look at me."

Tito glared at Arn. "I don't know who that is." A tic at the corner of Tito's eye.

"She was one of those girls found in your quarry... did you tie her up? Whip her to get your rocks off?"

"Even if I knew her, I, uh, I don't do that." Again, Arn saw a micro tic—nearly imperceptible—at the corner of Tito's eye.

Arn's gaze met Tito's and Arn knew the man was lying. How much he was lying about he wasn't sure. Yet. "International Dating, Inc. What can you tell me about how hard it is to get a woman across the southern border?"

"Why the hell should I tell you anything?"

"Look," Arn said and raised his shirt. "I have no wire. No recording. There's no one here who would corroborate your story. Just you and me."

"Why—"

"Because few men would have the moxie to actually have a woman brought over illegally."

Tito smiled, and Arn knew he'd cast his net for an egocentric bastard and had caught Tito. "It does take guts. Lots more than most men have. And money." He whistled. "A lot more. You couldn't afford it."

"You claim you didn't bring over Paquita Robles?"

Tito looked away for a brief moment, then back at Arn. "The first I knew of her was when I saw she'd been killed in the park. Now, if you don't have any more silly questions for me, I'll take my cat and go home." He stood, his hand on the doorknob. "You ain't the only one who can pack a gun. You come around me or mine again, it just might be the Gunfight at the O.K. Corral for you and me. And I don't plan to be Frank McLaury."

41

"Can I go to bed early, Gunny?" Darwin, leaned against the hall wall and rubbed his head. "I think talking with Dr. Land sort of tuckered me."

"Go ahead," Danny said. "You worked your tail off today on the lawn and the least I can do is let you go to sleep early."

Danny watched as Darwin shuffled down the hall like he had weights in his pockets before disappearing into his room. "He did too," Danny said. "Work his tail off."

"Looks like it," Ana Maria said. "That front lawn is going to actually *be* a lawn. And the weeds… I didn't realize we had so many."

"I think they were planted by my dad when I was a kid, that's how long those weeds have been growing," Arn said.

Danny leaned closer to Arn and lowered his voice. "You know Darwin's got a real talent for landscaping."

"I can see that."

"What do you think when ol' Darwin there gets back on his feet that we just might…"

"Have a room for him?" Arn said. "That what you were going to say?"

"You a mind reader?"

Arn stood and refilled his coffee cup. "No, I'm a retired cop used to reading people."

"That's right," Danny said, "you were going to tell us how your little tete-a-tete with Tito Hondros went today."

"You bring enough of those killer brownies for all of us into the TV room and I'll tell you."

254

"I'll meet you there," Danny said.

Arn walked out of the kitchen and heard Ana Maria curse from the TV room. When he entered, she was bent over the documents spread out on TV trays in a manner only she could decipher. "You still looking at all those clippings and police reports."

"Still," she said. "DeAngelo is madder'n a wet hen. I promised him I would have finalized outlines for both my Businessman Special featuring Alex and the Mail Order Murders."

"As I recall, you always did work better under pressure. When you were butting up against a hard deadline."

"I usually do." She sat in her chair. "This time I might have bit off more than I can chew proposing two specials back-to-back."

Arn sat in his own recliner and turned to face her. "Could it be you're too anxious to get national attention that you've taken on too much?"

She nodded. "I might have. But in case you haven't noticed, I'm no spring chicken. TV anchors on a national scale landed their gigs when they were far younger than me."

"Ana Maria, you act like you're some old maid or something. Hell, you've got talent to go with beauty."

She turned away and Arn said, "That's the blush and a smile I haven't seen in a few days."

"Damn you," she said, her smile spreading across her face, "you did it again. You made me turn red when I didn't want it. Especially now."

"Why especially now?"

She turned away and Arn saw her wipe tears away with her hand.

"What's wrong?"

She remained silent.

"Go ahead," Arn said, "tell me or I'll get you down and tickle the hell out of you."

"You wouldn't?"

"Watch me," Arn said and stood.

"All right, all right, I'll tell you." She wiped tears again. "It's Alex. He hasn't called me for days. I call him and it always goes to voice mail. I leave messages but he never returns my calls."

"Do you think," Arn said, "that Alex is still grieving over the loss of two of his employees? After all, their funerals were only today."

"I know," Ana Maria said. "I thought if I were there for him he could cry on my shoulder—everyone needs someone in times like this. I tried to get away to attend the services thinking that Alex would probably be there, but DeAngelo sent me and my cameraman down to Bennett, Colorado to interview a guy who specializes in restoring old Fords. When we got back, the funerals were over and no sign of Alex."

Arn laid his hand on her shoulder and said, "Give him a few days. Then if he doesn't return calls I'd start worrying."

"What are we worrying about?" Danny asked as he came through the door carrying three plates with a huge brownie on each topped by whipped cream. He handed a plate to Arn and Ana Maria and sat in his recliner. "Well?"

"Ana Maria's just concerned that she hasn't heard from Alex."

"I don't blame her with that Jesse Brown still on the loose," Danny said.

"Perhaps I should contact Kubek tomorrow," Arn said. "If Alex isn't answering your calls, maybe it is more than grief. Maybe Brown found him."

"That's what I am worried about," she said.

Arn sat and pulled his TV tray close before tucking a napkin under his chin. "You should be worried about those threatening texts you've been receiving. You still haven't told DeAngelo?"

"No," Ana Maria answered. "I'm starting to think that it's just some weirdo getting his jollies off sending a TV personality texts."

"I wouldn't dismiss it so soon," Danny said. "As for Alex, I bet the next time you hear from him he'll more than a mere date. Maybe set *the* date."

"Speaking of dates," Arn said, "have you talked with that lady in Longmont?"

"Not yet," Danny said. "I sent her another Visa card—"

"You didn't."

"I had no choice. She needed money so she could get her practice sanitized for the reopening. This COVID crap's been taking a lot out of her medical business, too."

Ana Maria looked at Arn and shook her head. "Doctors can't afford that on their own?"

Danny remained quiet, taking delicate bites of his brownie when he said to Arn, "You were going to tell us more about your little chat with Tito Hondros."

Arn set his plate on the TV tray as he looked at Danny, not seeing how the man could eat so slowly. "When I asked Tito about Ivana, he said he didn't bring her into the country. I think he was telling the truth."

"Doesn't mean that he didn't know her intimately," Danny said. "You said Dr. Land gave you some possible tells to identify a psychopath."

"He did but he also said that—just because a person's a psychopath—doesn't mean he criminally acts out his desires. But," Arn said, "when the subject of Bonnie Peters came up, Tito denied knowing her and all sorts of red flags went off in my head. He flat lied to me and did so looking like a choirboy."

"What's your next move?" Ana Maria asked.

"By now, Kubek may have had the pathologist do the autopsies on Bonnie and Melissa. I'm dying to read the lab report."

"Speaking of lab reports," Ana Maria said, standing over her documents. "There's got to be something in these police reports and newspaper clippings that I'm missing."

"Will you give it a rest for one night," Arn said. "You're working yourself up for no good reason."

"I suppose you're right."

"Good," Arn said. Let's talk about something more pleasant, like where you found Sonny today?"

She took a bite of brownie, the whipping cream sticking to her upper lip like a Monopoly Man mustache. "I found him in my car."

"No, I mean where did you find him before that? Did someone turn him into the Animal Shelter?"

"I didn't find him anywhere besides my Bug. When I got out of work, there he was warming the passenger seat. I assumed you found him and had to put him somewhere while you did whatever you were doing."

Arn stopped mid-mouth with a fork full of brownie. "You came out and found him in your car?"

"Sure," Ana Maria said. "If you didn't put him there, then someone must have found him roaming around and put him in my VW."

"How would anyone know what you drove?"

Ana Maria put down her plate and wiped her lips. The color drained from her face and she said, "They wouldn't know."

"Then somebody took Sonny from right here. Right from the house."

"No one could get past the security system?" Danny said. "I've been faithful in arming it whenever I leave the house."

Arn couldn't see himself, but he was sure the color drained from his pale face as well. "Somebody had to have bypassed the security system and took Sonny from inside the house."

"And later put him in my car," Ana Maria said. She began trembling and she hugged herself to stop it. "Someone wants me to know they can get into the house. Anytime."

"Danny," Arn said, "double check the alarm system. Ana Maria, come upstairs and I'll show you where I keep a shotgun. Just in case."

42

Arn didn't chance being able to bypass Lucille to get to Kubek and he asked Officer Smith, "Could you page her down here?"

"Not me," Smith said. "The last time she had to leave her office, she got a mad-on and threatened to give me a day off without pay."

"Can secretaries do that?"

Smith shrugged. "As long as she's been here, she knows where all the bodies are buried, and she can damn well ask someone to reprimand me."

"Maybe what I have to tell her will earn you a day off *with* pay."

Smith hesitated before asking, "It's that important?"

"Like the Sermon on the Mount, Lt. Kubek will want to hear what I have to say."

Smith picked up the phone and paused. "That important?"

Arn crossed his heart and Smith punched a number. "Arn Anderson's here and he says it's real important that he talk with you." Smith hung up and said, "Put a good word in for me."

Arn sat in the lobby looking at vintage law enforcement pictures hanging on the wall when he heard Kubek stomped down the hallway. "This better be good," she said.

Arn checked his watch and said, "a little early for lunch but we can talk over a latte."

"Why should I interrupt my work..." She stepped closer to Arn. "This is serious, not like some of your other cockamamie requests?"

"It's serious."

"All right. I'll grab my purse and meet you out front."

They were half-way down the block to Starbucks when Arn said, "Ana Maria's being stalked."

Kubek snickered. "That comes with the territory of being a local personality—groupies hanging over you. Doing what they can make you notice them. That is, if you were a local *celebrity* like Ms. Villarreal."

"I want protection for her," Arn said as they crossed the street and headed into Starbucks.

Kubek looked sideways at Arn. "My officers are not bodyguards. If you think she needs protection, I can give you phone numbers of firms out of Denver who specialize in that sort of thing—"

"She's in danger right now!"

Two women on break from their capitol jobs gave Arn a wide berth as he made his way to the order line. He glanced around the store and people stared at him. He lowered his voice and said, "Guess we better talk about this outside."

After they'd ordered, Arn led the way to the chairs outside. A man in a boonie hat glared at them as if they were intruding on his private spot. He stood and tossed his cup in the trash before leaving them the only people in outside seating.

"You're really serious that she's in some kind of danger?"

Arn told Kubek how Sonny had come up missing—presumably when someone opened the door to let him out. But he'd somehow found his way into Ana Maria's car. "Frida, I have a top-of-the line security system. I've had bad actors get inside before and I wasn't going to have it happen again. But it did."

"Where is Ana Maria now?"

"I followed her to work. She usually takes lunch at about one o'clock."

Kubek took the phone out her purse. "Excuse me a moment," she said and walked to the far end of the parking lot. When she returned she said, "I can spare a patrol officer for two days, then you're on your own. That should give you time to find a civilian security firm that'll protect her."

"Tell your officers not to be too obvious—she'd hate me if she knew I'd asked for protection for her."

"She doesn't know you're coming to me with this?"

Arn shook his head. "She only knows that I'm meeting with you to find out about the autopsies on Melissa Roush and Bonnie Peters."

"What makes you so sure I'd meet you?"

Arn batted his eyes. "Ol' irresistible me? I knew you'd want a latte. So, about the autopsies…"

"There wasn't much left *to* autopsy. After a fall from that height into a rock quarry, bouncing and rolling no telling how many times, the bodies were, to put it mildly, mush."

"But they were autopsied?"

"They were." Kubek sipped her latte.

"Were their hyoid bones broken?"

Kubek looked away as if she were teasing Arn with an answer. "Both had broken hyoid bones that could have been caused by the fall. Melissa had no marks that indicated someone might have strangled her—"

"I wouldn't imagine it. With rigor setting in," Arn said, "the discoloration would be hard to see after a fall from that height. Especially the way she ended up down in the quarry. And Bonnie?"

Kubek dug her notebook out of her purse and flipped pages. She showed Arn a sketch she'd made from the pathologist's description. "Bonnie showed distinct discoloration on her neck, Here," Kubek demonstrated on her own neck, indicating manual strangulation. "A thumb mark and three fingers showed faintly on the side of her neck. Plus," she flipped another page, "there was considerable tissue under three of her fingers and her thumb. Bonnie put up one hell of a fight. Now all we have to do is find someone who looks like a mountain lion clawed the hell out of them."

"I have a prime suspect for their deaths," Arn proclaimed.

Kubek's eyebrows raised, and she pinched her nose with her fingers. "Who might that be?"

"Tito Hondros. I… leaned on him a little at his quarry office last night."

"Let me guess—he didn't admit to killing the two girls?"

"No, but he did admit—in his own way—that he knew Bonnie."

"In what way did he know her?"

Arn shook his head. "Can't say. But when I asked him if he knew Bonnie Peters, he said he didn't, though he was clearly lying to me. He knew Bonnie."

"Was he all clawed up? 'Cause the amount of tissue under her nails—"

"I can't say that either but," Arn paused, "a matter of fact, he wore a turtleneck sweater and it was still blistering hot when I confronted him."

Kubek guffawed. "Thank you for that piece of evidence. That's all I need to go and swear out a homicide warrant on him."

"You don't think he's good for it?"

"I think he's for Ivana Nenasheva's murder—"

"He didn't kill her."

"That remains to be seen. As much as I'd like him to be the killer of the two girls, I can't stand in front of the judge and hand him my probable cause statement with flimsy information. I can just picture it, 'Lieutenant Kubek, what information can you provide the court that indicates Tito Hondros is the killer of little girls?'"

"'Well, Judge,' I'd say, retired cop Arn Anderson said Tito knew Bonnie, though he lied to Anderson.' But, here's where I'd hit a home run on the warrant seeking game, 'Tito Hondros wore a turtleneck sweater to hide his gouges that Bonnie Peters gave him when he was strangling her.' That about do it?"

Arn did see it. No judge in the world would issue an arrest warrant based on what Arn observed with Tito. Or even a search warrant for his DNA. "The ME sent the tissue under Bonnie's nails to the lab?"

"Of course he did."

"Then there could be a match with Tito."

"Of course, that's a possibility."

"Can you put a rush order on it?" Arn asked.

"With the lab," she laughed. "I'm afraid I burned to many bridges asking them to put a rush on those other samples. The soonest the lab ladies said they could get to it is the end of the week. Unless new information puts a real rush on it. And Tito Hondros wearing a sweater in this heat won't cut it."

"Even if it's homicide related?"

She nodded.

"Call Agent McDonald. See if he can grease the wheels."

"I'll do my best is all I can promise."

Kubek finished her latte and said, "I need to get back. You actually caught me working hard—"

"One more little thing."

"Nothing is 'little' with you. Let's hear it."

"Alex Barberi. Ana Maria's been calling him, but he doesn't respond. She drove to his house but no one answered the door, and his restaurant is still closed out of respect for his two waitresses. She's concerned… I'm concerned… that something's happened to him."

"Big strapping guy like that," Kubek said, "what could possibly happen to him?"

"Jesse Brown could happen to him. I take it your bloodhounds driving those patrol cars haven't found him yet."

"Look, Arn, believe it or not our patrol officers are busy with calls every single day. They look for Brown when they can, but to tell you the truth, he is low on the to-do list for us. There's not even any proof that he's in town. Or ever was."

"And those death threats that Alex had been receiving… those aren't real?"

"Didn't say they weren't. It's just that those threats can't be tied directly to Brown. Like Alex said, they could be competitors who wanted to buy that business before he outbid them."

"Could you at least have a squad car do a welfare check on Alex. Maybe… you know, see if he's inside and okay."

Kubek sighed. "I'll have an officer run by his house and check. What's the address?"

Arn shrugged and grabbed his cell. "I'll ask Ana Maria—"

"Don't bother her," Kubek said. "I'll just look it up on the city-county property records."

Thanks," Arn said. "Can you let me know what they find?"

"I will," Kubek said, then added, "sorry I can't do more, but law enforcement today is a lot different than when you were in. We can't do things by the seat of our pants anymore like you… old timers."

"We used to make a lot of collars operating by the seat of our pants as you call it."

"And there are Supreme Court rulings that barred many of those procedures."

"I'd like some of that 'seat of the pants' about now. It might solve these homicides."

43

A rn sat a block away from the TV station under a low hanging tree in his plain rental car. Inconspicuous. With no one even glancing his way.

The police car—on the other hand—sat on a side street not thirty yards from the television station, its emergency lights atop the car and the uniformed rookie behind the wheel reading a book. The scene shouted, 'Here's a damn cop!' to the person who was sending Ana Maria threatening texts, if he were watching. Anybody smart enough to defeat the alarm system at the house would be smart enough to spot the cop tailing Ana Maria. Arn thought of phoning Kubek and telling her to call off her officer then decided not to. Even a rookie who landed the shit detail of watching Ana Maria was better than nothing.

Arn drove away from the TV station towards downtown when his cell phone buzzed. "Damn you Arn Anderson!" Ana Maria said.

"I'm afraid to ask what."

"You know damn well why I'm mad—you asked for a police escort for me."

"Look, you think you're bulletproof but you're not. If this stalker sending you messages turns out to be the same one who entered our home and took Sonny, he's not going to be satisfied until he hurts you. He may have already found Alex—"

"Did you talk with Kubek about sending officers to his house to check on him?"

"She could spare one officer. She'll call me and tell me what he finds."

"That'd be a good time to tell her to call off her officer."

"But—"

"I mean it," Ana Maria said. "Tell her to order the officer to quit following me or so help me I'll pack my shit and be out of there."

"All right" Arn, said. "But at least let him escort you home tonight. I'll feel better once you're behind locked doors where Danny can take action if needed."

"That's all the concession I'm making. And you're not off the hook yet. We'll have a discussion about this when you get home."

Arn hung up, dreading the talk he and Ana Maria would have when he got home. All the more reason, he thought, to spend some time talking to street people, find out if there has been anyone matching the description of Jesse Brown.

* * *

Arn started walking the alleys, knowing many street people practically lived in the alleys. It was the place where most dumpsters were kept. He had walked four blocks and was about to cross the street and head to the other alley when the sound of a whistle stopped him. "Yo, my man, Arnold."

Nappy the Pimp stood from the milk crate he was sitting on in back of the Albany Restaurant.

"You're not lifting any more catalytic converters?

He smoothed his dress and said, "Arnold. Arnold. I haven't. Swear."

"Then what are you doing hiding out back here?"

"Ever see the choice cuts folks leave on their plates, especially at a high-class joint like the Albany?"

"Guess I never paid any attention," Arn answered. "I was just too busy finishing what I paid for."

Nappy tilted his head back and laughed heartily.

"Do you remember the FBI wanted bulletin Danny handed out to folks?" Arn asked.

Nappy grinned and reached inside his bra. He came away with a copy of Jesse Brown's wanted poster. "I got it etched into my massive brain."

"We'll let that pass," Arn said. "Did you, or anyone on the street, see anyone even remotely matching this man's description?"

"Nobody," Nappy said. He took out a silver cigarette holder and flipped it open, selecting one of the half-smoked cigarettes. "When Danny said it was *urgentento*, we knew we had to find this dude. But I'm telling you, Arnold, this man is not in town."

"Unless he's hiding somewhere in the ritzy section of Cheyenne."

"That's a possibility. Ol' Nappy's like most folks hereabouts—we don't shop where the neat and elite live."

Arn thanked Nappy and gave him a ten spot to buy cigarettes before resuming down the alley. Every street person he came across he asked about Jesse Brown. And every person Arn spoke with had scoured their contacts to find the wanted fugitive but to no avail. By the time he got back to his rental car, it was dark. Arn sat in the car, wondering where Jesse Brown may be in hiding if he were in town. Thinking of the places where Arn hadn't gotten the word out about him. After the better part of twenty minutes, he started the car and headed for home.

When he pulled to the curb in front of his house, he saw that Kubek had, indeed, taken Ana Maria's tail off, for there was not a squad car anywhere in the neighborhood. And Ana Maria's car was nowhere to be seen, either. He cursed himself and slapped the dashboard. "I should have never let her talk me into calling off the tail."

He punched in the security code and entered the house. Danny sang to himself from the kitchen while the television blared out some war movie in the TV room. *Has to be Darwin.*

"What're you making?" Arn asked.

Danny turned around and wiped his hands on his apron. "Catfish casserole. Ana Maria's favorite for when she gets back."

"Where'd she go?"

Danny shrugged. "She never even said goodbye, just ran out of the house like she seen a blue light special at Kmart."

"Why the hell didn't you stop her?"

"Arn, she's a grown woman. Besides, as pissed off as she was the moment she walked through the door... I'd be careful when she gets back if I were you. She's madder'n hell that she had a police escort."

Arn took off his hat and ran his fingers through his hair. "Damn it, she knows there's a stalker out probably biding his time to make his move on her."

*   *   *

Danny put the rest of the catfish casserole in the fridge while Arn dried the dishes. "I just don't understand why she doesn't answer her cell phone."

"I can give you one big reason," Danny said, "and it's not a good one."

Arn knew just what Danny meant. Arn had thought the same thing. When he worked Metro Homicide, the investigators would brainstorm. Toss out possibilities as to how a crime happened or how a scroat managed to evade them. In the end, it always came down to what was the absolute worst possibility that could happen. Right now, Danny and Arn were thinking the same thing—the worst possible thing that could happen was that Ana Maria's stalker had caught up with her. Taken her cell phone. Tied her up like the killer had done to the mail order brides.

"Maybe you can call Kubek again," Danny said.

"And tell her what—that Ana Maria Villarreal turned down her police escort and now she won't answer her cell phone? How about that the last communication we had with her was a single word before her cell phone went incognito?"

Arn sat at the kitchen table. He cradled his head in his hands, replaying that one word call over and over in his mind. "Arn..." Ana Maria couldn't have been more explicit if she'd have talked for an hour. Her voice had been strained. Painful. Then the line had gone dead.

She was in trouble.

"Piss on it, I'm calling Kubek." He dialed her personal number and she answered on the first ring. "I wondered when you were going to call—"

"Ana Maria's missing."

"Whoa, there. Slow down and tell me what you know."

"That's just it, I don't know anything." Arn explained that two hours ago, Ana Maria had called Arn's cell number and had gotten that one word out before her line went dead. "It's not like her not to answer her phone. Can you have an officer run out to Alex Barberi's house. That's the only place I can think she'd go to."

"I can," Kubek said, "but it won't do any good. My officer couldn't get anyone to answer the door when he did a welfare check this afternoon. Have you thought of the probability that she simply doesn't have cell service, wherever she went? I've learned there are more dead spots in and around this area than any other place I've been. Hate to say it, but it serves her right calling off her police escort like she did."

"Can you at least put out a BOLO for her Bug?"

"That I can do. Relax, Arn. She's a big girl. I suspect she can take care of herself."

Arn thanked her and disconnected. "She's going to put a 'Be On the Look Out' for Ana Maria's Volkswagen."

"That's something," Danny said. "Might as well wait in the TV room for the police to call."

"Might as well," Arn said and followed Danny into the TV room.

Darwin sat watching a black and white war movie and said nothing when Arn and Danny entered the room. That was all right by Arn. He wanted to think, and engaging Darwin at a time like this wasn't going to help.

Arn closed his eyes, replaying Ana Maria's phone call and her one-word cry for help—for it surely was pleading. "Damn!" he said, and hit the arm of his recliner and turned to Danny. "Was Ana Maria talking with anyone right before she stormed out of the house?"

"Not to my knowledge, but then I wasn't in the room with her. Darwin was."

"Darwin," Arn said, "turn off that television for a minute."

Darwin hit the remote and faced Arn. "You were in here when she ran out?"

Darwin nodded.

"Did she talk with anyone on her cell?"

"The only one she talked to was herself and was she mad. Called herself a dumb ass for missing it."

"Missing what?" Arn asked.

Darwin shrugged. "Whatever she was looking at on the card table.

She was hunched over it looking at papers when she started cursing herself right before she ran out."

Arn stood abruptly. He bent over the card table studying her paperwork. "Was she looking at this bunch of documents?" He pointed to the paperwork she'd compiled on Alex Barberi.

"No, I think that she was looking at the police reports on the Mail Order Murders. The ones you suspected me for."

"I was a bit misguided to consider you," Arn said. He picked up the top document, Ivana Nenasheva's autopsy report. "What do think she missed?"

"I wish I knew. All I know is that she stormed out of the room like she was on a mission." Darwin's face downturned in sadness. "I'm really worried about her."

Arn sat in his recliner and held the report to the light. "What did you miss," he said. "Tell me, what did you miss…" and then he saw it. A bottom notation that the Medical Examiner made referenced six animal hairs embedded in Ivana's sweater. Possibly dog or car hairs. Black hairs.

Arn stood. "Danny, look at this. The ME found several hairs. My God, Ana Maria skimmed over that like I did. Like Kubek did. Black hairs. Possible cat hairs." He stood and said, Grab that shotgun for me. This might take more than this little .38 if my suspicions are right."

"Where the hell you going off to like a wild man?" Danny asked.

"Tito Hondros," Arn breathed. "Kubek was right—the bastard killed Ivana after all."

Danny reached behind the door of the TV room and handed Arn the shotgun, "How can you be so certain?"

"That fat cat of Tito's has the longest and blackest hair I can think of. If he killed Ivana, he would do whatever he could so that the sketch of the killer was never aired on TV."

"Tito's not the only one with a black cat," Danny said. "But it looks like Ana Maria's ruse worked—it flushed the killer out."

"Apparently," Arn answered. "Tito has to be keeping her. And Lizzy may be in on it," Arn shucked the bird shot and replaced the shells with buck shot. "She had some deep claw marks on her neck. I couldn't see that obese Winston jumping up and mangling her neck.

That's something I missed."

"You're thinking Lizzy got those scratches from a struggle?"

Arn nodded. "Make more sense than that fat cat jumping her."

"Should I call Kubek?" Danny asked. Have her order a patrol officer to meet you at Lizzy's."

"No," Arn said as he cradled the shotgun under his arm. "One of those young rookies will only get in my way. Sometimes it just takes an old timer working by the seat of his pants to get the job done."

44

Arn darked out and pulled the rental into the empty driveway a half-block from the Hondros' house. He sat and watched, not sure how much time Ana Maria had. Not sure what her condition was. Only remembering that strained one-word call she'd gotten to Arn's voice mail.

He stepped out of the car and grabbed the shotgun. Using trees as cover, he walked towards the house and stopped at the edge of the garage. He looked up at the security camera and slammed it with the butt of the gun. Plastic and glass showered onto the pavement, and as he peeked around the corner of the garage, he realized Tito and Lizzy would never be able to hear him. The house was constructed to keep sounds of the world out. But they would be able to see him on their security monitors.

He crouched down and looked at the camera covering the front door. There was just no way to approach it safely. No way to get to the front door without passing right under the camera. The best he could hope for was to run to the camera and disable it like he did the one at the garage. Would Tito or Lizzy just open the door if he rang the bell?

Arn's alternate plan didn't look so promising—blasting the dead bolt off the door and charging in. He hesitated, yet hesitating could cost Ana Maria her life. Was she suffering even as he waited, unable to know just what to do?

Arn looked at the security camera. Perhaps he could use it to his advantage. Perhaps if Tito knew Arn was on his doorstep... he recalled the last time he and Tito talked at the quarry. He had warned Arn he would be met with gunplay if he ever stepped foot on Tito's property again. Would Tito's Greek machismo override his need to keep Ana Maria hidden? Would his machismo convince him he could handle Arn and still return to Ana Marie?

Arn held the shotgun tight against his leg away from the security camera, his body shielding it, hoping Tito wouldn't see it. He rang the doorbell. If it chimed inside, Arn couldn't hear it and he held it in before releasing it. He looked up at the camera and grinned, flipping the camera the middle finger. When Arn heard the deadbolt slide open, he stepped back and shouldered the shotgun.

Tito flung the door open, screaming, his revolver pointed at Arn, Arn's shotgun pointed at Tito. "Who do you think would win this Mexican standoff? Drop the pistol."

Tito, his face the color of a stop light, his angry breaths coming in great gasps, seemed to weigh his chances and he dropped his gun.

"What is it?" Lizzy hollered. She saw Arn standing in her doorway and ran screaming towards him. When she saw the shotgun pointed at Tito, she stopped and her hands went to her face. "My God, don't kill my husband."

"I should do just that," Arn said. "Back up."

They moved several paces back; Tito's gaze fell on his gun in the hallway, then to Arn's shotgun. "Don't even think about it." Arn squatted and grabbed the revolver, shucking the cartridges out and tossing the gun aside.

"Now, where the hell's Ana Maria?"

Tito looked at Lizzy and said, "that TV reporter?"

"Where is she!"

"Why the hell should we know?"

"The lab results on Ivana Nenasheva... the ME found hairs. Long black hairs from a dog or a cat, like Winston's long hair, on her body."

"You think I know where she is based on that?"

"Lizzy," Arn said, "where'd you get those scratches in your neck, 'cause a lot of tissue was found under Ivana's fingernails where she gouged the hell out of her attacker."

"I told you before... can I sit down? My legs are a little wobbly—it's not every day some crazy bastard busts into your home, threatening to kill you."

"Sit on the floor then."

When Lizzy sat, she looked up at Arn and said, "Winston clawed me, just like I said. I came out into the kitchen one day last week… needed a drink so I went into the study. After I poured some bourbon, I sat on the sofa. Right on Tito's damn cat. I didn't see Winston as he's black as Hades and he clawed the hell out of me. Just like I told you before."

"What the hell's that got to do with Ivana?" Tito asked.

"I already told you, but that's not all. When we had our little chat at your quarry a few nights ago, you lied then I asked you about Bonnie Peters. You knew her."

"Did you, Tito?" Lizzy stood and stared up at her husband. "You knew her? I thought we had an arrangement whereby you quit your damn running around."

"She was just a… little diversion. She never meant anything, not like the other girls." He turned to Arn. "I paid her a couple hundred dollars for a night a couple times and that's all."

"A couple hundred dollars?"

Tito nodded. "That's all I'd give a little bitch like that. A couple hundred bucks for a happy ending."

Arn felt that he had busted into the wrong house and he said, "You're telling me Ana Maria's not here?"

"I will personally show you around," Tito said. "And when this is all over, you and me will meet at the quarry. Just us. Two grown men settling their hatred like in the old country."

"Deal," Arn said, "but don't forget who holds the gun right now. Let's start looking. You, too, Lizzy."

* * *

"It's a good thing you didn't go for your other option and blow the dead bolt off," Danny said.

Arn felt his headache growing, and he started to tremble. He had almost made the wrong call. If he had blown the lock off and rushed into the house with Tito confronting him with his own gun, there would have been bloodshed. And Arn would have been on the wrong side of the law.

"You're certain Tito's not going to make a complaint?" Danny said.

"Not much to make a complaint about," Arn said. Arn's cell phone buzzed again. It wasn't Ana Maria and he didn't recognize the number. "They'll leave a message if it's important. But getting back to Tito, greeting a person at his doorway with a loaded pistol wouldn't go good for him, especially since the court ordered Tito to give up all his guns until his trial as a condition of his bail. If he reports me, I get my tit in a ringer but he gets his bail revoked. Besides, Tito hates the cops for arresting him more than he hates me. This way he'll have his chance to kick the shit outta me after this is all done."

Arn hit the arm of his recliner. "Damn it all to hell, where have I gone so wrong? Ana Maria's still out there somewhere. Needing us, if she's even still…"

"Alive?" Danny said. He laid his hand on Arn's shoulder. "I've tossed that possibility over in my mind, too. It's been hours since she called you."

"Maybe it wasn't the autopsy or the lab report that set Ana Maria off," Danny said. "Maybe something else… the police report or the crime scene photographs or… *something*."

Arn stood and rubbed his temples, but it did little to ease his growing headache. "What the devil set you off?" Arn said as he stared at the tables, one with the documents on the Mail Order Murders, the other table displaying documents Ana Maria had compiled for her special on Alex Barberi.

He picked up the initial officer's report, the first one to respond to the Barberi murders. It was straightforward, precise. Like other reports the Denver Police Officers wrote, but she had set it aside. Was this what sent Ana Maria out the door in such a rush? There didn't seem to be anything out of police protocol. They had sealed off the crime scene until investigators arrived, and it had been worked by the Metro Denver evidence techs.

Arn flipped pages held together by a large black clip. The written statement that Alex had given the investigators had been laid aside and Arn put them with the rest of the investigative documents and set it on Ana Maria's TV tray.

He picked up the autopsy report and read through it before replacing it. Nothing.

He grabbed the last piece of paperwork, the evidence list. Paintings and gold and coin collections and jewelry and collector guns had been stolen by Jesse Brown and his brother, Aaron. The investigator had listed everything taken in the home invasion. Including Mrs. Barberi's prized broach and earrings and matching watch that Alex said was special to the woman. The appraiser twenty years ago had taken a photograph of the photograph Alex provided at the time to document the set, unusual that it was. The photo grainy. The picture faded through the years. Arn held it to the light.

And gasped.

Much as, he was certain Ana Maria must have done right before she ran out of the house.

The watch Paquita Roble wore on the day of her murder was the missing watch from the Barberi home invasion. And Arn recognized that Katya Petrov's earring belonged to that set, the same one she wore when her body was discovered in Optimist's Park in Laramie. "Jesse Brown," Arn breathed.

He punched in Kubek's cell number, but it went to voice mail. He hung up and called the police department. The dispatcher told Arn that Kubek had taken two days off. "I need Alex Barberi's home number."

"I'm sorry," the dispatcher said, "but I can't give out people's address. Perhaps when Lieutenant Kubek returns—"

"I need that address!" Arn yelled a moment before the dispatcher hung up.

He pocketed his phone and said to Danny, "where's Darwin?"

"Sleeping."

"Wake him up and bring him into the kitchen."

"Why?"

"He knows where Alex Barberi lives. I don't know if Ana Maria is there or not, but it would be my best guess. And Jesse Brown may have her and Alex hostage."

"I don't know—"

"Remember that Ana Maria hasn't been able to get through to Alex the last few days? What if Brown's killed or taken him hostage in his own house? And here comes Ana Maria to Alex's place to check on him and gets taken as well. Brown *has* to be there. Now go get Darwin."

"But Dr. Land said Darwin can't talk about—"

"Danny," Arn said, "Ana Maria's life could be in danger! I need that address. Now go wake Darwin up."

"Okay," Danny said, "but let me do the asking."

He ran down the hallway and soon returned to the TV room with Darwin. He stood rubbing the sleepers out of his eyes when Danny eased him into a recliner. He stood in front of Darwin and said, "Ana Maria's missing. She may have been taken by a fugitive who murdered Alex Barberi's parents."

"That is terrible. Ana Maria's a nice lady."

"Sergeant Ness, Arn needs to go to Alex Barberi's house—"

Darwin stood suddenly and brushed Danny aside. Darwin looked down on him, his fists clenching and unclenching. His jaw muscles tightening, his teeth gritting so that Arn thought he'd soon break teeth. "Dr. Land said I wouldn't have to talk about working for Alex. He fired me."

Darwin started out of the room when Danny said, "Sgt. Ness, come back here."

Darwin hesitated before he finally turned around and walked back into the TV room.

"It is of the utmost importance that Arn have the address. Or Ana Maria may die."

Darwin rubbed his temples with his knuckles, his face flushed. Thinking. After long moments when Arn was unsure whether Darwin would tell them. "Give me a piece of paper and a pencil."

Arn grabbed the notepad that Ana Maria kept beside the documents. He tore off a blank page and handed it to Darwin. After jotting the address down, he said, "You will be able to spot Alex's house—it is at the end of a long driveway lined with flowers and foliage that I planted."

Arn took the paper and said, "Thanks, Sgt. Ness. Sorry you had to think about the bad times."

Darwin trembled and sat back in the recliner. "Just find Ana Maria."

"Get hold of Bobby Ryerback. I'll need some back-up and I'm just praying he's on duty," Arn said to Danny as he ran for the door, grabbing his shotgun from behind it. "Tell him Jesse Brown has Alex and Ana Maria somewhere where neither can call for help. Probably at Alex's house. Tell him to bring help when he comes."

45

Arn thought about taking his Oldsmobile tarped in the back. It would be a lot faster to drive out to the subdivision where Alex's house was, but a lot louder. Tonight, Arn needed to be quiet when he approached the house. After that, he expected all sorts of uproar as he felt the cold barrel of the shotgun alongside him in the seat.

He hopped on the interstate, pedaling as fast as the tiny rental would allow, the engine rapped as tight as Arn dared. He slid taking the off ramp, side swapping a delineator post, and floored the accelerator. "Lord, this is another of those times where I swear… I swear, I'll attend church if you just keep Ana Maria safe until I find her. I swear," and he unconsciously crossed himself like his mother had done whenever she invoked the power of the Lord.

A hundred yards before he reached the subdivision Arn cut the lights. A quarter moon faintly illuminated the roadway and Arn drove slowly, checking the numbers on the mailboxes as he went, yet he didn't need to check the numbers as Alex's house was just as Ana Maria and Darwin had described it. Two oak trees—looking as if they'd been planted within the last growing season—stood like juvenile guards on either side of a long, curving driveway.

Arn drove slowly, using the rental's emergency brake to avoid the brake lights giving him away, the crunch of the pebbled drive under the tires loud in the still night air. Did Alex have security cameras like Tito had? Arn had to believe the son of parents murdered in a home invasion would have a sophisticated system.

When he'd arrived within twenty yards of the house and just out of the fringes of the yard light he stopped. Above the entryway was a single camera pointing to the front door, illuminating it as if a warning to anyone forcing their way in.

Arn grabbed the shotgun, stuffed his .38 in his trouser pocket and paused for a moment to formulate his plan. When he worked Metro Homicide, he often let younger piss-and-vinegar street officers make the entry into a suspect's house. Arn was more like the proverbial bull in a 7-Eleven—just a bit too rough around his Norwegian edges for smooth entry. Right now, right this time, Arn wished he had some of those patrol officers to go in with him. He hoped Danny had gotten ahold of Officer Bobby, yet Arn knew he couldn't wait for backup that may never come. Ana Maria couldn't wait for backup.

"Lord, I'm serious as a heart attack," he whispered to himself a moment before he opened the door. He hurriedly shut it before anyone looking at the security camera would notice the dome light. "Let her be alive."

He squatted beside the fender of the car, expecting some reaction from the house. But no lights came on, no one opened the door to see who'd driven up the drive darked-out. The house remained as Arn first saw it—large and looming over thick, manicured bushes that Darwin had planted.

Arn drew in a deep breath, steeling himself for what needed to be done, the sweet fragrance of the flowers that Darwin had planted on either side of the walkway leading to the front door. Arn clutched the shotgun tightly. What he was about to do he had almost done at Tito's house, and Arn stood and ran as fast as a fifty-five-year-old man can run towards the doorway.

He smashed the security camera.

Stuck the muzzle of the shotgun against the deadbolt.

Turned his face away.

And touched off the round. Lock and door splintered, a piece embedding in Arn's cheek, sticky blood running down onto his hand. He put his shoulder to the door. His wrestler namesake Arn Anderson would have been proud as 200+-pounds smashed through the door, busting one hinge. Momentum caused him to hurl his body through the door and he fell to the floor. Rolling over, he shouldered the shotgun expecting Jesse Brown to come running down the hallway with one of the Barberi's stolen guns.

Yet, all that greeted Arn was silence. Darkness.

He grabbed the small penlight from his trouser pocket and shined it down the hallway. Nothing.

He began searching the house, cautiously entering each room in succession, going on to the next room when he found no one.

When he'd searched the last room, the kitchen, he sat on a stool at the counter. Sweat from the exertion and from expecting gunplay within each room searched had caused sweat to drench Arn's shirt front, dripping down from his head. He wiped his damp eyes and said aloud, "Where the hell are you, Alex and Ana Maria?" He jumped at the sound of his own voice, the only sound he'd heard since bursting through the door.

He glanced at what had to be the basement door, thinking back to Ana Maria telling him about water seeping into the foundation and flooding the basement. As he turned to leave, out of his periphery vision a faint light escaped from the bottom of the door where carpeting had been tramped down from use.

"What the hell," he said to himself and stood to one side as he opened the door ever so slowly. He did a quick peek around the corner and back just as quick, closing his eyes. Remembering what he'd just seen. The basement steps were wooden with no carpeting, as was the basement. The concrete floor showed no water on the floor of the room he'd just seen. Light came from somewhere down a hallway, the only illumination that he saw in his half-second look.

He pocketed his pen light and shouldered the shotgun before he started down the stairs. The first step creaked, and he stayed to one side where his weight wouldn't alert someone he was coming down.

Twelve steps, Arn counted, as he descended the stairs. Twelve steps where he was in the 'fatal funnel' where he was most vulnerable, but he reached the bottom without seeing anyone.

A faint noise reached him then, coming from somewhere down the hallway.

He stepped. Stopped. Peeked inside a large room. Nothing,

He continued down the hall, the noise becoming louder, like a dog scratching at the wide door that spanned the hallway.

Arn put his ear to the door, the scratching louder. And a whimper that was not a dog.

He put his hand on the doorknob. Testing it. Turning it when… cold steel shoved against his ear, accompanied by… the unmistakable sound of a revolver being cocked.

"Go on in and join the festivities but leave your shotgun out here."

"Alex?"

"Of course, who'd you expect, Jesse Brown? Now put the gun on the floor and slip that little gun of yours out of your trouser pocket and drop it as well."

Arn did as Alex ordered and walked into the room dressed only in boxer shorts with red polka dots on them. Hanging from the ceiling of the spacious room were eight small monitors hooked to his surveillance cameras. Photos of nude women in various poses of submission took up an entire wall and Arn recognized Paquita Robles. On closer examination, he saw a picture of Ivana Nenasheva looking over her shoulder as she hung from a ring. Deep, bleeding welts covered her back, as did Bonnie Peters, their photos showing a terrified look in their eyes.

A variety of straps and slings took up another wall, a larger sling dangling from the rafters overhead with strands of hair stuck to the leather restraints. On the far wall, two eye bolts with large rings had been anchored.

And Ana Maria was shackled to one, her hands tied overhead by hemp rope.

Encircling her head was a wide leather band connected to a red plastic ball the size of Arn's fist held tight against her mouth by the straps. Stripped to her bra and panties, dark red welts covered her shoulders and back. She turned towards him with a pleading look in her eyes. Arn resisted the urge to run to her and said, "Can you at least take her gag off? It looks like she'll choke at any time."

"Maybe, as soon as you walk over to that other ring beside her."

Arn walked slowly, looking over his shoulder, Alex too far away to try to disarm him.

"Stop, "Alex said and tossed Arn a set of police handcuffs. "Slip one cuff through the ring and then put 'em on your wrists."

Arn took the cuffs, a standard set most rookies carried. Smith and Wesson brand. He'd used any number of things to defeat them in training, and he could defeat them here. *If* he could find something to slide between the face and the teeth of the lock. *If* he had the time before Alex killed them.

Arn put a handcuff on and reached overhead, slipping the free one through the large ring before clicking the cuff on his other wrist. When he finished, he turned around and saw Alex for the first time. Festering gouges along his neck and face shown where he'd gotten into a fight that looked like he'd lost. He wore no shirt, and only a pair of boxer shorts as he moved the muzzle of his gun in a lazy figure eight across Arn's body.

"The gag," Arn said. "She doesn't need to suffer like that."

Alex shrugged. "Why not. Might do me good to have you two talk over where you screwed up."

He walked to Ana Maria and carefully, almost lovingly unhooked the strap and ball that covered her mouth. She took in gulps of air and tried speaking but couldn't. "That happens now and again when people scream and holler like you did."

Alex turned to Arn. "You can scream all you want, too. This house is about a block away from my nearest neighbor. Might as well be soundproof. Now tell me who else have you told that you were coming here?"

"You going to strip me and whip me, too? Arn asked.

Alex stepped forward and slapped Arn hard across the face. The last time he'd been slapped that hard was when he sneaked a kiss on Georgia Spangler's cheek in the eleventh grade. It pissed him off then and it pissed him off now, yet he forced himself to remain calm. At least as calm as he could being handcuffed to a ring in a basement wall with death looking like the only way to escape.

"Well, big man, you going to tell me?" Alex said.

"We can make this an... exchange of information. You tell me something I want to know, and I'll tell you something."

Alex slapped Arn again. "You're in no position to bargain."

"And you're in no position to assume I have no help coming."

Alex took a step back and met Arn's gaze. "All right, I'll play your little game, Ask away."

"Where's Jesse Brown? Did he come after you someplace in town?"

"Jesse Brown," Alex began, "was an… acquaintance I met in college. For as big and bullish as he and his brother Aaron were, they were geniuses with all things electronic. I met them when I took an electives class in computer science."

"I would wager they taught you how to defeat a security system?" Arn fidgeted, moving his hand ever so slightly so the jaws of the handcuffs were against his shirt collar. "Like that security system in my house."

Alex waved the air. "*Yours* was nothing."

"When did you bypass my system and come in and take the dog?"

"You knew it was me?"

"Not until now I didn't."

Alex's eyebrows raised. "I was just glad you didn't have a system like the one my parents installed. Foolproof doesn't even describe it."

"He was in on his parent's home invasion, "Ana Maria said, her voice hoarse.

"That so?" Arn asked.

Alex shrugged. "I had to help them with the codes. Even the Brown boys couldn't defeat my parent's security system. Your turn. Who did you tell?"

"I called Lieutenant Kubek," Arn said, moving the cuffs slightly. If he could work the fabric of his collar between the face of the cuff and the teeth… "She's—"

"She's gone for a couple days," Alex said. "Went to Chicago to test for Captain."

"How'd you know—"

Alex reached over and patted Ana Maria on the cheek. She jerked away and he said, "Ana Maria's been most talkative. Said that when she went to interview Kubek at the police station she found out the lieutenant had taken a couple personal days." He slapped Arn's face hard, the sting of the last slap still lingering. "That's what you get when you lie to me."

Arn shook his head violently to get his blood flowing in his face. "Believe me, Kubek picks up her cell phone whenever I call her."

"Oh?" Alex said and patted Arn down. He came away with Arn's cell phone and flipped it open. "You did call her... tonight it seems." Alex frowned and scrolled through Arn's messages. "You never opened this voicemail."

"Didn't recognize the area code."

"I do," Alex said. "Colorado." He tapped the play button. "Arn. Agent Barnes. I researched that private investigation firm that you said Alex hired to find his parent's killers. There is no such PI firm here in Denver or anywhere else."

The message ended and Alex broke the phone in half before tossing it away. "You should have checked that message before busting in here. Now give me something credible."

"I already told you, Kubek. She intends on sending an officer here," he lied.

"Did she elaborate?"

Arn shook his head. "Like you said, she's out of town. But she promised to call dispatch to send officers this way."

"If that's the case, I think we have a little time to get to know one another before a patrolman shows up."

"Now you," Arn said. "Where's Jesse Brown or is his coming to Cheyenne all a fabrication, too?"

"You are half-smart, aren't you," Alex said. "After I tracked Jesse and Aaron to a flophouse in Denver, I facilitated Aaron's... suicide with one of my dad's guns as a matter of record. But Jesse was gone when I busted in. Took me a goodly while to find him in the Miami area."

Things that had been right under Arn's nose that he missed were coming to a head and he said, "You took some of your mother's costume jewelry to a pawn shop. The same costume jewelry that was listed as stolen."

"My bad. I did that and gave the pawn shop Jesse's name. The FBI still thinks he's down in Miami, but I know for a fact that he was chum for sharks a few miles off the coast."

"All the threatening notes were just cover?" Arn asked.

"Just to throw the law off track."

"After you killed Paquita Robles and Katya Petrov—why leave expensive jewelry on them?"

"I gave Ivana my mother's earrings—and she must have promptly given them to her buddy Petrov. When Petrov and I… danced in Optimist's Park in Laramie, one of the earrings was lost. I panicked when I saw other walkers. Didn't have time to look for it and had to leave Petrov wearing the other one." Alex shrugged. "So, I'm human. Same with Paquita—when she was with me, I gave her the watch. Not like I was out anything—the insurance check had been long cashed."

"You should have taken the watch—"

"But I panicked. Again. When I saw other joggers in the park— Alex jerked suddenly and turned to his bank of security screens. He looked closely at the one he'd set up to monitor the end of his drive and tapped the screen. "Just to satisfy your curiosity, this is how I knew you were here long before you destroyed my door."

Ana Maria turned her head so she could see the screen. "That's Bobby!"

Alex hurriedly slipped on jeans and a shirt. "Know him?"

"He's just a kid," Ana Maria pleaded. "Don't hurt him."

"Not if don't have to," Alex said. "Killing a cop… now that puts a person in a different category. The law will hunt me relentlessly if I do." He smiled and winked. "Don't you two go anywhere. I'll be right back."

Alex shut the door and his footsteps grew fainter as he walked to the basement door. Ana Maria wiggled and massaged her wrists as best she could. "Do you think he'll hurt Bobby?"

"What's he got to lose?"

46

"We need to get outta here before than maniac comes back," Arn said as he kept an eye on the door.

"This is all my fault," she said. "When I saw that evidence list describing the same jewelry as Alex listed as stolen from his parents, I thought he must be in danger of Jesse Brown. Until I realized that the threatening notes Alex claimed to have received from Brown looked like his handwriting when he filled out the statement to the police after the murders. That's what I realized. Finally."

"Why did you come here to confront him on your own? I would have come with you and would have come properly armed."

Ana Maria winced and moved the rope around as best she could to relieve pressure. "Truth was, I didn't want anyone to suspect Alex for anything unless I *knew* one way or the other. When I did confront him, he led me down here to his basement and..." tears flowed, and she turned her head away. "As you can see, he beat me as a prelude to... raping me. If you hadn't come along... he would have done so already."

Arn scrunched his shoulders up as a part of the shirt collar slipped under the face of the handcuff. "Looks like you put up a fight by the looks of Alex's face and neck."

"Wasn't me." Ana Maria focused on the monitor just as Alex appeared on screen and waited at the front door for officer Bobby. "It was Bonnie Peters who clawed hell out of his face. Alex told me Melissa Roush came to him with a proposal that night she drove into the parking lot as he I was leaving. 'Give me ten grand or I won't tell that you hired Bonnie for sex and what you did top her,' Melissa threatened Alex. See, Bonnie figured out about Alex, but it was Melissa who was putting the bite on Alex. Melissa saw Alex slip the note into Bonnie's coat that night offering money for sex with her. Smug bastard told me he agreed to pay Bonnie and Melissa the money but when he met them Melissa went down easy, but Bonnie didn't go quietly into the good night but fought him like hell."

"As I bet Paquita did," Arn said, working the collar of his shirt into the teeth of the cuffs. "Now when I think back, I recall Alex wearing a turtleneck in his restaurant despite the damn heat. If we ever get out of this, Kubek will need to compare Alex's DNA with the tissue found under Paquita's fingernails.

"Damn it!" Arn said. "I should have been smart enough to figure it out. Bonnie told me the person who beat her drove to his house and the odor of lilacs was strong. She thought it was the man's cologne, but Darwin planted all those flowers that Bonnie smelled while she was blindfolded."

Ana Maria stood on her tiptoes to lessen the pressure on her bleeding wrists and said, "where's the other policeman Kubek promised to send?"

"There is no other policeman. I never got hold of Kubek. My guess is that Bobby's here 'cause I told Danny to call him."

Ana Maria watched the monitor showing Alex calmly walking to Bobby as he waited on the hood of his squad car. "Bobby won't know until it's too late—"

When the blow came, it came remarkably quick. Alex lashed out and caught Bobby on the point of the jaw. When the young policemen slumped, Alex grabbed him in an arm choke before turning to the camera. Alex smiled before... twisting Bobby's head. There was no sound from the monitors, yet the snap of his head couldn't have been any louder if there had been. Alex scooped Bobby up in his arms, and put him in the back seat before climbing into the squad car himself.

"We've only got a few moments before he hides the police car out back and returns," Arn said. "Tell me something to help me when he comes back."

"Help you how? I can't tell you anything except he admitted to killing Paquita and Katya Petrov and Ivana Nenasheva. He brought Paquita into the country illegally first, followed by Ivana later when he tired of Paquita. He kicked her out and threatened to kill her if she went to the authorities."

"This handcuff... I've had arrestees slide the seatbelt between the face and against the teeth to open it. My collar's going to do the same thing if... if I can work it round. He squirmed, feeling the fabric catch in the teeth. "I can just imagine a young woman like Paquita worlds away from home with no way back and now she's being threatened with death. Must have been hell for her."

"Not any worse than Ivana," Ana Maria said. "Alex was particularly 'feisty,' is how he put it. She had free reign of his house and could go shopping with narrow restrictions he placed on her. That's when she met Petrov—grocery shopping."

Arn wiggled, jamming the edge of his collar deeper into the handcuff, feeling the teeth give way. "She should have run away from him then. Came to the police."

"Being from Russia, Ivana was even more frightened of the police that she was of Alex.

Until she found guns among Alex's things hidden in the basement that was supposed to have been stolen in the home invasion. Ivana wasn't as dumb as Alex thought—she'd read the police reports of the home invasion. *That's* when she got the nerve to run away. And Petrov's lover, Tito, put Ivana up and kept her hidden."

"Why Petrov? Alex didn't even know her by the sounds of it."

"Alex said he was afraid Ivana was *too* friendly with Petrov and told her about the beatings. And about her suspicions that Alex was involved in his own parent's murders—"

The sound of the basement door echoed loudly as Arn squirmed against the cuff. "Just about got it..."

The door opened and Alex stood framed in it.

"Did you have to kill Bobby?" Ana Maria asked.

"Didn't have to," Alex said with a grin. "But he was cocky and I just... wanted to."

He took his belt off his trousers. He wrapped his hands around each end and advanced towards Arn. "As you can see by my face, I'm not about to be clawed up like this again. Besides," he held up the belt, "this'll be so much easier."

Arn wiggled. The fabric pressing against the teeth of the handcuff just as Alex suddenly moved around Arn's back and threw the belt over Arn's head. But Arn thrashed about, keeping his head tight against his chest.

Alex threw his arm around Arn's head, pulling it back when suddenly, the handcuff sprung open.

Arn shook his wrist to rid himself of the cuff, hung up in the ring.

He turned and smashed his fist into Alex's face. When he reared back to hit him again, Alex hit Arn hard in the kidneys.

Intense pain shot through Arn's body, his head coming away from his chest.

Alex's belt looping over Arn's neck as he clawed at the belt. His hand now between his neck and the belt.

Ana Maria screaming.

Alex setting his weight back. Tightening the belt. Arn losing consciousness... What little air coming in faint, deadly gasps...

Flashes of lightning shot across his eyes as... the life... squeezed from him. The last thought Arn had was that he'd failed Ana Maria when...

Arn dropped, his weight held by the single handcuff still hung up in the ring.

Ana Maria yelled.

Alex screamed. A loud *thud* reached Arn's barely conscious brain then. He shook his head to clear his mind as he sucked in deep, wonderful breaths when... Alex crashed into him a moment before he screamed again, and Arn thought the sound of Alex's breaking collar bone... intoxicating.

"Don't kill him!" Danny yelled. "Sgt. Ness, stop hitting him."

Arn got his legs under him and worked his hand through the ring. Darwin stood over Alex, one hand holding him off the floor by his shirt front, the other bloody fist poised to hit Alex again.

"Sgt. Ness," Danny said, "stand down!"

Darwin looked up at Danny standing beside him and let lose his grip on Alex. He fell to the floor, his head hitting the concrete, splitting his head. A pool of blood engulfing his face as his eyes rolled back in his head.

Darwin picked up a blanket, dirty though it was, and turned to Ana Maria. He gently draped it around her to hide her nakedness. "I couldn't hardly have let Alex hurt you none." A sadness came over his face and he said, Looks like I was too late. I am sorry," He looked about for something to cut the ropes around Ana Maria's wrists. "I was too late."

"No," Ana Maria said, "you were just in time."

47

Ana Maria slipped her top back covering her healing welts and Danny washed his hands of the salve the doctor had prescribed her. She winced as she turned back to the kitchen table. "You knew DeAngelo canceled my special about the Mail Order Murders?"

"I figured he'd do as much when he learned you'd almost died," Arn said.

"I didn't almost die," she said, "my guardian angel came along just in time."

"You mean," Danny said, "Darwin came along just in time."

"That, too," Ana Maria said. "By the way, where is Darwin? I was wondering how his interview went with the VA."

Danny used a spatula and put an omelet on their plates before taking off his apron and sitting across from Arn and Ana Maria. "Dr. Land called and said Darwin was a hit with the hiring board."

"Then the VA will start to look a little friendlier with Darwin taking care of the grounds," Arn said. "He said he plans to plant a lot of fragrant flowers." When Dr. Land heard that Darwin, with Danny driving Arn's Olds to Alex's, had rescued Arn and Ana Maria, he went out on a limb and suggested Darwin put in for a groundskeeper position open at the VA. "Plus, he'll be close enough that I can fit him into a therapy session whenever I have an opening," Dr. Land had told Arn.

"Speaking about positions, I understand Lieutenant Kubek's going to be Captain Kubek of the Chicago Police."

Arn checked his watch. "We'll soon know for certain in a minute."

Arn was half-way through his omelet when Sonny tried to emit what he considered a howl, announcing somebody at the door. "I'll let her in," Danny said.

He returned within a moment with Kubek behind him, and Danny said, "Sit. I can rustle up another omelet—"

"Not for me," she said. "Where I'm going, I'll have to wear a uniform, and I want to make sure I look good."

"Then you are headed to Chicago?" Ana Maria asked.

Kubek nodded. "I gave the Chief my two-week notice."

"Well, don't go without telling us what Alex confessed to," Arn said.

She accepted the cup of coffee Danny handed her. "That's the least I could do, not being there when you needed me."

Arn waved it away. "Can't do anything about it now. Tell us about Alex, for Pete's sake."

"Where to begin... for as much money as that man has, he didn't want an attorney. It was like his ego wouldn't let him keep quiet. It was like he was bragging."

"Just like Dr. Land said psychopaths often do," Arn said.

"Alex made a full statement to me and the FBI at the PD here... this is good coffee."

"I'm spoken for," Danny said, and Kubek gave him a sideways glance as she continued.

"He and the Brown brothers conspired to steal everything they could fence from Alex's parents. There was no intention to kill them in their initial plans. But it went sour, and Aaron overreacted to Alex Sr.'s fighting with them, and Jesse killed him, then killed the mother as the only other witness. They agreed to lay low fencing the stolen items and Alex put them up in a ratty house in Denver. It got him thinking that—even though he hadn't planned it—the murder of his parents was advantageous for him. Now he could inherit their businesses and holdings and never have to risk fencing the loot. So, he killed Aaron, staging it so it looked like a suicide."

"But brother Jesse saw the writing on the wall and cut a choagie down to Florida—"

"Where Alex found him and killed him. Fed him to the sharks just like he bragged. Pawned some of his mother's stolen jewelry under Jesse's name."

"What I don't understand," Danny said, "is why start killing. With the brothers gone, there were no witnesses."

"Another thing Dr. Land said about psychopaths," Arn volunteered, "is that psychopaths are sexual addicts. And they are thrill seekers." He held his cup and Danny refilled it. "I guess that his first… sex slave was Paquita Robles, am I right?"

Kubek nodded. "Brought here under the ruse of marriage. He brought her into the restaurant as a waitress—not because the family needed money but to better keep an eye on her."

When Alex tired of her, he kicked her out, but she was a woman scorned and intended on reporting Alex. That's when he found her working at the Cadillac Motel and strangled her, then hurriedly dressed her to make it look like an accident."

"If he just had taken the watch he'd given her?" Ana Maria asked. "But why tell Darwin when he was his dishwasher to take the jewelry to Burri's?"

"Insurance," Kubek answered. "In case he got sloppy, there'd be someone to pin it on—Darwin, and later Jesse who was thought to have fenced the items."

"I would almost offer condolences for not being able to go to court on Tito for Ivana's murder," Arn said. "I know how badly you wanted him to be her killer."

"I'd have loved to," Kubek said. "But Alex came clean with that, too. Ivana was another mail order bride he'd brought in illegally after Paquita. Alex abused her as he did Paquita, and restricted Ivana to just grocery shopping. One day she'd poked around the house and found stolen items from the home invasion. She put two and two together and knew she had to escape him. She went to the only man she could trust—Tito, and that was only because he was lovers with her friend Katya Petrov."

"Whom Alex was sure Ivana told about the stolen items and her suspicion about Alex killing Paquita?" Arn asked. "When I spoke with Josephine at Diamond Lil's Motel, she was sure Ivana and Petrov planned on fleeing Cheyenne."

"Alex said he was certain of it, too," Kubek said. By the time he found out about their escape plans, Petrov was already in hiding in

Laramie. He tracked her down and dumped her in the park. Just for thrills." Kubek smiled. "I knew you'd figure something out eventually."

"Even a stopped clock is right twice a day. But the thing I couldn't figure out," Arn said, "is why Darwin was so terrified of Alex."

"Paquita," Kubek said. "She and Darwin became close as either could be close to someone. During one of those trips to the VA, she confided in him. Darwin said she told him how dangerous Alex could be. Her suspicions, too, concerning the home invasion eight years earlier. Only when Anna Maria was in danger did he overcome that fear to save her life."

"And it was during that time Darwin worked at the restaurant that Alex told him to take the jewelry to Burri for cleaning and to give him Alex's name—"

"Which I presume angered Alex."

Kubek nodded. "At which point he promptly fired Darwin."

Kubek checked her watch and stood. "I have an exit interview with the Police Chief in fifteen. If I don't see you guys again…" she kissed Arn lightly on the cheek and shook Danny and Ana Maria's hands. As she started for the door, Danny said, "you never said what's to happen to Darwin on that officer assault charge?"

Kubek stopped and said over her shoulder, "At Bobby's funeral, the officer involved said the Darwin had been through enough and urged me to drop it."

"And are you going to? "Danny pressed.

"I can hardly do anything from my desk in Chicago, now can I?"

Epilogue

A rn stayed in the church after Wednesday Vespers service ended, after the rest of the congregation had shuffled out to do what they did after the weekday service at the Greek Orthodox Church. When he was the last one left besides the priest, he walked toward the front of the church and sat. Thinking. Thanking God once again that Ana Maria had survived yet another ordeal. Praying? He thought as much as he thanked the Lord that Danny and Darwin had saved them in the basement of Alex's private hell hole on earth.

He became aware of someone standing beside him and he looked up. Father Chris Xanthos smiled down on Arn and motioned to the pew. "Mind?"

"Not at all, Father." Arn moved down to allow the priest to set, and they both remained silent. Both quiet in their own thoughts until Arn said, "Do you believe in miracles?"

Father Chris smiled knowingly. "I would not be in the business I am if I did not. Why?"

"Because I think I lived through one. A... dear friend and I nearly died until God sent a miracle in the form of a troubled Iraq veteran." He looked over at the priest. "Is that possible—that God gifted me a miracle? Even though I've let Him down so many times, not attending services like I promised I'd do—"

Father Chris held up his hand to stop Arn. "For today, for this time, know that God's miracles come in even the simplest of packages. Even the miracle of one man who is *not* lost sitting quiet with a humble priest."

296

Arn could only nod as he sat beside Father Chris, and after some time, Arn became aware that tears had started flowing freely thinking how close he and—especially Ana Maria—had come to being Alex's next victims.

How long Arn and Father Chris sat together silently praying he did not know until he stood and wiped the tears from his cheek. "Thanks for sitting with me, Father," he said, and started out the church when the priest stopped him. "Would you like to go somewhere to talk, perhaps over a cup of coffee?"

Arn checked his watch. "Another time, Father. Right now, I have to meet a man at the quarry east of town. Tonight, he and I are going to have our own kind of discussion."

Father Chris looked sideways at Arn and said, "This sounds serious, as if you and this man were enemies."

Arn stood. "Perhaps we were a moment ago. But now... after being *here*, I think that he and I will bury the hatchet if that is possible. A man can have too many enemies."

"You are free to come this Sunday for Divine Liturgy," Father Chris said as Arn walked toward the doors.

He stopped and said over his shoulder, "I will, Father. This time... this Sunday I'll be sitting on the pew listening to what He has to say to me."

About the Author

C. M. Wendelboe entered the law enforcement profession when he was discharged from the Marines as the Vietnam war was winding down.

In the 1970s, his career included assisting federal and tribal law enforcement agencies embroiled in conflicts with American Indian Movement activists in South Dakota.

Curt moved to Gillette, Wyoming, and found his niche, where he remained a sheriff's deputy for more than twenty-five years.

During his thirty-eight-year career in law enforcement, he served successful stints as a police chief, a policy adviser, and other supervisory roles for several agencies. Yet, he has always felt most proud of "working the street." He was a patrol supervisor when he retired to pursue his true vocation as a fiction writer.

Curt writes the Spirit Road Mysteries, the Bitter Wind Mystery series, the Nelson Lane Frontier Mysteries, and the Tucker Ashley Western Adventure series.

If you enjoyed reading this book,
please consider writing your honest review
and sharing it with other readers.

Many of our Authors are happy to participate in
Book Club and Reader Group discussions.
For more information, contact us at info@encirclepub.com.

Thank you,
Encircle Publications

For news about more exciting new fiction, join us at:

Facebook: www.facebook.com/encirclepub

Instagram: www.instagram.com/encirclepublications

Twitter: twitter.com/encirclepub

Sign up for Encircle Publications newsletter and specials:
eepurl.com/cs8taP

Eccentric Circles: Short Stories
Free Download

CPSIA information can be obtained
at www.ICGtesting.com
Printed in the USA
BVHW070919170522
637226BV00006B/43